No longer the property of the
Boston Public Library.
Sale of this material benefits the Library.

Praise for *Nothing but the Rent*

"Mitchell, who clearly loves her characters, charges their exchanges with such a sisterly warmth. . . . [She] has given us characters we lean toward caring about, and that, in itself, is an achievement."—*The Baltimore Sun*

"One of the newest novels to follow in the footsteps of such previous bestsellers as *Waiting to Exhale*. . . . An entertaining and illuminating study of female bonding."—*Philadelphia Tribune*

"Publishing's new elite club [is] a collection of black female authors that includes Terry McMillan (*Waiting to Exhale*), Bebe Moore Campbell (*Singing in the Comeback Choir*) and Sharon Mitchell (*Nothing but the Rent*), who write a new brand of commercial fiction based on relationships."—*The New York Post*

"Reading this novel will be like hanging out with old friends. A very enjoyable tale filled with lovely, vibrant characters in a narrative that will have readers laughing out loud and talking about the experience from coast to coast."—Eric Jerome Dickey, *New York Times* bestselling author of *Liar's Game*

"Psychologist and first-time author Mitchell offers a highly entertaining and unusually illuminating study of female bonding. . . . This one has heart and, even rarer, soul."—*Kirkus Reviews*

"Many readers will sympathize with the problems these women face."—*Publishers Weekly*

"Mitchell . . . is about to surprise the literary world as the next Terry McMillan."—*Delaware Today*

Also by Sharon Mitchell

Nothing but the Rent

SHEER NECESSITY

SHARON MITCHELL

A SIGNET BOOK

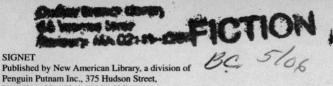

FICTION

BC 5/06

SIGNET
Published by New American Library, a division of
Penguin Putnam Inc., 375 Hudson Street,
New York, New York 10014, U.S.A.
Penguin Books Ltd, 27 Wrights Lane,
London W8 5TZ, England
Penguin Books Australia Ltd,
Ringwood, Victoria, Australia
Penguin Books Canada Ltd, M4V 3B2
Penguin Books (N.Z.) Ltd, 182–190 Wairau Road,
Auckland 10, New Zealand

Penguin Books Ltd, Registered Offices:
Harmondsworth, Middlesex, England

Published by Signet, an imprint of New American Library, a division of Penguin
Putnam Inc. Previously published in a Dutton edition.

First Signet Printing, October 2000
10 9 8 7 6 5 4 3 2 1

Copyright © Sharon Mitchell, 1999
All rights reserved

Ⓢ REGISTERED TRADEMARK—MARCA REGISTRADA

Printed in the United States of America

Without limiting the rights under copyright reserved above, no part of this
publication may be reproduced, stored in or introduced into a retrieval system, or
transmitted, in any form, or by any means (electronic, mechanical, photocopying,
recording, or otherwise), without the prior written permission of both the copyright
owner and the above publisher of this book.

PUBLISHER'S NOTE
This is a work of fiction. Names, characters, places, and incidents either are the
product of the author's imagination or are used fictitiously, and any resemblance to
actual persons, living or dead, business establishments, events, or locales is entirely
coincidental.

BOOKS ARE AVAILABLE AT QUANTITY DISCOUNTS WHEN USED TO PROMOTE PRODUCTS OR
SERVICES. FOR INFORMATION PLEASE WRITE TO PREMIUM MARKETING DIVISION, PENGUIN
PUTNAM INC., 375 HUDSON STREET, NEW YORK, NEW YORK 10014.

If you purchased this book without a cover you should be aware that this book is
stolen property. It was reported as "unsold and destroyed" to the publisher and
neither the author nor the publisher has received any payment for this "stripped
book."

In memory of my brave and giving friend,
Janice Jordan Coleman.
Your spirit lives on in the people you taught and nurtured.

ACKNOWLEDGMENTS

The first person I must thank is my father, Curtis Mitchell. Daddy, it was a long tearful ride back from the DMV when I flunked my driving test. It didn't escape me that by the time we got back home, you were practically in tears yourself. And the extra lessons did the trick! I've always known you've had my back.

I would also like to thank the rest of my family: My mother, Bertha Mitchell, who is my one-woman cheering section and public relations director. My sisters, Christine Clark and Marita Mitchell, and my brother, Curtis Jr., who despite their many differences share the same sense of humor and love of family.

To my friends—and you know who you are—your understanding when I was unavailable for long stretches of time and turned down numerous invitations has been phenomenal. Speaking of understanding, thank God I know a lot of psychologists. The patience, empathy, and free therapy I've gotten from my colleagues at the University of Delaware has helped me immensely. Then there's Vernese Edghill, Norma Gaines Hanks, and Tracy Cooper, three people who can spread the word about anything faster than an Internet virus. This kind of virus I like. And you really know who your friends are when, despite infrequent contact, the love keeps coming. Leah, Berniece, Blanca, Mable, and all of Boston University folks, your enduring enthusiasm and genuine pride in my success has really touched me. Michael Sims, just when I thought I have myself all figured out, every interaction with you results in me learning something new. Thanks for the lessons learned.

I really benefit from feedback as I write, and I want to

thank a number of people for giving me what I needed in that respect: the members of Julianna Baggott's Dining Room Table Writer's Group, Julianna, Jacquie Juers, Sharon Moore, Denise Verderosa, Kathryn Clarke, Heather Suchanec, Lisa Spera, Merle Shao, constantly challenged me to stretch as a writer. A more vocal, frank, funny and rowdy bunch of women would be hard to find. I also want to thank Kathy Bishop, Cindy Carroll, Lisa Sweder, and Amy Alfred.

It's been a "team effort" by the Ralph Vicinanza Agency. Special thanks to the hard work of Eben Weiss, Ralph Vicinanza, and my agent, Sharon Friedman. My editor, Jennifer Moore, has been a godsend. Jennifer, you have been so supportive, invested, and helpful. It has been a real pleasure working with you. Thank you so very much.

SHEER
NECESSITY

chapter
1

Graduations are such happy occasions, and coming home for her brother's had Toni daydreaming about her own commencement ceremony in the following spring. I can hardly wait, Toni thought as she peered out the window of her parents' car. Her father let them—Toni, her mother, and Darius—out in front of her parents' house, then left again to run some last-minute errands for the graduation party. Two cars were in the driveway. The Civic hatchback was Aunt Hester Ruth's, but Toni had never seen the beat-up black Porsche before. The thing was ancient. A JESUS IS MY CO-PILOT sticker clung for dear life to a bumper that was about to fall off, and splinters of red plastic marked where one of the taillights was supposed to be.

Darius and Mama were walking toward the house when he suddenly stopped and turned to her. "Oh, I almost forgot. Congratulations. Here's your diploma." He pressed the rolled paper into his mother's hands. Toni watched the tears well up in her mother's eyes. The diploma would be framed and placed on the living room mantelpiece along with hers, Joy's and Lynette's.

Darius planted a wet, messy kiss on his mother's cheek, then headed for the house. Toni figured he wanted to change out of his cap and gown before his friends started arriving for the party.

Anna Mae wiped away evidence of the kiss as if she didn't like it, but Toni knew better. Her mama had a soft spot for her baby and one and only son. Anna Mae continued up the path with Darius's diploma held firmly in one hand. Yet instead of going in, Anna Mae took a seat on the cement stoop, leaning back against the wrought iron banister.

She looks tired, Toni thought. Mama had been doing a lot of running around to prepare for this bash. She usually didn't know how tired she was until it snuck up on her.

"Why don't you go on in the house? Lie down and rest a bit before the party starts."

"But I was gonna help Lynette—"

"Mama, I don't want you lifting a finger. Let us wait on you for a change."

Her mama's eyes graced her as only they could. "You really are a sweet child," Anna Mae said. She patted a spot next to her, inviting Toni to sit.

As Toni took a seat, the hem of her dress brushed against her mother's bare legs. As she took in her mother's long shapely legs and full hips, Toni thought, she puts me to shame. Toni had plenty of hips, but the legs? No way. How come I have to be the shortest in the family? All the other women in the family were five-six at least. Toni was only a couple of inches over the five-foot mark.

Her mother reached out and touched Toni's hair. "Your hair looks nice."

Toni ran a hand through a swath of her shoulder-length hair. It was thick, silky, and colored a rich walnut brown. She usually wore it short but had decided to let it grow this past winter. "One day when we were bored, Chris decided to experiment with it."

Anna Mae laughed, "I don't know when y'all had time to be bored. I'd think opening a beauty shop—"

"Hair salon," Toni corrected.

Anna Mae rolled her eyes. "Same difference. I'm really proud of you."

"You must be pretty proud of Darius, too," Toni said, deflecting the praise.

"I'm proud of all my kids," Anna Mae said. "Lynn's a wonderful mother, and Joy just got a job at that wig store at the new mini-mall they put up at the corner of Seventy-ninth and Euclid."

Lynette had better be a good mother, with two kids under five and another baby on the way. And of course, Joy had a new job. She was *always* getting new jobs, because she couldn't keep one for more than a month or two. Lately, it seemed like she was changing jobs every few weeks.

Toni watched as her mama rested her back against the stone stoop, settling in. Would she ever get this woman to go in the house? "Mama, are you going to get some rest before this party or what?"

"Child, what do you think I been doing? Once I go through those doors, I'm not going to have a moment's peace. There are grandkids inside that house, and Hester Ruth's gonna talk my ears off. I declare, the older she gets, the less sense that woman makes."

Toni laughed. Her mama wasn't lying. Aunt Hester Ruth had a stuttering problem, and even those people who'd been around her for years had a hard time figuring out what she was saying half the time. But she didn't let her disability interfere with business. Her cooking spoke for itself.

"Don't worry. I'll keep everybody away from you."

"If you succeed, you're a better woman than me."

"Nobody's a better woman than you, but I am a meaner woman than you. Besides, they have to listen to me because I'm the oldest." Toni and her mother shared a smile.

Toni stood up. "Are you ready to go in?"

"In a minute. It's nice out here, isn't it?"

"Uh-huh." Obviously, her mama wasn't going anywhere

just now. Toni's gaze strayed back to the Porsche in the driveway. "Mama, whose pitiful-looking car is that?"

"Bruce's."

Bruce, Toni's brother-in-law.

"What happened to the other car?"

Anna Mae rolled her eyes. "Child, I don't even know. One day he just showed up with the thing. Him and Lynette didn't make no mention of the other car, and I didn't ask no questions."

Toni could believe that. Bruce hadn't wanted the family to know that he'd told Lynette to quit her job as a legal secretary, either. She had only found out when she tried to call Lynn at work and had been told she didn't work there anymore. Thinking she had been fired or something, Toni called her at home. Lynette explained that Bruce felt that she didn't need to work now that they were married. Her full-time job would be learning how to be a good wife to him.

That was two and a half kids ago, and unless being assistant manager at a pizza parlor was paying beaucoup bucks, Toni didn't see how they were making it. Hell, Lynn's job had probably paid better than his. He should have been the one to quit work and stay at home.

Toni eyed the car with disgust. "How do all of them fit in there? What about the child seats?"

Anna Mae again rolled her eyes and shrugged.

Toni shook her head. A Porsche was not what a family of five needed. She could understand Bruce's stupidity. She'd never known him to be any other way. But Lynn? The girl used to have sense. Now she was acting like some brainwashed cult member who couldn't make a decision without consulting her leader.

Anna Mae finally stood up. She was about to open the white storm door when she turned back to Toni and made a motion toward where she had been sitting.

"Oops, I almost forgot the diploma."

Toni handed it to her. "Diploma number four. Now your set is complete."

Anna Mae's smile faltered.

"What?" Toni asked.

Anna Mae sighed. "I don't know . . . education opens doors . . ."

"And?" Toni coaxed, wondering what was on her mother's mind.

Another sigh. "And I sometimes wonder what my life would have been like if I'd finished high school myself."

Toni gave her a little hug. "You don't need a piece of paper to tell me that you're the smartest person in this family."

Darius had brought his boom box outside, and the music was pumping. Two lines had formed, and those watching clapped for the ones gyrating their way to the end of the line.

"Go, Jackie! Go, go, go, Jackie!" Toni said, encouraging her sixty-five-year-old uncle who had joined the impromptu dance competition.

Uncle Jackie was not shy, especially after a couple of beers, and there was no telling how many he'd had while watching the NBA playoffs earlier. Now he was alternating between flapping his arms in the Funky Chicken and bumping hips with some young thing whose bad luck it was to land him as a dance partner. But the girl was taking it in stride. She held her arms over her head and rhythmically touched hips with him.

"Mama, take a look at Uncle Jackie."

Anna Mae was sitting next to Toni, feeding her granddaughter Montana from her plate. She gave a small shake of her head and laughed. "Jackie know he need to sit down before he breaks something. He so busy trying to *get down* this afternoon, tomorrow morning he ain't gonna be able to get up."

"I don't know. He looks pretty limber to me." Toni could keep a beat with the best of them but she had no idea what the latest dances were. The only smooth moves she'd been making lately had involved trying to pick up Sanji, her six-year-old daughter, from day care on time so she wouldn't be charged a late fee.

"Eat! Eat!" Montana said, then reached for more watermelon when her grandmother didn't move quick enough for her. She squeezed the fruit in her chubby fingers before stuffing it in her mouth. Juice and pulp ran down her chin.

Anna Mae calmly grabbed a napkin and wiped her face. However, a struggle ensued when she tried to pry the rest of the watermelon from Montana's clenched fingers.

"No! No, Bam-mama!" Montana fought and wiggled in Anna Mae's lap. Holding fast to Montana's forearm, Anna Mae hugged her body into her chest and tried to straighten the toddler's fingers with her other hand.

"Mama, do you want me to take her?"

A quick shake of the head. "Naw, I got her. But this here's a greedy child. Pretty soon she be and caught up with her big sister. Ain't that right, sugar puss?" she asked while tickling Montana's stomach.

When Montana laughed, Toni saw nothing but a few white nubs and a mouthful of chomped-up watermelon. She was cute without a doubt. But Mama wasn't lying, Montana was probably going to be tall and big-boned like her father. Her sister, Dakota, on the other hand, was frail-looking and slender like Lynette.

Toni frowned as she looked over at her younger sister. Lynn was still flipping burgers on the grille. She was too thin. Instead of gaining weight with her pregnancy—like a normal person—she looked like she had lost a few pounds. Dark smudges made her already large eyes look even bigger. Three kids in less than five years probably could do that to a person. Her husband, Bruce, walked over and said something to her. Lynn nodded and mashed down on a few of the hamburgers with a metal spatula. She was tall, but Bruce's bulk and height seemed to dwarf her. With the passing years, he seemed to be getting bigger and bigger and Lynn seemed to be getting smaller and smaller.

Bruce was wearing an old pair of gray sweat pants that had been cut off just above the knee, a muscle shirt, and a pair of mirrored sunglasses, like the kind state troopers sported. His thighs were like tree trunks, and his massive arms were crossed in front of his chest. Lately, he had gotten into this bodybuilding stuff, so he was looking pretty buff. Toni suspected he knew this because he held his position for so long it was almost like he was striking a pose.

Toni looked down at the small bowl of fruit salad in front of her. She used her fork to pick out the seeds in a chunk of watermelon and offered it to Montana.

Her small hand eagerly closed over it. "Eat!" she gurgled happily. Montana hadn't warmed up to her yet. Toni was hoping that food was the way to her heart, but when she held out her arms, Montana looked at them, then buried her face against her grandmother's shoulder.

Toni softly stroked one of her chubby legs, and the little girl burrowed even deeper into Anna Mae. "Oh, so now you're trying to act all shy." More than likely, she doesn't know who the hell I am, Toni thought. Six months out of a two-year-old's life was a long time. She wished she could get home more often.

Some of Darius's friends were starting to gather around the food tables. No doubt to refuel before their next round of bootie shaking. Toni's view of them was obliterated when Bruce sat down in front of her.

Ignoring Toni, he smiled at Anna Mae. "Enjoying yourself, Mother Rollins?"

Toni hated when he called her that. It made her sound like

an elder in the church. She was surprised he had joined them. Neither one of them could stand the other.

"Yes. This is really nice. Folks are really enjoying themselves. I forget how popular Darius is. And you know how it is, you invite one person, then they invite a friend to come along. Make sure you get some food before Darius's friends eat it all," she said, but was joking—there was enough to feed a small army.

Bruce slapped a mosquito on his wrist. He wiped his blood and the remains of the insect on his thigh. "I asked Lynette to fix me a plate. I don't know what's taking her so long. Sometimes that girl is slow as molasses."

Lynn was no longer at the grille but waiting in the food line with three or four other people. "Well, she has had her hands full helping Aunt Hester Ruth with the cooking and trying to keep an eye on the kids," Toni said. Besides, was something wrong with his hands?

"Hester Ruth is doing most of the work. Lynn moves around like she's in slow motion."

"Well, it is hot out here. Lynn probably shouldn't even be on her feet this long. She is pregnant, you know."

"Pregnant?" he said dismissively. "Back in slave times a woman would pick cotton, give birth right there in the field, then go back to picking cotton."

With lightning speed Toni's head tilted to one side. *Are you crazy?* She would like to see his big ass walking around with a bowling ball pressing against his bladder.

Her mama must have seen the look on her face. "Oh, here comes Lynn."

Lynn weaved her way through two other tables and placed a plate in front of him. "Here you go. I got the chicken—Bruce doesn't eat red meat," she explained as if they cared, "some pasta salad, cole slaw and a roll, and I put some extra sauce on the side 'cause I didn't know how much you wanted." She set a blue paper cup, some napkins, and some utensils on the table as well. "I have to go back for the—"

Bruce hooked a finger over the rim of the cup and peered inside. Frowning, he let go of the cup.

She looked from him to the cup. "Wh . . . what?"

He held the cup up, practically under her nose. "What is this?"

"I . . . I think it's Coke or Pepsi—" Lynn said.

"Have you ever seen me drinking any kind of cola?" When she didn't immediately reply, he said, "Have you? Have you?"

Lynn's eyes darted away. "I'm sorry . . . somebody started talking to me while I was in line . . . I guess I picked up the wrong kind."

"You guess? You guess? It ain't about guessing. You did get the wrong kind. I swear, Lynn, sometimes you act like you're retarded or something."

She eased the cup out of his hand. "Sorry, baby. I'll drink this one. I'll get you some ginger ale, okay?" Despite her appeasing words, his angry expression didn't change. "Can . . . can I get you anything else?" she offered.

Bruce picked up a knife and fork and began shredding his chicken. Lynn slunk off like a dog with its tail between its legs. Bruce gave Toni a hostile glance before spearing a piece of chicken.

Toni wanted to ram it down his throat. A gut feeling told her that her sister put up with this shit day in and day out. If he was like this *in front of* her family, there was no telling what he was like when they weren't around.

Toni turned to her mama, her eyes searching for answers. Anna Mae shrugged and buried her face in Montana's neck. Noticing this, Toni thought, *Fine, Mama can put me off for now, but we will definitely talk about this before I leave.*

Montana wiggled out of Anna Mae's embrace. "Daddy!

Daddy!" She held out her arms, wanting to be picked up by her father.

He waved her off. "No, I'm eating, stay with Mother Rollins."

She called to him one more time. "Daddy!" Bruce shifted the contents of his plate around with his fork, trying to decide what he would devour next.

Rejected, Montana's little face fell.

Anna Mae kissed her on the neck again. "It's okay, baby. Bam-mama gonna get you cleaned up. Do you want to go swimming again? Or do you want to go in the house and get some nice, clean shorts?"

"Sh-wimmen," Montana replied, and Anna Mae was rewarded with a grateful kiss.

Toni was left to listen to Bruce noisily enjoy his food, feeling more and more irritated by the minute. Then he had to make it worse by opening his big mouth.

"What's taking Lynn so long? All I asked her to do was bring me something to drink before I choke to death. How hard can that be?"

Lynn had stopped to check on Dakota, who was sitting next to Aunt Hester Ruth.

"She's coming. She's making sure Dakota is okay. Why don't you stop sweatin' her, Bruce? Kids need a lot of time and attention, you know."

"At least I'm willing to financially support mine," he said between bites. "By the way, how's Marvin doing?"

Now, why he gotta bring my ex-husband's name into the conversation? Like he is so much better than Marvin. Toni had had just about enough of him. "You know what, Bruce?"

He paused in mid-bite. "What?"

"Screw you."

A half hour later, Toni found Lynn back at the grille. Rings of sweat near her armpits. Looking drawn and tired.

Toni took the long-handled fork from her. "Lynn, you look exhausted. This heat isn't good for you. Why don't you go inside, get out of the sun for a while?"

"Thanks, Toni," she said, stepping aside. "It is hot out here. But I got to stick around and watch the kids."

"There are plenty of people to watch the kids. And now that Bruce's basketball game is over, he can keep an eye on them."

Lynette quickly shook her head. "Bruce needs to rest. He works hard."

"And you don't?"

"That's different. I love taking care of my kids. It's not work . . ."

Yeah, right, and that's why you look like you've dropped about ten pounds.

"Bruce has a difficult job. It's hard trying to schedule all the shifts and work with all those different personalities. Not only do the kids that work for him get an attitude and come to work when they feel like it, but then he always has customers complaining—"

"Should I start playing the violin right about now?"

Lynette shot Toni a look, clearly hurt by her lack of sympathy. "No," she said slowly, "but you could try to be a little more understanding."

Toni understood perfectly. Like understanding that Negro wouldn't do anything that looked like work until after he'd tried to get someone else to do it for him. He was just using work as an excuse not to do anything around the house.

Still, Lynn had to be tired and Toni didn't want to make life more miserable for her by arguing about her stupid husband. She insisted that Lynn let the rest of them do the cooking and babysitting. Lynn thanked her for taking over. But instead of resting, she ran right over to Bruce, looking nervous and eager to appease. Toni tried not to let it bother her—but it did.

Toni was playing Simon Says with Dakota, Montana, and a couple of other kids when Joy showed up. Nobody could tell from looking at them that the thirty-year-old Toni was two years older than her sister.

"Did somebody say there was a party over here!" Joy cried, taking in the crowd. She started snapping her fingers and moving to the music. She waved and smiled at her mama and Aunt Hester Ruth, displaying a slight overbite, which a lot of Toni's male friends had told her was sexy. Joy was several inches shorter than Lynn. Where Lynn was lean and elegant, Joy was a series of uncontrolled curves. Half of her ass was hanging out her Daisy Duke shorts, Toni noticed, and she really didn't need to be wearing a short-cropped T-shirt. There comes a time in people's lives, when they don't need to let it all hang out, and from the roll of exposed flesh around her stomach, it looked like Joy had reached that point.

Joy set a bag down on the nearest table, then joined the dancers. A lit cigarette dangling from one hand, she shouted the usual cries about who was "in the house" and "the roof " being on fire. Joy followed that up with cuss words to really make her point.

Toni spied her mama over by the inflated kiddie pool. Anna Mae scowled, clearly disapproving of Joy's way of conveying her party mood.

The other dancers responded to Joy's call: "Burn, mother-fucker, burn."

Joy started doing some kind of freaky dance with a couple of Darius's friends. She rubbed her butt against the front of one guy's pants while positioning herself between the thighs of another. The two boys were trying to keep up, but from the stupid look on their faces they didn't know what had hit them. Joy's laughter rang out as she reveled in her sexual power.

"Auntie Toni?"

"Huh?"

"What does Simon say? My leg is tired."

Toni returned her attention to Dakota, Lynn's elder daughter. She and the other kids were still standing on one leg. Toni smacked her forehead. She was so engrossed with what Joy was up to, she had forgotten all about them. "Simon says, bring me Auntie Joy." The kids skittered away.

After the next song, Joy sauntered over. "Hi, Sis." She wiped her glistening forehead with the back of her arm. She had changed her hairstyle since Toni had last seen it. The braids were gone, replaced by a short bob that tapered in the back. Her hair color was different, too, a lighter brown that was much better than the unnatural yellow color she used to have in it. This shade complemented her caramel-colored skin. "Whew! It's hot out here," Joy said, handing Toni the brown paper bag she was carrying.

Inside it were two bottles of Colt .45. "What's this for?"

"It's my graduation gift to Darius. I figured he and his friends would be thirsty on a hot day like this."

"Joy, I don't know why you brought beer. Most of Darius's friends are underage."

Her eyes mocked Toni. "Just 'cause they aren't supposed to drink don't mean they don't drink, Goody Two-Shoes."

"Call me what you like," Toni said, setting the bag in front of her. "I don't care what Darius and his friends do elsewhere, but you know Mama and Daddy ain't gonna allow no underage drinking at their house."

"You know, Sis, you're starting to sound like Mama," Joy laughed. "Underage drinking? Most of Darius's friends are over eighteen. How can you be old enough to vote but too young to drink? Now, that don't make no kind of sense to me."

Toni suddenly remembered something. Her eyes scanned the crowded yard, then came back to Joy. "Where's Jesse?" she asked.

"Oh, he's with Fonzo."

"Who?"

"You haven't met Fonzo?"

Toni stared at her blankly. She hadn't seen Joy since Christmas, and anyway, she would need a scorecard to keep track of her list of boyfriends. The last she'd heard—from Mama—Joy was seeing a suspected car thief.

"I thought you were seeing someone named Greg."

Joy picked up a nearby plastic cup, peered inside to make sure it was unused, then twisted the top off one of the beer bottles and poured herself a drink. "Greg? Greg is in jail. Ain't nothing he can do for me now. So I had to move on."

Toni could see she was all broken up about it. Joy raised the cup to lips that were darkened from years of smoking. Her pupils were in constant motion and a little glassy. It looked like she'd already had a little something a lot stronger than beer before she joined the party.

"You say Jesse is with this Fonzo. Does that mean he's not coming to the party?"

"Naw, he'll be here. Fonzo just had to pick something up and Jesse went with him."

"Oh, that's good. I can't wait to see him." Joy finished off her drink and poured herself another one. Toni shouldn't have worried about her corrupting influence on Darius and his friends, because neither they nor anyone else would get a drop of the beer at the rate Joy was going.

"So tell me about Fonzo. How did you meet him?"

"I met him at the unemployment office."

"Oh . . . does he work there?" Toni knew that was a stupid question even before she finished asking it.

"Not hardly. He was trying to find out why his check was late."

It figured. But if he was collecting unemployment, that meant he had a job at some point. "So what kind of work does he do?"

"He used to be an electrician till he hurt his back."

"Will he be able to go back to that line of work, or will he try to do something else?"

"Naw, girl. He makes good money on unemployment."

An unemployment check was *good* money? Now Toni had heard everything. "Hey, there they are now."

Joy started waving someone over. Toni turned to see Jesse walking beside a rangy man dressed in a Tommy Hilfiger polo shirt and a pair of baggy shorts that stopped several inches below his knees. Toni assumed this was Fonzo. What really caught her attention, though, was the three children tagging alongside them.

"Is that Fonzo?"

"Yeah, that's Fonzo and three of his kids."

Three of his kids? Does that mean there are more?

As the group neared them, Joy said, "Fonzo, come and meet my sister."

"Whaddup?" he said, nodding in Toni's direction. He twirled a toothpick that hung from the side of his mouth. He had one of those old faces, like he'd lived a hard life. He could have been twenty-seven or forty-seven.

"Nice to meet you. I'm Toni." She felt overwhelmed by his woolly appearance. His shoulder-length processed hair was in need of a touch-up. He had hairy legs and forearms, and a mat of curly hairs escaped the top of his shirt.

His kids shifted restlessly at his side.

"Joy, aren't you going to introduce me to everybody else?" Toni asked.

She pointed at the eldest boy. "This is Alphonso Jr. He takes after his daddy, don't you think?"

With his lanky frame, he was the same build as his father. Toni only hoped his face wouldn't look as beat up by the time he was his father's age—whatever that was.

"And this one," she pointed at the other boy, "is Owen."

Owen had his mind on other things as he enviously

watched the other kids playing with the ball. He was probably around seven or eight years old.

The toddler was still clinging to Jesse's hand. She pulled up her dress with her other hand, revealing matching green and blue bloomers. "And . . . this is . . ." Joy faltered, searching her memory. "This is . . . baby, what's your name again?"

Toni slowly shook her head. *Lord, how long has Joy been dating the man? She doesn't even know his kids' names.*

"It's Princess," Jesse answered for her.

"Yeah, that's right. Princess," Joy said. "Y'all go over there and fix yourself a plate."

The three children hurried off, and only Jesse remained. The round framed glasses that he'd started wearing in kindergarten made him took like a wise elf. More serious and somber-looking than any little boy should be. "Don't you want something to eat?" Toni asked.

He shook his head.

"No? Then come talk to Auntie." Toni held her hand out to him, and he silently took it, stopping in front of her knees. She hugged him tightly to her, bending down until her chin touched the top of his close-shaven head. "Are you having fun this summer?" she whispered to him.

She felt him nod.

"What have you been doing?"

"Cooking," he said shyly, pressing against her legs with his body.

"Cooking? Are they teaching you that at day care?"

Joy interrupted before he could answer. "Don't pay that boy no attention." She returned to Fonzo, who was drinking from her cup.

"Fonzo, why don't you go make sure all the kids get something to eat? Alphonso Jr. will probably fix himself a plate and forget about his brother and sister." Joy turned to her son. "Jesse, go say hello to your grandma."

The little boy looked at Toni, clearly reluctant to leave his comfortable spot. *At least, Mama will see to it that he gets something to eat*, Toni thought, equally reluctant to let him go. She gave his thin shoulders a little push. "Go ahead, Jesse, I'm not going anywhere. I'll talk to you later."

Joy scooted over closer to Toni and put her arm around her shoulder. She usually didn't cozy up to her unless she wanted something, and Toni immediately tensed up.

"It's nice to have you home, Sis."

"It's good to be home."

"How is my spitting image?" Joy asked, referring to Sanji.

Sanji did look a lot like Joy. And she already was a flirt with men of all ages. But that's where the similarities would end, if Toni had anything to say about it. "She's sleeping. I think the traveling and staying up late finally caught up with her."

Joy's eyes swept over Toni, sizing her up. Then she said with a sunny smile, "Say, big sis, how about lending me a few bucks?"

Just as Toni had suspected, Joy did want something. Her request for money came as no surprise. Every time Toni came home, Joy hit her up for money. "Yeah, sure, Joy, just as soon as you pay back all the other money you've *borrowed* from me."

The ingratiating smile left Joy's face, but she didn't look shamed in the least. "Aw, now why you even got to go there? You know I'd pay you back if I had it. Things are just a little tight right now."

Weariness engulfed her. Toni got so tired of this shit. "Things are tight all over. Why don't you have any money? Didn't you just start a new job at a wig store?"

Joy reached for her cigarettes. "First of all, it's a discount beauty-supply store, not a wig store. And secondly, I don't get paid for another week. You know how it is." The begging look returned. "I'll be all right once I get paid. In the meantime, Jesse needs a few things. He's outgrown his shoes and a lot of his summer clothes."

Mentioning Jesse got to Toni, as she was sure Joy knew it would. "How much are you talking about?"

"A hundred?"

Since when did "a few bucks" become a hundred dollars? "Try again," Toni told her.

"Fifty?"

Toni could manage that. She nodded in agreement.

"Thanks. You're my favorite sister."

Toni felt no pleasure at this. Of course, she was Joy's favorite—she was the only one stupid enough to give her money that she would never see again.

Joy jumped up. "I feel like dancing. You coming?"

Toni shook her head no. The quickness with which Joy grabbed her beer and left let Toni know just how much of a *favorite sister* she was.

Her friend Fonzo returned with food heaped like pyramids on his two plates. After placing them on the table, he reached for the second bottle of beer. Leaning forward, he hunkered down over his food like he was afraid somebody might try to take it away. Toni watched, vaguely fascinated, as a hot dog disappeared in two bites.

Fonzo noticed her watching him. "You're not tall like Joy. Come to think of it, you don't look that much like her."

Toni's gaze swung from Fonzo to where Joy had resumed her nasty dance amid a flock of admirers. Fonzo got that right. She and Joy were two *very* different kinds of people.

c h a p t e r
2

"Please, Sanji, hurry up!"

Toni was waiting for her daughter to finish her cereal. To say that Sanji was not a morning person would be an understatement. But she was really outdoing herself this morning. Toni'd had to practically drag her out of bed. And even after she had sat Sanji on the toilet, her eyes had remained closed, her chin resting heavily on her chest. Then when she'd finally gotten her dressed, Sanji spilled orange juice down the front of her shirt, which meant a change of clothes. Now she was staring unhappily at the bowl of Crunch Berries in front of her.

"I don't like cereal, Mommy."

Toni sighed. "Sanji, what are you talking about? You have cereal every morning."

"But Chris *made* breakfast."

On Sunday, Sanji had spent the day at Chris's place. Called up and invited herself. Sanji claimed they needed "quality time together." Toni had no clue where she'd picked up that expression. Toni wasn't invited. She told Chris that Sanji could stay home if he didn't want to be bothered, but he seemed to want her around. Sanji stayed so late, Toni had to call and ask when he was bringing her back. Still, it had been nice to have a lazy Sunday afternoon for a change. Since they'd opened the salon, free time was a precious commodity.

Toni watched as Sanji swirled the increasingly soggy pink spheres in her bowl. Expelling a major breath, Toni said, "Is that right?"

Sanji nodded. "Yes, we had pancakes with syrup. And . . . and sausages. And Chris let me cook . . . and we made orange juice, too . . ." She paused to frown at her newly refilled glass. "Chris says fresh squeezed is the only *real* juice." She pushed the glass away. Toni held her breath, hoping she didn't tip it over yet again.

"I don't want this juice, Mommy. I want *real* juice like Chris's." The look she gave Toni was one of pure defiance.

It was almost seven o'clock. On Tuesday mornings Toni did hair at one of the local nursing homes and then worked at the bookstore from one to six. But first she had to drop Sanji off at the babysitter's. She felt tired just thinking about the day ahead. One more year of this, she vowed. After graduation she'd be ready to dedicate all her time to running the salon.

"Sorry, Sanji, but this is all you're getting. Do you want it or not?" Later, Toni was going to have a little talk with Chris about spoiling Miss Thang.

"No," Sanji said, folding her arms across her chest. At least Toni wouldn't have to fight with her over her hair. Chris had cornrowed it and fastened the ends with barrettes. The style should last several days, providing Sanji didn't take a notion to unbraid it—as she frequently did.

"Fine," Toni said, grabbing her juice glass, then putting it in the fridge. She poured Sanji's untouched cereal down the sink and briefly flicked on the garbage disposal. Over the metallic roar she said, "Sanjari, get your backpack, so we can get going."

Rolling her eyes, Sanji slid off her stool at the breakfast nook. Toni despaired as she watched her walk away. Sanji's blue overalls hugged her rear and dipped in dramatically at the waist. *If she has hips and curves plus a surly attitude now, what will her teenage years be like?*

During her absence, Toni checked her bag to make sure she had all the necessary supplies. When she worked out of people's homes or at the nursing homes, she had to bring her own stuff, and she was shit out of luck if she forgot something. She kept two portable dryers and all her scissors, clippers, combs, and brushes in the trunk of her car. But she didn't like to keep chemicals out there. Extremes in temperature affected them, so she always had to remember to re-stock her perms, shampoos, et ceteras. Even then she was just "guesstimating" what she would actually need when it came to the nursing homes. Unlike her individual clients, the clients at the nursing home didn't place their orders in advance.

She saw a few things she was low on. She'd get more when she stopped at the hair salon to pick up Chris.

Sanji returned with her backpack. Taking it from her, Toni grabbed two breakfast bars from the glass cookie jar on the counter and stuffed the bars in one of its zippered pockets. "Sanji, eat these if you get hungry before snack time."

"Hurry up, Mommy. We gonna be late."

Toni laughed. "Sanji, you got a lot of nerve rushing me."

Toni winced as Sanji slammed the car door, rattling its window, and then skipped up to Flo's front door. She sat in the semicircular drive, waiting for Flo to let Sanji into the white ranch-style house. Just beyond, a smattering of cows munched lazily on green tufts of grass. Only a wire fence kept them out of Flo's front yard. Not that a stampede looked imminent, Toni thought as one cow awkwardly bent at the knees, lowering her heavy girth to the ground. A fully equipped playground was on the other side of the house. Newark, Delaware, was such an odd place, a mixture of college town, farmland, and suburban refuge for people who worked in Philadelphia or Wilmington.

"Bye, Mommy," Sanji called before disappearing through the door. She didn't look back to see Toni's answering wave. Toni put the car in drive and had started to pull away when she heard Flo call her name. Toni glanced out the window and saw the fifty-something woman walking toward the car. Dressed in a nylon jogging suit and sneakers—sensible clothing for a baby-sitter, she supposed—Flo was only a few inches taller than some of the kids she watched. Toni braked and leaned over to roll down the window of her Saturn.

"Hey, Flo, what's up?" she asked. "Did Sanji forget something?" Flo rested short, plump fingers across the edge of the door and leaned in. Brown freckles dotted caramel skin.

Dark, inquisitive eyes gave the car's interior the once-over. Flo was very clean. Toni didn't know how she did it with a house full of kids.

"No, no," she said in her twangy, high-pitched voice. She reminded Toni of a Munchkin. "I just came to tell you that I'll be on vacation next week."

Toni stared at her. She couldn't have heard right. "Vacation?" Toni repeated stupidly.

"Yeah, I'm going down the shore to spend a week with my sister."

"But . . . but, Flo," Toni stammered, both panicking and pissed. "What about the kids?"

Flo hunched her shoulders. "Everybody's gonna have to make other arrangements."

Make other arrangements? Like that was a piece of cake. Toni sucked her teeth. Bit her lip. Tried to stifle the urge to strangle her. "Flo, this really puts me in a bind."

Another shrug. "I'm sorry, but I need time off, too, ya know." Then she added, "Besides, I thought you were taking Sanji to day camp for the summer."

What does that have to do with anything? Toni turned to

watch the cows for a moment, so that Flo wouldn't see the daggers in her eyes. Flo's damned vacation was not coming at a good time. "Flo, camp doesn't start for two weeks. What am I supposed to do about *next* week?"

"I dunno," she replied without a smidgen of sympathy. "What am *I* supposed to do when disloyal customers take their kids someplace else for the summer?"

Disloyal? Toni looked at her in earnest. Flo was drumming stubby fingers along the inside of the window. The tap, tap, tapping noise against the plastic panel only intensified Toni's irritation. "Flo, I'm sending Sanji to camp because it's cheaper and because she'll be doing a lot of structured activities like arts and crafts, learning about nature and going on field trips. She can't do that here."

"You don't seem to have a problem leaving her here during the school year," she said. Abruptly she straightened and stepped away from the car. "I can't leave the kids in there by themselves for too long."

On her way back to the house, Flo fired a parting shot: "And, Toni, since I won't be here next week, can you drop off what you owe me this Friday?" Confident that Toni wouldn't refuse, she walked away.

By the time Toni pulled in at the mini-mall on Route 40 where the salon was located, she was feeling a bit overheated. Not from the early summer weather, but from the conversation she'd just had. Flo was an excellent child-care provider and had more flexible hours than most day-care centers. But the woman needed to work on her professionalism. How could she give less than a week's notice that she was going on vacation?

Toni sat behind the wheel for a moment, trying to calm her nerves. That's when she noticed the patch of fine red bumps that had appeared out of nowhere on her forearm. It hadn't been there when she got dressed this morning. She resisted the urge to scratch and instead opened the car door. She'd deal with it and Sanji's day-care crisis later.

Shear Necessity was wedged between a grocery store and a video store. The mini-mall also had a large hardware store and a couple of fast-food restaurants. She and Chris were hoping to attract people who wanted to get several errands done at once: the wife who got her hair permed while her husband went home-repair shopping or the kids who after their haircuts were rewarded with pizza or a burger.

Toni's fingers trembled slightly as they traced the black lettering etched into the glass—Shear Necessity. Owned and operated by Antonia Carleton and Christopher Van Aken. She turned the key in the lock and pushed open the door. Her heart quivered with pride, and anticipation coursed through her. It happened every time she entered the salon—even though it had opened almost three months ago.

Part of her couldn't believe that a long–wished-for dream had come true. It was ironic that being mowed down by a car last fall had turned out to be one of the best things that ever happened to her. Thank God she only came away with a concussion and a couple of cracked ribs. She still had occasional nightmares about the accident. Lights coming at her. Lying in the street, gasping for air. The worst nightmare of all had Marvin, her ex-husband, performing emergency surgery on her. Since it was completely the driver's fault, his insurance company had provided a settlement that was just enough seed money to start her own business and pay off her car loan.

Toni flicked on the lights. To the right of the entrance was a chest-level reception desk. Toni placed her oversize bag on it. Chris should be here soon, and they'd head off together from here.

Chris and Toni had met in a technical writing class almost five years ago. They sat next to each other every Monday, Wednesday, and Friday, exchanging idle chitchat and notes.

Then one day she made some offhand remark about the professor's hair looking like a bird's nest, and they really began to click. Toni had gotten her cosmetology license before she married Marvin and moved to Delaware. It turned out that Chris was a hair stylist, too. They both had eventually declared business as a major. Chris still wasn't sure what he was going to do with his degree, but he had some inherited money, which took the edge off of "finding himself."

A loud crash came from the storeroom in the back of the shop. It was followed by a string of muffled curses, which caused Toni's heart to leap to her throat. *Who the hell is back there?* Toni reached for the nearest object: a blow-dryer. The sound of footsteps heading her way sent her racing over to the front door. Just as her hand clutched the doorknob, she heard her name being called. She whirled around to find Chris standing there, using a wad of paper towels to dry the outside of a recently washed coffee carafe.

"Chris, you scared the hell out of me!" she accused, holding the blow-dryer against her heaving chest.

He smiled, and even though she was annoyed with him, she couldn't help but appreciate his good looks. Chris's longish, thick golden hair was naturally streaked by the sun. It was the envy of some of her customers, who wanted the same done to their hair and then were disappointed to learn that it was a color created by God, not Clairol. His skin was golden, too. Chris had a year-round tan that came from lazing around his backyard in the summer and courtesy of a local tanning salon in the winter.

His green eyes scanned her from head to toe. He chuckled when he saw the blow-dryer in her hand. "What were you gonna do with that? Comb and fluff me to death?"

"Ha-ha, very funny. I didn't think you were here yet. I didn't see your car outside."

"I took it in to get new brake shoes. Marsh dropped me off."

Marshall and Chris had been together for three years, lived together for two. "Why didn't he stick around?" Toni asked.

"He's putting the finishing touches on the new deck he just built. He couldn't wait to get rid of me. A home-repair project is more appealing than my company, can you imagine that?"

Yes, she could imagine it. Chris's boyfriend spent every free minute working on the townhouse they shared. Marshall and Chris were a classic case of opposites attracting. Chris was easygoing and definitely not into working up a sweat. Marshall, a corporate banker, had been born with an appointment book in his hand. Everything had to be planned with him. Naturally, in between the lovey-dovey moments they complained about the other. Always trying to get Toni to choose sides.

It sometimes surprised her how easily she bantered back and forth about relationship stuff with them. Toni had never had a gay friend before she met Chris. Acquaintances maybe but never actual friends. Maybe the comfort she felt around them was due to the fact that Chris had been unattached when she first met him. He'd been her friend long *before* Marshall and had stayed pretty low-key about who he was dating. Looking back, she suspected he was protecting her somehow by not talking about his love life. Then Marshall came along and a serious relationship started. By that time who Chris loved or slept with didn't matter to Toni.

Chris started waving a small white waxed-paper bag in front of her. "Croissant?"

Toni raised an eyebrow, then took the bag from him. Usually he showed up with some grease-soaked doughnuts. After she took a bite out of a chocolate-laced croissant, she murmured, "Chris, you're too good to me."

He shrugged and took the bag. He wrapped a paper napkin around a croissant and pulled it out. "I just know how you are. You run around like a madwoman, and though you never forget to feed Sanji, you often forget to feed yourself."

He was right. But Toni ignored hunger when she was busy and didn't feet hungry when she was tired. Unfortunately, both circumstances occurred a lot. "It's not like Sanji would let *anyone* forget to feed her."

"Be glad. That means she's assertive."

Toni rolled her eyes. Assertive. That's not the word she would have chosen. Chris was always defending Sanji. And the feeling was mutual.

"Fine. She's assertive. Now, we better get going. We don't want to keep our customers waiting."

The nursing home ran on a tight schedule. Lunch was served at twelve sharp, so they had to be done with everyone's hair by eleven forty-five. When the elevator reached the basement, Toni pressed the hold button, then quickly unloaded her stuff. A small room off the laundry served as their temporary styling salon. She didn't know what it was normally used for—Chris thought it might have been a kitchen at some point—but the two stainless steel sinks it boasted made it ideal for their purposes.

The drone of washing machines and the smell of detergent and bleach greeted them. While Chris put out chairs in the hall outside the door of their makeshift salon, she opened her bag and took out a stack of magazines and flung them on a nearby table. A lot of the old folks at River Bend Villas had failing eyesight and couldn't read regular-size print. However, looking at the pictures was better than staring at the walls and vending machines while they waited.

She loaded their supplies onto one of the two portable carts that they left on the premises—they were so old and beat up no one would steal them. Nearby, on a rectangular folding table, was another dryer.

When Chris returned, Toni asked, "So how many heads

we got today?" He picked up a brown clipboard from the table. The residents signed up for their appointments the night before.

"Twelve."

"Twelve heads in four hours? Think we can do it?"

"No sweat. Almost everybody is coming for a wash, cut, and set." He checked the list again and cocked an eyebrow. "I have to warn you, Mrs. DuFour is coming in today."

Toni groaned. Mrs. DuFour could be sweet with her cute French accent—when she was in her right mind. The last time she'd been a handful, screaming that Toni was hurting her, yanking her scalp, when she knew she wasn't. "I'll flip you for her."

Chris shook his head. "I don't know. I think she likes you better."

"Thanks a lot. Little do you know you're adding insult to injury."

He was unraveling the cord to his blow-dryer. Pausing, he looked at her. "What do you mean?"

"For the past two days, all I've heard from Sanji is 'but Chris says this' or 'Chris did this' or 'Chris did that.' By the way, are you deliberately trying to turn her against me, or is it just an unconscious thing?"

Chris laughed. "My, my, somebody is in a stank mood," he said. He'd picked up that word "stank" from Toni and now ran it into the ground.

She threw a box of curler tissues at him. On reflex, he caught it. "I am not in a stank mood. I just been around stank people today . . . present company excluded, of course. Like I said, first Sanji then Flo . . ." The elevator dinged, then the sound of people talking as an attendant brought down their first customers.

Chris looked at her quizzically, waiting for her to finish her sentence.

"I'll finish telling you once we get the first group settled."

Toni reached for the faded blue smock she wore to protect her clothing.

"Okay," he said.

The aide, a black woman in her forties, wheeled in the first resident. "Mornin,'" she said. "I got one more coming down the hall. She's using a walker. When you think you be ready for the next group?" Three other women and an elderly man took a seat in the "waiting room" chairs.

"Maybe in an hour and a half, two hours tops. Tell you what, I'll use the phone in the rec room to call upstairs and let you know when we're ready."

The woman nodded before turning away.

Chris had already started washing the first woman's hair. The other four chatted with each other. They were laughing and actually seemed happy to be here, which lightened Toni's mood. Generally, she found the older people easier to work with. Getting their hair done was a treat that many of them looked forward to, and it gave them a chance to talk to somebody new.

She smiled as she beckoned for the woman sitting closest to the door to follow her. She was a petite little thing, shorter than Toni. Her hair was hidden behind a red paisley cotton scarf. Toni remembered her from the last time. She'd worn a scarf then, too, explaining that she didn't like to go out in public if her hair wasn't fixed. Toni didn't know what she meant by "out in public," but she liked a woman who still cared about her appearance even if she was old and not going anywhere special.

Toni picked up the clipboard and glanced at it. The nursing home staff had to approve the use of chemicals ahead of time to avoid negative interactions they might have with prescription meds a resident was on. Her first client, Miss Reynolds, was getting her hair colored, cut, and styled.

Toni pulled the cart closer to the sink and gathered the supplies she would need: a pair of rubber gloves, a bottle of

semi-permanent color, the color energizer, a plastic applica-
tor bottle, and comb. After mixing the hair color with the energizer, Toni set the bottle aside. She tied a thick wad of
cotton around the edges of Miss Reynolds' hairline to keep
the dye off her face. With the end of the comb, Toni parted
her hair in quarters. She evenly distributed the solution,
mostly on the roots since there was still color at the mid-
lengths.

Miss Reynolds' hands rested on her lap. A humongous di-
amond was on the ring finger of her left hand. Toni had always called her "Miss," but seeing the ring made her
wonder if the woman had ever been married. She didn't ask,
though. Toni had found that clients told her what they
wanted her to know, and what they didn't bring up was none
of her business. She never knew what kind of bad memories
an innocent question might dredge up. "That's pretty nail
polish you have on, Miss Reynolds."

She held gnarled, blue-veined fingers out. "You like? It's
called Crimson Tide."

Once the color was in, Toni put a clear plastic cap on Miss
Reynolds' head. She turned to see how Chris was progress-
ing. His client was a black woman. She was very fair-
skinned, kind of reminded her of Lena Horne. The woman
was dressed in a housecoat and fuzzy white slippers. Chris
was lucky: it looked like a simple wash, blow-dry, and curl.
Two sets of curling irons were stuck in the heating plate on
his cart.

Strands of her hair flew as Chris held the dryer in one
hand and used a comb to detangle a targeted section of her
head. He could have been a walking advertisement for
Surfer Magazine, yet he was perfectly at home doing an old
black lady's hair. He'd been trained at school in West Philly,
so he had learned to do all types of hair. That's why they
made such a terrific team. Toni and Chris didn't want to set
limits on who their clientele could be. Race, creed, color,

didn't make any difference to them. Shear Necessity was about artistry, customer satisfaction, and making money.

Toni used a towel to dab a thin trail of dye that threatened to ooze onto Mrs. Reynolds' forehead. She asked her if she was doing okay, any stinging or burning. Mrs. Reynolds said she was fine. A crackle and then the pungent smell of singed hair as Chris began curling.

He noticed her watching him. "How's it going?" he asked.

"Fine."

He grabbed another lock of hair and quickly tightened the curling iron around it. "So finish telling me why you're in a stank mood," he invited.

Toni put Miss Reynolds under the dryer. As she adjusted the heat on it, she said, "Well, Sanji was just being Sanji, but I get her over to Flo's and Flo announces that she's going on vacation next week. That puts me in a bind. I signed Sanji up for day camp, but that doesn't start for two weeks."

Chris frowned. "Can Flo do that? Just leave without warning?"

Toni looked at the clipboard, then beckoned the next client to come in. A Mrs. McElrath. A simple wash and cut. "Flo runs the day care out of her house, and she's licensed. But it's not like we have a written contract or anything." She shrugged. "Flo can do whatever she wants." Toni settled the woman in her seat. "But you know what I think?"

"What?"

"I think Flo's just doing this out of spite. I think she's mad because I'm putting Sanji in day camp for most of the summer, and that's money out of her pocket." If Flo was mad now, she was really going to be pissed come September. Sanji would be starting school full-time and Toni would be paying for only a couple of hours after school each day, if that.

"Do you really think she'd do that?" Chris looked at her

in disbelief. Toni envied him. He didn't have a vindictive bone in his body, so he wouldn't understand how petty people could be sometimes.

"Hell, yeah—"

Mrs. McElrath's head moved under her hands as she chuckled.

"Oh, excuse me, Mrs. McElrath." One of her professional rules was no cussing in front of clients.

"I'm not offended," she said. "My daughter Irene had to raise three kids when her husband got killed in Vietnam. Owen, Claudia, and Mark. They're all grown now. Did your husband die, too?"

Only in my revenge fantasies. "We're divorced," Toni said.

"Oh, that's too bad," she murmured.

Toni shrugged. There was really nothing to be sorry about. Marvin had never been much of a husband. It was him not being much of a father to Sanji that really got to her. "Anyway, Chris, Flo gave me some little speech about loyalty before she dropped this bomb on me. I don't mean to be disloyal, but if I get Sanji into a free day camp, why would I spend a hundred and fifty dollars a week?" Toni rinsed Mrs. McElrath's hair, then carefully checked to make sure all the shampoo was out before applying the conditioner.

"So what are you going to do?"

"I don't know. I was hoping you or Marshall could keep her a couple of days." Marshall sometimes worked at home.

"I might be able to keep Sanji on Thursday, and Marsh will be in and out of town for the next couple of weeks . . ." His eyes were downcast as he added, "In fact, he'll be in Santa Fe next week."

She tilted Mrs. McElrath's head to the left with one finger, then held her head steady as she clipped the hair close to her split ends. "I guess I'll have to take Sanji with me to the nursing homes next week," she went on. "And on the days when I can't find a baby-sitter, I'll have to take a sick day."

"Do you really have to do that? Why don't you ask Marvin to keep her?"

Toni's answering look said it all. Asking Marvin would be like spitting out the window of a speeding car. It would just fly back and hit her in the face. He'd have a million and one excuses why he couldn't do it, and hearing them would only piss her off. Toni asked Marvin to help out with Sanji only if she was really desperate, and she wasn't desperate—yet.

She had a few days to find out what his new excuse would be.

chapter
<u>3</u>

When a loud, persistent banging shocked her awake around midnight, Toni knew it could only be one person. Marvin. He'd done this "just dropping by" stuff before. She had fallen asleep on the couch while reading some trade catalogs for the bookstore. And she didn't appreciate the interruption. She was just hitting her REM sleep groove. In her dream, she had been sailing around the world on a yacht with an all-male crew that catered to her every whim.

Toni hit the hallway light switch to better see the recurring nightmare at the door. Through the peephole stood a shadowy figure. She had been meaning to ask the landlord to replace the light but hadn't gotten around to it.

She put the chain on the door and opened it a crack. She then went through the motions of asking who it was—as if she didn't know.

"It's me, Marvin."

Dressed in a Chicago Bulls jersey and matching jogging pants, his baseball cap on backward, her ex-husband was looking much younger than his thirty-two years. Despite the time of night, he looked like he was ready to go shoot some hoops. Marvin was an inch shy of six feet, and a neatly trimmed goatee surrounded his full lips. Thick brows and wide-set eyes, in coffee-colored skin, were so like Sanji's, it looked like he spit her out.

Those eyes were now boring into her. He leaned against the door frame, at ease and melding with the night. "Why did it take you so long to open up? You got a man in there or something?"

What? Is he the jealous ex-husband now? "How is it your business if I do?" was her swift retort. "I don't ask you about the company you keep."

"Yeah, but I got a right to know if you bringing unsavory people around my kid." Toni was tempted to laugh. The most unsavory character she interacted with was him. "So you gonna let me in? Or what?" he asked.

"Or what," Toni said under her breath. But she didn't really mean it. Marvin was the only person left that she could ask to keep Sanji. She had been paging him for days, but he hadn't bothered to call her back. She closed the door and took the chain off. Toni opened it again but blocked his entrance. "Marvin, what do you want?"

"I want to know why you haven't brought my daughter over to see me."

Since when has it become my responsibility to take Sanji to you? Marvin lived fifteen minutes away in Wilmington, sometimes with his younger brother, sometimes with his woman and her kids and their kids. It depended on which one of them was mad at him about something.

"Marvin, when have I ever stopped you from seeing Sanji?"

"C'mon, Toni, you won't let her set foot in my house."

"That's because that bitch you're living with is crazy." The words came from a deep well of pain that refused to dry up despite the passage of time. Then again, maybe she should thank Tiara for forcing her to wake up and see that Marvin was playing her for a fool. *Stupid, trusting me thought all those late-night hang-up calls were the work of a crank caller*. Not even when someone keyed and egged her car did she suspect anything. Toni was certain she didn't have any enemies. So she shelled out the five hundred–dollar deductible to have the repair shop smooth, sand, and paint over those deep grooves, believing all the time that she had been the victim of random vandalism.

She felt a rush of anger all over again thinking about how genuinely baffled Marvin had seemed by all the strange goings-on. How long, she wondered, would the lies have gone on if she hadn't decided on the spur of the moment to take Sanji on a picnic at Lums Pond? No sooner had they settled themselves in near the Nature Center than they spotted Marvin. His brother Leroy had picked him up that morning. Marvin never bothered to tell Toni how he was spending his time, so when she saw him in the park, she thought maybe they'd come to do a little fishing. He and Leroy did that sometimes.

Toni was surprised and maybe curious rather than suspicious when she saw him standing near a woman and a gaggle of kids. The woman had a newborn in her arms. Toni thought she was an acquaintance. Marvin had met a lot of people through the jobs he kept quitting, but then the woman leaned toward him and kissed him and, from what Toni could see, he wasn't exactly fighting her off.

Toni didn't know how she ended up standing right between them. Then she hit him. She punched him so hard, her hand came away with blood from his lips and her split knuckles. Then with all her might she kneed him in the nuts. Marvin's eyes opened wide in shock as he doubled over, one hand clutching his groin and the other his bleeding and rapidly swelling upper lip. The woman started to say something, but Toni held up her hand and suggested the woman shut the fuck up before she got beat down, too.

Marvin's voice pulled her back to the present. "Why you got to call Tiara a bitch?"

Toni's bitter eyes stared back at him. If he didn't know the answer to that question, then he was a bigger fool than she thought. Not only was that newborn Marvin's baby, but so was the oldest boy. Apparently, Tiara and Marvin went back a long way, and when he moved back to Delaware, they didn't let minor details like his wife and child keep them from resuming their screwed-up relationship.

"Toni, you gonna let me in or not?" He slapped his arm. "These gnats are driving me crazy."

"Keep your voice down. I don't want to wake up Sanji." Not that there was much chance of that happening. Sanji slept like the dead. Toni opened the door wider and stood aside. "Come on in. I need to talk to you anyhow."

Marvin preceded her into the living room. He pushed the catalogs she had been reading to the side and took a seat on the couch.

He smiled and said, "I smell onions. What y'all have for dinner?"

"Smothered pork chops."

Taking off his cap, he said, "Man, I love your smothered pork chops."

He gave her a hopeful look that Toni pretended not to see. *Do I look like I'm running a restaurant up in here?* "Marvin, I really don't appreciate you knocking on my door at this time of night. Since you haven't seen Sanji in almost two months, couldn't this burning desire to spend time with her wait until the morning?"

"Two months?" he frowned, then smiled, trying to charm her. "C'mon, it hasn't been two months?"

"April eighteenth, to be exact." She remembered the date because she had just picked up Sanji from a friend's birthday party and spotted him waiting for a bus on Kirkwood Highway. Sanji saw him, too—that's the only reason Toni had offered him a ride.

"Look, I don't know how you expect me to visit her if I don't have a car."

Was it her fault his drunk-ass brother crashed his car? Was it her fault that Leroy had been driving around uninsured and couldn't afford to pay the repair costs? "You might not have a car, but is anything wrong with your dialing finger? Sanji hasn't heard from you in weeks."

Marvin sat up straighter and stroked his goatee several times. A tic had started above his right eye. "Well, I am here now," he said.

"Yes, you are here. But it's a wasted trip. Sanji is in bed, and I'm not waking her up."

He nodded, surrendering without a fight. "So what you been up to?"

Toni bit back the answer that immediately came to mind. *Working my ass off at two jobs to support myself and the child that you abandoned.* "Not much. I went home for Darius's graduation a few weeks ago."

"For real?"

She nodded.

He shook his head in disbelief. "Darius is a high school graduate? Man, it seems like he was playing pee-wee ball just yesterday."

"He starts Ohio State in the fall."

"I always knew Darius would go far. How's Mama?"

It irked Toni that he still called her that. He'd lost all claim to her mama when the divorce papers were finalized.

"She's fine," Toni said. "How about you? Are you still working?" When she had seen him last, Marvin had a job as a dispatcher for a moving company.

"No, I am not. I can't be working for nobody that talks to me like I'm nothing." The smile had left his face. "My supervisor was this beer-belly redneck who thought he was still in the mountains of West Virginia . . ."

Toni tuned him out. She had heard the "Marvin Carleton

don't take no shit from nobody" speech many, many times before. But Marvin took offense at any hint of criticism. He was always coming home upset because a boss hadn't liked his ideas about how his job should be done. Sometimes she actually agreed with him. Sometimes the way a supervisor spoke to him did border on verbal abuse. But when you're working for somebody else, you rarely get to have the last word. Even if the work environment was "unbearable" like Marvin always claimed, you found another job first, *then* quit.

". . . so I told him what he could do with his job!" He stopped abruptly. "Toni, are you even listening to me?"

"Uh-huh. You were telling me you quit your job. How long ago was that?"

"About a month."

Toni said, slowly, "So, you're not working right now?"

His eyes narrowed, regarding her with suspicion. "I already told you that. Why you so interested?"

"Don't worry. I ain't trying to hit you up for money." Toni had long since learned not to rely on Marvin for child support. She took him to court once, and that was enough for her. Marvin had actually told the judge that he didn't have any money to support Sanji because he had to take care of his other two children—his two illegitimate children.

Toni repeated herself. "Marvin, I don't want any money from you, but I was wondering if you could keep Sanji for me next week since you're not working."

He was already shaking his head. "A whole week?"

This is exactly why I hate asking him for anything. "Marvin, it's not a 'whole week,' just Monday through Friday, and I'll take her with me to the nursing homes on Tuesday and Thursday morning."

He got to his feet, shaking his head. "I dunno. That's still five days, and I got things to do."

Toni stood up, too. She put her hands on her hips, challenging him. "Like what?"

He stared at her, helpless. Behind his eyes she could see that mechanism which served as his brain, trying to think up a good excuse. He shrugged. "I . . . I need to look for a job."

What a tired-ass excuse. "You been without a job for a month. Would it kill you to wait one more week? Marvin, you know I wouldn't ask if I could have found anybody else."

Toni watched as his entire body sagged. His resistance was weakening. She pressed on. "Marvin, you showed up tonight because you said you wanted to see your daughter . . . well, now here's your big chance."

"I dunno, I need to talk to Tiara first—"

"Tiara? What's she got to do with it?"

He regarded Toni uncertainly, his hands mangling his baseball cap. "I'm staying with Tiara right now, and if Sanji is coming over—"

Sanji staying at Tiara's place? The same Tiara who'd scratched up her car, schemed to break up her marriage, and refused to pass along messages to Marvin from his daughter? Even now she still called Toni's house and hung up as if Toni was the reason Marvin hadn't gotten around to marrying her. Toni didn't trust Sanji within ten feet of that psycho. Obviously, the man was confused. "Hold up a minute, I ain't said nothing about Sanji staying at that bit—" She corrected herself. ". . . woman's house. I'm willing to drop Sanji off at Leroy's. He's just around the corner from you, or I can pick you up and you can stay with her here."

"I'm on Leroy's shit list," he said. Toni regarded him levelly. She was not interested in his problems with Leroy. "I guess I'd have to come over here."

It was her turn to relax. Marvin would take care of Sanji next week. That's all she needed to hear. "Thank you, Marvin, I really appreciate it." She had gotten what she wanted.

He could leave now. Toni made a big production of picking up the clock from the table. She turned it so he could see its silver dial. "It's late."

Marvin put his cap on, and, as he passed the kitchen, said, "How about wrapping me up one of those pork chops for the road?"

You have to be joking. Let your woman feed you. "Sorry, I only have enough leftovers for me and Sanji."

Toni stepped around him and practically raced down the short hallway and opened the front door. When he caught up with her, though, he used a long arm to push it closed. Sighing, she turned around to face him. "Now what?"

"Well, since I came all this way, you might as well let me look in on her. Let me kiss her good night. And in the morning, tell her that her daddy was here."

"Fine." Sanji's room was just to the left of the front door. Toni opened the door to her room and ushered him in. "Make this quick," she whispered. "I'm tired." There was enough moonlight coming in through the mini-blinds to guide his way to the bed.

He bent over Sanji and placed a quick kiss on her cheek. "Good night, Miss Behavin'," he said, calling her by her nickname. As if reluctant to leave, he gave her yet another kiss. Something about the way he lingered, lightly touching her arm through the covers, tugged at Toni's heart.

As angry as she got with Marvin, she never really doubted that he loved Sanji. But it wasn't a grown-up love. He wasn't doing right by her popping in and out of her life like he did.

He straightened and turned toward Toni. Sanji stirred behind him.

"Daddy?" Sanji rubbed her eyes and sat up in bed.

Toni couldn't believe it. Sanji had slept through him banging on the door. She'd slept through them arguing in the living room. And now with the slightest touch from her no-good father, she woke up like Snow White after the prince kisses her.

A big smile on his face, Marvin turned back around. More awake than she ever was on the mornings when Toni had to get her up, Sanji quickly scooted over so that he could sit next to her. "Daddy, whatcha doing here?"

"I came to see you, Miss Behavin'. How's Daddy's heart?"

Toni leaned against the doorjamb. Marvin had started the question-and-answer game he always played with Sanji.

"Fine," she replied.

"Why do you have to go to school?" he asked.

"It's where you learn important information."

"And what do you need to do in school?"

"I need to study hard, be nice to the teacher, but even the teacher doesn't know everything." Toni wasn't sure she liked the answer they'd worked out to that question. Marvin, though, smiled in approval.

"What will you say when nasty little boys try to kiss you?"

"Back off, or my daddy will shoot ya!"

Marvin laughed. "That's right. And what will you be when you grow up?"

"A nun who lives in a convent."

"And who will you always love from deep down in the bottom of your heart, no matter what?"

"You, Daddy," she whispered before placing a kiss on his cheek.

Toni looked away before her daughter's unquestioning love for her father broke her heart.

c h a p t e r
4

Anna Mae drove the metal end of an old-fashioned wooden-handled chopper into an onion, creating a small pile on a cutting board. Nearby, cubed white potatoes were soaking in a large bowl. "If anybody asks you, where I am going . . . I'm going up yonder . . . I'm going up yonder to be with my Lord!" Her soprano filled the kitchen, amid the smells of cinnamon and nutmeg wafting from a couple of sweet potato pies that were cooling on the counter behind her.

With only her youngest, Darius, still living at home, the house was quieter than it had been in all of her thirty-two years of marriage. Darius was out with friends tonight, and her husband, Clarence, didn't get off work until ten. Anna Mae sighed contentedly. Lord knows, she loved her family, but it was nice to have the place to herself. She had been able to get an early start on her Sunday dinner. Then once she was done, she planned to color her hair. Gray roots were starting to resurface beneath the auburn rinse she'd put in it three weeks ago. It was times like these, she missed Toni. Being a hairdresser and all, Toni always made her hair look real nice, and the color lasted longer, too, when she put it in.

Toni had been her usual bossy self when she'd come for Darius's graduation in May. Not at all like the bruised and battered wreck she'd been at Christmas. She still couldn't believe Toni had gotten hit by a car and hadn't told anybody. Anna Mae shook her head, picturing how Toni had held her side and moved so gingerly around the house at Christmas. Toni was too closed-mouthed. Family was supposed to take care of each other. Toni didn't even give anybody a chance to. It just wasn't right—not telling her own mama. Toni had said she was all right, and Anna Mae reckoned she was.

With slender hands that had already begun to crook inward from too many years of cleaning up after other people's messes, Anna Mae scooped up the onions and dumped them into an empty bowl. She picked up the bowl of potatoes, walked over to the sink, and drained the water off.

When the doorbell rang, she jumped. Almost immediately, an impatient finger pressed the bell again, letting out a long, unrelenting buzz. Frowning, Anna Mae set the bowl on the counter. *Now, who is that ringing the bell like a doggone fool?* She dried her hands on a small towel that was hanging on a drawer handle.

In the sitting room, Anna Mae paused to switch on the light before entering the foyer. She blinked at the brightness that flooded the tiny vestibule. The bell continued its racket. "Hold on, I'm coming. Who is it?"

"Mama, it's me, Joy. Open up."

Surrounded on all sides by thick green foliage and flowering plants, Anna Mae fumbled with the two locks on the door, opened it, then unlocked the metal security door as well. Light from the front porch bathed Joy and Jesse, her son. "Joy, where are your keys?" Anna Mae asked, though she knew the answer. Joy moved around so much, she'd lose her head if it wasn't attached to her.

"Who knows?"

Anna Mae groaned as she stood to one side to let them in. "Joy, this is the third time you've lost the keys to the house. You know how that upsets your daddy."

"Then don't tell him," Joy said as she and Jesse headed past Anna Mae for the sitting room.

"Now what kinda attitude is that?" Anna Mae called after her. "Where will you be if the wrong person gets a hold of the keys and busts in here on us?" And that was a real possibility given some of the so-called friends Joy hung out with. Lazy bags of bones. Slouching around like just saying the word *work* would bring on a heart attack. Of course, Joy wouldn't see it that way. All she saw was how much fun her friends were.

Pausing before continuing through to the sitting room, Anna Mae picked up the tail end of an ivy plant that had started in a large straw basket overhead but now was creeping along the edge of the windowed side of the small hallway. "Samson is looking kind of sickly," she observed. "Remind me to give him a stick of plant food." She reached overhead to poke her fingers around the compacted soil in the planter. "Hmm, maybe I need to re-pot him. He has to have room to breathe. Don't you, baby," she said, stroking his brittle leaves.

Joy said, "Mama, will you stop talking to that darn plant and come in here?"

Anna Mae gently arranged the vines along the windowsill before following Joy's instructions. She stood near the closed door and regarded her second-born child. Though they were the same height, five-six, Joy was about ten pounds heavier, and after having Jesse, her flat, tight stomach was a distant memory. Joy laughingly called it her little pitcher's mound.

Her latest hair color was a brassy blonde. It was parted in the middle, knotted into a ponytail which was then thrown over one shoulder. Her dark brown roots were showing. There was no sign of her son. "Where's Jesse?"

"Huh?" Joy paused in the act of shrugging out of her leopard print jacket. "Oh, he went upstairs to find Daddy."

Six-year-old Jesse was such a quiet child. So unlike his cousins, Dakota and Montana, who were in constant motion. And Sanji . . . Sanji put a magpie to shame. Jesse and his grandfather had an odd relationship. On a good day, neither one had much to say. But Clarence was the only one Jesse actively sought out. Anna Mae would stumble across them sometimes: Clarence reading the paper and Jesse watching Clarence read the paper.

"He's not home yet," Anna Mae said.

Joy shrugged. "I guess Jesse will find that out when he gets upstairs." She sat down in her daddy's easy chair and propped her feet on the matching brown plaid ottoman.

Anna Mae nodded. Catching sight of the tiny gold nose ring Joy sported, her expression turned disapproving. Sticking metal in your nostrils was just plain nasty. It looked painful, too.

She took in Joy's blouse, a black fishnet that had a gold lining. Her black leather pants were so tight, she probably had to slather with Vaseline to get into them. "You look like you going out or something."

"It's Thekla's birthday. So me and the 'hos are going out to celebrate."

The *'hos?* Anna Mae cocked her head to one side. "You and who?"

Joy, who had been inspecting her tricolored nails, raised her eyes at her mother's tone. "Latifah, Michelle, and Kaye Jay. We gonna get our groove on."

"Why you calling them the 'hos? That don't even sound right. If they're 'hos, what does that make you?"

Joy waved a dismissive hand at her. "Aw, Mama, the name don't mean nothing. It's a term of endearment. Stop being so old-fashioned."

Old-fashioned? Since when did friends call each other 'ho? Anna Mae replied, "Well, I don't care what you call 'em to their faces, but I don't want you talking like that in my house."

"Fine." Just then a long buzz emitted from the kitchen. Her tone deceptively light, Joy said, "Mama, I think your time is up."

When Anna Mae opened the oven to look, she found that Joy had followed her into the kitchen.

"It smells good up in here, Mama. Whatcha cookin'?" Joy lifted one of the lids of a pot. "Hey, now . . . greens," she said as steam dripped from the lid into the steel vessel. She peered into another pot. "Red beans and rice? Mama, who is gonna eat beans in the summer?"

"Your daddy asked for 'em." Anna Mae smiled. Clarence loved beans. Pinto, lima, butter beans. Didn't matter. He ate them year-round. Beans made her feet like she was carrying around a lead weight in her stomach, but they didn't bother him.

Putting on a pair of oven mitts, Anna Mae took out the fudge coconut brownie surprise she was taking to church to-morrow. Only her daughters knew that the "surprise" was two shots of rum instead of vanilla extract. Reverend Turner would have a fit if he knew about the rum, but what he didn't know wouldn't hurt him. Besides, all the alcohol burned off during the cooking. "Joy, clear a space on the counter so these brownies can cool." Joy quickly reorga-nized the foil-covered dishes and pies. After she set a blue and white enameled trivet on the counter, Anna placed the rectangular baking pan on it.

"So what you gonna do with Jesse while you out 'gettin' your groove on'?"

Joy inspected one of the pots again. "Are the greens done yet?"

Anna Mae nodded, aware that her daughter had ignored her question.

Joy opened a cabinet door above the sink and took out a

small ceramic bowl. Anna Mae silently handed her a serving spoon. Joy filled her bowl with the steaming vegetables and the chunks of smoked turkey Anna Mae had used to season it.

She grabbed a bottle of Red Devil hot sauce that Anna Mae always kept on the table and liberally doused her food. After the first forkful, she rolled her eyes heavenward. "Umm . . . This is *so* good."

Anna Mae was accustomed to being complimented on her cooking. After all, she cooked for a living. She was a cook at a private girls' school and then on weekends worked for her sister, Hester Ruth, with her catering company. She cut a two-inch square of cornbread, put it on a small saucer, and handed it to her daughter. Within minutes, Joy had cleaned the bowl and held it out for a second helping. Anna Mae refilled it and handed it back. Joy immediately dug in. "Girl, you eating like there's no tomorrow."

Before answering, Joy reached for a napkin to wipe her mouth. "I didn't realize I was hungry until I started smelling all this good grub. I don't think I ate anything all day."

Anna Mae's eyes widened in alarm. "What do you mean, you ain't had nothing to eat? It's nine o'clock. What did Jesse eat today?" When Joy scrunched up her face as if she had to think about it, Anna Mae felt anger well up inside her. She threw the pot holder she just picked up toward the table, barely missing Joy's fork, which was posed for another bite. She walked over to the stairs leading to the second floor of the house. "Jesse! Jesse, baby, come downstairs!"

"Okay, Grandma," he called back.

Anna Mae returned to the kitchen to find Joy cutting herself another piece of cornbread.

"Mama, this cornbread is da bomb. What's the green stuff in it, jalapeños?"

"Joy, what the hell is wrong with you?"

Anna Mae rarely cursed, and Joy nearly dropped her cornbread in surprise. "Wh—what?" she stammered.

"Why you ain't feed that boy? It's almost a brand-new day! What is wrong with you? I didn't raise you like that."

"Mama, he did eat. He fed himself," Joy said with a hint of pride. "In fact, that's what woke me up today. I heard him moving around, banging stuff in the kitchen."

Anna Mae stared at her in open-mouthed amazement. How could Jesse feed himself? He was only six years old. "What do you mean, he woke *you* up? What time of day are you talking about? Besides, the boy needs more than one meal a day. And you sound like you don't even know what he ate."

"Come on, Mama . . ." Joy purred, trying to snuff out the flames of her mother's anger. "Why you getting all mad?"

Anna Mae's scowl remained in place. Joy didn't used to be like this. As a child, she was the most helpful of Anna Mae's three girls. She never had to get on her to do her chores, and she followed Anna Mae everywhere she went. Responsible and a regular mama's girl. Then she hit her teens and all signs of that little girl vanished. Anna Mae didn't understand what had happened to her. That lack of understanding was mirrored in the took she now gave her.

Sighing, Joy said, "Oh, for God's sake, Mama, I ain't gonna let my own child starve—"

"Well, you could've fooled me," Anna Mae muttered. She lowered her voice as she heard Jesse thumping down the stairs. "Joy, Jesse shouldn't have to scrape up a meal. That boy can't raise himself."

"Aw, Ma—"

Anna Mae interrupted her as Jesse stepped into the room. "Joy, your foolishness has got to stop."

The boy's round eyes were magnified behind his round wire rimmed glasses. They shifted uncertainly from his mother to his grandmother, not sure what he had walked in on. He was a skinny little thing with a head shaped like a peanut.

Anna Mae held out a hand, beckoning him to come closer. He didn't move. "Joy, we'll finish this conversation later."

"Whatever."

Whatever? Anna Mae's eyes swung around to her again. *If Jesse wasn't here, I'd go upside your head with one of these saucepans.* Anna Mae turned to her grandson. "Jesse, are you hungry?"

Jesse regarded his mother's empty bowl, licked his lip, then nodded. "A little."

Anna Mae laughed. "Well, we got plenty. Come here, let Granny help you out of that coat." As Jesse began to take the coat off himself, Anna Mae noticed the small navy backpack he had placed on the floor. "What you got there?"

Jesse's finger held onto the back of one of the chairs. In answer to his grandmother's question, he looked at his mother, who was finishing off the last of her cornbread. It took Joy a moment to feel his gaze upon her. "Oh, that's his stuff," she said.

"What stuff?"

"His clothes for church tomorrow. I figured since I'm going out tonight, I might as well bring him over here just in case I oversleep. He's supposed to give his speech, and I wouldn't want him to miss it."

Anna Mae wasn't falling for this. "The children's program isn't until three in the afternoon. How late you planning on sleeping?"

A car horn honked loudly and repeatedly. Joy jumped up from the table. "That must be my ride." She kissed the side of Jesse's head. "See ya tomorrow, little man." Not waiting for him to respond, she left the room at a trot.

Anna Mae followed her into the sitting room. As Joy slipped on her shimmery jacket, she asked, "Mama, you seen what I did with my purse?" When Anna Mae shook her head, Joy started searching under the throw pillows on the couch.

"Joy, you were sitting in the chair, not the couch."

"That's right." Joy moved her search over to the recliner. She straightened suddenly and patted herself down. Anna Mae detected the anticipation in her eyes, the wide grin, and wondered if Joy got excited about anything besides partying.

"Oops, I forgot. It's in my pocket." Joy reached in and pulled out a small gold purse. She snapped it open, looked inside. "I got my cash and I got my cigarettes, so I'm good to go."

"Joy, wait," Anna Mae said, stopping her daughter before she got to the door. Joy gave her a questioning, slightly impatient look. "Joy, I really don't appreciate you dropping Jesse off like you delivering Sunday's newspaper. I have a lot of stuff to do tonight."

"Aw, Ma. Jesse ain't gone get in your way. Just put a kiddie tape in the VCR—*Hercules* or *The Lion King*—and he'll be fine. Besides, in a little while it'll be time for him to go to bed."

"That's not the point. I know Jesse ain't no trouble. But did it ever occur to you that I might like having some time alone every once in a while?"

Joy finished zipping her coat and walked over to her mother. Enveloping her in a bear hug, she said, "I'm sorry, Ma. We didn't decide to go out until the last minute, and I couldn't find a baby-sitter on such short notice."

Anna Mae slowly shook her head. When she and Clarence couldn't find a baby-sitter, they stayed home. Who was keeping Latifah's and Kaye Jay's kids tonight? she wondered.

The horn honked again. "Kaye Jay is waiting for me. I

gotta go . . ." Joy turned on the light and entered the foyer. "Kiss Jesse good night for me."

Anna Mae nodded. "You want me to pick you up for church?"

Joy waved to the passengers in the already crowded, dented Ford Escort that idled at the curb. "Huh?" she said. "Naw, Ma, that's okay. I'll take the bus. Like you said, I've already put you to enough trouble. I'll see you tomorrow."

With Jesse waiting in the kitchen, it is a little late to be worried about inconveniencing me. Anna Mae shut the front door. She needed to finish making her potato salad, and there was no point attempting to color her hair with a child under foot. If Clarence wasn't too tired when he got home, maybe he could keep an eye on Jesse and she could do it then.

When Anna Mae returned to the kitchen, she found Jesse seated at the table, his hands clasped in front of him like an old man, worry etched in his brow. Anna sat down next to him and turned over his hands, touching and smoothing his palms. "What's the matter, baby?" she asked him.

Without looking up, he said, "Grandma, Mommy was supposed to practice my speech with me. I got six lines but don't 'member all of them."

Is that what he's frettin' about? Jesse—though usually not his mama—went to church every Sunday, and Anna Mae was the one who had given him his speech. The kids were doing a program on the great stories of the Bible. Jesse's speech was about the Good Samaritan. She had a copy of it upstairs. She patted him on the head. "Don't worry, baby, Grandma will go over your speech with you. You gonna be the best speech-giver up there by the time we done finished practicing. But first I want you to have a little something to eat." She pushed away from the table.

Jesse released a big sigh, then nodded. Anna Mae busied herself fixing him a plate. She gave him a little of everything that was done cooking. No point in asking him what he wanted because he always asked for one or two dishes and that was it. But she knew he'd eat more if she gave it to him.

Anna Mae set the plate down in front of him and handed him a fork. She watched him as he took a bite of the macaroni and cheese and slowly chewed it. When at long last he swallowed, she asked, "How's it taste?"

"Good." Then he smiled at her, the first smile she'd had from him all night. "Grandma?"

"Yes?"

"Is Mommy coming to hear my speech?"

The longing in that simple question made her want to weep. Anna Mae placed a hand on one of his thin cheeks. "If she can make it, baby, she'll be there. If she can make it. And me and Grandpa Clarence gonna be in the front row."

Jesse considered this for a moment, then stabbed at his macaroni again. "I hope she can make it, Grandma," he said solemnly.

"Me, too, baby," Anna Mae echoed. "Me, too."

chapter
5

Toni tugged on the hem of the black V-neck sheath she was wearing. The mid-thigh dress hadn't looked so skimpy when she'd tried it on in Macy's dressing room. She was paranoid that one false move and her goodies would be on display for all the world to see. She had Chris to thank for that, since it was his brilliant idea that they get all decked out tonight. He said they needed to do something to celebrate the grand opening of Shear Necessity. Toni thought the celebration was coming four months too late. Besides, a more practical way to get the word out would have been to send flyers to the neighborhoods near the shop, but Chris had nixed that idea. "Bo-ring" had been his exact word.

He said, if they wanted Shear Necessity to be seen as upscale, then they needed to act upscale. Something about spending money to make money had figured into his argument as well. Furthermore, he insisted it was never too late to party. Toni could never resist him when he got fired up. Chris's enthusiasm was contagious.

Not that he had waited around for her to agree. The plans for the party were already in the works by the time he told her about it. His family were charter members at a local country club, and Chris had already rented out one of the reception rooms before telling her about his "idea." He had shrugged off Toni's concern that they couldn't afford a big party right now. Chris said not to worry, he had it covered. He had explained that the trip he'd planned to take to Paris with Marshall had fallen through because Marshall couldn't get away from work. So they had decided to use the money for this party instead.

Toni shook her head as she slowly edged her way through the crush of people. There was no way the money he'd saved from this trip had paid for all this: the fancy room, the caterer, and a DJ. The only thing that he hadn't sprung for was the liquor. If people wanted to get lit, there was a cash bar.

The high heels of Toni's T-strap shoes sank into the intricately patterned carpet as she moved over to the buffet table. It was hard to believe that there was a time when most of her shoes had towering heels. Standing on her feet all day had forced her to learn to accept her five-foot stature.

Once at the buffet she picked up a plate. She had already said her hellos to a few people and probably should be schmoozing more, but that was not her thing. Besides, she was starving. She worked a few hours at Shear Necessity, waited until the last minute to buy something to wear tonight, and then had packed some stuff for Sanji, who was staying with her friend Brittany overnight.

People were enjoying themselves. In the dimmed lighting, Toni watched small groups at the crisp linen-covered tables that sat eight to ten talking and laughing. Each table had a small floral centerpiece and lighted candle. A spacious square of parquet flooring had been left in the front of the room, where the DJ, one of their customers, was mixing it up, playing a little R & B, a little techno, and some pop music. Toni wondered if Chris had schooled him on who was going to be there, or if Brandon had just quickly pegged this crowd. Toni had invited a few people from the bookstore, some of her neighbors, and, of course, all of Shear Necessity's regular customers. But by far most of the people were folks Chris had invited.

It looked like the United Nations up in there. That's the way Delaware was, Toni mused. When Marvin had first talked about moving back to his home state, she hadn't been too keen on the idea. "They got any black people besides you and your family there?" she had asked. But surprise, surprise. The First State was a former slave state, so a sizable number of blacks had been living there for centuries, especially in the southern part of the state. And wedged between Philly and Baltimore on the Interstate 95 corridor, plenty of blacks had migrated from those larger cities. Then you had the yuppies who came to work for the big banks who profited from the lenient corporate tax laws, and the engineering and pharmaceutical companies like du Pont, Merck, and Gore had imported nerds of all creeds and colors. And everybody was representin' tonight. Toni estimated that there were between seventy-five to a hundred people milling about.

She stopped fussing with her dress long enough to sample the tortellini and sweet pepper salad and a honey-lime salmon dish. "Umm, this tastes good," she murmured. It had been a while since her taste buds had been treated to anything that took more than thirty minutes to prepare. In fact, the selection of food was pretty overwhelming. Fancy focaccia bread and quesadilla appetizers. Besides the tortellini, there was a couscous salad with chicken and peas. Another pasta salad with tomatoes. Sesame noodles, sautéed scallops, grilled pizza, some kind of vegetarian stir-fry. And Toni hadn't even checked out the dessert table yet. At any rate, this was no run-of-the-mill rubber chicken affair. Toni was starting to suspect that this little shindig had cost more than a trip to Paris for two.

A pair of strong arms suddenly encircled her waist, taking her by surprise. Toni craned her head around and found herself staring into Chris's smiling eyes. He released her, and she turned around to face him. He wore an olive pinpoint oxford shirt and a pair of off-white microfiber cuffed pants. She had barely seen him all night because, unlike her, Chris had been making the rounds. Every time she caught a glimpse of him, he was chatting with someone different.

"Wanna dance?" he said.

Toni finished swallowing her most recent bite of the salmon. "You lied to me," she accused.

"About what?"

She gestured with her free hand. "About how much all this is costing."

He shrugged. "Don't worry about it. It's not coming out of Shear Necessity's budget."

"That's not the point. It's . . . it's . . . too much."

"Hey, it's only money. And if I want to throw us a party, why not?"

Toni could only stare at him in puzzlement. Chris was such a good friend, she sometimes forgot they came from different worlds. His family had made a modest fortune farming mushrooms in Hockessin. "Must be nice to be born with a silver spoon in your mouth," she said dryly, but not really begrudging his good fortune.

"Yeah, it is. So stop worrying. I'm not going bankrupt. Besides, Marsh will probably find some way to write it off. You know us filthy rich, we are always looking for ways to beat the tax man."

So was Toni, but somehow she hadn't managed to figure out how to do that. Toni returned a wave from Dottie, a cashier at the bookstore, before answering. "So where is Marshall?"

He and Chris had come in separate cars. When she'd spoken to Chris earlier, he'd mentioned that Marshall was running a little late. Apparently, he had gotten caught up with his latest remodeling project: adding a bathroom in the basement.

"Oh, he's around somewhere."

A cheer from the crowd rose when Brandon put on a remixed version of Lauryn Hill's "That Thing." More people poured onto the dance floor.

"Let's dance," Chris said again.

"In a minute. Can I finish eating first?"

"Well, make it quick because I'm ready to get down and get funky."

Toni laughed. Chris was an enthusiastic, albeit rhythmically challenged dancer. He had three left feet, if you included the fingers he insisted on popping totally off the beat.

His eyes narrowed suspiciously. "Did I say something funny?"

She shook her head, then changed the subject. "So did Marshall finish the bathroom today?"

The people on the dance floor were starting to get loud, so Chris moved closer to her and practically shouted, "Here's a little secret. We don't really need another bathroom. Marsh just gets off on all that hammering, sanding, drilling, and scraping."

Just then Marshall appeared behind Chris. He was just under six feet and had curly light brown hair that was combed away from his ample forehead and just beginning to gray. He was ten years older than Chris. "Did I hear my name being maligned?" he teased. He leaned forward to peck Toni on the cheek.

"Well, I don't know about being maligned," she replied. "But Chris thinks you have a secret desire to be a carpenter."

"Some of us like to be a little more productive in our free time. There are other ways to unwind than guzzling a couple of beers and sitting in front of the TV."

Toni had seen Marshall's work. He really could be a carpenter if he ever gave up banking. "If you ever finish fixing the place up, y'all gonna have the best-looking house on the block," Toni said. She put her empty plate down on a small table that was there for that purpose. Someone from the catering staff immediately removed it. Dah-am! Dirty dishes disappeared like magic. Toni wished she had someone who could do that around her house.

"I'm glad somebody appreciates my hard work. By the way, you took great, Toni." He took a swig of his Heineken.

She looked down at the inches of exposed brown thigh. "You don't think my dress is too short?"

Chris scoffed. "How do you ever expect to get a man if you don't give him a taste of what he'll be getting?"

Toni rolled her eyes at him. Why did Chris insist on viewing her as desperate to find a man? Women did have other things on their minds. "And here I was thinking I needed to have brains and a good personality. Besides, I'm not out to catch a man. This is supposed to be a business-related event." She took in the charcoal lightweight blazer and gray slacks that Marshall had on. "You clean up pretty nice yourself."

"You think so?" Marshall unbuttoned the jacket and twirled around.

The sight of the sag in the rear of his pants brought a smile to Toni's face. She'd seen the outfit before on Chris. Marshall was a couple inches shorter than Chris, but it still fit him nicely. "Yes, y'all make a cute couple."

"Yes, we do," Marshall agreed, putting an arm around Chris's waist.

Toni saw Chris stiffen, then go very still. Marshall felt it, too, because his eyes immediately began searching Chris's face.

Chris quickly glanced around the room. Toni knew he was checking to see if anyone had noticed. No one was paying them any attention. But that didn't stop him from taking a step away from Marshall. "Not here, Marsh," he said, apologetic.

"Why not here?" Marshall challenged. His voice was level but the eyes that had regarded Chris with affection just moments earlier now teemed with anger and hurt.

She watched a fake smile play around Chris's lips. "Like Toni said, this is a business event and . . ." he paused. ". . . You know."

Marshall replied, "No, I don't know. Maybe you can explain it to me."

Chris suddenly hailed a college-age kid from one of his classes who came up to say hello. His plate was laden down with food.

"Nice party, man." He popped a Swedish meatball in his mouth even as he spoke. "We don't get this kinda grub at the frat parties."

Chris slapped him on the back. "Glad you could come, Charlie. Eat up."

When Charlie ambled on his way, Chris turned back to a stony-faced Marshall. "C'mon, Marsh, cut me some slack," Chris pleaded.

"Why don't you cut me some?" Marshall retorted. "This is just like Christmas. And your grandmother's birthday party . . ."

Toni looked from Chris's pained expression to Marshall's angry one. She didn't know what had happened at Christmas or Chris's grandmother's party, for that matter, but this was not the time to get into it.

Toni grabbed Marshall by the arm. "They're playing my groove," she said, dragging him out to the dance floor.

She danced to a couple of songs with a barely moving Marshall. She spent as much energy.trying to cajole Marshall into a better mood as she did making fancy dance moves. Her attempts to lighten him up didn't work, so when she felt a trickle of sweat on her forehead, she called it quits.

She didn't want to get all hot and funky and stink up her new dress.

Toni paid the tuxedoed bartender for a cranberry spritzer and wandered through a set of French doors that led to a patio overlooking the golf course. Surprisingly, only a few people had been tempted by its relative quiet. She took a seat on a low stone bench that bordered the patio railing, not caring that her dress hitched up. At the end of the patio farthest from her, a middle-aged man was playing octopus with a girl half his age. She wasn't fighting him off, though. Red tips of cigarettes glowed in the darkness as a couple of smokers indulged their craving a few feet away. A comfortable summer night's breeze was blowing. Toni closed her eyes against the sight of a full, orange-tinged moon. Intermingled with the cigarette smoke was the lemony smell of roses in the air. She took a sip of her drink. *It's nice out here*, she thought, glad to be away from the noise and the strain of smiling as people she knew and didn't know came up to wish her good luck with Shear Necessity.

"Toni."

She opened her eyes with a smile. Chris had materialized at her side as if he knew she was thinking about him. He wasn't alone. Marshall and another man were with him. Curious, Toni gave the newcomer the once-over. A brother, probably around her age, in his early thirties. Average height, upright posture like a military man. Her eyes traveled up from the small cleft in his chin to the intelligent brown eyes that seemed amused by her open inspection of him.

"I told Marsh you would be out here," Chris said.

She nodded. "I needed a break from the noise."

"Uh-huh. Anyway, we wanted you to meet someone. This is Beale."

"Hi, Bill," Toni said and extended her hand.

He grasped her hand in a firm handshake. "No, Beale," he

corrected in a voice that was surprisingly deep. James Earl Jones deep. His eyes flickered appreciatively over her crossed legs, then back to her eyes.

Toni sat up a bit straighter and placed her hands at the edge of her dress. *Like that is going to make my dress hem any longer.* The guy noticed the futile gesture, and a smile lurked in his eyes. "Beale? Is that your first name or your last name?" Toni asked.

"It's a family name that I got stuck with. It's a long story—"

Chris cleared his throat. "Well, since it's a long story, we'll let you tell it. Marsh and I need to get back to the other guests."

And I don't? Toni challenged him with a look. Chris's matchmaking was not subtle. When the other two men disappeared back through the French doors, Toni rose from the bench. She wasn't comfortable with the way her dress kept riding up. "So tell me about your name," she invited.

"Actually, it's Beale Jefferson. Beale is my mother's maiden name, and there were no more males on the Beale side. So I got the name to keep it going."

"Beale," she said, trying the word out on her tongue. "It certainly is unique."

"Especially when you say it."

Toni's hand went up to finger the small opal she wore around her neck. Opals were supposed to bring luck to people born in October. Her hand landed on the pulse that was fluttering erratically at her throat, and she jerked it away. "Uh, so how do you know Chris and Marshall?"

"Actually, it's Chris. He used to cut my hair when he worked at Frank's place, Fresh Look. But we kinda developed a friendship, too."

"Really, then why haven't I seen you around? I know most of Chris's friends."

"Probably because I'm so busy."

"Doing what?" His eyes widened at her tone. Now, that did sound rude, Toni had to admit. Had she gone so long without socializing that she had forgotten how to talk to people? Toni softened the question. "I meant, what do you do?"

"I'm an art teacher."

"Wow." She was genuinely intrigued. She had never met a male art teacher before. A male industrial arts or shop teacher, but that was not the same. But hell, did that mean he was gay? It wouldn't be the first time Chris had tried to hook her up with someone who later turned out to be gay. She realized that the silence had stretched on a little too long, and said, "Most teachers have regular hours. Where do you work that keeps you so busy?"

"Laurel. It's a private school."

Toni had never heard of it, but that wasn't surprising. Delaware probably had as many private and parochial schools as public. Desegregation hadn't gone over well, even if the school Sanji attended was about fifty-fifty.

"It's not the teaching that keeps me busy. I'm also a photographer."

"Oh, really? Now, that's an interesting job. You're probably surrounded by beautiful women all the time."

He leaned back against the railing and crossed his legs at the ankles. "I wouldn't say that. I work with models sometimes—both male and female. But mostly I do photography for local advertising, so it can be a picture of anything from a side of beef to side-by-side refrigerators. I do weddings, too, which means that the most beautiful woman in the room is unavailable."

Toni tried to interpret that statement. So did it mean he wasn't gay? Get with it, Toni, this is the new millennium, he could be bi. *And why do you care anyhow?* she asked herself The man was just making conversation.

"Well, it still sounds interesting. You get to meet people in different professions."

He laughed, a rich, hearty sound that left a lingering echo in the air. "So do you."

She smiled. "That's right. But shampooing a pilot's or banker's hair is not the same as getting to see how they work. Which is what you do."

"Oh, I don't know, your job sounds pretty interesting, too. Hair stylists and barbers rank right up there with bartenders and therapists. People trust you with their secrets."

True, people did tell her all their business. And she didn't blab. So, it did sound kind of important when he put it that way. The couple that had been making out at the far end of the patio walked by them on their way back to the party. The octopus had one hand on his woman's butt and the other on her breast.

Toni sighed, glancing wistfully at the moon. Octopus or not, it had been a long time since anyone held her like that. She turned back to find Beale staring at her intently. "Well, I should get back to the party. Chris has been doing most of the work. I'm not much of a hostess," she said apologetically.

"Oh, I don't know if I agree with that. I've found you to be pretty good company."

Toni ducked her head. She hoped he didn't think she'd been fishing for a compliment. "Uh . . . well. Thanks for saying so," she mumbled, mortified because she couldn't even look at him. Lord help her, she'd been off the market way too long.

When she made to walk past him, he stopped her with a light touch on the arm. "Toni, since you expressed interest in my work with models, I'll keep you in mind the next time I'm doing a shoot with models." At her startled expression, he said, "I know you're busy and all since you just opened the shop, but if you're interested . . ."

Her eyes lit up. "Of course, I'd be interested!" When he laughed at her enthusiasm, she lamely added, "I mean, I'd love to. It sounds more glamorous than what I usually do. I'm always looking for ways to branch out."

"Great. Well, like I said, I'll give you a call."

"I should give you my card." Then she looked down and remembered, she'd left her purse in the car. "I don't have any with me, but they are scattered all over the tables inside. I'll get you one."

"Don't worry. I know where to find you. I told Chris I'm going to start coming to Shear Necessity to get my hair cut."

"Oh," was all she could think to say. Then, "Speaking of which, don't you want to see my work before you hire me to work for you?"

"Did you do your hair tonight?" he asked.

"Yes," she said. Her face warmed as his eyes moved over both her hair and her face.

"Then I've seen all I need to see. You look beautiful."

"Oh." This time it came out as a croak, and Toni knew it was time to get back to the party. She was pathetic. The man was just being nice and she was getting all flustered. She took a long sip of her drink, and prayed that her tongue would be untied by the time she had to say good night to their guests.

chapter
6

Lynn smoothed out the small puckers in the needlepoint canvas that rested on her knees. She had a lap frame but rarely used it. The cross stitches were slowly bringing to life a lithe caramel-colored dancer who was caught in the sinewy ebony arms of her male partner. Her body was arched backward, her outstretched arms poised above her head. His hands supported her just beneath her rib cage. Lynn had painted on the design herself. Powerful and romantic. "Not bad, if I do say so myself," she murmured. The canvas was for Mrs. Ewing, her way of congratulating her teenage daughter Maureen for getting the lead in her dance academy's latest production. With a new baby on the way, the hundred and twenty dollars Mrs. Ewing was going to pay would come in handy. Since she wasn't working, Lynn tried to supplement the family income any way she could, mostly by baby-sitting the neighbors' kids and with her needlework.

She had learned needlepoint in a home ec class and fallen in love with stitching. She had moved from buying pre-painted canvases to creating her own designs. Needlepoint was something she could do when she was around other people. She even came to realize that people were less bothered by her silences when she was needlepointing. Not that she ever got much opportunity to say what she was thinking, growing up with Joy and Toni, she reflected. Those two could trade words and insults for days at a time. But she wasn't into verbal battles. And when she did venture an opinion, people had a way of out talking her, making her point of view seem weak or silly because she wouldn't defend it hard enough. From what Lynn had observed, once people made their minds up about something, they weren't likely to change it. So what purpose did arguing serve?

Lynn hummed along to Tracy Chapman's "Revolution" as she pushed the needle through the canvas and firmly yanked the gold thread that made up the dancer's leotard. The CD player was down low because she didn't want to wake Bruce. He had closed the restaurant last night and hadn't gotten home until after two. He'd been up for a few hours earlier in the day and then fell asleep watching ESPN in the bedroom. Lynn looked at her watch. Six o'clock. Bruce had been out for a while, almost four hours. He must have been really tired, she thought.

To make sure she hadn't missed any stitches, Lynn held her handiwork up to the light filtering through the windows. Most of her pieces were much smaller than this one. She'd been working on this piece every chance she got for almost two months straight; in the doctor's waiting room, in the car when Bruce was driving and at night when she finally got the kids to bed, or quiet moments like this when the kids were playing in their room. If she kept up her current pace, she should be finished with this one by next weekend. Mama could give it to Mrs. Ewing when she saw her in church on Sunday.

Lynn sighed, feeling guilty. She hadn't been going to church much lately. Too tired. Sometimes just getting out of bed was a challenge.

She glanced around the small living room. They lived on the second floor of a rented two-bedroom duplex. Examples of her work were everywhere from the throw pillows on the couch and armchair to the potpourri-filled wildflower pouches that hung on small hooks. But she was especially proud of the family supper scene above the television. She had intended to give it to Mama as a present but found she couldn't part with it because it reminded her of her Sunday dinners, the only time the entire family had sat down for a meal together—because Mama had insisted.

Slender fingers worked deftly, adding yarn to cloth. Lynn found needlework relaxing and could scarcely believe that people were willing to pay her to do it. Her specialty was making ornaments as Christmas gifts, using black folk art as a motif. Toni was the one who had convinced her she should start charging people. Toni went so far as to help her develop a list of fees based on the size of the project and the materials used. Lynn had only four customers at the moment, for which she was extremely grateful. Every little bit helped. And it eased her guilt about Bruce having to work so hard.

When she first met Bruce, he had been so committed to starting and raising a family. He talked about all the kids he wanted to have and the things he would do with them. Family trips. Going to church. Coaching their Little League team or being a Scout master. Lynn had the same dreams. All she ever wanted was to be a good wife and mother. And at first they lived that fairy-tale existence. But Bruce's idea of family became more and more narrow. He'd never gotten along with his folks, and with each passing year he complained about the time she spent with her family—or anybody except him and the kids. He said it was confusing for the kids to get different messages from everybody when they misbehaved. He thought Mama in particular was too lenient. He also felt the kids would be better off with a stay-home mom and so did she. So she quit her job even though they really needed the money.

Bruce started working longer hours to compensate for the

loss of income. He didn't hang out with friends. He didn't go to bars. His only outlet was going to the gym. He was a good man. He just worked too hard. Got so wound up trying to take care of them.

Lynn shifted in her seat. Sweat from her legs made them stick uncomfortably to the couch cushions. She lifted up for a second to free her khaki shorts. Barefoot and dressed only in a ribbed white T-shirt and shorts, she still felt overheated. The two window fans recirculated moist, heavy air, making Lynn wish they had air conditioning. It was scorching inside and out. She paused to push back a few strands that had escaped her ponytail. Being pregnant in the summer was not fun, and this pregnancy had really slowed her down compared to the others. She couldn't remember being this tired when she was carrying Dakota and Montana. She had liked being pregnant then, marveling at every little sign that life was growing inside her and feeling more alive because of it. It was different this time. It was hard. And now the doctor was saying she needed to gain weight—

"Gimme! Gimme!"

She recognized Dakota's war cry immediately. It was followed by a high-pitched wail of pain. Pooh, the little boy from down the street. Lynn was watching him this week because his regular baby-sitter had the flu. She tossed the canvas on the couch and stood up. Too quickly, her spinning head informed her. She grabbed the arm of the couch to steady herself. The wails stopped for a moment, followed by what felt like a lengthy silence. Then Pooh let out one of those I-sucked-in-as-much-air-as-possible-before-screaming screams.

Through the cracked door of the master bedroom, Bruce bellowed, "Lynn, what the hell is all that racket?"

She didn't stop to answer but went directly into Montana and Dakota's room. The three kids were in the middle of the floor between the two twin beds and surrounded by an assortment of games and toys. Pooh was holding his arm and still yelling his head off. Despite the deafening howls, he didn't have any obvious injury, Lynn was relieved to see. Dakota was trying to get him to be quiet without much success. Montana was hugging a Blues Clues doll to her chest.

"What's going on in here?" she asked, and they all turned. Lynn spied surprise, guilt, and worry flashing in the rounded eyes of those small faces. "Well?" she repeated more softly, now that Pooh was at least trying to stifle his tears.

Lynn grabbed a couple of baby wipes from the nearby dresser and took him gently by the shoulder. She wiped his nose and mouth and said, "Blow." He did. The tears had turned to hiccups. She caressed the locks of his curly light brown afro; there was an unexpected patch of almost blond hair at the nape of his neck. "So tell me what happened?" Though she was asking him, she was looking at the other two.

"Pooh," Dakota said. "Pooh took my Blues Clues."

"Dakota, you know you're supposed to share," her mother reminded her.

"But I wasn't done playing with it," the four-year-old explained. Clearly expecting that to override the sharing rule. "Pooh wasn't playing nice," she added for good measure, regarding the little boy severely.

"Still, you didn't have to make him cry. You should have come and told me," Lynn said. "What did you do to him anyway?"

"Nothing."

"Nothing?" she repeated, her tone disbelieving. She hoped Dakota was not about to turn into a little liar. Lynn tilted Pooh's chin up. His fat yellow cheeks were streaked with tears. She wiped his face with a second baby wipe. "What did Dakota do to you, Pooh?" she asked.

"Nothing."

Another "nothing." Lynn said, "Don't be scared. You can tell me the truth."

"I am. Dakota didn't do nothing. It was Montana. She bit me." He held out his arm to show the evidence. Three red marks on his fleshy forearm.

Montana? Lynn had to stop herself from laughing. To protect her big sister the two-year-old had taken on somebody twice her size? She flashed on a memory of herself at seven. Craig, the preacher's son, had cornered her in the basement of the church. He had taken candy out of her Easter basket. All her jelly beans. She was crying. Then Joy showed up. She whacked Craig upside the head with her own basket. Craig got an Easter egg he hadn't expected. A big one on his forehead. Joy took back all of Lynn's jelly beans *plus* Craig's *and* his Cadbury egg.

Lynn wanted her daughters to stick up for each other, but wasn't it supposed to be the other way around? Lynn tried to keep a straight face as she confronted her ferocious toddler. "Montana, it's not nice to bite people," she scolded. "Tell Pooh you're sorry."

The little girl shook her head. "No."

Lynn sighed. "Give me that doll and tell him you're sorry."

Montana clutched the doll to her even harder. "No."

Lynn pretended to give up. "Okay, but when Pooh and Dakota get their freeze pops, you can't have one because you've been bad." The kids had already had dinner, and she had promised the freeze pops to them for later.

Montana still wasn't prepared to give up. She searched Lynn's face to see if she was serious. After a pause, she handed over the doll and said, "Sorry," more to her mother than Pooh.

"Okay, then no more fighting now and y'all can have freeze pops in a few minutes."

Bruce burst out of their bedroom as she walked by it.

They collided, and she bounced off the rock-solid wall of his naked chest. He was wearing only a pair of shorts. The left side of his face was creased from where he'd been sleeping on it, and his eyes were red with sleep.

"Oops, sorry," she said, smiling. He looked down his broad nose at her and marched into the living room without saying a word. Holding her breath without realizing it, Lynn slowly trailed behind him.

Bruce stopped abruptly in the center of the room, almost making her crash into him again. With his strongly muscled thighs and barrel chest, he made the small room feel even smaller. Though Lynn was tall, she had to look up at him. She had always liked the height difference between them, because it made her feel less gawky about her own height. She was always the tallest girl in her class. Some of the kids used to call her Olive Oyl.

"I'm sorry the kids woke you up," she said as his red-rimmed eyes seemed to look through her.

"This is my one day off all week, and a man can't get a little friggin' rest," he said.

"Sorry, honey. The kids just got into a little argument. Everything is fine now."

"Maybe for you. But you know once something wakes me up, I can't fall back asleep."

True. Lynn bit her lip. The kids had been playing quietly up until a few minutes ago. Maybe she should have checked on them a little sooner. Maybe the whole biting incident wouldn't have happened.

"You sit on your ass all day long, and the *only thing* you have to do is watch the kids. And you can't even do that right," he groused.

That stung. Taking care of two kids all day—sometimes more when she was baby-sitting, like today—wasn't exactly "sitting on her ass." Before she could say as much, Bruce said, "And what the hell is all this shit?" He was talking about her needlepoint. Bruce didn't like clutter. Lynn had thought she would have it put away before he woke up.

"For God's sake, why can't you keep it clean in here?" Before taking a seat on the couch, he pushed the discarded canvas and her toolbox onto the floor. The lid flew open, and her carefully sorted yarns, needle threader, and needles spilled out on the carpet.

Lynn silently stooped to pick up the tossed supplies, the walnut and cherrywood trim box. She raised hurt eyes to her husband's as she ran her fingers lightly over the case, checking to make sure it hadn't been scratched or worse yet broken. It was a gift from Mama. "Bruce, why did you do that? I was gonna straighten everything up. You didn't give me a chance."

"I'm not going to apologize for wanting a place to sit in my own house without needles and shit jabbing me in the ass."

There was no talking to him when he was like this. When he had literally woken up on the wrong side of the bed. Lynn closed the case and placed it and the canvas she'd been stitching on the coffee table.

"What's for dinner?"

"Meat loaf."

His expression said: Well, what the hell are you still standing here for? After a few seconds, Lynn lowered her eyes and mumbled, "I'll go fix you a plate."

Her hands were still trembling as she cut a thick wedge of meat loaf with a plastic spatula and laid it on a plate. She added a generous helping of cabbage and a slice of cornbread. Bruce was changing. Yelling and impatient all the time. Maybe she shouldn't have quit her job. They had agreed that they wanted to have a big family. But maybe working six days a week and all the overtime was too much for him.

Lynn took a glass out of the cabinet and went over to the

refrigerator, which was covered with childish squiggles and splashes of color. Lynn encouraged their interest in art, liking the idea that they had inherited their creative side from her. She sighed as she filled the glass with lemonade. But according to Bruce, she wasn't doing anything worthwhile.

When she returned to the living room, he had his feet propped on the coffee table. Her passionate dancers were crushed beneath his size-twelve feet. Lynn handed him his food and set the glass on the end table next to the couch.

"Bruce, please move your feet," she said.

He lifted them an inch or so, just enough for Lynn to pull the canvas free. Almost immediately his feet descended with a thud.

As she straightened, she felt a pull in her stomach. A wave of nausea hit her. Her hands tightened around the canvas as she struggled to keep it down. She could taste the wash of bile in her mouth. Then the pungent smell of cabbage hit her, making her struggle for self-control even harder. A chill went through her, making her palms sweat and dampening the skin on her face.

Upon noticing his wife's pained expression, Bruce said, "Lynn, what's wrong with you?"

"I felt sick for a minute. But I think it passed," she said, still not daring to move.

"Why don't you sit down, then?" he suggested.

Lynn wanted to believe these words of concern, but they were edged with impatience. "Actually, I don't feel well at all. I think I might lie down."

"I thought you said it had passed."

She licked her dry lips. "I didn't throw up. But I feel shaky, and my head is pounding all of a sudden."

"Well, you can't go to bed because Pooh is still here. And you know that hyper little bastard gets on my nerves. Besides, it's time for me to go to the gym."

Bruce went to the gym almost every day, usually before

work. He had joined almost a year ago. Even though it was a luxury they really couldn't afford, Lynn had thought it might help him relax, like her needlepointing did for her. "Bruce, I really need you to look after the kids," she insisted.

"This is just fucking great. First I can't get my rest, and now I can't go out and do the one thing that I enjoy."

Her head was really pounding now. Tears welled in her eyes. "Bruce, I can't help it if I'm sick."

He blew out a disgusted breath. "Fine. Go to bed, Lynn. Just go to bed."

Lynn did as he ordered, but she didn't feel good about it. A little understanding would have made her feel a whole lot better.

c h a p t e r
7

Without taking his shoes off, Marvin had stretched out full length on Toni's couch. Sanji, her bare feet curling around the edge of a cushion, perched on his stomach like an eagle. She was watching a TV show. Something about kids speaking with an inside voice, not an outside voice when they were in the house. Sanji was so totally into the lesson, she didn't notice that she was squeezing all the breath out of her father. But Marvin didn't mind. This was the quietest she'd been all morning. Other than possibly being talked to death, hanging out with his daughter was no problem at all.

Getting away from Tiara every morning was a whole other issue. For three days in a row, his morning had started with an argument. Tiara had been riding his ass about spending time at Toni's place. She didn't like it one bit. That was too bad. Marvin didn't like half the shit her silly ass did, either.

Toni was tripping, too. She refused to pick him up at Tiara's place but would wait for him a block away in front of Leroy's house.

Sanji's butt dug into his ribs. Marvin shifted positions to make himself more comfortable. Like a self-absorbed cat, Sanji plopped right back onto his stomach. A whoosh of air escaped him. Man, she was heavier than she looked.

"Sanji, you trying to kill Daddy or what?" Sanji paid him no attention. A tendency she shared with her mother.

After two straight hours of cartoons, it was time for a change. It would be different if she was watching something good like *The New Adventures of Batman and Robin* or maybe *Spider-Man*, but Toni didn't allow her to watch anything that wasn't "educational." Hell, knowing the difference between good and evil was educational. That was a superhero's main message. Absently, Marvin played with Sanji's hands, matching her much smaller palms against his. That Toni was something else. She had even gone so far as to hand him a list of acceptable and unacceptable TV programs. She really needed to take that stick out of her ass. "Say, Miss Behavin', when this goes off, how 'bout letting me watch something?"

This time Sanji actually looked his way. Her brown eyes with thick brows—like his—considered him thoughtfully. "You mean, you want me to share?"

He said, "Yeah."

Sanji squinted and touched a finger to her bottom lip, thinking about it.

She was so dramatic. Such a little actress. When it seemed she'd take forever to make up her mind, Marvin asked, with a little laugh, "You got a problem with that?" He stuck a hand between two of the cushions, searching for the remote.

Sanji shrugged. "I guess not." She finally raised up off him, pushed his legs aside, and took a seat where his feet had been. Propping an elbow on the arm of the couch, she waited for him to change the channel. He clicked to a talk show.

What time was it? Marvin didn't own a watch. He picked up a glass-encased clock from the end table. A little after eleven-thirty. He gave the white and gold metal a second glance. If he remembered correctly, somebody had given them the clock as a wedding present. There used to be a framed wedding picture next to it. Now there was nothing. Just an empty space with a thin layer of dust on it. If it wasn't for Sanji, Toni would have erased all trace of my black ass, he thought to himself. Momentarily full of regret, Marvin returned the clock to its place.

Sanji pulled on the leg of his jeans. "Daddy, those people are fightin'. The fat man pushed the other man off the stage. And they are yellin'. They're supposed to use their inside voices. Not scream and yell."

Sanji hopped off the couch and moved closer to the TV. Marvin turned his attention to the screen. Somebody had just confessed that he had slept with his brother's wife before and after the wedding. No wonder all hell had broken loose. The guy who'd been pushed off the stage had made his way back onto it and was now pointing at his brother, telling him he was an educated fool. "All book sense and no common sense," he yelled.

Marvin laughed. This was better than watching a fight on Pay-Per-View. And Fat Boy needed to take a seat before he got beat down again.

With eyes full of wonder, Sanji turned to him. "Educated fool? Is this show educational?"

Amused by her interest, Marvin was tempted to let her watch, but Sanji had a big mouth. If Toni asked her what she did today, the talk show would be the first thing she said. "No, it's not," he told her. "Your mama said *you* have to watch something educational, but she didn't say nothing about me. Since it's my turn to watch, why don't you go play in your room? Draw me a picture or something—"

"But, Daddy—" The phone rang just then, interrupting what was surely destined to be a protest.

Marvin reached for the phone. "Hello," he said.

"Why you pickin' up that bitch's phone?"

"Tiara?"

"Where's that bitch? Is she waiting for you in bed?"

Marvin closed his eyes and only wished he could close his ears as well. Tiara was trippin' hard. She was all right most days, but she was insanely jealous when it came to Toni. He ran his fingers through his hair tiredly. Toni in bed waiting for him? Didn't he wish! That was about as likely as him being voted Husband-of-the-Year. Marvin's jaw clenched and unclenched before responding. "Tiara, you seriously buggin'. Toni is at work."

As he had predicted, another fight broke out on the show. Sanji had inched closer to the screen and was now waving her small fist in the air. "Hit 'im! Hit 'im in the nose!"

Damn! Toni was gonna kill him. Marvin pressed the phone against his shoulder. Tiara's muffled rants were still audible as he cried, "Sanjari Carleton, I thought I told you to go to your room!"

Startled, Sanji swung around in surprise. Marvin hardly ever raised his voice with her. He jerked his thumb in the direction of her room. Sanji scrambled to her feet, gave him a confused look and, with shoulders slumped, left.

"Damn," Marvin muttered. It killed him to see the hurt radiating from her eyes. He hadn't meant to yell at her.

He put the phone to his ear again.

". . . Marvin! Marvin, answer me, damn it!"

Marvin had no idea where Tiara was in the flow of her insecure raving. And he didn't much care. She'd made him upset his baby. "Tiara!" he shouted. She stopped in midsentence. Good, he'd gotten her attention. "Tiara, I repeat: Toni is not here. She is at work. Ain't nothing going on between us. I don't know how many times I gotta tell you that. I'm just doing her a favor. I'm just taking care of my daughter. Can you understand that?" Silence. "Can you?"

A sob, then, "You have a daughter here, too. She needs you, too. She—"

Marvin hung up. Tiara cried at the drop of a hat, and this

time she was crying over nothing. He didn't need this shit. He began massaging his forehead with his palm.

A small hand unexpectedly touched his shoulder. He automatically snatched away from it. "What?" He immediately regretted his reaction when he saw the uncertainty and fear on his daughter's usually smiling face.

"Daddy? You mad at me?" she asked.

"Come here." He pulled her over the back of the couch onto his lap. "I'm not mad at you. I just don't want us to get in trouble." He chuckled. "You were getting just a little too excited watching that show. Pumping your fists like Evander Holyfield. That's why your mama don't want you watching stuff like that."

"Too violent?"

He nodded. "That's right."

She grinned. Her top two front teeth were missing. "So, we shouldn't tell Mommy."

"Definitely not." She gave him another gap-toothed smile, and he hugged her to him.

"When are those teeth gonna grow back? I'm gonna start calling you Count Dracula." She smiled again, and Marvin was happy. They were back on good terms. "Maybe I'm a vampire, too," he said, diving for her neck. "I vant to suck your blood, Count Dracula." Marvin playfully nipped at the soft skin on his daughter's neck.

Sanji giggled, twisting and turning, trying to get away from him. "Stop. Stop. The hair on your face tickles—"

The phone rang *again*. Annoyed, Marvin raised his head. That. had better not be Tiara calling again. He was tired of her silly games. He snatched the receiver off the base and snarled, "What?"

"Marvin?"

"Oh, Toni, it's you."

"Were you expecting someone else?" Then she added, with a hint of suspicion in her voice, "What's going on?"

"Nothing," he mumbled. Only a fool would mention that Tiara had called, and the last thing he wanted to deal with was another hysterical woman. "What's up?"

"I forgot to put Sanji's Social Security number on her summer camp application. I need to give it to the community center today."

Sanji had begun to watch the talk show again. When Marvin quickly switched channels, she gave him an indignant look. He tweaked one of her braids. A cooking show. That should fit Toni's educational requirement. "So where is the card?" he asked.

"There's a drawer in one of the nightstands in the bedroom—the one closest to the bathroom—where I keep all my important papers."

"Hang on, I'll be right back." He held the phone out to Sanji. "Hey, Miss Behavin', you wanna holler at your mother?"

Sanji took the phone. He gently shifted her from his lap to the couch. "Hi, Mommy." Marvin listened to her side of the conversation as he walked away. "No, we didn't eat lunch yet. . . . Yuk, I don't want no yucky leftover liver and onions. . . . I'm gonna tell Daddy to buy me a Happy Meal."

Marvin's heart sank when he heard this. Sanji could forget it. He didn't have two nickels to rub together. He really needed to learn the fine art of getting fired from a job rather than quitting. At least that way he could collect unemployment. If people would let a black man be a man, maybe he wouldn't have to quit all the time.

The bed groaned under his weight as he sat on the edge and began sifting through the contents of the drawer. Bills, old bank statements, scotch tape. He picked up a folded paper that was starting to age. He opened it. Their divorce decree. He folded it again with a heavy sigh, thinking, *Well at least she considers it to be an "important paper." Shit, where is that Social Security card. Those things are so little anyhow*. Marvin finally pulled the drawer out and tipped everything onto the bed. He scattered the mess of papers and odds and ends until his hands located a small, neatly typed card. He picked up the bedroom extension.

". . . and after *Arthur*, we watched—"

Marvin interrupted his daughter before she could spill the beans about the talk show. So much for it being their little secret. "Toni, I found the card," he announced. He read the number to her.

"Okay. Thanks, Marvin. I'll see y'all around six."

"You can hang up now," he told Sanji when he still heard her raspy breathing over the line.

After Marvin hung up, he began throwing the papers back in the drawer. Sanji ran into the room and jumped on the bed. "Let's talk, Daddy," Sanji pleaded.

Marvin smiled as a plastic bank card fell out of an envelope. "About what?" he asked, reaching for the card to put it back in its holder. When they were married, they used Sanji's birthday as the PIN number of all their cards. Marvin wondered briefly what PIN number Toni was using now. Maybe she hadn't even changed it.

"I wanna go on a lunch date," Sanji declared, interrupting the tangent his mind had wandered onto. "I don't want no stinky liver for lunch."

Before she could set her throttle on full whine, Marvin said, "Sanji, Daddy's money is funny right now. Maybe we can do lunch some other—"

"But you never take me to lunch no more. You live with Marvin Jr. and Daisa. You do stuff with them all the time."

"Look, Sanji, this is not a good time—"

"Don't you love me as much as you love them?" she asked softly.

Marvin swallowed hard and fingered the card and trifold paper he was about to put it in. Sighing, he stood up, shoving the card into his pocket. He threw the rest of the stuff in the drawer and slammed it shut.

The noise made Sanji jump. "Daddy, you scared me," she complained.

"Sorry, baby. Go put your shoes on. Daddy needs to stop by the bank first, and then we can go to Mickey D's." He could hear her excited whoop of joy as she ran in search of her sneakers.

It had been hectic at the bookstore all day. A huge order had come in, and they'd had to put it out. Toni was grateful that Sanji was subdued for a change. Her daughter sat quietly between her legs, as she removed her colorful barrettes from the ends of her braids. When Sanji's head rolled forward, Toni tilted it back and said, "Man, Sanji, you look tired. What did you and your daddy do today?"

Yawning and resting her head against her mother's knee, Sanji said in a sleepy voice, "We went to McDonald's and Discovery Zone . . . then Daddy played basketball with his friend in the park . . . he let me shoot some baskets, too . . . I was good . . . then we had some ice cream"—she yawned again—"rocky road."

Sounded like they had an expensive day. Somebody, maybe Tiara, must have floated him a loan. Better her than me, Toni thought. *Marvin takes his sweet time repaying debts.* On the other hand, she conceded, loosening Sanji's braids with her fingers, he could be a good dad when he put his mind to it. She wished Marvin and Sanji had more days like today. "So y'all had a busy day, huh? Ate junk food for lunch. I guess that explains why you didn't eat much for dinner." She felt Sanji's nod of agreement against her leg. "I'm glad you had a good time, sleepy head."

"Uh . . . huh," Sanji murmured as she curled her arms around her mother's leg. "Daddy loves me. Daddy said he would do anything for me."

chapter
8

Thanks to a harsh winter, the school year had gone a week longer than usual to make up for all the snow days. The low hum of teenage voices, the chairs scraping against the white-tiled floor, and the clink-clank of utensils hitting plates were signs that the Upper School lunch period at the Hayworth School for Girls was in full swing. Anna Mae set two more pans of chicken tetrazzini on the stainless steel counter. One of her jobs was providing any extra napkins, cutlery, and food the girls might need.

A shriek of girlish laughter pierced the air. Anna Mae looked up but couldn't locate its source. All around her, uniformed girls chattered, barely pausing for a breath. They seemed so innocent in their plain blouses, kilts, and knee socks scrunched down to the ankles to give them a cool and casual look. The girls sat in groups of eight at round tables that had yellow or orange tops. The brightness of the tables was accentuated by the sunshine which streamed in from the French doors and high windows that overlooked the ball fields at the rear of the school. Anna Mae, Delia, Mary, and Bebe set the tables before the girls came in. Bud vases with fresh flowers, along with the crystal salt and pepper shakers, the food, and heavy off-white crockery were put out twice a day. The Lower and Middle School girls came in at eleven-thirty. The freshman through senior classes filed in after they'd cleared out.

Mrs. Strauss, the dietitian, wheeled over a cart loaded with desserts. She planned the menus. Anna Mae and the rest of the kitchen staff did the cooking, cleaning, and serving. "Anna Mae, please put these in the window," she said in the thick German accent she had never shed despite living in the U.S. for over twenty years. Anna Mae had worked alongside her for twelve years and knew just as much about Mrs. Strauss today as she did the day she met her. Didn't bother her, though. As long as Mrs. Strauss kept treating her fairly, they would get along just fine.

One of the girls walked up to the window. With a student body of only six hundred, many of whom had been at Hayworth since kindergarten, Anna Mae knew most of them by name. "Hi, Mrs. Strauss. Hi, Anna Mae," Kirstie said, the silver metal of her braces glinting. "We ran out. I came for a second helping."

"Take whatever you need." Anna Mae bit back a smile. Kirstie was always coming for second helpings—sometimes thirds. Anna Mae didn't know where she put it, but she liked a child with a healthy appetite. Kirstie walked back toward her friends. Anna Mae saw her steal some crushed potato chips off the top of the chicken and pop them in her mouth. Kirstie was neat and a little curvy, just like a girl should look, Anna Mae thought.

Anna Mae put eight slices of apple pie on each tray, then set the trays on the counter. Usually, someone from each table came up to get dessert for everyone. She took a seat on a stool. She liked having counter duty, liked watching the kids.

Working at a girls' school reminded her how lively her own house had been when Toni, Joy, and Lynette were around. Joy trying to sneak in or out of the house long after curfew. Toni yapping on the phone when she was supposed to be doing her homework. Lynette complaining that it was her turn to use the phone and Toni ignoring her. Her kids probably wouldn't believe it if she told them she actually missed all the drama.

In her opinion, kids hadn't changed much in the last ten to fifteen years. They still thought they could put one over on the dumb adults. Anna Mae got a laugh out of the girls who hitched up their skirts the minute they stepped off school property, trying to entice boys from nearby schools who waited at the bus stops with them. Or the ones who hid in the bushes near the parking lot to sneak a smoke. Back when it had been her own kids, it hadn't been as funny, but at least she knew what they were up to—most days.

And now? Anna Mae shook her head sadly. Now she just didn't know. Toni lived hundreds of miles away, and she was as closed-mouthed as a clam. Joy lived in Cleveland, but who could keep up with her? Sometimes, Anna Mae didn't hear from her weeks at a time. Then there was Lynette, her baby girl. At twenty-three with a husband, two kids and one on the way, Lynn should have been the one she didn't have to worry about. She had always been the quiet one, like her daddy, but it was a contented quietness. Lately, she rationed her smiles as if she only had a few left in stock.

Across the room, Stephany Markum, one of Hayworth's smattering of black students, noticed Anna Mae at the window and waved to her. When she waved back, the entire table started waving then just as quickly turned their attention back to their conversation. A few months ago, one of the teachers had decided it was "unhealthy" for all the black students to "congregate" at lunch and had convinced the headmistress, Mrs. Boatwright, to have assigned seating at lunch.

Anna Mae could have told them it was a bad idea. Everybody was unhappy—the black students, the rest of the students, even the teachers. Any fool could see that the athletes sat with each other, the pretty girls sat with each other, the bookworms sat with each other. So, the black students must have something in common, which was why they sat with each other.

But nobody had asked her opinion—not that she expected them to. She could have told them that a handful of black students sitting together didn't mean they were planning a revolt. They were just doing what everybody else was doing: hanging out with friends. Anna Mae could have saved everybody two weeks of misery and the headmistress a flood of complaints from students and parents.

Students started bringing their dirty dishes to the counter, forcing Anna Mae back to reality. Clean-up was not a fun part of her job. Bebe, who had been washing dishes from the first lunch period, came over to give her a hand. Bebe's son was on leave from the Marines, so she was in an unusually helpful mood. They began stacking the dishes on trays which would later be wheeled over to the dishwasher. Some of the girls stopped for a minute to chat. Most of the time she enjoyed hearing what they had to say. Other times she was left speechless by how easily they shared personal problems with her. And some of those kids had problems with a capital P. Fighting parents, drugs, cheating boyfriends, worries about getting into the "right" college. Anna Mae wiped the counter with a damp towel, cleaning up some soda someone had spilled. One thing she had learned over the years was that money didn't buy happiness.

At the end of the lunch shift, Miss Doan, the assistant headmistress, entered the kitchen. She was fortyish, with light brown hair and thin, aristocratic features. She wore a hand-crocheted vest over a starched white blouse. Her skirt was gray, the heel of her shoe a sensible height, and gold clips discreetly peeked from behind a blunt haircut that stopped just below her chin. "Hello, Anna Mae, Bebe," she said.

The faculty and staff usually never got any closer to the

kitchen than the counter. Anna Mae exchanged a look of surprise with Bebe before returning the greeting. "Miss Doan," she said.

"Anna Mae, when you're done here, I was wondering if I could have a word with you."

Though the woman was smiling and nothing about her tone of voice was angry or harsh, it wasn't really a question. *Why does Miss Doan want to talk to me?* Anna Mae wondered. The only time they met was when it was time for a performance evaluation, and she'd already gotten her evaluation last month. She had gotten good marks as usual. Mild alarm registered in the pit of Anna Mae's stomach. "Is something wrong?" she asked, though she couldn't imagine what it could be.

Miss Doan hastened to reassure her. "No, no, nothing's wrong. There has been a change in school policy that affects you, and I wanted to go over it with you."

Bebe stopped pretending to work. She rolled the cart of stacked dishes a little to the left so that she could have a clear view of the two of them as they talked. "So, what's the new policy?" she asked.

Miss Doan paused, as if considering her words carefully before answering. "The new policy doesn't really apply to you, Bebe. That's why I want to talk to Anna Mae, privately."

"Oh," Bebe said, her round brown face showing disappointment that her curiosity wouldn't be satisfied.

Miss Doan looked around the kitchen. Then made up her mind about something. "Anna Mae, I can see that I've gotten you worried, and really you shouldn't be. Why don't you come down to my office right now and I'll tell you what's going on?"

Anna Mae smiled weakly. "I'd appreciate that, Miss Doan. 'Cause you do have me curious. You're sure nothing's wrong?"

"Absolutely!" Miss Doan said. "Bebe, if she asks, tell Mrs. Strauss that Anna Mae is with me."

Anna Mae took off her black hair net, stuffed it in the pocket of her white uniform, and followed Miss Doan through the cafeteria, then down the hall to her office.

The office was small, with lots of antique furniture and a leaf green and white carpet—the school colors. Miss Doan invited her to sit in a high-back chair that had a green paisley print on a cream background. Anna Mae waited, her anxiety building as Miss Doan stopped to turn on a brass lamp. Picking up a manila folder, she settled herself in her chair before swinging around to face Anna Mae. She fingered the folder, then crossed her legs.

Only a few feet separated them. Anna Mae saw that her name was written on the folder in black magic marker.

"Anna Mae, I want to apologize if I caused you any embarrassment or anxiety back there—in the lunch room."

Anna Mae glanced at her personnel file in Miss Doan's slender, neatly trimmed fingers. What on earth was going on? Had someone complained about her? She said, "Well, I have to admit, I am a little nervous. What's this all about?"

Miss Doan delicately cleared her throat. "Did you hear about the case a few months ago in the Shaker school district where a janitor mixed the wrong chemicals to clean the floors?"

Anna Mae nodded, still not sure what this had to do with her.

Miss Doan continued, "The next day, people started to complain of dizziness, headaches. Some people were taken to the hospital, and the school had to be evacuated."

"Yes, I remember hearing about it on the news. But—"

"I know, I know, you're wondering what my point is." Miss Doan curled the folder along its length, then uncurled it. "Well, our board of trustees also heard about it. Apparently, the janitor improperly mixed the chemicals because he was unable to read. As a result, some parents are suing the school system. Needless to say, this led some of our board members to wonder if something like that could happen here at Hayworth. The long and short of it is the board has decided that a high school diploma or high school equivalency will be the minimum requirement for non-professional staff at the school. That includes maintenance, clerical and dining services staff."

The significance of what Miss Doan had said hit her like a sucker punch. Anna Mae had a tenth-grade education. Miss Doan was telling her that she was no longer qualified for a job she'd been doing for twelve years! She tried to let go of a tense breath that was stuck in her chest. After all these years of working at Hayworth, they were changing the rules on her. Because some janitor at another school couldn't read, *she* was being punished.

When she finally released the trapped breath, she asked, in a tremulous voice, "Are you firing me?"

Surprise leapt into Miss Doan's eyes. She leaned forward as if to comfort Anna Mae. "My God, no," she said. "We would never do that, Anna Mae." With compassion-filled eyes, she apologized again. "I'm sorry. I'm not explaining this very well. All employees must have a diploma . . . but you have until the end of the year—December," she clarified, "to get yours."

Anna Mae closed her eyes in relief. She wasn't being fired. Still, she had to get her GED, and that was a lot of work. She'd have to study math, science, history. Everything. The fear returned. She opened her eyes. "Miss Doan . . . if it's a matter of proving I can read, can't I just take some kind of reading test?"

Miss Doan slowly shook her head, shooting down the idea. "If it were up to me, you wouldn't have to do anything. But unfortunately, the decision was not mine to make. The new policy specifies that employees must have a high school education."

"But it's been over thirty years since I set foot in a classroom . . . as a student, that is," she tagged on. Anna Mae felt like she was babbling. Miss Doan obviously knew what she meant the first time she said it.

Miss Doan opened the folder and took out a piece of paper. "Anna Mae, I've written down the names of some adult-education programs near you. I feel badly. It's obvious this has been an unpleasant shock to you." She handed the paper to Anna Mae, who took it with shaking fingers. She stared at the page, seeing only a series of squiggly lines. Maybe she couldn't read. Then Anna Mae blinked and Miss Doan's precise penmanship came into focus.

Anna Mae turned her attention back to the assistant headmistress, wondering what she'd missed when her mind had gone blank. " . . . and I have every confidence that you will be able to get your GED in the interim. And Anna Mae, please, please, let me know if there is anything I can do to help you achieve this very important goal."

She could exempt me from this crazy new policy. But Anna Mae knew that was impossible, so she didn't bother asking again. It would sound too much like begging. And she was too proud to beg. Getting up from her seat, Anna Mae clutched the paper in her hand. She appreciated the reluctance and concern in the woman's eyes. Miss Doan was a nice lady, but she didn't run the place. She was just enforcing the rules. And if she wanted to keep her job, Anna Mae would have to play by those rules.

After washing up, Clarence Rollins went directly to the kitchen table. He and Anna Mae always ate in the kitchen now that all of the kids except Darius were out of the house. And Darius was hardly ever at home.

His wife got home around four, but she always waited

until he got home to eat. Sometimes, he didn't get in until after eight. On those nights she would put the food in the oven, turn it on low, and wait for him. Anna Mae wouldn't listen when he tried to convince her to eat without him. She insisted the food didn't taste the same when she ate alone. That it tasted better when she had company—his company.

He didn't have the words to describe how that made him feel. Happy. Grateful. It wasn't like he had much to say at dinner. He figured Anna Mae did enough talking for the both of them. His heart swelled with pride. He thanked God for her continued devotion—he was lucky to have it after more than thirty years of marriage.

Clarence, well over six feet, eased his lanky frame into one of the chairs at the kitchen table. It was Wednesday, the middle of the week. He watched Anna Mae cooking up a storm. Over at the stove, she added a little flour to the skillet. She was making gravy for the biscuits.

"Anna, what you need me to do?" he asked.

"You can set the table. Dinner will be ready in a minute," Anna Mae said without turning around.

Clarence pushed back from the table, walked over to the cabinet next to the sink, and took out some dishes. After getting two of everything—plates, glasses, and silverware—he walked back to the table. "How was your day?" he asked.

She didn't answer. Instead, she put on a pair of oven mitts and took out the pan of biscuits. She set it on top of the stove. Clarence gave her back a questioning look before walking over to the fridge. Surely she had heard him? He was a little worried. Anna had been acting peculiar since yesterday.

"What do you want to drink?" he asked.

"Water's fine."

Clarence filled their glasses and sat back down at the table. They were having dirty rice, one of his favorites. Anna had even thrown in the chopped chicken livers, which she didn't like. Last night she'd made brown bread and red beans and rice. While he appreciated her thoughtfulness, he knew something was bothering her. He could always tell. When she started cooking down-home meals for no reason—it wasn't his birthday, a holiday, or even a weekend— she had something on her mind.

Anna Mae sat across from him, said a halfhearted blessing. Clarence picked up a homemade biscuit and turned it around in his big, callused hand. Golden, so flaky the buttery crust clung to his fingers. Clarence took a bite. Soft as a cloud and just as close to heaven. Then he noticed the lines across her usually unmarked brow. Anna Mae, a hearty eater, hadn't even picked up her fork yet.

Not taking his eyes off her, Clarence returned the biscuit to his plate. He wiped his fingers with a paper napkin. He'd thought that whatever was bothering her yesterday would pass, but it hadn't. "Anna, tell me what's wrong."

Anna Mae swung her eyes to his. Clarence's uncustomary bluntness jolted her out of her funk. She told him about the new policy at the school. "I gotta get my GED or I'm gonna lose my job."

Clarence thought, *So that's what the long face is all about*.

Anna Mae sighed. "I wish that I'd known how important a good education was back when I was young. I didn't even think about finishing school. That's how unimportant it was."

"C'mon, Anna. You being too hard on yourself. Consider the time and the place. Fort Deposit, Alabama, wasn't turning out a lot of black high school graduates back in the sixties. Why, we wasn't even black yet, we was still colored."

Anna Mae nodded but seemed to be only half listening. "I remember when my cousin Nell wanted to stay in school— she was in the tenth grade, I think. People started talking about her like she was lazy or crazy or both. So, she quit and started helping around the farm more."

Anna took a sip of her water. She held the glass in hand, her eyes faraway, remembering. "When the kids first started school, I could help them with their homework. . . . Pretty soon I felt like they were teaching me, not the other way around. By the time they got to algebra and world geography, I was lost. I thank God, none of them had any real problems in school 'cause I couldn't have helped. I would have been totally useless."

Clarence reached across the table and gave his wife's hand a little squeeze. How could Anna Mae, of all people, be putting herself down like this? A man couldn't ask for a better wife, and the kids had one hell of a mother. "Anna, you did the best you could with what you had. And that's pretty damn good if you ask me."

Anna Mae raised an eyebrow, a smile appearing on her face. Clarence had said more tonight than he had all week. It didn't really surprise Anna Mae that he had gotten all riled up on her behalf. He was like that when it came to his family. Playfully, she wagged a finger at him. "Clarence, what would Reverend Turner think if he heard you cussing?"

"Damn good or darn good? All I'm saying is that me and the kids appreciate everything you've done to make this house a home. We left Alabama and most of our family behind so we could have a better life. And we did. Our kids were fed, clothed, had a roof over their heads, and had two hardworking, loving parents. That's more than a lot of people could say."

Anna Mae bit her lip, chewing on what he had to say. Clarence continued to watch her, his heavy-lidded eyes willing her to see the truth in what he'd said.

"I know, I know." Anna Mae responded as if he had said something more. "But the thought of going back to school is scary. Clarence, if I lose my job, what will I do? What else am I trained to do? Who is going to hire a fifty-year-old woman who doesn't even have a high school education? What if I don't pass the test? What if I fail—"

Clarence wasn't used to seeing Anna all churned up like this, and he didn't like it. Unable to listen for another moment, he interrupted the flow. "Calm down, Anna," he ordered. Heeding him, Anna Mae stopped in mid-sentence. He held out a hand to her. "Now come here."

Without letting go of his hand, Anna Mae walked around to his side of the table. Clarence patted his thigh, inviting her to sit. Anna Mae settled in, resting her head against his cheek, curling into him like one of their grandchildren, trying to absorb his quiet strength.

"Anna, you're worried about failing this test, right?"

She nodded, her reddish-brown hair brushing against the side of his lean jaw.

"Anna, just one question. When have you ever failed at anything?"

In the silence that followed, his arm encircled her waist, pulling her closer to him. The few pounds that Anna had gained over the years had only made her more shapely, more womanly. He touched the warm copper skin of her face, smoothing away the worry lines. She was still beautiful—inside and out, he thought. "While you rack your brains for an answer, how 'bout I warm up the food? I think it's gotten cold."

Anna Mae nodded, allowing him to stand up, allowing him to take care of her.

c h a p t e r
9

Toni always made her weekly call to her mama first thing Saturday morning—before things got crazy at Shear Necessity. She picked up the cordless phone and dialed her parents' number.

"Hello?" a child's voice answered.

Surprised, Toni asked, "Hi. Who is this?"

"It's Jesse."

"Hi, Jesse. This is Auntie Toni. What are you doing over there?"

"Helping Grandma wash clothes."

Toni laughed at his literal answer. "Well, that's nice of you. You should tell Grandma not to work you so hard. It's too early to be washing clothes. It's Saturday morning, you should be watching cartoons."

"But I like washing clothes. I like taking out the trash, too."

The kid definitely was not normal. But he was oh, so sweet. "Well, I'm glad you're having a good time. Where's Grandma?"

"Grandma!" he shouted. Toni held the phone away from her ear. "Grandma, Auntie Toni wants you!"

A brief silence was followed by rustling noises. Moments

later, her mother's voice came over the line, slightly out of breath.

"Hi, Mama. Why are you breathing so hard?"

"I had to come up from the basement."

"Well, you didn't have to rush on my account. I could have talked to Jesse a little bit longer. What is he doing over there so early in the morning, anyway?"

"Visiting. Joy dropped him off a few days ago."

"Uh-huh." Toni knew her sister. "And just how many days is a 'few days'?" she asked.

"He's been here since last Sunday. Joy said Jesse wanted to go to church with us."

Last Sunday? He'd been there almost a week. "I know Reverend Turner can give a long sermon, but I've never known him to preach for seven whole days. Why hasn't Joy picked up her child?"

"She called on Wednesday, but me and Jesse were at Kmart. I was buying him a few summer things to wear."

I'll bet, Toni thought to herself. Mama was probably out buying Jesse clothes because whatever he had he'd outgrown.

"Joy told your daddy that she didn't have a ride over here."

"She found a way to get him over there in the first place. Besides, don't buses run every fifteen minutes?"

Anna Mae sighed. "I don't mind, really. Jesse is an angel. Ain't that right, sugar? Ain't you Grandma's little angel?"

Damn! Toni hadn't meant for Jesse to hear any of what was being said. She should have known he'd stay under Mama and not run off and play like most kids would.

"Mama, send Jesse out of the room. I want to talk to you." She slowly counted to ten as her mama spoke to Jesse. It pissed Toni off the way Joy constantly took advantage of her and then Mama, who normally wasn't stupid, acted like she couldn't see what Joy was doing.

"Jesse, would you go see if the dryer has stopped?" Anna Mae asked. He must have said yes, because then she said, "If it's stopped, put the clothes in the basket for Grandma. Huh? Okay, you can fold them if you want to."

Speaking of washing clothes, Toni needed to make sure they had enough clean towels for the customers. But she wanted to finish this discussion. She'd check the supply room in a few minutes.

"Okay, he's gone," Anna Mae said. "Now, what's so top-secret Jesse can't hear it?"

"You know how kids are. They hang on your every word, and I just don't want Jesse to get the impression that he's unwanted. Even though Joy doesn't seem too concerned about that."

Anna Mae started to protest, "But he's not unwanted. All my kids and grandkids are welcome at my house any time."

That's exactly what Joy was counting on. She was forever getting evicted for not paying her rent. Then she'd stay with friends for a while until she wore out her welcome there. Finally, she'd end up on her parents' doorstep. "Mama, that's not the point. I thought you were supposed to be starting your GED classes this weekend?"

Anna Mae took her time answering. "I was," she said. Then she gave a long, drawn-out explanation as to why she wasn't going to the class. "Both Darius and your father are working this weekend. Lynn's got her hands full, so I didn't want to bother her. And I couldn't take Jesse to class with me. . . ." She trailed off, then added, "But it's all right. They got another session starting in a couple of weeks."

Toni swallowed an impatient sigh. Her mama needed to stop putting everybody else first. "You say another class is starting soon?"

"Yes, in two weeks."

"That's good," Toni told her. "Mama, I know how important this is to you. I know you want to sit for the exam before the school year starts. Don't keep putting off the class. Don't let Joy screw this up for you."

"But, Toni . . ." her defense began.

While she made excuses for Joy, Toni surveyed the shop, trying to decide what needed to be done before the customers started showing up. She picked up a hand mirror and examined the hair at her temple. Damn, those gray strands had cropped up again. And she'd discovered a hair or two under her chin last week. Her attention wandered back when Anna Mae started talking about the problems Joy was having at her new job. Joy's boss was "harassing" her because she'd been showing up late.

"So, why is she late?" Toni asked.

"Her new boyfriend—Fonzo, you met him. Anyway, he had been driving her to work, but they had some kind of argument and now she has to catch the bus."

"And?"

"And the bus either gets to her stop way before she supposed to start work or a little bit after. Maybe I should let her use my car? I don't really need it during the summer."

"Mama, Joy can take the early bus. It won't kill her to get there early. What time does the store open? Nine? Ten o'clock? Even if she gets there early, it's broad daylight and it's summer. So it's not like she's gonna be alone or freeze to death."

"Maybe you're right," Anna Mae said, but she still sounded doubtful.

Toni was positive that Mama was more irritated with Joy's selfish and irresponsible behavior than she was letting on. But she also knew that Mama didn't believe in bad-mouthing one of her kids to another. She didn't want anyone thinking she had a favorite. Trying to get her to talk about how she was really feeling about Joy would be like trying to squeeze the toothpaste back into the tube.

Praying for patience, Toni walked over to the reception

desk. She loosened the leather strings of her purse and took out a pile of magazines. They were starting to develop a thumbed-through look from too many trips from the shop to her purse to the nursing homes and back again. Toni divided the pile and spread them out like fans on the two tables at the ends of the couch and love seat. She smiled, remembering how Chris had let her have her way when it came to decorating. They could have gone with your basic boring waiting room chairs, but she had chosen a Southwestern style instead. Lots of sunset colors, cacti green, and landscapes.

Her mother had moved from Joy to Lynn. "Your sister's finally starting to show a little. Most of her weight gain has been in her stomach. I'm a little worried about her. She's been looking kinda peaked lately. Real tired. I think she's doing too much. It's hard on her having two little kids to take care of, too. Her face is so thin. Remember how chubby you got when you were pregnant with Sanji?"

"How could I forget?" Fat had attached itself to every part of her body. "Thanks for reminding me, Mama."

"What?" Anna Mae asked, clearly surprised that Toni had taken exception to her comment. "Toni, you were beautiful when you were pregnant. There's nothing prettier than a woman who's expecting."

Swollen feet, thimble-sized bladder, and the inability to move unassisted from the seated to the standing position. Yes, you couldn't get more attractive than that. "If you say so, Mama. Is everything okay with everybody else?"

"I think your daddy is working too hard. He doesn't really have to work on Saturday. But I don't suppose I could get *you* to tell him to slow down. You're just like him."

There were a lot worse things she could be besides hardworking. Joy or even Marvin might want to try it some time. "Speaking of work, I gotta run—"

"Wait a minute," she said before Toni hung up. "Where's my grandbaby? Where's Sanji?"

Normally, Sanji came with Toni on Saturdays. When she was in the mood, she served as their salon assistant by greeting customers, holding tissue papers as Toni set people's hair, or doing some half-hearted cleaning up. And she had the nerve to charge them a fee, too. Sanji had informed them that her name was not Cinderella and she did not work for free. The part of Toni that wasn't indignant was glad that her daughter placed a value on her skills at the tender age of six and expected others to do the same. "She went to a pajama party last night. She's staying with her friend until I finish here."

"Oh," Anna Mae said, disappointed. "Well, have her call me tonight. I miss Sanji. It would be wonderful to have her sassy behind around for a few days."

Toni missed Mama, too. It was hard not having any family close by. "I'll tell Sanji you asked about her," Toni said. "She's doing fine. Sanji spent the week with her father. Can you believe that Marvin came through? Granted, he emptied my refrigerator and ran all the gas out of my car, but he took good care of Sanji."

"Hmm . . . It's about time," Anna Mae said. Despite Marvin's attempts to charm her, she had never liked him. Mama felt strongly that a man should provide for his family, and Marvin's frequent job changes marked him as irresponsible and shiftless in her book. Of course, she didn't share these feelings with Toni until after the divorce because "it wasn't my place to be in your business."

"I'm just glad he took responsibility for once. I really didn't want to have to take sick time or vacation time just because I couldn't find a baby-sitter."

"Shouldn't have to beg a man to keep his own child." Toni could see her shaking her head in disgust.

"Tell Daddy I said hello. Talk to you soon." After Toni hung up, she turned on the TV facing the couch. She wanted to catch the news. Delaware had only one local station, and it only aired at certain times of the day.

The bell over the front door tinkled. Toni turned toward the sound. It wasn't even eight-thirty yet. Chris was early.

"Hi, gorgeous," he said. He was dressed in typical work gear: loose-fitting jeans and a green T-shirt that matched his emerald eyes. Those eyes had none of their usual sparkle today, but overall, he still looked pretty good. It wasn't fair. He ate like a pig but was naturally slender. His idea of exercising was walking to the kitchen to get more pizza. On top of looking good, Chris had somebody and she didn't. Good thing she liked him so much. Because he would be so easy to hate.

"Hi, yourself. Whatcha got in the bag?" Toni said.

Chris took a seat in one of the hydraulic chairs. He tossed the bag to her. Toni caught it and peered inside. "First croissants and now muffins. Are you trying to hint that I should give up the donuts?"

He shrugged. "Not at all. I was in the mood for something different." He rested an elbow on one of the chair arms and crossed his legs.

Something in his tone of voice made her give him a second, more probing look. This time she saw past the attractive features, noticing the glum expression, the slumped shoulders, and false calm that he was fronting. Toni put the bag down on the counter and moved directly in front of him. "What's wrong?" she asked.

"What's right?" was his dejected reply.

After the party, Toni had grilled him on the almost-argument between him and Marshall. That's when Chris had admitted that they'd been having problems lately. Some big problems at that. He'd told her that Marshall was job hunting. Shocked the hell out of her. And Toni said as much. Chris hadn't told her before because he hadn't wanted to believe it himself Not surprisingly, he was still upset about it.

Toni could only imagine how tense the atmosphere at their house must be. "How's Marshall?"

"Pretty damn happy. Two New York banks called him back for a second interview."

Her heart went out to him. Chris had been hoping that Marshall's job prospects would fizzle out, forcing him to give up on the idea. But Toni wasn't convinced that Marshall would give up so easily. From what Chris had told her, Marshall had reached the conclusion that the gay community in the Newark-Wilmington area wasn't big or unified enough for him. He also wanted to live somewhere where they could be "more out." In recent lengthy conversations, Chris had been trying to help her understand what that meant. Toni thought either you were out of the closet or you were in, but apparently it was more complicated than that.

"Oh, Chris," she consoled, "I know you must be disappointed that things are moving in that direction. Do you think Marshall would accept a job if he got an offer?"

He rubbed a hand over his tired face. "Why not? He's from Brooklyn, so he'd be going home. And he doesn't have anything to keep him here."

Toni shook her head. The Chris she knew was a die-hard optimist. Why was this happening? It seemed that Chris had finally found somebody who made him happy. Toni was happy for him. She had never seen two people happier. Marshall's sudden desire to relocate just didn't make any sense to her.

"Okay. Help me understand this. What does this move to New York mean for your relationship?"

"Marshall says he doesn't want to break up."

"So how are you supposed to have a relationship if he's there and you're here?"

Chris smoothed his hair back with his fingers, a nervous habit of his. "That's a good question. I don't want to be apart, but it's not like he's giving me much choice. I couldn't leave

Delaware right now even if I wanted to. I still have to finish school."

Toni waited, hoping Chris would mention Shear Necessity. But he didn't. Instead he stared into space, not quite seeing her or the mess she would be in if he up and left anytime soon. Unlike him, she was supremely aware of all the what-ifs. Like, what would happen to Shear Necessity if Chris moved to New York? She certainly wouldn't be able to come up with the money to buy him out.

Chris said, more to himself than Toni, "I really wished he'd talked to me before he started looking for jobs. Now I feel like I'm just being dragged along."

He was right, and she was pissed. "Marshall is a fool if he throws away a relationship like yours! He is wrong. So wrong for putting you through this."

Chris laughed. "You know what you look like right now? A cross between a Chihuahua and a pit bull." He clasped his hands in front of his heart. "Toni, my hero and defender."

Toni slapped him on the knee. "You making fun of me? This is what I get for taking your side?"

He grasped Toni's hand and looked at her with no trace of his previous amusement. "No, you get my undying gratitude."

"You're welcome," she replied with equal seriousness. "But I still think Marshall is being a jerk. Y'all usually talk out your problems. Why not this time?"

"Toni, don't blame this all on Marshall. A lot of this is my fault. I think Marshall could live without a huge gay community. It's me not being completely out that he's unhappy about."

"But you are out—" Toni broke off when he started shaking his head.

"Not at work. Not to most members of my family—and that's the part that really gets him. He wants me to be totally comfortable with our relationship. I just don't think it's necessary for everybody to know my personal business. We've talked about it a lot, and I guess this job search was Marshall's way of saying he's tired of talking."

"Well, what he's asking you to do is easier said than done."

Chris stood up, inadvertently brushing off her hand. "He feels I should have more personal integrity."

Toni bit her lip, not knowing what to tell him. She hadn't walked in the shoes of a gay man. Were his blues sung in a different key?

Sensing her uncertainty about how to respond, he grasped her by both shoulders. "Toni, Toni, Toni. Don't look so worried. Marshall and I aren't dead in the water yet." Toni tilted her head up to get a good look at him. Chris's eyes were no longer clouded, and his easy smile was back in place. Was he really as okay as he suddenly sounded and looked? And how had they gone from Toni comforting him to the other way around?

chapter
10

Joy smiled. She was so proud of herself. She'd persuaded her parents that she could get herself home. She knew how to take the number three bus down Superior, and she knew what street to get off at. After all, she was twelve years old now. Big enough to take care of herself. Shoot, they had let her go all the way to Rochester by herself. And even though Mama had told her not to get off the bus when it stopped in Buffalo, she had done it anyway—both going and coming. On the way, she went into the terminal to get a Coke. Then coming back, she wanted to buy her mama a souvenir. Mama's gonna like the ashtray I bought her. It had a picture of a buffalo standing next to the Empire State Building.

The heavy suitcase in Joy's hand knocked against her leg, making it difficult for her to walk. She was on Thirteenth Street headed toward Superior Avenue. She stopped and re-gripped the bag, which was making her upper arm and shoulder start to hurt.

The two weeks she had spent in Rochester with her father's youngest sister, Aunt Laura, had been a lot of fun. Aunt Laura didn't have any kids, so she spoiled Joy. She let her stay up as long as she wanted, even let her place her own bets when they went to the racetrack with Uncle Hank. This visit she had taught Joy how to play spades. When Aunt

Laura had card parties, Joy served the beer. And they sold dinners to people who got hungry, because the gambling went on for hours. Best of all, Aunt Laura had bought her some new school clothes. Joy was gonna be the finest-looking girl in the seventh grade.

Those new clothes were weighing down her suitcase. It was a lot heavier today than it had been when her mama and daddy had dropped her off at the Greyhound Bus station two weeks ago.

Joy stopped again. She set the suitcase on the pavement. It was hot out. She wiped the sweat from her brow then flexed her aching arm. She picked up the suitcase. Just a few more blocks to the bus stop.

She marched on, thinking how glad she would be to get home. Toni would be so jealous when she saw all the stuff Aunt Laura had bought her. Maybe if she wasn't so bossy, Aunt Laura would invite her to come every summer, too. Still, she missed Toni even if she was bossy.

A low shadow crept alongside her as she walked. Joy didn't notice it. She just wanted to get to her stop. She hoped there was a bench there, so she could sit down while she waited for the bus.

A horn honked. Joy jumped, then looked in the direction the sound had come from. A long, shiny red car—a Cadillac—had pulled up beside her. The man behind the wheel said, "Hey, you look hot. Can I give you a ride?"

He was wearing a gray suit, and his gray tie had little maroon lightning bolts. She stared at his broad face. He had lines in the corner of his eyes, and there was a shiny brown spot on the front of his head where hair should have been. He was old, Joy thought. Older than Daddy even. A gold band gleamed on his left hand. He looked all right, but Joy knew her parents would be upset if she accepted a ride from a stranger. She shook her head, continuing to walk. "No, thanks, I'm just going to the bus stop."

The sweat on her forehead was trickling again, running into her eye, stinging. Joy swiped it against the back of her hand. Her new cotton blouse was stuck to her back. She was tired after sitting on a bus for six hours, and her thighs scraped together as she walked. I'm gonna be a stink box by the time I get home, she thought. Toni would make sure she knew it, too. She would probably say something stupid like, "Whew, did you take a Greyhound bus or a garbage truck home?" Joy put the suitcase down again. She raised her arms above her head, stretching them.

"Little girl, you look about ready to pass out." It was the man again. He had stopped the car. Smiling, then leaning over, he opened the car door. "C'mon, hop in. I'll take you to your bus stop."

Joy looked at the open door, then the empty street. The heat from the sidewalk shimmered, and leapt at her like fire claws. The bus stop seemed a million miles away. Joy swooped the case up under one arm and walked over to the car. It's okay, she told herself. You're perfectly safe. He is just a man who is trying to be nice. She put the case in the back seat then got in. . . .

. . . Joy twisted from side to side, trying to break free of the strong hand held over her mouth. He was lying on top of her, so much heavier than her, trapping her against the seat. She couldn't breathe. Fear and the friction of the leather seat had her drenched in sweat. Another hand unzipped her shorts, pushing them down past her knees. A prying hand, trying to spread her legs apart. His aftershave, sweet and musky, suffocating her. She squirmed, trying to bite the hand at her mouth, and clamped her legs tightly together. His fingers dug into the soft flesh of her thigh. The soft material of the shiny gray suit she'd admired earlier stuck to her damp skin as he pressed against her. Joy's cry of pain was muffled. He yelled at her to shut up, to stop fighting and to enjoy it. Then his hand moved from her mouth to her throat, squeez-

ing, threatening to cut off the flow of air. She stared in wild-eyed terror into the face of the Devil. Am I gonna die? Is this how I'm gonna die?

"Yo! Yo, Joy," a male voice said, close to her ear. Joy jerked away, then raised a hand to bat way the marijuana stink of his breath. Disoriented and scared, she sucked air into her lungs. Her breath came in quick little gasps. She scrambled away, her hands feeling the grit of an unwashed floor.

Her heart racing, Joy curled up in a ball, resting her head against a wall where disintegrating wallpaper scratched her face.

A hand clamped on her shoulder, and Joy screamed. "Get off me. Get your hands off me. Don't touch me. Don't ever touch me," she yelled, then threw herself at her imagined attacker.

Her balled fist was caught in a much bigger hand. Joy struggled to break free. "Hey, hey, Joy, why you trying to kick my ass? You on a bad trip?" came the voice again, this time with a tinge of laughter in it.

Joy grew still, trying to clear her fogged senses. *Who is that?* "Lance?" she said uncertainly. Now she could smell the strong, closed-up musty scent of the place. Her eyes opened to a gloomy darkness. Around her were other bodies on the floor or sitting on broken-down furniture. They were asleep or nodding or giggling as they sucked on their pipes. Sucking like babies.

Her throat tightened in reaction to the sight. She wasn't like them. She just needed to dull the pain sometimes. She needed a place to smoke and to forget. That bitch at the store had fired her. Fired again. Feeling the strong hands around her wrists, Joy looked down at them, then stared into the eyes of Lance, the burly, much tattooed owner of the house. She pulled away from him.

Lance smiled while Joy rubbed her wrists. "I see you finally returned to the land of the living."

Joy watched him wearily. Her throat was dry. *How long have I been here?* she wondered. She glanced around the room again. A couple of white kids, probably from the suburbs, were sharing a pipe. There was no place to go in their neighborhood to do poor folks' drugs, so they came into the city. Joy's head ached. She didn't see anybody she knew. Hadn't she come here with Fonzo? She didn't see him. She licked her lips and tasted the sourness of her own breath.

"Joy, maybe you should go home. You looked fucked up."

"Thanks," she muttered.

"You been here two days—" Two days? No, it couldn't be. Joy scrunched up her face, trying to remember. She had been two hours late for work. That bitch had followed her around the store all day—like she expected her to steal something. Then fired her. Told her she wasn't reliable. Let her work all fucking day, then fired her. And then . . . *Concentrate, Joy,* she told herself. *Then I told her to give me my damn money. I got Jesse. Called Fonzo.* What happened after that she couldn't remember. Joy grimaced. *Mama is gonna be disappointed. Mama never said anything, but her face always did. Sad, pitying, worried—Joy messed up again.*

Lance hauled her up by the arms. "C'mon, Joy. Girl, you could use some sleep. Take a look in the mirror."

Joy pulled away. She didn't want to know what she looked like. "Leave me alone, Lance. I ain't ready to go home."

"Well, what you gonna do? You already smoked up everything you had."

Joy's eyes widened. Not believing him, she stuck her hands in the side pockets of her jeans, turning both inside out. Then felt around in her back pockets as well. "I spent all my money?" *An entire week's pay?*

He nodded.

Shit! Shit! Her expression took on an edge of desperation. Joy didn't want to go home. She couldn't go there. Didn't want to face Jesse or Mama or Daddy. Her hips swayed as she walked over to Lance, her eyes half closed, assessing. She stood in front of him, close enough to brush against the bulge in his pants. "C'mon, Lance, help a sister out."

An assessing gleam had entered Lance's eyes as well. Joy knew he was interested. *They are always interested.* Lance cleared his throat, then laughed. "Now, Joy, you know I don't sell rock in here. The vice squad is my boss, and selling is not allowed on the premises."

Smiling, her intentions very clear, Joy moved closer. Her round breasts touched his chest. "I know you don't sell, but you can send a runner. Get somebody to pick up the stuff."

Lance scratched the back of his head, pretending indecision. "Yeah, but what do I get out of the deal?"

Joy pressed her full length against him. Her arms went around his neck. "Whatever you want, Lance," she purred. "Whatever you want."

The white noise from the television woke Jesse up. His glasses had become crooked while he slept. He readjusted them and sat up. His eyes immediately turned to the door of the apartment. A thin crack of yellow light from the hallway came under it. He listened, straining to hear the slightest sound. He didn't hear the creak of his mother's footsteps as she came up the stairs. Every night he listened for her, but she still hadn't come.

Sighing, Jesse got up from the couch.

He turned the TV to another channel. A movie was on. The people were only in black-and-white. But that was okay. The voices kept him company.

It was hot. He took off his dirty socks, leaving them on the couch, then went into the bedroom. He returned moments later dragging a fan that was almost as tall as he was. He plugged it in, and the fan began to swirl the warm air of the room.

In his T-shirt and underwear, he padded over to the refrigerator. He opened it and surveyed its skimpy contents. Eggs. Bologna. Peanut butter. He'd had peanut butter earlier. Bread. The milk was sour. Jesse reached for an opened package of bologna—there were only a few slices left, the bread, and an almost empty jar of mayonnaise. He thought about cooking the bologna. He liked his bologna cooked, but the last time the grease had popped everywhere and it scared him. He decided to eat it cold. Jesse made his sandwich and went into the living room with it.

He climbed back on the couch. Taking a bite out of his sandwich, he watched the black-and-white people on the screen. They had two kids—two boys and a dog. Everyone was happy. They were going on a vacation to the Grand Canyon. Jesse didn't know what the Grand Canyon was, but it sounded like a lot of fun because everybody was so happy.

He glanced at the door again, then back to the screen. *Where is Mommy? When is she coming home?* he wondered. *She'll be home tomorrow*, he whispered to the empty room. *Mommy will come home tomorrow.*

chapter
11

The merest of frowns wrinkled Toni's brow as she gazed at her and Sanji's reflection in the dresser's mirror. She was wondering if the red ankle-length sundress she had on was too casual. This was a business luncheon, after all. That Beale guy had actually followed up on his promise to call her about some possible jobs. When she heard that one-of-a-kind baritone coming over the line, she knew exactly who it was. She just wished she hadn't sounded so surprised. Some guys were true to their word and knew how to keep a promise.

Once she got over the surprise, she felt this inexplicable sense of relief. Maybe she was just excited by the prospect of working with models. She knew Beale's photos were mostly for local publications, but she liked the idea of a lot of people seeing her work and then spreading the word. At least, that's what she hoped the fluttering in the pit of her stomach as she talked to him was all about. Maybe she just needed a pleasant break from working side by side with an extremely lonely and depressed Chris.

Marshall had accepted a job at a bank in New York. Within two weeks he had moved up there. He was heading up a year-long special project for the bank, and though he hadn't taken a permanent job with them, Chris was not taking the separation well. A long distance relationship was the last thing he wanted.

She reached for the lipstick Sanji handed her. The shade was a warm brown with just a hint of red. Sanji had excellent taste. Some of Toni's excitement must have rubbed off on her. Sanji had insisted on helping Toni pick out her clothes and makeup. *And I've already changed my mind three times about what to wear*, Toni thought as she inspected her lightly made-up face. Her skin was fairly smooth and even-toned, so she had skipped foundation, but she had really gone to town on her eyes. Eye liner, mascara, shell eye shadow on the entire lid, and a dusting of wine on the lower lids made her brown eyes look bigger and more . . . exotic than usual. Toni bit her lower lip, then stopped because she didn't want to gnaw off her lipstick. She couldn't help but wonder if she had gone overboard.

Stepping away from the dresser, she said, "Well, Sanji, what do you think? How do I look?"

Sanji moved away from the dresser as well. She stuffed her hands into the pockets of her overalls and walked completely around her mother. That's when Toni noticed she'd been playing in her lipstick. A shade of plum covered Sanji's mouth. "You look very pretty, Mommy, but you forgot earrings." She hurried over to the dresser and rummaged through Toni's modest collection. She held up a pair of gold hoops. "How 'bout these?"

"Thank you, ma'am," Toni said as she accepted them and attached them to her ears. "How about now?" she said.

"Perfect," Sanji said with a lipsticked smile. "Your date will fall in love with you. And kiss you until your lipstick is all gone."

That caught Toni completely off guard. What did her six-year-old know about being kissed until your lipstick was gone? "My . . . my date?" she finally got out.

Sanji nodded.

"Sanji, I'm not going on a date. This is a business meeting." It wasn't like Beale was picking her up at the apartment or they were going out for the evening. Dinner was a date. Lunch . . . well, lunch was lunch.

"Chris is your business partner, and you don't get all dressed up to lunch with him," Sanji said.

"This is different."

"I know. This is a date."

Toni groaned. Sanji had put two and two together and come up with five. *Why am I trying to reason with a child, anyway?* Toni asked herself "This is not a date," she repeated. "And don't go saying anything like that to your father when he gets here." Marvin was keeping Sanji while she met with Beale, and she didn't want him changing his mind.

"Okay," Sanji said, sensing with a child's sometimes adult-like intuition that telling her dad probably wouldn't be a good idea. "But, Mommy, why don't you go on dates?" she asked. "Vivian's mom is divorced, and she goes on dates all the time."

Toni sighed and put her hands on her hips. Sanji just wasn't letting this rest. Why was it so vital to her that Toni go on a date all of a sudden?

"Well, I'm not Vivian's mom," Toni finally said, since Sanji was still looking at her as if she expected an answer.

Sanji's rebuttal was cut off by the sound of the doorbell ringing.

Good. Marvin had finally arrived. "Sanji, go open the door for your father," Toni said.

"Daddy!" she squealed, then left Toni like she was yesterday's newspaper.

When Toni finally emerged, she expected to find Sanji and Marvin in the living room, but they were sitting in the breakfast nook, where Marvin had helped himself to one of the sandwiches Toni had set out for Sanji's lunch. Sanji was sitting on his lap, gazing up at him like a pooch waiting for a crumb to drop.

"Sanji, why don't you get off your father and let him have some elbow room?" Toni said, taking a juice glass from the cabinet.

His mouth full of chicken salad, Marvin said, "Miss Behavin's fine where she's at."

Sanji rewarded him with a broad smile and then turned to glare at her mother.

Oh, so it was like that, huh? Was this the same little girl who had been so enthralled by Toni's every move only minutes before? Toni opened the fridge and filled the glass with orange juice. She handed it to Marvin. "From the way you're wolfing down those sandwiches, I thought you might need something to drink before you choked."

"Thanks," Marvin said, draining the glass in three gulps. He let out a loud belch that sent Sanji into a fit of giggles.

"Daddy, you so funny," she said.

"Yeah, a regular comedian," Toni said dryly. "Marvin, I appreciate you taking Sanji off my hands for a few hours, but I hope that belch is not an example of the kind of behavior you'll be exposing her to." She was smiling as she said it. Marvin was such an over-grown kid himself, it was no wonder he and Sanji got along.

Placing the glass on the counter, Marvin gave her an easy smile. "You need to lighten up, Toni." He bent to nuzzle Sanji's neck. If Sanji's fresh set of giggles were any indication, his mustache tickled—just like it used to tickle her when they were fooling around. Whoa, where had that thought come from? She hadn't had a sexual reaction to Marvin in ages.

To hide her confusion, she handed Marvin a paper towel. "You have lipstick on your face," she said. She handed one to Sanji as well. "Wipe that lipstick off before you leave the house," Toni softly commanded.

•

"Miss Behavin', you gonna get me in trouble," Marvin said as he started wiping his cheek and neck where he thought Sanji's kisses might have landed. He missed a spot near the base of his throat. Toni had a sudden image of a time when she used to place little kisses there.

Shocked by those memories, she asked herself, *What the hell is wrong with me? Am I ovulating or something?* She had to say something, to distract herself from her own thoughts. "So what are you and Sanji going to do today?" she asked.

Instead of answering her, Marvin reached for another sandwich, lifted the top slice of bread, and sniffed the turkey and Swiss filling. Toni had always thought that was a peculiar and rude habit of his. After verifying that the sandwich was edible, Marvin said, "I was thinking that maybe we could go to the Please Touch Museum."

Seeing her raised eyebrow at the mention of the children's science museum in Philly, Marvin said, "I thought you would approve of that, since it's educational and all."

"How are you going to get to Philly? Are you driving, or did Leroy drop you off? I hope you weren't planning on borrowing my car. I need it to get to the restaurant."

"I got my own transportation," he assured her.

"Good. Good," Toni said, while looking at her watch. She had plenty of time. It was eleven-thirty and she wasn't meeting Beale until noon. And since this was Delaware, just about everything was within twenty minutes' driving distance. "The museum probably has an admission fee, and if I know Miss Greedy Gut," Toni said, referring to Sanji, "she's going to want something else to eat before dinner. So, how much money do you need, Marvin?"

His head whipped up, and he scowled at Toni.

"What?" she said, confused by his hostile look.

"Did I ask you for any money?" he snapped. Sanji looked from one parent to the next. Noting her curiosity, Marvin said, "Miss Behavin', it's kinda cool outside. Go get a jacket with a hood on it and maybe an umbrella, too."

Marvin stood up and set Sanji on her feet. Sanji ran off to do as he had asked. Marvin's eye was twitching, so Toni knew he was mad about something, but for the life of her she couldn't figure out what. "Why are you looking at me like that?"

Shaking his head, as if he couldn't believe she even had to ask, Marvin replied, "Because you're something else."

"Meaning?"

"Meaning, why are you always trying to make me look bad in front of my child?" Toni stared at him. "Why are you offering to give me money in front of Sanji like I'm some kind of bum or something?"

Where was all this coming from? she wondered. The truth be told, he usually *was* broke. "Listen, Marvin, I was just trying to be nice. After all, you're doing me a favor."

"And why can't you let me do it? You always have to do something to even the score. I swear, Toni, sometimes I think you'd rather die than admit that I actually helped you with something. Even when I try to do right, you won't let me."

Marvin's anger took her by surprise. He never got this fired up about anything, least of all the offer of unearned money.

He turned his back to her as if he was through talking to her. He called out to Sanji, "Hurry up, Miss Behavin'."

Toni touched his arm, and Marvin turned around. With the height difference, she had to crane her neck so he could see the apology in her eyes. "Marvin, I don't know why you're getting all offended. It's not like I haven't given you money before. Sometimes, you've actually asked me for money when you take Sanji out."

"I didn't ask for anything this time," was his brief retort.

She backed away. "Whatever, Marvin. Sorry if I hit a nerve."

"You should be. You might try keeping in mind that whether I'm flat broke or rolling in the dough, I always try to do my best by Sanji."

Toni felt ashamed. Not that she agreed that Marvin was doing his best. Still, she didn't need to belittle what effort he did put forth, especially in front of Sanji. She extended a hand to him. "How about we declare a truce?"

Her eyes widened as Marvin took her hand. An easy grip replaced his earlier stony look. He began to trace slow circles on her palm. Toni took a step back, yet registered relief that his touch did absolutely nothing for her. Those earlier flashbacks about the mustache and kissing him must have been temporary insanity.

"I don't have a white flag . . . and I was thinking we could seal this truce with a kiss," Marvin said, flirting.

"A kiss?" Wasn't he supposed to be spitting mad? Toni laughed as she slipped her hand from his. "A minute ago you wanted to strangle me, and I thought maybe you were losing your mind. Now I *know* you have lost it. I'll go get Sanji," she said with amusement. Marveling at his nerve and complete lack of shame, she left him standing in the middle of the floor, staring at his empty hand.

chapter

12

As Toni made for the heavy wooden doors of the restaurant, she noticed Beale getting out of a silver Integra near the entrance. He had grown a mustache since the party. It made him look more mature and a little dangerous. She liked it. Though he was only average height, he had long, muscular legs. Her eyes moved up to his backside. Toni wished she had a butt that compact and tight. His posture was soldier-erect.

When Beale noticed her, he quickly pressed the remote button on his key chain that locked the doors and turned on his alarm system. He walked over to her and said, "Like I said when we first met, you are a walking advertisement for that salon of yours."

The simple compliment and the male appreciation in his eyes melted away most of the nervousness she had felt while driving over. "Thanks," she said, a pleased warmth infusing her face.

Once settled at a table under a large green and white umbrella, Toni ordered a cobb salad and iced tea. Beale opted for the crab cakes. As they ate, he described the jobs that he had coming up. He had two shoots for different local clothing stores. One was a children's store, the other for a designer who had her own boutique. He explained that he always had a regular lineup of male and female models who were hoping to be "discovered" one day by a modeling agency in New York or Philly. He offered to pass Toni and Chris's name along to them.

Toni opened her purse to take out a pile of business cards. It was like that commercial, she no longer left home without them. After passing them over to Beale, she was surprised to see that she had eaten most of what was on her plate. She had thought she'd be too nervous to eat, but she had been so absorbed in what he was saying, she hadn't been paying any attention to what she was doing.

She loved the deep timbre in his voice. Such a powerful sound was so unexpected coming from a regular-sized Joe like him. And Beale had a way of looking at her so directly, so intensely, she couldn't have looked away if she had wanted to.

"I also have a shoot for a bridal shop," Beale said as he slipped the cards into his pants pocket.

"It's July," Toni said. "I would have thought the bridal stuff would have come out in the spring."

"This is for a fall sale," he replied. "Not everybody can be a June bride," he explained with another one of those dazzling smiles. Pearly whites surrounded by smooth chocolate skin.

Damn, he was cute! Toni silently acknowledged. And attentive and interesting and employed.

Was she smiling like an idiot? She hoped not. What was with her today? Why was she salivating over this man when he hadn't said anything to indicate that he was thinking about her in the way her dirty mind had been thinking about him? Attraction and desire strummed in her veins. It was like when a numb hand or foot started coming back to life. You knew you'd feel better once it had, but in the meantime those initial pricks and tingles didn't feel good at all.

"Speaking of brides, Chris tells me that you're divorced."

Toni felt a frisson of tension creep up her spine. The last thing she wanted to talk about was Marvin. "I am," she said.

Noting her two-word response, he said, "Still a sore subject?"

"It depends on the day."

Beale's smile was sympathetic, apologetic. "Sorry I brought it up."

Toni suddenly felt a need to set the record straight. She didn't want him to have the mistaken impression that she was pining over Marvin's worthless behind. "You didn't say anything wrong. Marvin and I are through," she said, her gaze not wavering. "My biggest beef with Marvin these days has to do with his parenting skills. But he's been more involved lately, which is good."

Beale nodded. "That's right. You have a little girl . . . Sanji."

Toni raised an eyebrow. He knew her daughter's name? Then Toni smiled because she already knew who had been blabbing. "So what else has Chris been telling you about me?"

"Uh-uh. We males stick together. I'm not giving you any ammunition that will get Chris in trouble."

"Fine," she said. "Why don't you tell me about you? Are you married?" Now, why did that have to be the first question to pop out of her mouth? Toni picked up her fork, stabbing at the few surviving pieces of lettuce she'd left on the plate.

"Nope. I'm not married. Never been."

"A confirmed bachelor, huh?"

"I wouldn't say that. Granted, in my twenties, I was all about getting my education. So, I probably wouldn't have been the guy to go out with if a woman was looking for commitment. But now that I'm thirty-five, I'm . . ."

Then he paused to drink from his lemonade. Toni could have strangled him. That is, if she hadn't become mesmerized by the tangy liquid pushing past those lips and then easing down the strong column of his throat. Ice cubes clinked as he set the glass back on the table.

"Now that you're thirty-five?" she prompted.

"I think I'm ready to settle down and focus on something . . . someone other than myself." Strong brown fingers stroked the condensed moisture on the side of his glass, rolling the wetness between his fingers.

Does he have any idea how erotic that is? Toni wondered. She voluntarily licked her lips. Whew, she was suddenly feeling a little warm. She picked up her iced tea which was more water than tea. Because, like her, the ice was melting.

Beale continued to tell her more about himself. He had majored in art in college and had dabbled in different mediums: graphic design, painting, and photography. He eventually discovered that photography was his strong suit but didn't really want to make a career of it. He'd always loved working with kids and looked for a way to combine those two passions.

He laughed. "It's funny. Everybody says there's no money to be made if you major in art, but I've had better luck finding photography work than as an art teacher."

"I know what you mean. Art, music, and physical education are the first things to be cut when a school system's budget gets tight. It's a shame."

"Well, it took a while, but I feel blessed. Every day I get to do something I enjoy. So many kids get turned off from the arts at a young age because other people don't understand what they are trying to express . . . because they're not encouraged . . ."

His words made her think of Lynn and the beautiful craft work she created. Lynn had been a late bloomer. One of those kids who hadn't discovered her talent because she hadn't had the opportunity to take any art classes until high school. Toni felt sad and worried for her sister, wondering what turn her life might have taken if she'd discovered her passion a few years earlier. Before she bought into Bruce's limited vision of herself.

A light breeze caused tendrils of hair to billow softly along the outline of her face. Beale's life story floated past her ears. He was born in North Carolina. She smiled a little when he confirmed her suspicion that he was ex-military. He'd been in the Air Force ROTC. The sound of his voice and the lazy heat of summer had her feeling calm as the Brandywine River that flowed nearby.

"I wish I had my camera right now," Beale said.

Toni was startled to find his eyes flickering with some emotions she couldn't identify. "Why is that?"

"Because you're as pretty as a picture. Maybe you should be one of the models."

"If you say so, but I learned as a teenager that I don't have what it takes to be a model."

"Says who?" he asked.

"Says the Zilber School of Modeling. I begged my parents to let me take a six-week course. And after they took my five hundred dollars, what do you know, they told me I was too short to be a model."

"Were you crushed?"

She shrugged. "Not really. I never really wanted to be a model. But I was really into clothes and makeup back then, and me and two of my friends had saved up money from our summer jobs to do it."

"Well, I'm somewhat of an expert on the subject, and I say beauty comes in all shapes, sizes, and colors. And you definitely have something that I would love to capture on camera. But frankly, I don't know if the camera could do you justice."

Toni finally blushed. His flattery was just too much. "Uh, not to question your expert eye, but I think I'll stick to the behind-the-scenes work."

His voice was teasing as he said, "Toni Carleton, I think you're shy."

Shy? The word shy had never been linked with her name in her entire life. She was the older sister, the leader, the go-getter. Yet something kept her from protesting. Maybe she felt shy when she was around *him*.

"Beale, you said something about studying in Paris. That must have been exciting. I've never even been out of the country. Not to the Islands. Not even to Canada."

"It was a lot of fun. The French aren't as anti-American and stuck up as most people think they are. But there's no place like home."

Toni nodded. But she wasn't sure where home was. She'd lived in Delaware for almost ten years, but it still didn't feel like home. Her family was back in Cleveland and that felt more like home for that reason. But it still wasn't quite home. Did that mean she was homeless? A chuckle escaped her.

"Care to let me in on the joke?"

"It's nothing. I'm just thinking silly thoughts," Toni said.

His eyes widened in mock surprise. "A Renaissance woman like you, thinking silly thoughts? How could that be?"

"Renaissance woman?" she echoed.

"That's right. Mother. Business woman. College student. Freelance hair stylist. Now thinker of silly thoughts. That makes you a Renaissance woman."

"I thought it just made me a busy woman, who sometimes doesn't know if she's coming or going," Toni said. Then she tested the new label on her tongue. "Renaissance woman." She laughed. "I think I kind of like the sound of that."

"Your laughter. I think I kind of like the sound of that," Beale said.

She had expected to see humor lurking in his eyes, but his expression was serious as all get out. The tingling sensations came back. She hoped she wasn't reading too much into his comments, but the attraction didn't seem one-sided. *There's only one way to find out*, a little voice inside her whispered. She was going to take those jobs he was offering. "Beale, you're like good medicine for my tired soul. I'm going to really enjoy working on the shoots with you." And maybe she could get this tingling and twitching taken care of, too, while she was at it.

chapter
<u>13</u>

Though Chris was the one telling the joke, his smile didn't quite reach his eyes. Marsh, though, threw his head back and laughed. Chris was telling a story about the woman who had brought her poodle to Shear Necessity for a shampoo and a trim. Chris's attention was not on the story but on who was coming and going in the dimly lit, trendy Manhattan restaurant. He was wondering when Seth, Marsh's ex, was going to show up. The man was a half hour late.

Chris had been the one who had insisted that the three of them meet for dinner. Now he wasn't so sure that was a good idea. He reached for his martini to wash down the lump that had formed in his throat. He still couldn't believe Marsh had "forgotten" to mention that Seth was a corporate attorney at the same New York bank where he'd taken the job. Yet it was really Seth's constant calls this weekend that had raised Chris's hackles. Maybe he was being insecure for nothing. But if they were "just friends" as Marsh claimed, there was no harm in them meeting—Chris glanced at his watch—that is, if Seth ever got here.

Chris forced himself to tune out the muted conversations of his fellow diners and the hustle and bustle of the wait staff. Normally, when he and Marsh went out to dinner, they amused themselves by trying to guess the relationships between the other people around them. Tonight Chris didn't care about what was going on with the rest of the room.

"So what did you tell her?"

"Huh?" Chris said.

Marshall scowled, pretending impatience with Chris's short attention span, "The lady with the dog? What did you say?"

"Oh," Chris replied, resuming his story, "I told her that my license didn't cover four-legged clients, but Mutton was welcome to wait while I gave her a shampoo and a trim instead."

We have actually enjoyed each other's company for a change, Chris told himself. His jokes were corny, but Marsh was laughing. Chris wanted to savor these moments. They hadn't occurred with much frequency this past month.

Marsh had come home most weekends as promised, but whenever they were in the same room for more than five minutes, the tension between them rose faster than desert heat on an August afternoon, making Chris feel helpless and sick at heart. Keeping busy at Shear Necessity sometimes took his mind off of how lonely and miserable he was. But not for long.

He frowned, remembering that Seth would be joining them any minute now. He hoped this meal would be just as carefree as the rest of the weekend had been, but he doubted it. Not feeling suspicious the way he did. Marsh and Seth had always remained in contact. They had mutual friends. And of course, now they saw each other at work. All of that Chris could deal with, but Seth had called three times since his arrival—once after midnight. Marsh told him he was being paranoid. Maybe so, but Chris wanted to make sure it was all as innocent as Marsh claimed.

However, as the prospect of meeting the guy grew more real, Chris started to feel even more insecure. He couldn't help it. Marsh's ex was readily available while he was hours away.

Marshall took another sip from his scotch and soda. Chris fingered his silverware and regarded Marsh in an enjoyable silence. A thatch of curly hair showed above his unbuttoned polo shirt. His eyes traveled back to Marsh's familiar face. He looked good. Rested, not tense or angry for a change. Marsh caught him watching and gave him a wink. A surge of joy swept through him. The easy camaraderie was one of the things he'd missed most.

Marshall looked past him, then held up a beckoning hand. "Here comes Seth."

Chris turned around, eager to get a first look at Seth Lundgren. He tried to hide his dismay when he saw that Seth was everything he had hoped he *wouldn't be*. A man about Chris's height was smiling as he waited for a tuxedoed waitress at a nearby table to move out of his way. His wheat-colored hair was close-cut, sculpting his head in small waves, and framing his face was the thinnest of sideburns. He had broad swimmer's shoulders and lean legs. A pair of loose-fitting jeans were cinched at his flat waist with a thick black leather belt. His white dress shirt was rolled up at the sleeves, showing off sun-browned, sinewy skin. Because he still had his sunglasses on, Chris couldn't see his eyes.

It struck him that Seth looked a lot like him—only better. He turned back to face Marsh. He'd seen enough.

Moments later, a surprisingly accented voice said, "Hey, guys, sorry I'm late." Chris looked up to find that Seth had removed his glasses. Chris guessed him to be five or six years older than himself. Midnight blue eyes gave Chris a cursory examination before he took a seat on Marsh's right.

Seth stuck out a hand. "So you must be Chris. Good to finally meet you." Seth's handshake was firm and hard like the rest of him.

•

"Nice to meet you, too," Chris said, then tossed down the last of his martini.

"So what took you so long?" Marshall asked.

Seth turned to him, his grin teasing. "Don't you remember what weekend this is?" Marshall looked at him blankly. "C'mon, is your memory really that short? What do I do the third weekend of every July?" he prompted.

Marshall's brow furrowed in concentration. Then an answer registered in his brown eyes. "The Columbia triathlon?"

Seth slapped Marshall on the back, then turned to Chris, smiling. "See, I knew he'd remember. Yeah, man, I was up at the crack of dawn; swimming, running, and biking. I spent the rest of the day recuperating. That's why I was late."

"Recuperating, my ass," Marshall scoffed. "I bet you won the damn thing."

Chris watched the interplay between them keenly. He didn't particularly like how Seth's hand lingered on Marsh's back. "So, how did you do?" he inquired, just to be polite.

Seth gave him an "aw shucks" grin, then said, "While I appreciate MJ's faith in me . . ." *MJ? Who is MJ?* Chris wondered. Then his eyes widened. *Seth has a nickname for Marsh?* "I didn't win the race but"—he paused for dramatic effect—"I did win for my age division. Not too shabby, huh?"

"Very impressive," Chris agreed. "I was wondering where a corporate attorney got such a deep tan. Now I know."

"Oh, triathlon training ain't the half of it," Marshall bragged. "Seth is into parachuting, waterskiing. You name it, he does it."

"So, Chris, what do *you* do when you're not putting perms in people's hair?" Seth asked.

Chris's face flushed, feeling mocked. "Nothing as excit- ing as you, I'm sure," Chris said dryly. "I go to school part-time. So I study a lot, and with Marsh in New York, I've been doing a lot more stuff around the house."

Signaling for the waitress, Seth said, "Ah, yes, MJ *is* a handy man to have around," he said with a laugh.

Seth was taking every opportunity to let Chris know that *he* knew "MJ" as well as Chris did—maybe better. *Why?* was what Chris wanted to know. He regarded "MJ's" smiling face. Was he catching any of this?

After they placed their orders, Seth regaled them with more tales of his athletic prowess. Chris noticed that a lot of the stories dated back to when Seth and Marsh were a couple. When the food came, Chris was relieved on two counts. One, since Seth needed his hands to eat, he had to remove his arm from around the booth that he and Marsh shared and two, hopefully, he wouldn't be able to eat and talk at the same time. Chris was getting tired of the trips down Memory Lane.

Chris pushed the soggy arugula around on his plate. Piled on top of it were microscopic bits of chicken and peppercorns in some type of bland cream sauce. He was going to order a pizza when he got back to Marsh's place. His head came up when Marsh laughed again at some joke Seth had made. Deciding to change the conversation to one he could join in on, Chris said, "Seth, I couldn't help but notice that you have an accent. Where are you from originally?"

Seth stopped, his fork poised en route to his mouth. "MJ never told you?"

Chris made a conscious effort not to roll his eyes. His first thought was, *No, believe it or not, "MJ" and I have better things to talk about than you.*

"I'm part German and part Norwegian. I spent my first ten years in Norway, and then my family moved here."

I had to ask, Chris thought ruefully. So not only was Seth athletic, but he was a Norse god along with it. The question was, which one? Chris summoned up what little he remembered from a mythology class he had taken ages ago. Was Seth like Thor with his big hammer? Or Odin, the king of the gods? Or maybe Loki, the god of mischief, the cunning trickster.

Seth said, "I notice that you have an accent, too."

"I do?" Chris replied.

"Yeah, sounds kind of . . . of rural." As in country or hickish, Chris presumed. "MJ told me that folks down your way say New Ark instead of Newark. Is that right?"

"Yesiree, Bob." Chris figured he might as well play the country bumpkin part all the way, since he'd already been typecast.

"How quaint," Seth said with a smile. "I shall have to visit there sometime."

Chris made some noncommittal comment. Seth made coming to Delaware sound like he was going to some backwater country. Yep, he was definitely Loki.

Seth asked Marshall a work-related question, effectively cutting Chris out of the conversation *again*. Chris rearranged his food around on his plate, only stopping because the waitress came over to see how they were doing.

She took Marshall's and Seth's empty plates and then turned to Chris. "Are you done with that?" He nodded his head miserably.

"Seth, can I get you and your friends anything else?" the waitress asked.

"I'm not sure, Erica," Seth said, turning those impossibly dark blue eyes on her.

Chris searched the front of the woman's jacket, looking for a name tag. Of course there wasn't one. Seth and the waitress were on a first-name basis. That meant Seth was a regular here. Undoubtedly, he had suggested this restaurant for dinner as well. No wonder Chris couldn't stomach the food.

Seth's eyes shifted to Chris. "You up for dessert? The chocolate mousse is top-notch."

Chris began shaking his head. He just wanted to leave. The place was pretentious and the food stunk.

Marshall, who was totally missing the distress signals in Chris's eyes, cheerfully said, "I don't know about dessert, but I would like some coffee."

"Me, too," Seth said. The arm had gone back up around the booth. His hand dangled, brushing against Marsh's shoulder. He saw Chris staring at it and smiled.

The waitress turned to Chris. "Nothing for me," he said. "Just leave my water glass."

"Let me out, Seth," Marshall said. "I think I had one too many scotch and sodas before you got here." Seth removed his arm and stood up to let Marshall pass. "I'll be right back," Marshall said. They both watched his departing back as he headed for the men's room.

A silence fell over the table. Chris had decided to say as little as possible to Seth. He didn't like the man.

Seth yawned and stretched his arms over his head. "I guess the meet took more out of me than I thought," he said.

"Maybe you should skip the coffee, go home, and get to bed early," Chris suggested.

Seth gave him a thin smile. "Don't worry about me," he said. "I'll be fine. I don't want to spoil MJ's evening. He works too hard. It's good for him to get out."

"He hasn't done any work since I've been here," Chris said evenly. "And I haven't heard him complaining," he added for good measure.

"What have you guys been doing?"

"Mostly hanging out at his place, relaxing, spending time together."

"Hanging out at his place?" Seth scoffed. "That can't be too much fun. MJ barely has any furniture there."

And Chris liked it that way. After all, Marsh's stay in New

York was temporary. "There is no point in him moving a lot of stuff up from Delaware," Chris said. "He's not going to be here that long."

"Really?" Seth said slowly. "But . . . the project's hit a couple of snags. It's probably going to take at least three months longer than originally projected." Noting Chris's look of surprise, Seth said, "Oops, I just assumed MJ had told you. Sorry for letting the cat out of the bag."

"Marsh and I don't spend much time talking about his work. It probably just slipped his mind," Chris lied, embarrassed that Seth knew more about Marsh's life than he did.

"Well, don't you worry about MJ," Seth said. "I won't let him work himself to death. I'll see to it that he takes a bite or two out of the Big Apple." His toothy grin was calculating rather than reassuring.

Chris said, "Marsh is a big boy. He can take care of his own social needs. And I'll take care of those that he doesn't. Besides, you wouldn't want hanging out with 'MJ' to take too much time away from you and your boyfriend." Marsh had moved to Delaware to lick his wounds after Seth had cheated on him.

"Boyfriend?" Seth said with a laugh. "Do you see any boyfriend here? I'm as free as a bird."

Chris hoped his dismay was not showing on his face. It was just as he had suspected. Seth was on the prowl. He shrugged. "I'm sorry," he said. "I just thought you were with the same guy you dumped . . . I mean, cheated . . . I mean . . ." He threw his hands up helplessly. "So whatever happened to that guy?"

Without a trace of shame Seth said, "He is ancient history. And the biggest mistake of my life."

"Really?" Chris said, not liking this news one bit.

"Yes, really. And I've told MJ that many, many times."

"I just bet you have."

Just then Marshall returned to the table, followed closely

by the waitress, who brought their coffee. Seth slid next to the wall, and Marshall sat on the outside this time, much to Chris's relief. Having Marshall on the outside didn't make him look quite as trapped by Seth.

Marshall had reached for his coffee when Seth suddenly cried, "Wait!" Both Chris and Marshall looked at him in surprise. Smiling, Seth said, "We've never really celebrated your new job, Marshall. We don't have champagne, but we can still have a toast." He picked up his mug and gestured for them to do the same. "Here's to Marshall's triumphant return to the Big Apple." Looking directly at Chris, his smile loaded with spite, he added, "May he continue to move on to bigger and better things."

Okay, that was it. No more of the innuendo and cat-and-mouse bullshit. Chris calmly touched glasses, then flung his water in Seth's conniving face.

Marshall lashed out at him from the darkened interior of a cab. "Chris, what the hell is wrong with you?" He'd asked that question several times as he hastily paid the bill and apologized profusely to Seth. Chris hadn't answered then, nor had he answered when Marshall eventually caught up with him outside La Maison Verte, where he was attempting to flag down a cab without much success. "I can't believe you acted like such a dick!"

"Me? Me act like a dick?" Chris sputtered. "I was wondering the same thing about you and Seth."

"What the hell are you talking about? What did I do? What did Seth do?"

Chris turned toward his baffled voice. When had Marsh become so obtuse? "It wasn't what you did, but what you didn't do. What you didn't see," Chris said.

"Why don't you tell me what I supposedly didn't do, then? That would be a lot more helpful than slinging around all these vague insinuations."

He hated when Marsh talked to him like he was a two-year-old. "For starters, why did you let the guy drape himself all over you? Then every other word out of his mouth was 'MJ, remember this' or 'MJ, remember that.' And every time I tried to bring up something we *all* could talk about, he'd stop long enough to take a few stabs at my job and where I lived. Then he'd go right back to how much fun you and he used to have."

Chris glanced at the back of the taxi driver's head, wondering what she was making of this conversation. The woman's eyes were focused straight ahead. Clearly, yelling and screaming in the back of the cab was nothing new to her.

"So what?" Marsh said, finally responding. "That happens sometimes when old friends get together. That doesn't mean Seth deserved to have a glass of water thrown in his face. I can't believe you reacted like some diva on a soap opera. You embarrassed the hell out of all of us!"

"Us who? I wasn't embarrassed." Marsh must be talking about him and Seth. So great was his fury at the time, Seth was lucky he'd gotten off with only drenched hair and a mottled purple face. That icy water had sure wiped that smug grin from his face.

Chris looked at Marsh, then raked his hair in frustration. "Do you really think I'm so petty that I can't handle a little reminiscing? It was more than that, and you know it "

"I know no such thing!" Marsh roared right back. "You need to get a grip on reality. There is nothing going on between me and Seth."

"Not yet," Chris muttered thickly.

"Not yet? What is that supposed to mean?"

"Just what I said. That guy's intentions are more than friendly. He wants you back."

Marshall sighed heavily. "Chris, you're being ridiculous."

"I don't trust him."

"You don't have to trust him," Marsh said quietly. "You need to trust me."

Chris sought out Marsh's eyes in the darkened cab. He wished he could see them more clearly. He wished *Marsh* could see Seth more clearly, see him for what he was—a man who was prepared to ensnare him with all the skill of a seasoned hunter.

The cab finally pulled up in front of Marshall's building. Marshall proceeded to pay the woman. As Chris got out, an empty space above a tall metal pole that was embedded in the cement caught his eye. The street sign was missing. New York was a big city. Without a sign to guide you, it would be easy to get lost, he thought as he stuffed his hands deep in his pants pockets and waited for Marshall to join him on the sidewalk.

This discussion wasn't over. Not by a long shot.

c h a p t e r
14

As Toni waited for her bank's customer service rep to look up her checking account, she averted her eyes, not wanting to look at the mess on her desk. Lately, no matter how much work she did, there was always something else needing to be done. A few minutes earlier, before paying some bills, Toni had called the automated account information to find out which checks had cleared. It had seemed a simple enough task, but then she found out that there had been two withdrawals from ATM machines that she couldn't account for.

The woman came back on. She patiently reviewed all of the transactions Toni had made in the last month in an upbeat, helpful voice she'd probably been trained to perfect. "Wait," Toni said when the woman mentioned a withdrawal on June 4. "Can you tell me where I made that withdrawal?"

"There was a thirty-dollar withdrawal at Eden Square Shopping Center on June 4."

Eden Square? That's where she did her grocery shopping. Maybe she had picked up a few things at the store and forgot to write it down. She scratched her scalp with the tip of a pencil. It was itching. *I need to wash my hair*, she thought. Toni wrote in the thirty-dollar debit and put a check mark next to it.

"There is also a debit for fifty dollars on June 17. Where did that transaction take place?" Toni asked.

After a brief pause, the faceless woman said, "That one was at Delaware Park."

Toni dropped her pencil in surprise. It rolled under the desk. "Delaware Park? As in the racetrack and casino?"

Yes.

Her blood pressure rose a couple of notches. "Somebody has screwed up. I have never set foot inside Delaware Park!" *What in the world is going on?* Toni kept the card in her wallet all the time. She hadn't lost or misplaced it, so there was no way some gambling addict could have gotten a hold of it. Somebody at the bank must have entered the wrong numbers in a computer.

"Perhaps you forgot to write it down, like you did the first transaction," she offered helpfully.

"I think I would remember if I'd been to the racetrack," Toni repeated. When the woman didn't immediately respond Toni added, "The withdrawal was on June 17, you said?"

"Yes."

Toni glanced at the cat calendar on the wall in front of her desk. June 17 was the day she had taken Sanji and two of her friends to Six Flags in New Jersey. Toni explained to the woman that she had been out of town on that day. Though the customer service rep didn't appear as concerned as Toni was about the possibility that someone was stealing money out of her account, she did obligingly describe the procedures for correcting the discrepancy. As she droned on, Toni's mind pored over all the transactions she had made recently. *Have I goofed somewhere? I don't think so. But then why am I coming up short? Lord, I hope nobody has gotten a hold of my account number.* Toni had seen the movie *The Net.* With a Social Security number and a little computer know-how, a person could get access to your entire life. Sighing, she hung up the phone.

Toni picked up an invoice slip that Carla, one of the people she supervised, had brought to her attention as soon as she got to work. Standing up, she reluctantly approached the small cubby hole where her boss, Elmer, the trade manager, was supposed to be doing his work. Toni needed to ask him a question. The space she called her office was really just a black countertop anchored to the wall directly behind the customer service desk. Elmer's office was formed by two floor-to-ceiling bookcases which intersected with the solid wall that his desk faced.

Toni peeked through the entrance made by the two cases. Elmer was slumped over his desk fast asleep, with his head resting on his arms. His computer's multicolored screen saver twirled restlessly in the background. Elmer's rear hung over the sides of his chair like worn-out saddlebags. His striped short-sleeved shirt heaved with each breath he took. A pair of round tortoiseshell glasses lay on a small pile of books near his head.

That two-hour lunch break must have really wiped him out. Toni rapped loudly on the side of one of the cases and walked in. Elmer merely stirred, then shifted to rest his left cheek rather than his right cheek on his folded arms.

No one would ever accuse Elmer of working too hard, but his laziness had reached ridiculous proportions. He had progressed from showing up late to not showing up at all. Sometimes he took lunch and never came back. Complaining to his boss hadn't helped.

Toni was getting fed up with doing his work and hers, too. She would be so glad when she was done with her degree and could get the hell out of here.

In the meantime, the work wasn't going to get done by itself. Toni ventured farther into Elmer's cramped office. Frowning with distaste, she shook him by the shoulder, then quickly let go. This time he shot straight up.

"Huh?" he said, reaching for his glasses. He pushed his overlong, not too clean brown hair off his pimply face. If it were anybody else, Toni would have offered to trim it a long time ago, but she tried to touch Elmer as little as possible. His eyes were red from deep sleep. "Oh, Toni, it's you."

"Yeah, it's me. I hate to interrupt your nap," she lied, "but Carla was having trouble figuring out which company to send these returns to." Toni showed him the invoice. "We need to get the publisher's exact name. I'd never heard of 'em. They haven't updated my computer code, so I can't pull up this particular screen. I thought maybe you could run a check on your computer."

He stood up with the invoice in his hand, then moved to the side of his desk. Elmer's bulk shrank the available space in the room exponentially. All the bookstore offices—except the manager's—were tiny. Office space had been sacrificed to create more sales floor. Elmer started smoothing out his crumpled clothing. His attempt to stuff the tails of his shirt into the waist of his pants in some semblance of neatness was laughable. He was a forty-five-year-old man who was still living at home with mother. You'd think in all that time, the woman would have taught him a thing or two about personal grooming. Then again, that was assuming Elmer's mother was any better.

He handed the invoice back. "Sure, Toni, *you* can use my computer to check it out," he said. Ever helpful, he wrote down his access code for her.

Elmer possessed an amazing ability to hear only what he wanted to hear. But it no longer surprised her. Toni had known from the start that she would be the one looking up the information.

Elmer squeezed past Toni as he moved toward his desk. "Say, would you watch the fort? I'm going to walk over to the Union for a soda. I got cottonmouth, and I need to stretch my legs."

Toni didn't bother reminding him that there were soda machines in the building. She simply nodded in agreement. He was of no use to her anyway.

After Elmer left, Toni tried to match the book to publisher

as quickly as possible. In addition to his laziness, Elmer was a heavy smoker. The surrounding bookcases kept in the smell of body funk and cigarettes. But that didn't bother her as much as his collection of vampire memorabilia. The fangs and coffins and crucifixes that lined two of his bookshelves gave her the creeps. Nervously, she eyed a velvet painting of a cloak-draped Dracula leaning over his latest victim—a semi-nude young woman—with blood dripping from his mouth.

She had tracked down the tiny publisher and returned to her station when her phone rang.

"Hello, University Bookstore," she said, picking it up on the second ring.

"Toni?" came a hesitant voice on the other end.

"Mama?" Toni immediately went on red alert. Her mama never called her at work. "What's wrong?"

"It's Joy . . . she's missing."

Joy was always missing, but the catch in her mama's voice relayed that this time was different.

"Mama, what's going on?"

"Jesse called me last night. Joy hasn't been home in days. She left him . . . left that baby in that apartment all by himself " The tremor in her voice threatened to dissolve into tears. "Clarence went over and brought him home. Lord, Toni, that child was scared and hungry."

Toni could hear the anger in her mama's voice, but her fear was stronger. Joy had never left Jesse alone like that.

"Did you call her job?" Toni asked.

"I went over there this morning. They said they fired Joy last Friday. That's the last time they saw her."

Oh, God, Toni thought, *what kind of trouble is Joy now?* "What about her friends?"

"We called everybody, all her friends. Don't nobody know where she is."

Pressing her ear to the phone, Toni reached underneath

her desk, fumbling for her purse. She snatched up the purse. She looked inside to make sure both her wallet and check-book were in it.

"I hate bothering you at work—"

Toni halted the apology: "Mama, please. I'm glad you called. I would want to know." She craned her neck, trying to see around the bookcases. *Has Elmer come back from the Union yet? Where is his worthless ass when I need him?*

"Mama, you need to make a police report."

"Your daddy did that last night . . . after he brought Jesse home. The police weren't no kind of help. Since Jesse is the only one who knows how long she's been gone, that made it kinda sticky. We didn't want to tell them she'd left Jesse by himself, and they kept saying that if she was an adult, she may have just have taken off on her own—" She ended on a sob, finally breaking down. Toni forced herself to be quiet, letting her mama release some of the terror she'd kept bottled inside. As she listened, Toni was on the brink of tears herself. Her mother weeping was one of the most painful sounds in the world.

After a few minutes, Anna Mae regained control. "God, Toni, I'm worried sick . . . Lynn is here. But she hasn't been feeling well. Did I tell you that she had some bleeding and cramping?"

She hadn't. All hell was breaking loose in Cleveland. Toni waited for her mama to continue. "I hate to ask you this. I know how busy you are," she paused. "Toni, can you come home?"

Toni's purse was already closed, and the note she had scribbled for Elmer on a large yellow Post-it was in her hand. "Hang in there, Mama. I'll be home as soon as I can."

chapter
15

Toni didn't know Lynn had entered the room until she heard
the dry rustle of papers as they landed in front of her on the
table. The dining room was used only on special occasions
like Christmas and Thanksgiving dinners. With the house at
full capacity, Toni had hid out in it, hoping to get a moment
to herself. A moment to think and clear the swirls of fear that
clouded her head. Lynn and her kids were here, plus Sanji
and Jesse. Then there was Aunt Hester Ruth, who spouted
Bible verses and sung snatches of spirituals at the mention
of Joy's name. Toni knew she meant well, but Aunt Hester
Ruth was not helping.

"Here's what is left of the flyers," Lynn said quietly.

As Toni straightened her shoulders, the bones in her neck
cracked like twigs. She slowly twisted it from side to side,
loosening any remaining kinks. Her fingernails had been
chewed to the quick, she noticed as she reached for a picture
of Joy that the family had been posting and passing out all
over the city for the past forty-eight hours.

Toni stared tiredly at the color flyer. They had used the
most recent photo of Joy they could find. A Polaroid that had
been taken at one of her favorite clubs by one of those ama-
teur photographers who for a small fee documented everybody's night out on the town. One shiny shoe was poised on

the edge of a wicker chair, showing off the curves of her thigh. The clingy red dress could have doubled as a long, tight-fitting T-shirt. One hand was on her hip, her head tilted to one side, the other hand curled around a tall, golden-colored drink, and her blackberry-painted lips were curved into a Delilah smile.

Toni glanced over at Lynn, who had slipped into a seat next to her. The thin elastic of her bra strap was visible where her too loose maternity dress fell off her shoulder. Lynn's skin was a dull beige, her large eyes made even more deep-set by the dark shadows underneath them. "Where is Mama?" Toni asked.

"Still sleeping."

Sleeping? Is that what you call it? Toni let the flimsy paper fall to the table and rubbed her temple with two fingers. Mama hadn't recovered from watching the news last night. A story had come on about a woman's decapitated body being found near the Fifty-fifth Street train station. It wasn't Joy. It was a white woman in her forties. Mama had crumbled anyway, succumbing to her worst fears. Daddy and Darius had to help her into bed.

It was almost eleven o'clock, and Mama still wasn't up. Mama never slept this late. On the other hand, she needed the rest. The past few nights, Daddy said, she had been tossing and turning, crying, pacing, and praying. Toni used the pad of her thumb to press a spot on her head that was throbbing. She had been on the go nonstop ever since the call from Mama. After picking up Sanji from day camp, she threw some clothes in a suitcase and drove the seven and a half hours to her parents' house. She hadn't remembered to let Chris know what was up until after she got to Cleveland.

Joy had been missing for eight days. Mama couldn't take much more of this. None of them could. They had been running all over the city talking to Joy's friends. No one had seen her. And Lynn, who looked like a gust of wind could blow her away, kept trying to take care of the kids when she was supposed to be resting.

Toni reached over to touch the stringy hair that Lynn had pulled back into a hasty ponytail. Frowning, she rubbed the limp strands together. Lynn's hair was thinning like the rest of her. "Lynn, how are you feeling?"

Lynn clasped her bony hands on the table. Her answering smile was wan. "I'm okay. Still bleeding a little."

Bleeding a little? She had been bleeding "a little" for two weeks. And was acting like it was no big thing. Toni released her hair and moved her hand to her sister's face. With a finger she lifted her chin so that she could have a better look.

Toni felt like crying at what she saw. Her "little sister" looked old and worn out at twenty-three. Lynn's hollowed eyes and cheekbones reminded Toni of pictures of the people standing in soup kitchen lines during the Depression. Lynn looked ten times worse than she had only a few weeks ago at Darius's graduation party. She would lose the baby if she wasn't careful. "Lynn, you should be in bed."

"But I need to help Aunt Hester Ruth with the kids—"

"Aunt Hester Ruth is fine. Daddy and Darius can help her."

"But Bruce doesn't like it when other people look after the kids."

Like Toni really could give a shit about what Bruce liked. This was an emergency situation, and people had to be flexible. "If he's so concerned about them, then he should be here to look after them himself."

"Oh, Toni," Lynn sighed. "You know he would. But he can't just take off work."

"Why not? That's what I did." Toni tried to take the edge out of her voice. "Lynn, what's the point of having a husband if he doesn't help you raise the kids? Sanji's here with me because I have nobody else to take care of her. You shouldn't have to do it alone—"

A spasm crossed Lynn's face.

Whether hurt or pain, it made Toni partially regret her words. Toni sometimes forgot how thin-skinned Lynn was. But shit, she was only telling the truth. Lynn just didn't want to see it. Bruce only cared about Bruce. Forget about taking off from work. He wasn't doing *anything* to help. He wasn't watching the kids. Hell, he hadn't even offered to tack up a flyer.

Now with Joy missing, Lynn was getting anything but rest. Toni gritted her teeth in frustration. Where the hell was Joy? Aloud she asked, "Where are the kids?"

"Sanji's in the backyard with Daddy, and Aunt Hester Ruth is fixing the kids something to eat."

Like Mama, Aunt Hester Ruth cooked when she was upset. She'd been cooking sit-down meals ever since Toni's arrival.

With a smile that was a ghost of her normal self, Lynn said, "I think she's trying to fatten us up to make herself feel better."

Sanji was never one to turn down a meal. But Jesse. Toni was worried about him. He was already skinny, and she hadn't seen him eat more than a bite or two. He only perked up when he heard someone talking about his mama. Yesterday, Darius had taken him to the basketball court to get him away from all the tension in the house. And Jesse wasn't the only one who needed looking after.

Toni eyed the tiny stomach bulge in Lynn's otherwise skeletal frame. "Well, it looks like Aunt Hester Ruth has her work cut out for her with you."

Suddenly self-conscious, Lynn pulled her drooping strap up and smoothed the front of the print dress. Then she crossed her arms in front of her. "What do you mean?"

"I mean you're too thin. Come to think of it, when was the last time you ate anything?"

Lynn leaned back in her chair, pondering her older sister's question. Seconds passed. Finally, she stammered, "I'm . . . I'm not sure." When Toni gave her a disapproving look, Lynn threw up her hands. "I haven't felt hungry. Really," she tagged on when Toni's expression didn't change.

Toni drew a deep breath, ready to lecture her on prenatal care. The doorbell rang before she could get the words out.

"Saved by the bell," Toni said. "I'll see who is at the door. You go get something to eat."

Toni was surprised to find Fonzo standing outside the screen door. Her father had already talked to him a couple days ago. So what was he doing here? Had he heard from Joy? She hurriedly unlocked and opened the door. She pushed him aside, hoping that he'd brought Joy with him. When all she saw was an empty stoop, she took a step back and gestured for him to come in.

"Y'all heard from Joy yet?" he asked as he crossed the threshold.

"No. No. I thought you'd brought her with you." Still, he was here for a reason, and Toni was eager to find out what it was. She led him into the living room and sat down in her father's leather easy chair. "Have a seat," she told him. As Fonzo sat across from her on the low settee, his long legs nearly came up to his chest.

A hairy hand scratched at his mid-morning five o'clock shadow. His muddy eyes became disbelieving. "Y'all still ain't found her yet? I thought she be and come home by now."

Toni sprang forward in the chair. Her fingers dug into his arms. "What do you mean, you thought she'd be home by now? Do you know where she's at?"

His expression was shifty. Not looking directly at her, Fonzo said, slowly, "Well, I ain't for sure . . ."

He knew something. She was sure of it. Toni crossed over and sat next to him on the couch. "I don't care . . . I'm not asking for guarantees . . . just any place you can think of . . ." Her eyes searched his, trying to figure out what he was hiding.

"Well, she might be over at Lance's," he said.

Finally, some information they could use. "Who is Lance?" Was this a new man Joy had taken up with? Toni swore to God, she'd kick Joy's ass if she had driven them crazy with worry while she was shacking up with some man.

"Well, I ain't wanna tell yo'old man this, but . . . Lance be running a smoke house over there on Eighty-first and Carnegie. And Joy, she be hangin' there sometimes. Go there to smoke rock."

"Smoke house?" Toni's eyes widened with shock. What was he talking about? Joy wasn't no crack head. She couldn't . . . wouldn't be that stupid. Toni grabbed a fistful of his T-shirt. "A smoke house," she repeated. "As in crack house?"

He held up both hands in a defensive gesture and moved out of her grasp. "Not exactly. You can't buy the stuff there. People just go there to smoke."

Shut up! Shut up! she wanted to scream at him. *I don't want a lesson on drug culture. I just want to find my sister.* "Fonzo, are you trying to tell me that my sister is a crack head?"

"I ain't saying nothing 'cept you might want to check out that place and see if she's there. It's an apartment above where the old Rexall drugstore used to be."

Toni was about ready to explode. She felt the heat scorching the place where her skin made contact with the cloth of the couch. "You're supposed to be her boyfriend. Why didn't you check it out?"

"Boyfriend? I ain't her man." Fonzo's bushy eyebrows arched as if she'd accused him of being the anti-Christ. "Joy ain't got no papers on me. I didn't even know she was missing until your old man came around looking for her."

Toni lunged at him again. She stabbed his chest with a pointed finger. "You told my father you hadn't seen her. How could you do that, you asshole!"

Hurriedly, Fonzo leapt off the couch. Toni got to her feet as well, her eyes slicing him like laser beams. "Damn, baby. Why you bugging? Last time I saw Joy she was fine. In fact, she told me to fuck off."

"You mean, you were with her and you left her in some . . . some . . . drug den!" Toni didn't wait for him to answer. "You let us worry ourselves sick for days, and you knew where she was?"

"I figured she was where she wanted to be. And I ain't wanna hear no shit from her about blabbing to her family. But then when she never showed up . . ." He shrugged one shoulder.

What a fucking asshole! Joy might be dead somewhere, and he was worried about having her pissed at him? Toni shook her head in amazement. "Well, better late than never, I guess," she said sarcastically.

Totally missing the irony, he said, "That's exactly what I was thinking. That's why I came over today."

Lynn called out from the dining room. "Toni, who was that at the door?"

"Nobody!" she replied.

So thorough was her disgust, Toni couldn't even look at him. "Fonzo, just leave." Finding her legs no longer able to support her, Toni flopped back into the recliner.

"Huh?"

"Just leave," she repeated.

There was silence, then he mumbled, "Uh, well, I hope you find her."

With her head bowed, Toni listened to the sounds of his retreating feet as he headed for the front door. Even after it slammed behind him, she couldn't muster up the strength to stand. She needed a moment to gather her thoughts.

It all made a horrible kind of sense: Joy's inability to hold down a job, the constant begging for money, not hearing from her for days. The chair enveloped Toni's overheated body. Toni sawed at the corner of what was left of one of her nails. How was she gonna tell her parents that Joy was probably holed up in a crack house somewhere?

Toni glanced nervously at the way her father's work-scarred brown hands gripped the steering wheel. He looked like he was holding on for dear life. His back was ramrod straight, not touching the seat. He stared straight ahead. The broken glass on the sidewalks, the potholed streets, and aging houses of the urban landscape went by at twenty-five miles an hour. His droopy eyes looked sadder than ever. Though he had called in sick before Toni told him about her conversation with Fonzo, perhaps out of habit he had donned his dove gray work shirt. A color that perfectly matched his shattered expression.

Her father had insisted that the two of them follow up on Fonzo's lead without telling her mother. He didn't want to say anything to her until they had some real news. More important, he didn't want to upset her unnecessarily. As always, protecting Mama.

Toni reached over and turned down the Shirley Caesar that was playing in the cassette deck. "Daddy, are you okay?" she asked.

He blinked and gave her a sideways glance. "About as okay as a man can be when he learns that his child is a drug addict," he said sadly.

"But we don't know that. We don't even know that she is at this place. We've only got Fonzo's word on it, and I don't know him from Adam. He could be lying." Toni was grasping at straws and she knew it. She just hated to see him looking so . . . so despairing.

"This is my fault," he said in a quiet voice.

"Daddy?" He couldn't have shocked her more if he had said he was a Martian. She stared at his profile, from the crinkled salt-and-pepper hair to the square jaw. "How is it your fault?"

"I knew something was wrong. I knew that girl wasn't living right. And I didn't say nothing."

"Daddy, it's not your fault. She's been wild for years, and plenty of people have tried to talk to her. Joy is a grown woman. I just think she finally got involved in something she couldn't handle." Toni placed a hand on the solid muscle of his upper arm. "Please . . . please, don't blame yourself, Daddy," she begged him.

"It's kind of hard not to. I raised her."

Toni sank back against her seat. She couldn't believe he was blaming himself. She didn't know how to talk to him when he was like this. And if Daddy was acting like this, what would Mama be like?

In the side-view mirror, Toni noticed the lights of a police car flashing behind them. Her first thought was that they were about to be ticketed for speeding. The siren was off, and the car was moving at a pretty good clip. But a quick glance at the speedometer quashed that idea. Still, her father put his signal on and pulled over to the curb. The car whizzed by them in a black-and-white blur. After checking that it was okay to do so, Clarence pulled back into traffic.

When they got to Ninety-third and Carnegie, he made a left.

"Where on Carnegie did you say this place was at?" Clarence asked.

"I don't have the exact address. Fonzo said around Eighty-first and that it's an apartment above what used to be a drugstore." Toni hadn't spent much time in this part of

town. Carnegie was a funny street, one-way or two-way de-
pending on the time of day. It was a major thoroughfare for
people who commuted into the city from the eastern suburbs. There was not much traffic this time of day, noonish.
"You look for it on your left and I'll look on my side," she
told her father. Another police car flew by them in the left
lane.

They stopped at a traffic light. Out her window, Toni saw
a check-cashing place with a large, gaudy orange and white
sign. A group of hard-looking brothers stood in front of a
mom and pop store. There were a lot of old abandoned
stores, but she didn't see anything that looked like a drugstore. Through the windshield she spied a number of flashing lights twirling a few blocks away. Something was up.

An unwelcome suspicion popped into her head, causing
her stomach to tighten. They were at Eighty-sixth Street.
Eighty-first was only a few blocks away. She looked over at
her father. His fingers were in a death grip around the steering wheel. Was he thinking what she was thinking? "Daddy,
do you think they're going to the building Joy is supposed to
be in?"

Clarence's Adam's apple bobbed. His voice came out in a
croak: "I hope to God they ain't." A pool of sweat had
soaked the fabric of his gray shirt at the armpits, betraying
his worry. He pulled the car over at Eighty-third Street.
There was no way he was going to get any closer. A swarm
of cop cars had blocked off the street at Eighty-first. He
snatched his keys out of the ignition and didn't bother to
lock the car doors. Clarence and Toni bolted from the car
and raced toward the brownstone that the police had surrounded.

Fueled by adrenaline, Toni was too scared to be winded
from her two-block sprint. She reached the group of gawk-
ers before her father did. Not waiting for him, she elbowed
her way through to the front of the crowd. She came to a

sudden halt and put a hand to her chest to still her hammering heart. Four uniformed police officers were talking to each other in front of a boarded-up Rexall drugstore. No guns were drawn and they seemed at ease, but the cops didn't come out in force in the hood unless they were actually doing their jobs—for a change. On the curb, she saw people sitting in the back of some of the squad cars. One girl was crying, unable to wipe her snotty nose because her hands were shackled from behind. Toni's eyes darted anxiously to the open door to the right of the store. As if drawn by a magnet, she moved toward it. She could see a narrow set of stairs leading to an upstairs apartment.

Panting and sweating, her father materialized at her side. Looking up at him, she saw her anxiety mirrored in his transfixed brown eyes. "What . . . what's going on?" he gasped.

"I don't know," she murmured. "I don't know." Toni turned to the person closest to her. "What's happening?"

A teenage boy dressed in army fatigues answered. "They raiding Lance's."

"Oh, God!"

"Toni?" her father said. The single word conveying a wealth of concern when he saw her stricken face. "What is it?"

"Lance. Lance, that's the name of the guy Fonzo mentioned—"

Raised voices and the sound of feet stumbling down wooden steps cut off her next words.

All eyes were trained on the door. A young white cop with a fiery red bruise on his forehead emerged, followed by a hulking black man in his late twenties. He smiled in malicious delight at the bruised officer. Noticing the crowd for the first time, he acknowledged them with a defiant nod of his head. A second cop behind him saw the gesture and stuck a leg out. The big guy went down like a sack of potatoes, the side of his face hitting the broken pavement.

A roar of protest came from the crowd. "Yo, man, he knocked Lance down."

"Police brutality!" someone else shouted.

Ignoring the outrage of the crowd, the same cop who had tripped Lance brought him to his feet by yanking on his cuffed wrists. Lance grunted in pain. Suddenly a very pregnant woman with a scarf on her rollered head and house slippers on her feet rushed forward. "You're hurting him, damn it! Get off my brother," she screamed, lunging at the officer. He did let go—to defend himself from the three-inch fingernails that were aimed at his eyes. The cop grabbed her by the wrists.

"He's beatin' down a pregnant woman!" someone cried.

Holding the woman's hands high above his head, the beefy cop yelled, "I'm not hurtin' her!" The woman continued to strike out at him with her thrashing feet. One of the house shoes had come off. "The chick is going psycho on me."

Two of the neighborhood people jumped in. Toni edged away and pulled her father with her, not wanting to get hit. The cops who had been milling around the storefront joined the fray.

Two officers tried to contain the crowd. "Get back! Stay back!" they warned the people, who seemed ready to riot. Though the police were soundly cursed and their mothers' morals called into question, no one else got into a physical altercation with them. The skirmish was over in a matter of minutes. Lance, his pregnant sister, and those who came to their assistance were hustled into the backseats of patrol cars. "Break it up. Go on home, folks. The show is over," the police said. Though they backed up a few paces, no one showed signs of leaving.

"Daddy, this is crazy," Toni whispered, watching the police's futile attempt to disperse the grumbling crowd. "We got to get out of here." When he didn't answer, she whirled around, looking to her right and her left. He was no longer with her. *Where did he go?* Then she saw him sprinting over to one of the squad cars. She ran after him. Had he found Joy?

As she neared the car, she saw her father bend down and tap on the rolled-up window. "Joy, it's Daddy," he said over and over, his voice laced with desperation. A woman she barely recognized as her sister sat catatonic-like, oblivious to his attempts to communicate with her. Joy's matted hair weave fell in a messy cloud around her face, and her eyes stared at the iron mesh in front of her. The white blouse she wore was coated with gray as if she'd rolled around on a dusty floor. Her lips were dry and caked white.

Clarence raised his frantic eyes, noticing his eldest daughter was at his side. "Toni, she's not answering me," he said. He turned back to Joy. "What's wrong with her? Joy, baby, it's Daddy."

Toni called along with him, drumming on the glass. Joy remained motionless. Was she really that out of it, or was she pretending to be because she was embarrassed?

"Hey, you. Step away from the car," a voice bellowed.

Toni jumped and turned toward the raised voice. Her father did not. "That's my sister in there," Toni said to the Clint Eastwood look-alike that had addressed her. "Something's wrong with her."

The cop glanced at Toni, then Joy. He shook his head without much sympathy. "Ma'am, I'm sorry that's your sister, but I still need you and"—he gestured toward her father—"him to move away from the car."

His nonchalance was pissing her off. Now Toni knew how Lance's sister had felt. "Look at her! She's not moving. She doesn't recognize us—her father and her sister. I think she needs medical attention."

"We'll get her checked out when we get her to the station."

"The station? What station?" Toni asked.

"The Fifth Precinct."

"Oh, God." She had been so relieved to find Joy, she had forgotten what sitting in the back of a squad car meant. Joy was going to jail. She felt physical pain when she saw her father's hand splayed against the window of the car, waiting in vain for Joy to respond.

Toni gave his shoulder a little shake. "Daddy, you gotta get up. You'll be able to talk to her in a little while." For a moment it was as if he didn't hear her. Then his hand fell away and he stood up. Toni put her arm around the waist of the worn old man that her father had become and slowly walked him back to the car.

c h a p t e r
<u>16</u>

Anna Mae peered out the living room window. When she saw no sign of her husband's car pulling into the driveway, she let the curtain fall and went back to pacing restlessly around the room. *What was taking them so long?* Clarence had called hours ago to let her know that they'd found Joy. Her tears of relief immediately dried up and turned to shocked silence when he told her where they were and why.

She shook her head, still not quite believing it. Joy had been arrested on drug charges. When Clarence had given her the specifics, it was like he was speaking a foreign language, Greek or something. Joy had been charged with criminal trespassing, possession of a controlled substance, and possession of drug paraphernalia.

Anna Mae crossed over to the window yet again and stared out into the dusk. She wasn't a naive fool. She knew Joy was no angel. Joy partied and liked to have a good time. She'd never been the most responsible person when it came to keeping a job. But never in a million years had Anna Mae suspected that it was because she was doing drugs. *Are there signs that I missed? Should I have questioned Joy about her whereabouts after those times when no one heard from her for days?*

Anna Mae tried to shake off the guilty thoughts that began

to close in on her. *It's bad enough that Joy didn't care about herself, but what about Jesse?* At the thought of her grandson, a flame of anger ignited within Anna Mae. *There's no telling what that child has witnessed and heard in his young life. He doesn't deserve—*

The glare of approaching headlights interrupted her silent condemnation of Joy. A car pulled into the driveway, and the lights were quickly extinguished. Anna Mae rushed to the front door and threw it open. Standing on the stoop, she watched Toni open the driver's door and come toward the house. Clarence's familiar lanky frame emerged from the backseat. His shoulders were stooped as he went around to the other side to open the door. When she saw Joy, Anna Mae let out the week-long breath. Tears of relief welled up in her eyes. Drug charges aside, her baby was alive and home in one piece. And that was the most important thing.

"Hi, Mama," Toni said tiredly as she pressed a kiss on her mother's cheek. "Come into the house. You shouldn't be standing out here in your nightgown."

Anna Mae looked down, only now aware of the thin flowered house dress she wore. She'd been in such a daze, she wouldn't have been surprised if she had answered the door butt naked. But she had a feeling this particular reunion should take place indoors. She was so full up, had so many questions. Anna Mae wasn't sure what she'd say or do when she was face to face with Joy. Before reentering the house, she glanced behind her, as if afraid Joy might disappear again.

Toni had sat in the first chair she got to. Her eyes were closed as she rolled her head around on her neck. She looked rumpled, like moist hands had bunched her clothes from top to bottom. Even the laces of her tennis shoes were undone— both of them.

"What took y'all so long?" Anna Mae asked.

Toni opened tired eyes. "Mama, I ain't never had to get nobody out of jail before, and I hope to hell I never have to again. Me and Daddy had to ask questions every step of the way. Where were they holding her? When could we see her? What were the charges? How much is the bail? Who do we pay? People at the police station were so unhelpful and confused, you'd think this was the first day on the job for all of them."

These were not the kinds of details Anna Mae cared about. "How is Joy? Is she okay?" In the background, the security door slammed.

Toni shrugged. "Here she comes. See for yourself."

The pitiful creature a step or two in front of Clarence didn't look like Anna Mae's Joy. Her hair was a tangled, matted mess. Anna Mae had seen wild dogs that looked better fed. Though not exactly skinny, Joy looked like the stuffing had been pulled out of her. Cheeks that were once fleshy were now hollow. Her eyes were sunk deep in their sockets, showing no sign of their usual devilish gleam. Empty, vacant, unfocused pupils gazed into space. Had it only been a week or so since she'd last seen her?

Anna Mae's stomach lurched. The smell of sweat, urine . . . and an unwashed body leapt across the short distance that separated them. It was obvious from the layer of grime on her soiled clothes that she had been living in them for days. Anna Mae's eyes sought Clarence's. His thin face was pinched, and his sleepy eyes were mere downturned crescents. He looked dead on his feet. She had never seen him looking so exhausted, not even after a double shift at the plant. Sad eyes met hers. Clarence slowly shook his head as if he, too, could not believe how Joy had deteriorated since they last saw her.

Motherly concern overtook revulsion as Anna Mae staggered forward, enveloping Joy in her arms. The embrace was not returned. Anna Mae took a step away but didn't break contact. She took Joy's cold hands and stretched her arms out in front of her body, inspecting her, searching for more signs of physical and emotional damage. They were the same height, so her worry was reflected back at her from Joy's empty eyes. "Joy, are you all right?" Anna Mae asked.

"Fine," Joy replied in a voice with about as little expression as her face. No explanation. No apology. Still, Anna Mae was glad to hear the sound of her daughter's voice. There had been dark moments in the last week when she feared she would never see Joy again.

She abruptly released Joy's hands. After almost driving them crazy with worry, all Joy had to say was "Fine." Anna Mae said, "Well, you don't look fine. You look like you been through the wringer." Anna Mae twisted her lips, regretting her bluntness. Criticizing wouldn't help anything. When Joy didn't react one way or the other, she added, "We need to get you cleaned up." To see her reduced to such an inhuman state made Anna Mae want to cry. A hot bath would be the first step in helping Joy rejoin the human race.

"Where are the kids?" Toni asked in a weary voice.

Anna Mae looked past Joy's stone-still body. Toni was hunched forward in the armchair. Her elbows rested on her knees, the palms of her hands supporting her head. She didn't look much better than Clarence. Remembering she hadn't had a good night's rest since Joy's disappearance, Anna Mae figured that she was beat, too. The trials of the past few days had taken a toll on all of them. "I asked Hester Ruth to keep them tonight," Anna Mae said. "I was keeping some supper warm for y'all in the oven. I bet you're hungry, Joy."

"I don't want nothing."

Anna Mae didn't know what to do. The girl was looking like death warmed over, and she was refusing food?

Toni got up from the chair. Anger edged her voice as she glanced in her sister's direction. "I'll take Joy upstairs," she said. Though Toni made the offer, Anna Mae sensed she had little enthusiasm for the job. And Anna Mae didn't begrudge her that. Dealing with the police sounded like a nightmare, and just by being here Toni had done plenty.

"You two have done enough for Joy. You been running around all day . . ." Anna Mae paused. She'd done it again—the implied criticism. It just kept popping out of her mouth. She gave Joy a sideways glance. Her expression was still blank, making Anna Mae wonder if there was anything she could do or say, anything to wipe that unseeing look from her face.

"C'mon, baby. Let's go upstairs and get you out of those grimy clothes," Anna Mae said, taking her by the hand and leading her away like she was a child.

Joy said nothing as Anna Mae ran her a bath. She disrobed and sank into the heated water. Equally silent, Anna Mae, from her seat on the toilet, used a pitcher full of water to wet Joy's hair. The liquid in the tub instantly turned a darker shade of gray, causing Anna Mae's heart to break just a little bit more.

Sounds and images of summer nights flooded through her. Dirt-streaked faces, ashy knees and elbows, gap-toothed smiles. In the days before Darius, and when Lynn was still a lap baby, Joy and Toni had ripped and ran all day, then had an allergic reaction to the word *bath*. To save time and to make sure they were doing more than splashing around in the water, sometimes Anna Mae had bathed them together. Slick with soap, brown skin shiny and ripe with youth, their protests soon turned to giggles.

Now stretch marks were etched in Joy's sides, crawling toward her belly button. There was no laughter. Only Joy's withdrawal and Anna Mae's heartache.

Joy had been the sweetest of her babies. Always eager to help. Always interested in what Mama was doing. *Lord, where has my child gone?*

Anna Mae asked Joy to raise her arms so that she could wash underneath. Joy couldn't even keep them lifted. After trying, her hands hit the water with a noisy splash. Anna Mae felt a tear prick her eye and blinked it away.

Slowly, she lifted one of Joy's arms, resting it on her shoulder. Anna Mae scrubbed as hard as she could, trying to wash away the stench of a life that was trying to steal her daughter from her. She scrubbed, hoping to blot out the worrisome thoughts that kept coming at her. She didn't want to think about what Joy might have done to keep the drugs coming. Anna Mae wasn't naïve. She had heard Darius and his friends bad-mouthing girls—strawberries, they were called—who traded sex for drugs. Anna Mae's lips tightened, and she pulled the comb a little harder through Joy's hair than she had intended to. She apologized when Joy cried, "Ouch." Still, it angered her to think about the vultures who took advantage of people when they were at their lowest point. What kind of person would do that? She hated even to think about it. But her next thought was along the same vein. What if Joy was one of those strawberries? And if she was, what diseases had she exposed herself to?

Anna Mae's hand shook as she deposited the pitcher and comb on the floor and reached into the tub for the soap and a washcloth. Though she wanted to go easy on Joy her first night back, as her fears started to feed on each other, Anna Mae's need to have some questions answered overpowered her. While lathering the dry, scaly skin on Joy's back with soap, she cried, "Joy, what happened? What were you doing in that house? How did you end up in that place?"

"Ain't it obvious, Mama?" Joy said in a wooden voice.

Anna Mae scowled at her. Nothing about this situation was obvious to her.

Her eyes glittering unnaturally, Joy added, "I didn't 'just say no' to drugs. I didn't say no." Then she began laughing as if amused by her little joke. Anna Mae gazed at her, first in confusion, then in alarm when Joy's laughter continued, rising in pitch.

"Stop it, Joy!" Anna Mae said. Joy kept laughing, then gasped as if she couldn't catch her breath. The laugh became a grimace of pain as she clutched her stomach and doubled over. When she lifted her head, she was laughing again.

"Joy, stop. You gonna make yourself sick," Anna Mae pleaded, softening her tone.

The laughter became a hyena's bray. Of its own volition, Anna Mae's wet hand rose from the water and slapped her daughter's haggard face. Joy's laughter disappeared. The smack echoed in Anna Mae's ears. She stared at her stinging hand, then at the swollen imprint that slowly materialized on Joy's face. No longer vacant, Joy's eyes were glazed with shock.

A stricken look crossed Anna Mae's face. A part of her had wanted to do that—slap the taste out of Joy's mouth—since she'd first learned that Joy had left Jesse in that dingy apartment all by himself. But now that she'd given in to that urge, it didn't feel good. There was no relief, only guilt and regret. An agonizing thought gripped her: *What kind of mother kicks her own daughter when she is down?*

Anna Mae knelt next to the tub, then cradled her naked, motionless child and began rocking her. "Oh, baby, Mama is so sorry." Within seconds, her thin nightgown was soaked. "I don't know what came over me," she murmured, holding Joy close, tightly pressing her face against her bosom. "Mama is so sorry," she repeated. The steam off the water dampened Anna Mae's skin, mixing with her tears.

When Anna Mae laid a gentle hand on Joy's face, she felt tremors beneath it. She pulled back in surprise and peered into her daughter's face. Joy was crying. Her eyes were brimming, hot tears trickled down her face. Then to Anna Mae's surprise, she wrapped her arms around her mother.

"I'm sorry, too, Mama," she said softly, and then repeated the apology, becoming incoherent as her sobs got louder.

They sounded strange to Anna Mae's ears. Joy hadn't cried since she was a girl. Not even when she was in labor with Jesse. The boy's father had already been in jail by then, doing twenty years to life. Still, Joy had fought to keep the family out of the delivery room. She wanted to go through it alone. But Anna Mae had stayed whether she wanted her to or not. Now that same strong girl held onto her like she was a lifeline. And Anna Mae wasn't about to let go.

"You go ahead and cry, baby," she encouraged as she stroked Joy's damp hair. "You can always cry on Mama's shoulder." This simple fact only made Joy cry harder.

chapter
17

The court-appointed attorney ushered them into a cramped meeting room in the public defender's office. Mama and Daddy had offered to hire an attorney for her, but Joy wouldn't hear of it. That was the only sign of protest Joy had made since they had found her five days ago. Toni didn't care if she was being agreeable or not. She wanted to hear what Joy's lawyer had to say. She didn't want anybody calling her in a few weeks asking for more help in sorting out the mess Joy had created.

Toni was well aware that her emotions were running about as regular as a city bus on a holiday schedule. One minute she was cussing Joy out and calling her all kinds of names, then the next she insisted on being involved every step of the way in getting her help.

They had moved Joy's stuff out of her apartment the day before. The hand-me-down furniture wasn't worth saving. The couch and the two sets of mattresses were left out on the curb for the garbage men to haul away. The rest of Joy's worldly possessions fit into six large trash bags. While they were packing, Joy's landlady had shown up, demanding two months in back rent.

Joy hadn't completely lost her spunk. She tossed out a "So sue me," then showed the loudly cursing woman to the door. Mama had been so embarrassed. She told Joy that what she'd said to the woman wasn't right. As far as Toni was concerned, Joy was just being her usual uncaring self. Toni wasn't embarrassed, she was disgusted. Who was Joy to think she could sit up in somebody's place month after month and then get an attitude when the person asked for the rent money? Joy didn't know what a charmed life she'd led—up until now. And even now Mama and Daddy were prepared to clean up after her. Mama had promised the land-lady that she'd get her money.

Then there was the matter of Joy's health. Mama was too embarrassed to bring it up with her, so she'd asked Toni to do it. And their suspicions about unprotected sex were confirmed because Joy hadn't said a word when Toni insisted that she see a doctor. The terror that had briefly flickered in Joy's lackluster eyes hadn't escaped Toni's notice. Besides having her general health checked, Joy took pregnancy and AIDS tests. Despite her anger, Toni was happy to learn that Joy wasn't pregnant and hadn't contracted any garden-variety forms of VD, but they wouldn't get the results of the HIV test for a while. And she would have to be tested again in six months. Toni knew this from personal experience. She had been tested herself after she found out Marvin had cheated.

Mama and Daddy took a seat on the same side of the small wooden table. Mama clutched the straps of her purse, trying to encourage Joy with a smile. Toni sat opposite her sister. When her mother caught Toni's eye, she frowned. Mama probably wanted Toni to fix her face. To mask her feelings about being here. Toni had no doubt displeasure was written all over it. Toni turned her gaze to her sister. Joy might want to readjust her own features, she thought. Maybe she might try aiming for a "frankly-I-do-give-a-damn" look. After all, this was *her* life. And Toni didn't appreciate the fact that the rest of them seemed to care about it more than Joy did.

Toni looked around the no-frills room. Scratched-up table. Uncomfortable chairs. Institution-colored painted walls. Anxious family members. The mock cool pose of the accused.

Joy's weave couldn't be salvaged, so Toni had taken it out. The short natural suited her. Joy wore a short-sleeved button-up shirt and a pair of jeans. Both a smidgen too tight. What else was new? If only Joy could understand that less was more. She was an attractive woman without all the goo and loud, cheap clothing.

A chair scraped as the bespectacled attorney pulled it up to the table, sitting across from her parents. Todd Vaughters was extremely young looking. His hairless face with its rounded cheeks hadn't lost its baby fat. The plain gold band which circled his ring finger caught her eye as he smoothed his tie and reached for a stack of folders in front of him. Toni guessed that if he was old enough to be married, he was old enough to practice law. Mr. Vaughters pulled out a folder from the middle of the pile. "Let me see what we have here," he murmured, opening Joy's case file.

Oh, God, this was not starting well. The man hadn't even looked at the file yet. Joy might want to reconsider paying for a lawyer. It was worth the money if it meant getting someone who could give her case the attention it deserved. And it wasn't Joy's money anyway.

After adjusting his glasses, he looked at Joy. "Miss Rollins, it says here that you had drugs and drug paraphernalia on your person when you were arrested. Is that correct?"

Joy shrugged. "I don't know. I don't even remember being arrested."

Mama was unable to contain a groan at Joy's cavalier admission. Her purse began bouncing up and down like a jockey headed for the home stretch. Toni knew she was embarrassed—again. Daddy reached over and squeezed her knee. Mama blinked in surprise and then smiled and put her hand on top of his. The lawyer, on the other hand, nodded as if hearing this type of response was nothing new for him.

"Do you remember being at 8103 Carnegie Avenue?"

"Yeah."

Again Mama looked like she wanted to be anywhere but here. Toni knew the feeling.

"Well, unfortunately for you, the person living at that address"—he glanced down at the file again—"a Mr. Lance Leonard, didn't reside there legally. He was a squatter, which means that anyone staying there with him was trespassing. So you've also been charged with criminal trespass."

"That's a misdemeanor, right?" Joy asked.

"That's correct."

"And I didn't have much cr—" She glanced nervously at her parents. They were both listening intently. "I didn't have much . . . much stuff on me," she quickly improvised.

"According to the police report, the only drugs you had were in the pipe you were smoking."

Joy glanced around the table at her family and saw varying degrees of pained expressions. "So, those should be misdemeanor charges, too, right? So maybe I'll get probation or community service or something, right?" She said this with such certainty, it prompted Toni to wonder when she'd become so familiar with the legal code.

The lawyer thumbed through a few more pages before answering Joy's question. His eyes were encouraging as he said, "Yes, they are misdemeanors . . . but there is the matter of your prior record."

On her left, her father abruptly leaned forward. Looking puzzled, he said, "Prior record? What prior record?"

Toni herself wasn't particularly surprised.

"It says here that you were arrested for check deception six months ago, and two months prior to that there was another misdemeanor possession charge."

Mama's eyes swung around to Joy's, willing her to deny it. She didn't. In fact, Joy couldn't maintain eye contact, breaking off to look down at her hands, which looked oddly bare without her usual glittery tips attached.

Like Mama, Toni was realizing how little she knew about her own sister. *How could Joy be arrested not once but twice and I—none of us—knew a thing about it?* she asked herself. Maybe she should have paid even more attention rather than shutting Joy out when she started to live the fast life.

Since Joy seemed to have lost her know-it-all attitude and couldn't respond, Toni asked, "So how does her prior record affect the new charges?"

Though Joy was his client, the lawyer responded to the authority in Toni's voice. He addressed his comment to her. "Well, Ms. Rollins—"

"Carleton," she quickly corrected him.

He nodded, flicking his eyes to her, then back to the file in front of him. "Ms. Carleton, your sister got off lightly with her prior offenses. Restitution for writing the bad checks—which she hasn't paid yet . . ." He turned to Joy. "You got lucky on that one. You could have been charged with fraud, which is a felony." Redirecting his comments to Toni, he said, "She received a suspended sentence for the possession charge." He peered at the file, bringing it closer to his face, then continued. "This is her second drug offense. And a case probably could be made that the check deception was directly related to her drug addiction."

Mama winced at the words "drug addiction." They were hard to hear. Everyone in the family had probably been thinking them, but no one had uttered them aloud, at least not in Joy's presence.

Noticing her mother's discomfort, the lawyer's brown

eyes were full of sympathy as he continued to deliver the bad news. "So I doubt very seriously if Ms. Rollins will get off with a slap on the wrist this time—"

"Hold up," Joy said, panic edging her voice. "Are you saying I could do jail time for this? But I wasn't even doing anything. Just getting high. It wasn't like I was hurting anybody."

Only yourself and everybody who cares about you, Toni thought. Joy hadn't believed she could go to jail? She was starting to sound just like all those people out there in the waiting room. "I been set up," one person had claimed. Another had cursed a blue streak about his "motherfuckin' lawyer" being late.

Joy fidgeted in her chair and tugged on her clothes, as if just now realizing they were too tight. Toni saw that reality was finally sinking in. Now Joy knew why they were sitting with a lawyer. She was beginning to understand what happened to people who broke the law.

"Ms. Rollins, that is a possibility. But there may be another option," her lawyer said.

"What? What is it?" Joy asked, eager for a way out.

"Well, with a history like yours, your best bet is to plead guilty."

"Guilty?" Joy shrank back at the very thought. "They'll throw my ass in jail for sure if I plead guilty."

Toni's father glanced from his wife's troubled face to Joy. His eyes flashed a warning as he firmly said, "Joy, watch your language. And let the man finish."

Mr. Vaughters cleared his throat. "If Ms. Rollins pleads guilty and undergoes a drug assessment, I can probably get her case heard in Drug Court. I'm pretty confident that I can make a case that the crimes she has committed are due to her addiction." There was that word again, but Mama didn't react to it this time. Toni saw only her mother's determination to find a way to help Joy.

"Rather than punishing addicts, the trend these days is to try to rehabilitate them. If Ms. Rollins pleads guilty, she is likely to be placed in a diversion program, which means she avoids formal prosecution and conviction. Instead, she will receive counseling—"

"Thank the Lord," Joy said, placing her palms together and looking heavenward. She was smiling for the first time since coming into the room, making Toni realize just how nervous Joy had been about this meeting.

"Ms. Rollins, more than likely you will get six months to a year of counseling with some of it being on an inpatient basis at a facility of the court's choosing."

Joy's confident grin remained in place. "Whatever . . . I'm down for that," she said. "If it means not going to jail. Sign me up."

"You say that now, but if the court orders treatment, you have to take it with the same seriousness as a jail sentence. You will be monitored and expected to stay out of trouble just as if you were on probation. You'll probably also receive some job training and be expected to do community service."

"I'll do it," Joy said. She half rose from her seat as if ready to bolt from the room. Mama motioned for her to sit back down.

Not deterred by the small distraction, the lawyer gave Joy a level look. "It may not be as easy as you think. We're talking three to four months of court-supervised community living in a private or state-run facility. Think you can handle it?"

Joy rolled her eyes. Her old cockiness had made a comeback. "Piece of cake."

"Well, then, I suggest you get your affairs in order. Because once on this track, things move pretty quickly. You'll probably be ordered to a drug-treatment facility as soon as your case is heard. The assumption is that if you have a drug problem you should be taken off the streets ASAP before you get into more trouble."

"She's not going to get into any more trouble," Mama assured him. Toni knew that meant she wasn't gonna let Joy out of her sight while she waited to get help. "She's staying with us, and then she'll go wherever the judge sees fit."

"Mama . . . What about Jesse?" Toni asked.

Mama looked at her, puzzled. "What about him?"

"If Joy's going to be away for months, what's gonna happen to Jesse?"

"What do you mean, what's gonna happen to Jesse? He's gonna stay with me and your daddy."

"Yeah," Joy readily agreed. "Jesse loves spending time with y'all."

If looks could kill, Joy would have been dead on the spot. "As if he ever had another choice. You were dumping him off there every chance you got, anyhow," Toni said. "Mama, it's too much on you. What about your GED classes?"

"If Mama's not worried about it, then why are you?" Joy snarled.

Toni wondered what had happened to the cooperative attitude she'd been fronting. "Oh, I see you're finding your voice now that it's in your best interest."

"Girls!" their father said. "Stop acting like kids! We'll figure something out."

Toni was huffing and her chest was heaving, but she did shut up. So did Joy. Neither of them were used to their father raising his voice.

"Sorry, Daddy," Joy said, blowing him a kiss. "Y'all don't mind if I leave, do you? I'm gonna die, if I don't get me a cigarette. I'll meet y'all outside."

After the door closed, Toni turned to her mother. The anger in her eyes was unmistakable, as was her mother's intention to be unmoved by them. As Mama thanked the lawyer and picked up her purse, Toni felt totally unappreciated. After all she was only trying to look out for Mama's best interest.

Toni started to say more, but her mother held up a hand. "Not another word, Antonia. Jesse is staying with us." Clarence put an arm around his wife's shoulder, and they exited together.

Hurt, Toni grumbled. "Why did they ask me to help if they aren't going to listen to what I have to say?"

The lawyer shrugged his shoulders. Settling family disputes was not a part of his job description. She left him shuffling his papers and went in search of her ungrateful relatives.

chapter
18

Toni usually didn't get this lucky, but she had found a parking space on Fourth Street in downtown Wilmington without much hassle. Even better, she didn't have to worry about feeding the meter because it was Sunday.

Sanji had leapt out of the car and already turned the corner onto Market Street by the time Toni stepped onto the pavement. She would be all right. The Christina Cultural Arts Center was only a few yards away.

Sanji was beyond excited about the dance performance. Toni smiled ruefully: her daughter was always looking for an opportunity to be center stage. On the drive up, Sanji had insisted that she play a tape of the music she was to dance to. Despite the seat belt, she had thumped and gyrated all the way to Wilmington.

She wasn't as excited as Sanji, but she was glad to be back on her own turf, dealing with her own problems. As much as she loved her family, they sometimes took a lot out of her, especially since no one seemed interested in listening to plain old common sense. Joy was only worried about saving her own skin, and Mama seemed to think that she could be all things to all people and still have something left over for herself. Whatever. Toni had enough on her own plate before she went running over to Cleveland, and she had a lot of catching up to do when she got back. Sanji's dance recital was the first fun thing she had done with her daughter in weeks, and Toni was determined to enjoy it. For Sanji's sake and for hers.

There were a few adults, probably other parents, hanging outside the doors of the center. All of them were African-American, which wasn't surprising. Though this was a "community" center and everyone was welcome, a significant number of blacks lived in and around the downtown area. The center put on plays, dance performances, art exhibitions, and taught a variety of classes—dance, music, arts, and craft classes.

When Toni entered the lobby, she noticed that the ticket window was empty. Probably because this was a rare "free to the public" performance. Sanji were nowhere to be found. Toni assumed she had gone to change into her costume. Voices and the sounds of furniture scraping across the floor were coming from upstairs. A couple of people headed for the stairway, so Toni followed behind them. The recital was probably in the small theater on the second floor.

A woman dressed in a purple and gold African-style outfit greeted people at the top of the stairs and handed out programs. At a nearby table, several more women were pulling two-liter bottles of soda and small bags of chips out of grocery bags. They would be sold during intermission. Though the recital itself was free, this was a nonprofit, so they were always looking for a way to earn a buck or two.

The program was supposed to start in a half hour. Toni entertained, then quickly banished the thought of getting a textbook from the car and studying while she waited. She was sick of studying.

People were running around like chickens with their heads cut off, so Toni offered to help. She was told to put out some more folding chairs. They were expecting a large crowd. Toni always traveled with a sweater because while it was hot outside, the air conditioning might be on full blast inside. Toni put her blue cardigan down on a chair front and center of the stage. She wanted the best seat in the house because Sanji was sure to be looking for her in the crowd.

After helping to set up, she wandered back into the hallway and started talking to a few people who worked at the center. Though Sanji had been taking classes at the center for almost a year, Toni didn't know a lot of the other parents because she couldn't devote too much time there beyond getting Sanji up to Wilmington for practice once or twice a week. More and more people started to stream into the hallway.

Someone asked about Shear Necessity, so Toni fished a couple of business cards out of her purse and then excused herself. She wanted to make a quick pit stop before taking her seat. Because she knew how people could be. If it started to get crowded, somebody would throw her cardigan on the floor and plop down in her chair and dare her to say something about it.

She was hurrying back to the theater when someone called her name. Toni started at the sound of Beale's distinctive voice, then turned to face him. He was dressed in jeans and a white T-shirt. Toni's eyes lingered where the cotton clung snugly to his biceps and across his chest. He might be on the slender side, but he was all muscle. A fancy camera was hung from a thick strap around his neck.

His smile was broad. Clearly, he was happy to see her.

Toni hung her head and emitted a groan before she knew it.

"Dang! I know I ain't the greatest guy in the world, but women don't usually look that unhappy to see me," he joked. When she would have spoken, he took her arm and gently pulled her to one side so people could pass. Toni hadn't realized they were blocking the door to the theater.

At his touch, her arm jumped to life, and her head snapped up, meeting his eyes fully. "It's not you, Beale. I'm just embarrassed," she admitted. When Joy had done her disappearing act, Toni had completely forgotten about Beale and the models until she checked her messages while she was in Cleveland. Beale had left a couple of messages the day before and one after she had missed the first shoot. "I'm surprised you're even talking to me."

"Don't worry about it. I understand. You can't plan a family emergency."

"Still, it was very unprofessional not to contact you."

"Hey, you sent Chris to cover the next two shoots." When he saw that her discomfort was for real, he increased the pressure on her arm, just a little, to get her attention. "I forgive you, okay?" he said.

Toni stared into his eyes. She let out a little breath. "Okay."

He smiled again. "So, is everything all right with your sister?"

Toni hadn't gone into detail about the "family crisis." As much as she liked Beale, she didn't feel comfortable sharing her family problems with him. "She'll survive."

The lights flickered, signaling that the performance would be starting soon. They both asked at the same time, "So what are you doing here—" then broke off laughing.

"You first," Beale said.

"Sanji is performing."

Beale hefted—no, fondled—the camera, Toni decided, then gulped because her mouth had gone dry.

"And I'm here to record the event for all posterity," he explained. "No, actually, the video guy is doing that. I'm taking some pictures for the center's next calendar of events."

Despite Beale's claim that he did the photography on the side, it was obvious he had a lot of gigs. "So when do you sleep, Beale?" Toni asked. "You seem to have your finger in a lot of pies."

He laughed. A rich, hearty sound that drew the attention

of other people standing in the hall. "Talk about the pot calling the kettle black. You're not exactly a lady of leisure yourself."

The lights flickered again. Her prime seat was lost for sure, but oddly, Toni didn't take even one step toward the theater. Instead, her eyes roamed over Beale's strong jaw and easy smile. He was so open and relaxed, making him seem much younger than he was. Toni envied his openness. In the few years since the divorce, she had been more closed into herself than ever. She didn't want to get hurt again.

The hall had cleared out, and she was in la-la-land. With a jerky step she moved away from the wall and out of his grasp. "Well . . . I'd better get going," she said, and felt like a traitor to her daughter because she didn't want to go anywhere. She wanted to stay with Beale and let his positive energy flow into her. "It was good seeing you again, Beale—"

"Wait," he said, as if he was reluctant to walk away, too. "What does Sanji look like? I'll make sure I get some pictures of her."

He wanted to take pictures of Miss Thang? The mother in her responded to his interest in her child. The world-weary woman in her wondered if he was just trying to play her. Trying to get close to the mom by pretending to like the child. Toni immediately felt ashamed of herself. She was reading too much into a simple offer. It was possible that the man was just trying to be nice.

Toni held her hand in front of her waist. "Sanji's about yea high. And she has these two huge Afro puffs."

She saw his amused look and shrugged. "Hey, it's not my fault Sanji picked her braids loose yesterday." Toni would have mentioned Sanji's missing tooth, but that probably described half the kids in the dance ensemble. "And let's see. Oh, well, she's got these curvy little hips."

"Well, why didn't you say that in the first place? I'll just look for a miniature version of you."

"So, what you trying to say?" she teased. "I got big hips?"

"Did you hear the word 'big' cross my lips? You said curvy and I just agreed. In my book, a woman can't have too many curves."

"Nice save," Toni said. "But I've got to go. Sanji is in the first dance and"—she added as the thought occurred to her—"aren't you supposed to be taking pictures?"

"Uh, right," Beale said, looking embarrassed because he had to be reminded of why he was there. "Maybe we can get together for lunch sometime?"

The question was so out of the blue, Toni was too surprised to respond. She simply stared at him.

Filling the silence, Beale said "Or dinner . . . or for whatever," he finished, now looking uncertain because she hadn't said anything.

"You want to talk about some other projects?" she asked, testing him, trying to figure out if this was business or pleasure.

"Projects?" He shrugged. "I guess that could be one of the many things we talk about." Just to make himself clear, he added, "But not the only thing and certainly not the main thing."

The breath she'd been holding slipped out with her relieved smile "Sounds good, Beale. You know my number. Give me a call."

The music to the first song had started. The room was packed by now. Toni was positive that she would be watching the performance from the back of the room, but she didn't care anymore. Because Beale wanted to get together "for whatever." Though the house lights were off, the multicolored stage lights illuminated the chair—where her sweater was still draped.

Toni quickly took her seat, grinning because her new-found luck was holding out. Now she knew how Sanji felt about today's performance. Toni suddenly understood why Sanji had been singing, skipping, and dancing all weekend. Sometimes, that's what happened when you had something deliciously good to look forward to.

chapter
19

"I still don't see why Jesse had to be shipped off to Delaware," Joy said, her displeasure competing with the static of the bad phone connection. "Why do Montana and Dakota get to stay put? Nobody made them leave town."

Toni walked over to close her bedroom door so that Sanji and Jesse, who were eating lunch, couldn't hear her when she went ballistic on her selfish~ass sister. "Joy, you sound like a two-year-old. This isn't about playing favorites. Mama and Daddy are simply not able to take care of three kids right now." Not with Lynn holding on to her pregnancy by a thread. The spotting Lynn had been having earlier in the summer hadn't stopped. After Lynn's doctor had ordered complete bed rest, she and the kids had moved in with her parents. Not surprisingly, Bruce had opted to stay alone at their place.

Toni made a face. She hadn't bothered to question the thinking behind that decision because she already knew. Bruce didn't believe in doing any work when it came to his family. It looked like Lynn would be at Mama and Daddy's for the duration of the pregnancy.

The constant care Lynn needed plus looking after Jesse, Dakota, and Montana and working at their real jobs had quickly become too much for her parents to handle. Forcing them to reluctantly ask if Jesse could stay with Toni for a while.

That's why she had called Joy. She needed to be Jesse's legal guardian so that he could attend school in Delaware and for him to qualify as a dependent on her health insurance plan. Joy was foot-dragging, and she couldn't proceed without her cooperation. "What is the big deal?" Toni asked her semi-incarcerated sister.

"Lynn is going to have the baby in a month or so. It's too much of a hassle to uproot Jesse for hardly any time at all," Joy argued. "Now you're asking me to sign my baby over to you."

Toni gritted her teeth. Joy's one-track thinking was irritating the hell out of her. She looked down at what she was wearing. She needed to change out of the cream-colored slacks she'd worn to work. After seeing the skimpy contents of Jesse's lone suitcase, Toni realized that most of the stuff was too lightweight for the fall. Buying him some new clothes was the first thing on her agenda. And the single twin bed in Sanji's room would do for tonight, but Toni had bought a reasonably priced bunk bed set as soon as she'd learned Jesse was coming for an indefinite stay. Even though it wasn't really in the budget, she reasoned that Sanji was getting to that age where she would start inviting friends for a sleep-over, so the bunk bed was an investment. When they got back from the mall, she would tackle the job of rearranging Sanji's overflowing closet to make room for Jesse's things. She had a million and one things to do, and listening to Joy's drivel was not one of them.

As she shimmied out of the pants, Toni snapped, "Joy, you act like I'm trying to steal Jesse or something! I didn't ask for this." She yanked open a drawer and pulled out a pair of faded sweat pants and long-sleeved T-shirt. "I'm just trying to help. The guardianship is temporary," she told Joy for the umpteenth time.

"If Bruce would take his kids home, Mama would have time to take care of Jesse *and* Lynn. Jesse wouldn't have to be sent so far away," Joy argued.

"And if you had acted like a mother and not a drug fiend, we wouldn't even be having this conversation. You'd be in Cleveland taking care of your own child!" That shut Joy up. Finally.

It wasn't until Toni had pulled the shirt over her head and was bending to tie her sneakers that Joy spoke again. "Why did you have to go there?" she asked quietly.

Toni sighed. Great, now Joy was feeling hurt. "Because you weren't listening to me. I'm sorry if I hurt your feelings, but somebody's got to take care of Jesse for the next few months and you know you can't do it, so why get in the way of someone who is trying to?"

"I guess I just miss him. . . . He's all I got."

Toni shook her head wearily. If Joy had been thinking like that all along, maybe she wouldn't be in this predicament. Toni glanced at her watch. One more task came to mind: she needed to call Flo back. The baby-sitter had left a weird message on her machine. She sounded pissed but didn't say why. It had been too late to call her back last night, and, after a half day at work, Toni had driven straight to the Philly airport to pick up Jesse. Toni would have to see what Flo wanted, especially since she was about to ask her if she had room for one more child in her flock.

The bedroom door burst open. "Mommy, Mommy, tell Jesse it's my TV and he has to ask me to use the remote control," Sanji cried. She hurled herself onto the bed and then peeked around Toni's shoulder as if the devil himself was chasing her. Toni shook her head at the melodrama. Jesse was nowhere in sight. She wouldn't have Sanji making him feel unwelcome. Sanji would have to learn how to share—graciously.

"Sanji, what have I told you about making a racket when

I'm on the phone?" Toni said, trying to pry loose of her daughter's solid weight against her back. She resumed her conversation with Joy. "I know you miss him, but I need you to sign the guardianship papers. There's no telling what kind of shape Lynn will be in even after she has the baby. She might still need a lot of help from Mama. Jesse should stay here at least until the holidays, and then we'll see how things stand with you and with Mama."

Meanwhile, Toni pried the remote out of Sanji's hands. Red and yellow magic marker lines and all-purpose child-hood grime clung to her daughter's palms.

Shit! She had forgotten to tell the kids to wash their hands. The phone had rung just as they were about to eat lunch from the smorgasbord of "snacks" Mama had packed for Jesse's one-hour flight from Cleveland.

Jesse appeared in the doorway, staring silently at Sanji, who became even more excited at the sight of him. "It's my TV. It's mine," she chanted.

Toni should have known that Sanji wouldn't keep quiet for long. "Joy, I've got to go." She saw the solemn child's eyes flicker to life at the mention at his mother's name. What was she thinking? Of course the boy would want to speak to his mother. Toni said, "Jesse's here. I'll put him on."

"No . . . no, hearing his voice will just make me miss him even more."

Jesse started toward the bed, eagerness glittering in his eyes. "But, Joy—" Toni said to dead air. Her sister had hung up. Damn. Damn. Damn. Why was it always about Joy's feelings? What about how Jesse was feeling?

The child froze when he saw Toni hang up the phone. Sanji had draped herself around Toni's back like a little monkey. "Was that my mommy?" Jesse asked.

"Yes."

"She didn't want to talk to me?" he asked.

"Nobody wants to talk to you. 'Cause you wear glasses," Sanji said.

"Be quiet, Sanji," Toni ordered. Her daughter's legs tightened around her waist. Seeing the tears pool in Jesse's eyes, Toni longed to comfort him.

"Come here," she said, patting a spot next to her on the bed. His head was bowed as he approached. The mattress barely gave under his slight weight. Toni put an arm around him and gave him a fierce squeeze. "Of course your mommy wanted to talk to you," she said with a smile. "We just got disconnected. That's all." Damn that Joy. "I'll call her back," Toni assured him. And she better bring her ass to the phone, too. Toni would not have this poor child thinking his own mother didn't want to talk to him.

Toni looked up the number for the rehab center in her leather address book. It was under N for New Beginnings. Joy must have still been near the phone because she picked up.

"Your son was worried that you didn't want to speak to him, and I told him nothing could be further from the truth. But I think he needs to hear it from you," Toni said before handing the phone to Jesse.

Toni had spent more money than she had planned to, but Jesse needed a lot of the basics like new underwear, socks, and T-shirts. Sanji, being Sanji, had noticed all the goodies Jesse was getting and started whining. So she scored a couple new school outfits, too. Normally, Toni wasn't such a soft touch when Sanji begged, but she didn't have the energy to reason with her after the draining phone call.

Getting the kids settled in for the night took some doing. It was the same routine: reluctant bathing, and teeth brushing, only times two. And Sanji wasn't pleased about sharing her bed with anyone. But she relented when Toni assured her it was only for one night. The new bunk bed would be delivered tomorrow, and Chris was going to help her assemble it.

Toni yawned. She wasn't really sleepy, but she did want to relax for a while. It had been a hectic day. Determined to read for pleasure for a change, she picked up a mystery she'd started at the beginning of the summer.

Toni was only a few pages into her book when she heard a faint noise coming from Sanji's room. She paused, then glanced at the door leading to the hallway. It took her a moment to recognize the sound of crying. Toni threw the book on the comforter and went into the room. She touched a small lamp on the dresser, and a splash of light came on. Both Sanji and Jesse blinked. Sanji had the covers pulled up to her nose, trying to look innocent. Jesse had tears running down his face. "What's wrong?" Toni asked.

"Auntie Toni, Sanji said there's a monster in the room."

"Sanjari." Toni's voice rose in pitch as she said her daughter's name. "Why are you upsetting your cousin? You know there are no monsters in this room."

"I was just playing," Sanji said, avoiding her mother's eyes.

"Well, I'm not playing. You better be quiet and go to sleep."

"There are no monsters in here for real?" Jesse asked, still not convinced.

Not unless you count your cousin Sanji, Toni thought, giving her daughter a grim look. "For real. But just to make extra sure, I'll look," Toni told him.

She entered the walk-in closet and turned on the light. After moving around some sweaters on the shelf and peeking behind several pairs of shoes on the shoe rack, she declared, "All clear in here."

She turned the light off and closed the closet door. She knelt near the bed and peered under it. "Don't see any monsters under here. You look, too." Jesse slowly craned his neck, but then straightened up quickly, as if at the last minute deciding to take Toni's word for it.

"See anything?" Toni asked. He shook his head.

Toni stood up. "Okay then, it looks like this room is monster free."

"You didn't check the drawers," Sanji offered helpfully. Toni rolled her eyes at her daughter but walked over to the chest of drawers and open and shut them. "Nothing in here but clothes," she reported. She gave them both another good night kiss, then said, "Now, y'all go to sleep."

She shook her head as she made her way back to her room. That Sanji was wrong as wrong could be, preying on that boy's fears. No sooner had Toni climbed back in bed and picked up her book than she heard a knock on the door. Now what? She placed the book on her lap. "Come in," she said.

It was Jesse. "Yes?" Toni said.

"Auntie, I'm scared," Jesse said.

"Is Sanji still bothering you?"

"No."

"Then what are you scared of?"

"It's too dark and too quiet."

"It's supposed to be dark and quiet. That's what helps you sleep."

"But it's too quiet. . . . Mommy lets me sleep with the TV on."

So that's what kept him company while Joy ran the streets.

"Grandma and Granddaddy let me sleep with them," he said, eyeing the empty spot next to her hopefully.

Well, maybe they did. And though he looked so pitiful, he might as well get used to sleeping alone and without the TV. Besides, Sanji would pitch a fit if Jesse got to sleep with her. Then she would want to do it, too, and caffeine addicts were less restless than Sanji was when she was sleeping. "I'll tell you what, Jesse. You go back to your room and leave the door open. I'll leave my door open. My light is on, so you'll be able to see me and I'll be able to see you."

He squared his slight shoulders and with a resigned sigh breathed, "Okay." Like a new recruit the first day of boot camp, he marched back to his room, determined to be brave. Toni watched him go, feeling guilty. She picked up her discarded book. Was it so wrong to want a little peace?

A half hour later, she checked on him again and found that he was still sitting straight up, staring at the crack of light in the door. Sanji was sprawled helter-skelter on the narrow mattress, leaving little room for Jesse to get comfortable even if he hadn't been afraid of the dark.

Toni pushed open the door and beckoned to him. She could hear his sigh of relief from where she stood. "Come on, sweetie," she said when he joined her in the hall. "Let's go get some shut-eye."

c h a p t e r
<u>20</u>

Lynn couldn't concentrate. She turned the magazine she'd been reading facedown on the yellow and white bedspread. A mountain of pillows was propped behind her back to give it support, but she just couldn't get comfortable. Though she had slept in this very bed most of her life, she didn't remember it being so narrow and hard. Then again, she hadn't spent her every waking and sleeping moment in it, either, as she had been doing for the past month. And back then she had shared the room with Joy, which made for exciting if sometimes nerve-wrecking times. Joy had actually had a boy in here once while Mama and Daddy were downstairs playing dominoes. She promised a scared Lynn that they would never know if she didn't say anything. And Lynn hadn't.

Lynn gazed longingly at the empty twin bed across from hers. She missed those times. She missed Joy.

Her thin hands spread slowly over the small mound of her stomach. "You hang in there, little one," she whispered to the fragile life growing within her. "Hang on a little while longer and then you'll be home free." Her voice was creaky from infrequent use. She hadn't done much talking lately. Mama wouldn't let the girls visit unsupervised. They were too boisterous, jumping all over the bed, trying to get her attention. Darius was away at school, and Daddy was at work all day. With three kids in the house Mama checked in on her whenever she got the chance.

Mama's infrequent visits she understood, but what about Bruce? Lynn bit her lip. She hadn't heard from her husband in a few days. Her hand reached for the phone, hovered over it, then withdrew. It was best not to bother him at work, she decided.

Nor were there any friends to call. She'd never been outgoing like her sisters and brother. She had one or two friends, but had lost touch with them. It wasn't a conscious choice. It just happened.

Licking her dry lips, Lynn reached for a nearby glass. Cool perspiration from it dampened her hand, and ice cubes clicked as she raised the glass to her lips. "Ah," she said in appreciation. That hit the spot. Mama had sweetened the iced tea just the way she liked it. After another long sip she returned the glass to the coaster on the nightstand. She flipped the magazine over without much enthusiasm. There were other magazines and books within reach, and Daddy had brought in a small TV. That gesture had brought a smile to her face. Daddy hadn't allowed TVs in the bedrooms when they were growing up. Now one sat on the banged-up dresser. Even from here Lynn could see the faint marks on the bottom drawer where Joy had persuaded her to carve their initials. Lynn hadn't wanted to do it, but Joy had said her handwriting was neater. That one had earned them a whipping. In fact, most of the trouble she had gotten into as a child had involved Joy. The memory of both the pleasure and the pain of being Joy's baby sister lingered in her eyes.

What she wouldn't do for a little trouble now! Everybody kept teasing her, saying they were jealous, like lying around in bed all day was a luxury. It wasn't. It was boring and lonely. Her parents had done everything they could to make life easy for her. Mama had even given her a crystal dinner bell to ring if she needed something. Lynn had been horrified. Though she knew it was important not to overexert herself, she wasn't about to let her mother wait on her like she was helpless. There was no way she was going to ring that bell.

In fact, she decided, *the least I can do is help out some*. Lynn carefully rose from the bed and went over to Joy's old bed to fold the basket of clothes her mother had brought up earlier. She was happily engaged in this task when she heard the sound of small feet running up the stairs, then down the hallway. She smiled, turning just in time to see her two daughters burst into the room. Both were wearing overalls and matching hot pink T-shirts.

As if remembering their grandma's warning about their mother's delicate condition, they both pulled up at the last moment to avoid crashing into her. "Mommy, Mommy, you got a surprise," Dakota said, grabbing her hand excitedly. Montana wrapped herself around one of Lynn's legs. Lynn stroked her head absently, then smiled down at Dakota. She was practically skipping in excitement.

"A surprise? I love surprises. What is it?"

Dakota shook her head. "If I told you, it wouldn't be a surprise."

Lynn laughed. "Not even one little hint?" she begged. Dakota emphatically shook her head no. Lynn frowned, pretending to be disappointed.

Heavy footfalls echoed in the hallway.

"Daddy! Daddy!" Montana cried, detaching herself from Lynn's leg and rushing for the door.

"Montana!" Dakota wailed. "It was supposed to be a surprise! Now you messed it up. You always mess it up."

"It's okay, honey," Lynn assured her. "It's still a very nice surprise." Dakota shot Montana a look of disgust. She took a seat on the spare bed next to the clothes basket just as her father came in. Across the room, Montana, oblivious to her sister's disdain, held her arms out, wanting to be picked up. Bruce paused to scoop up his younger daughter.

Lynn's eyes teared up. It was silly, but when she hadn't heard from him, she was afraid he'd forgotten about her. She walked over to hug him, seeking the strong, solid feel of him. Though she tried to meld with him, there was no give in his body. The bulge of his biceps pushed into her, creating within her a vague sense of disappointment that she couldn't *really* touch him. Her protruding stomach was another barrier between them. She couldn't sink into him the way she would have liked. At any rate, Montana soon pried them apart, wanting a hug of her own.

Bruce moved Montana to his side and glared at his wife. "What are you doing out of bed?" he asked, his tone already implying that whatever reason she gave would not be good enough. "I thought you were supposed to be resting."

Lynn drew back, wrapping her arms around herself. This was not the greeting she had hoped for. "I am. I just got up like two seconds ago." She nervously smoothed her rumpled cotton nightgown, then changed the subject. "I thought you would be at work right now. Why aren't you?"

"John decided to show up for his shift for a change," he replied. Just then his eyes zoomed in on the neatly folded piles of clothes on the bed. Dakota had started to haphazardly fold what was left in the basket. "Looks like you been up longer than a few seconds," he said. "If you gonna do housework, you could do that at home. Your own house is a mess right now."

Her face flushed guiltily. This pregnancy had been hard on her. She'd barely had the strength to throw some clothes and toys in a suitcase when the doctor had ordered complete bed rest. And no doubt Bruce was much too tired after work to tackle housework as well. "I'm sorry, Bruce, but I wasn't feeling up to it when I left. Do you want me to ask Mama to go over and straighten up a bit?" she offered, all the while hoping he'd say no. Mama had enough to do. When he didn't answer, Lynn gave a little laugh before climbing back in bed.

"Really, Bruce, I just got up. I was afraid I'd get bed sores if I didn't get up and move around some," she joked. His face was carved granite. She drew the edge of the bedspread over her legs. The slippery magazine pile was disturbed and slid to the floor. "Oh, shoot," Lynn said, and threw the covers back.

"I'll get 'em, Mommy!" Montana cried.

"No, me!" Dakota said, dropping her grandmother's purple underwear back into the clothes basket. She rushed over, hoping to beat her younger sister to the magazines. They both grabbed an *Ebony* at the same time. "Let go. I got it," Dakota ordered.

"Noooo!" Montana countered. "Mine! Mine!"

Lynn's soft "Girls! Girls!" went unheeded. Montana yanked her end of the magazine. A loud ripping sound followed.

Dakota let go of her end, leaving Montana in sole possession of the tattered magazine. "Now look what you did." She pointed at the evidence of wrongdoing in her sister's hand.

Seeing her father's tight-lipped frown and narrowed eyes, Montana began to wail.

"Quiet, both of you!" Bruce's voice cut through the crying. Montana paused in mid-sob, and a startled Dakota flinched at the anger in her father's eyes.

"Mommy," Montana said, then dove into bed with Lynn. Following her sister's lead, Dakota scrambled toward the shelter of her mother's arms as well.

"Careful, girls," Lynn warned as sharp elbows and knees burrowed a little too closely to their unborn brother or sister. She felt a tinge of pain in her belly and sucked in her breath. The sensation passed quickly.

"Get out of that bed right now," Bruce ordered, almost as if the sight of his family cowering from him fueled his fury.

"Really, Bruce . . . they can stay," Lynn said, forcing a smile, an arm now around each of her daughters.

Ignoring her, he yanked Dakota out of Lynn's arms and gave her a whack across the behind. "When I tell you something, you do it. Don't go running to your mama." He set her down none too gently and said, "Now, go downstairs with your grandmother." At the sight of a fat tear silently rolling down Dakota's cheek, he added, "And don't even think about crying or I'll give you something to cry about." The child hurriedly wiped away the tear and ran out of the room.

Fearing that it was her turn to experience her father's wrath, Montana clung to her mother even tighter. Lynn could feel her small body trembling against her. She gently began twisting a braid that had come undone. The tightness in her stomach had returned. When Bruce reached for Montana, Lynn said, "You didn't have to hit Dakota. She and Montana were just being kids."

Bruce cocked his head, his square jaw came up. He was unused to his wife disagreeing with him. His expression grim, he picked up Montana, who stared at him in wide-eyed fear. After lowering her to the floor, he gave her a little push. "Go downstairs." Montana didn't have to be asked twice. She scampered out of the open doorway as fast as her plump legs would carry her.

Lynn breathed a sigh of relief. At least Bruce hadn't hit Montana as well. When Montana cried, it went on for what felt like an eternity and didn't stop until she had made herself physically sick. Lynn rubbed her stomach, which churned uneasily. A sour taste came to her mouth at the harsh look Bruce was giving her. Lynn had married a gentle man who had sweet, hopeful plans about the life they would have together. Where was that man? she wondered.

It made her nervous when he loomed over her like that.

She held both hands out to him. "Bruce, what's wrong?" she asked.

He stared for the longest time, then took her hands. She was unprepared for the punishing grip he inflicted. Lynn winced and tried to withdraw them. He held tight. "Bruce?" she said, her eyes panicked. "Bruce, let go."

He joined her on the bed and brought his face right up to hers. "Don't ever disrespect me in front of my kids," he said between clenched teeth.

Lynn tried to back away, but there was nowhere to go except against the puffed up pillows. Bruce had never hit her, but lately he had started grabbing her and pushing her around when he got angry. He scared her sometimes. Lynn tried not to tick him off. The problem was, she could never figure out what set him off. Like now. "What—what are you talking about?" she whispered, trying to calm him with her voice.

He moved his hands further down, to her wrists. Her fragile skin bunched where he gripped it. She could feel his touch bruising her to the bone. "When I tell the kids to do something, my word is law. Do you understand that?" His hot breath brushed her face.

"I'm sorry, Bruce," she said. "I didn't mean to disrespect you." Her wounded eyes pleaded with him. "You're hurting me."

Bruce abruptly let go of her. Lynn rubbed her sore wrists. Red imprints had formed on her skin. He said, "Lynn, I don't know what's come over you. Why you always gotta provoke me? Make me do things I hate to do."

Lynn shook her head and swallowed any words of protest she might have made. She didn't want to set him off again, and the pain in her stomach had returned, more frequent and sharper. Lynn took a few deep, slow breaths, trying to ride through the waves that crashed against her.

"I think it's your family," Bruce went on, oblivious to her crisis. "I know none of them like me."

"Bruce . . ." Lynn said, gritting her teeth. It's only cramps. Stay calm, she told herself

"Don't try and tell me anything different. I know they all think they're better than me. Like just now, I saw your dad in the driveway and he barely said two words to me."

"Bruce, Daddy's like that with everybody. He's just quiet, that's all."

"What about your mother? She's polite, but I can tell Mother Rollins doesn't like me much, either, and neither do your sisters. This whole family thinks they're better than me."

Lynn closed her eyes. He had to calm down.

"Lynn." She squeezed her eyes shut tighter. "Lynn, I want you to come home. Being here is no good for our marriage. They're trying to turn you against me."

She shook her head. "No, Bruce, they're just trying to protect me and our baby. You know I can't take care of the kids and myself right now. You know I can't go home." When he didn't respond, she said, "Bruce, what do you want me to say?"

He leaned over her again. His chest pressed hard against her stomach. Lynn shrank back, afraid she'd made him angry again. But the hand that cupped her face was gentle this time, and she breathed a shaky sigh of relief. "I want you to promise that you won't let them turn you against me. You and the kids are all I have."

Lynn did not understand where it came from, but the genuine pain in his voice touched her. Lynn's hand slowly came up to stroke the back of his neck, and Bruce relaxed, resting his face against hers. "Promise you'll never leave me," he whispered against her cheek.

Willing herself to ignore the cramping in her stomach,

Lynn continued to stroke his neck and back. "I promise, Bruce. I promise."

With a tired but satisfied smile, Anna Mae slowly closed the oven door. The two peach pies for the church bake sale were browning nicely. The thick juices bubbling near the edge of the crusts made her regret that she hadn't thought to make an extra one for the family. She hesitated before grabbing a mug and pouring herself a second cup of coffee. She usually didn't drink caffeine this late in the day, but recently she had found that she needed all the extra pick-me-ups she could get. Some mornings she got out of bed feeling every one of her fifty years. Taking care of two grandkids and a sick daughter was more than a notion. She sighed, trying not to worry about Jesse. She'd felt bad about sending him away, but she was certain Jesse was in good hands with his Aunt Toni.

She missed the little fella, though. The way he followed her around the house like an eager-to-please puppy both tickled and saddened her. His mama used to be just like him when she was his age. What had happened to make Joy change so drastically? She had gone from Mama's little helper to Mama's big headache in what seemed like the blink of an eye.

Anna Mae shook her head to steer away from the troubling direction such thoughts were taking her. Her heart ached for Jesse. He was missing his mama, poor baby. Though Joy had spoken to him on the phone, she did not want him to visit her at the rehab center.

After a sip from the steaming cup, Anna Mae ruefully admitted that she didn't have the same kind of energy she had thirty or even twenty years ago when her kids were young. This was the first moment of peace she'd had all day. She didn't know what had happened during Bruce's visit, but both Dakota and Montana had come downstairs all teary-eyed. And when she had asked what was wrong, Dakota had started in on Montana about "making Daddy mad."

Well, he made *her* mad. Wasn't here five minutes before he upset the kids, when he should have been keeping them occupied. Not that she was surprised. That man hadn't offered to lift a finger to help with them since Lynn took to her bed. Then when he came downstairs—after a very short visit, considering he hadn't seen his wife in days—he had the nerve to tell *her* that Lynn was resting. Ordered her not to let the kids bother Lynn—as if she didn't know how to take care of her own child. The kids certainly weren't going to be bothering *him*. Bruce was whistling as he walked out the door. He gave not a backward glance at the two little girls whose eyes followed him with a mixture of longing and fear.

For someone who insisted he wanted a passel of kids, Bruce wasn't very good with them. Anna Mae prayed for Lynn every night, hoping that she knew what she was doing, bringing another child in this world with Bruce as its father. Some people were in love with the idea of raising a family but weren't too keen on the work involved. Bruce was one of them. All talk and no action.

That's why she thanked God for Clarence. After he'd finished mowing the lawn, he had quickly realized that the kids were hindering both her cooking and studying. He had rounded them up and took them for pizza and a movie.

She didn't understand why her girls had such a hard time knowing a good man when they saw one. After all, they had lived with one all their lives.

Before taking a seat at the kitchen table, Anna Mae took off her red apron and draped it over a chair. With a small laugh Anna Mae regarded the dusting of flour that covered her GED study guide. In their effort to help her with the baking, Dakota and Montana had left more flour on the table and floor than in the mixing bowl. Anna Mae picked up the heavy book and, with slow deliberation, brushed away the flour using the palm of her hand.

The mailman had brought her some bad news yesterday. She had not passed three of five sections of the GED test: math, interpreting literature, and science. She had been hoping to do better but wasn't really surprised when she didn't. Joy got into her mess, and Lynn and the girls had moved in. Anna Mae had barely attended any of her classes after that—still, she had been half hoping that the few hours of studying she squeezed in at the end of the day when all the kids were in bed and things had quieted down would be enough. She should have known better. She had not gotten ahead in this life on luck. Every accomplishment, every possession, was hard earned. Why would her GED be any different? She had a lot to do. It was late September, and she only had until the end of the year to pass the darn thing.

Taking a deep breath, Anna Mae flipped the book open to the math section. She had bombed on the math. She frowned in concentration as she tried to make sense of the word problems before her. It wasn't until she felt paint flakes on her lips that she realized she'd been gnawing her pencil. Anna Mae wiped a hand across her mouth and tried to rid her tongue of the wood chips. She tossed the pencil into the crease between the pages, then stretched her arms over her head. Anna Mae loosened her shoulders and thought, *God, how I hate math. Maybe I can get Darius to spend a few hours helping me when he comes home next weekend for Kevin's birthday.*

Anna Mae checked the yellow and black smiley face on the wall clock next to the stove. Clarence and the kids would be home before she knew it. She stood up and took the pies out of the oven to cool. After resuming her seat, she rubbed a finger across her tired, bleary eyes. Anna Mae hunched over the book again.

A half hour later, she turned to the back of the book to

check her responses against the answer key. She slowly un-crossed the fingers of both hands after she learned that she'd gotten four of the five questions right. She did a little bob-bing dance from her seated position. "Not bad, Anna Mae," she said, congratulating herself. "It's amazing what you can do when you have no distractions."

The sound of a tinkling bell cut short her celebration. Anna Mae went still. What was that? It was too faint to be the doorbell or an alarm clock. Faint or not, it was insistent. Anna Mae got up from the table and moved in the direction of the sound. It was coming from upstairs. Oh, my God, it was Lynn ringing the dinner bell. The one she had sworn she would never use, Anna Mae reminded herself.

She took the stairs two steps at a time. She ran into Lynn's room. Her breath left her at the sight of the red stains soak-ing the white blanket at the juncture between her daughter's slender thighs. Though Anna Mae stood in the doorway, it was as if Lynn didn't see her. Lynn had not stopped ringing the bell clutched in her blood-soaked hand.

chapter
<u>21</u>

Chris was never this late, Toni thought. She was filling up another large plastic bag with clothes that Sanji had outgrown or thought she was too cool to wear anymore. He had promised to help her assemble the new bunk bed. But when he had failed to show up at four, Toni had busied herself thinning out Sanji's closets and dresser drawers. Marvin had volunteered to take Sanji for the day and included Jesse in the invitation. Offers like that were few and far between, so Toni decided to use the time to get caught up on her household cleaning.

Where was Chris? Toni wondered. She hoped he hadn't forgotten that he was supposed to come over. She was counting on his help. Toni hated putting furniture together. She didn't have the patience for it. Chris wasn't all that great with his hands, either, but with their combined brain power they were bound to figure out how to put the bed together. Plus, she was looking forward to hanging out with him, catching up on the gossip and nosing around to see how things were going with Marshall.

From Chris's distracted behavior—like his blowing her off today—it was obvious that all was not well with those two. That was too bad, for Chris and in this instance for her, since Marshall would have enjoyed a do-it-yourself project like putting the bed together. She cinched the clothes-filled bag and tossed it against the wall and out of the way. Unfortunately, things had changed. Marshall thought he could find something in the Big Apple that he wasn't getting in lowly Delaware, and now Chris had vanished, too.

Well, I can't wait for him all day, Toni told herself. Reluctantly she retrieved her seldom-used tool kit from the kitchen. She ripped open the two large boxes that the delivery guys had dumped in the middle of Sanji's room. Paper particles and dust flew into the air, making her sneeze. Toni rubbed her nose as she read the instruction sheet. Just great, she thought. Diagrams. Why couldn't the assembly instructions use plain English to tell her how to put the contraption together?

Yet despite a few missteps involving screwing parts in backward, Toni eventually put together the metal frames for the two bunks. After attaching them to the head and foot boards, she stood back to admire her handiwork. Not bad, Toni observed. She was glad she'd decided to get the bed with the built-in bookcase. Jesse liked to look at picture books and color. Toni was hoping he'd be a good influence on Sanji.

When a second hour passed, Toni surmised that Chris wasn't just late, he wasn't going to show up at all. She sighed, not knowing what to do about his recent behavior. His visit to New York had been a disaster. Rather than bringing them closer together, the fallout over Marshall's "friendship" with his ex had created even more distance between them. Not that she blamed Chris for being upset. Marshall was being a jerk. And the jerk had not been to Delaware since the argument. He used to come down every weekend.

Like his relationship with Marshall, Chris was quickly unraveling. He had been coming into work late, looked like hell, and interacted with people as if he was sending in his responses via tape delay. Toni wished there was something she could do to help. But after the first round of indignation and hurt, Chris had stopped talking about Marshall, the lock on his emotions sealed tighter than any bank safe.

Toni grunted as she tried to lift the top bunk onto the lower one by herself. She soon discovered that she wasn't tall enough nor were her arms long enough to get the height and angle she needed. She wrestled with the bed for several minutes, but all she got for her trouble were aching arm muscles and back strain. *If I had known Chris was gonna flake out on me, I would have just paid the extra fifty bucks to have the delivery guys assemble the bed.* In the end, Toni placed the two beds side by side. She didn't bother to put the mattresses and linen on because she knew they couldn't stay like that.

She thought about giving Beale a call. He had called earlier in the week, asking if she'd like to go out this weekend. With Jesse due to move in, Toni had said no. She hadn't even hesitated. Her mind had been focused on getting Jesse settled in. Now she was wondering if maybe she should call and ask *Beale* to help her out with the bed.

Toni shook her head. That wasn't right. The man didn't know her. Just 'cause he wanted to take her out didn't mean he wanted to come fix up her house. Besides, if he was still here when Marvin got back, Marvin was bound to say something idiotic or cop an attitude and refuse to keep Sanji down the road. He was petty like that. Now that he'd gotten around to being a somewhat responsible daddy, Toni didn't want to give him an excuse to be trifling again.

Toni had come into the kitchen to make dinner when the phone rang.

Toni pushed her hair back from her face and silently mouthed "Oh, shit!" when she heard Flo's disgruntled voice.

"So, were you ever gonna call me back?" Flo bellowed, without so much as a "hi, how are you."

Flo's message had slipped her mind. "Flo, I'm so sorry.

My little nephew came to stay with me for a while. I've been busy from the moment I picked him up at the airport."

In an abrupt change of conversation, Flo asked, "Why is he coming to stay with you?"

Shaking her head, Toni reached for a jar of spaghetti sauce. Most polite people wouldn't ask questions like that, but this was no polite person. This was Flo. "It's a long story," was Toni's brief reply. She set the jar on the counter and took out the dry spaghetti. The Italian sausage in the fridge and a few more cloves of garlic would spice up the sauce. "Flo, now that you got me, what's up?"

"Toni, I'm going to come right to the point. That check you gave me last Friday bounced harder than a rubber ball."

The pan Toni had been filling with water almost slipped from her hands. "What! But that's impossible." Toni immediately began to review recent bank transactions to figure out if she'd messed up somewhere. A kaleidoscope of activities flashed through her mind: buying Jesse's plane ticket, shopping for the bunk beds, putting Sanji's old bed in storage, plus the usual stuff, school and work. Toni remembered that she hadn't had time to deposit the check from the nursing home in the business account, so she had written the check to Flo *and* the one for her landlord at Shear Necessity from her own account—hell, was that going to bounce, too?

"Impossible?" Flo snorted. "Says you. My bank says something different."

Toni put the pan on the stove and turned the burner on. Flo didn't have to sound so disbelieving. It's not like she'd stiffed her before. "Flo, I am so, so, sorry," Toni repeated. "I've been having problems with my checking account for a while. I promise it won't happen again. I'm going to get this situation straightened out first thing Monday morning,"

"I ain't running no charity over here. I got my own bills to pay," Flo grumbled.

"I understand, Flo, believe me, I do." Flo was just starting to get used to the idea that Toni's bill would be smaller now that Sanji was in school all day; she didn't want her getting all pissy again.

"I'm glad you understand, and I hope you understand that I need my money."

"I'll bring it when I come to get Sanji on Monday night."

"See to it that you do."

Damn, she's acting like we just met, Toni thought. *Me, who has never written a bad check in all the years she's been keeping Sanji.* "Fine, Flo," Toni said, swallowing her annoyance. She still needed to broach the subject of Flo taking care of Jesse, too. This was not the time, though. She would explain about Jesse when she picked Sanji up on Monday.

Though Flo seemed pacified, she managed to get one more crack in: "Pay me in cash this time."

When Toni hung up the phone, she cursed. "Damn and double damn!" She had planned to take Monday off from the bookstore to enroll Jesse in school, and now she'd be spending time at the bank as well. She grabbed the jar of spaghetti sauce, slapped the bottom of it violently with her palm, and then tapped the sides on the kitchen counter. She grimaced as she attempted to twist the top off. Then the top popped off the jar, scattering red globs all over the counter.

Toni was balancing her checkbook for the third time when a series of knocks at the door signaled that Marvin and the kids were back. She opened the door to an evening that had grown cold. Sanji's mile-a-minute prattle began before she even crossed the threshold.

"Hi, Mom . . . Hurry up, Jesse . . . Daddy, I'm not ready to come home," she whined. "Let's go over to Uncle Leroy's house. We can play with his PlayStation."

Toni opened the door wider and ushered them in. "Hi, guys. Did you have a good time?"

Jesse said to his cousin, "Would he really let us play with

his PlayStation?" Toni noticed his eyes were more animated than usual. The outing had done him some good. Maybe getting away from Cleveland for a while would give him a chance to be a child while he still was a child. Toni didn't want him to grow up to be someone who as an adult tried to live the childhood he never had. She'd seen plenty of that in her day. And couldn't help glancing at Marvin as she had that thought.

"Uh-huh," Sanji said. The kids stopped at the hall closet to shed their jackets, then joined Toni and Marvin in the front room of the apartment.

"I made some spaghetti. Y'all want some?"

"We had pizza," Sanji volunteered. "Grotto's Pizza."

"How long ago was that?" Toni asked Marvin. He had sprawled out on the couch and propped his feet on the coffee table. When he saw the look Toni was giving him, he smiled and put his feet on the floor.

"'Bout a hour ago," Marvin said, answering her question.

Toni took a seat across from him, and Sanji plopped down in her lap, deeply gouging her thigh bone. With a rueful smile, Toni acknowledged that her child didn't know how to do anything daintily.

"We saw some gooses at the park," Sanji said.

"Geese," Toni corrected. "And what did you see?" she asked Jesse, who still stood in the middle of the floor. Toni realized that was often where he could be found: in company but not exactly with company. "Come here, Jesse," she bid, patting a spot on her lap. He came readily enough but stopped short of touching her, as if he doubted the sincerity of the offer. Toni pulled Sanji closer to her, making room for him. Jesse moved to the end of her knee.

"I saw some squirrels and a chipmunk. He was little," Jesse said.

"Like you," Toni teased.

"I'm not that little." Toni saw her reflection in his glasses. "It was really little."

Toni laughed. Maybe there was a spunky side to him. After all, he was Joy Rollins's child. In the meantime Sanji began to scale Toni's body like it was a mountain. When Toni realized her intent, she warned, "Don't even think about sitting on the back of this love seat, young lady. Look at your sneakers, they're muddy."

"Aw, Mom." As usual, Sanji looked toward Marvin for support. He was dozing on the couch. They had worn him out. *Good*, Toni thought. *Now he knows how I feel.*

Sanji had one foot on Toni's thigh and the other leg dangling against Jesse. Mud from her shoe had attached itself to Toni's sweat pants. "Don't 'aw Mom' me and stop climbing all over me." Sanji plopped down again, this time even harder. Toni got a whiff of her daughter on her way down. "Sanji, you smell fresh."

"Like roses?"

"No."

"Like lemon-fresh dishwashing liquid?"

"No, like damp air, dead leaves, dirt, and sweat."

Jesse giggled. Toni tickled his stomach. "I don't know what you're laughing at, you smell just like her. In fact, both of y'all are stinking up my living room." Jesse wiggled, trying to get out of her teasing grasp. Sanji tried to help him by grabbing her mother's hands. Amidst a fit of laughter and flying legs, they finally pried Toni's hands loose.

With a laugh Toni said, "Okay, Stinky Ones, you win."

"Yea! We win," Sanji shouted, and then performed a victory gyration she'd probably seen some football player do in the end zone.

Both kids groaned when Toni told them to go run a bath. Sanji claimed Toni's bathroom as her own—because it was bigger. She looked at Jesse as if daring him to challenge her. He didn't.

Still within the circle of Toni's arms, Jesse said shyly, "Auntie?"

"Yes?"

"Do you have any bubble bath?"

"Of course. I hope Mr. Bubble is okay?" Toni said. He nodded slowly, but his face brightened at the prospect.

"Me first," Sanji said, sprinting down the hall to get to the bubble bath before Jesse.

"Share with your cousin," Toni yelled after them. God, she was just realizing how selfish her precious daughter was. Jesse's slow shuffle down the hall said it all. He was used to coming in second.

Toni wanted to hug him and hold him and love him until the little boy who should have been giving Sanji a run for her money came to life. Instead, she called after him, "Let me test the water before you get in."

While the kids were bathing, Toni roused Marvin and asked him to help her set up the bunk beds. Marvin did a double-take when he saw the frames. They only needed to be fitted on top of one another. "You put this together by yourself?" he asked.

"Uh-huh. You don't have to act so surprised."

"No so much surprised as amazed."

"Yeah, yeah. Manual labor is not my strong suit. When you get over your awe, could you give me a hand? I don't like leaving the kids in the tub unattended." In fact, she opened the door that connected Sanji's room to the main bathroom. When she popped her head around the corner, she saw that Jesse was covered from head to toe in bubbles. "Everything okay in here, Jesse?"

He nodded.

"Good. Don't forget to clean behind your ears."

Together, Marvin and Toni took all of thirty seconds to fit the beds on top of one another, making Toni wonder why she hadn't waited for help in the first place.

Marvin went into Toni's bathroom to say good-bye to Sanji. When Toni saw him to the front door, she said, "I have to get the kids out of the tub before they shrivel up. Thanks again for helping with the bed, Marvin. I don't know what happened to Chris. It means a lot to Sanji when you spend time with her. You also really helped *me* out by getting the kids out of my hair for a few hours. You can stay and put Sanji and Jesse to bed if you want." Sanji had told her that Marvin did a better job at reading stories than Toni did.

From the open doorway, Marvin gave her a crooked smile. Rubbed at his scratchy-looking facial hair. "Naw, I better get home. I think Tiara saw me on du Pont Highway with the kids in the car. She was at a gas station with her sister. I might as well get the argument out of the way early. Then I can get to bed at a reasonable hour."

Spending a couple of hours with his daughter would provoke an argument? Toni summoned up a neutral took.

"Just know that I'm here for you if you need me," Marvin added.

"Uh-huh," she said. Toni wondered if Marvin even knew he was lying. "I have to see to the kids," she said, closing the door on him.

Toni fell asleep with the light on. A fist pounding at her front door woke her up fast. She hurriedly threw on her robe. She closed the door to the kids' room as she passed it. She was muttering under her breath as she unlocked the dead bolt, leaving the chain on. If Marvin was paying one of his late-night visits, she was gonna strangle him. "Who is it?" she hissed before the fist thudded against the door again.

"It's Chris," came the slurred reply. "Got your mass . . . ages."

Her mass . . . ages? Was he drunk? He couldn't be. She had never seen Chris drink more than a couple of beers.

Toni opened the door. The full moon behind him created

a spotlight—unshaven face, wearing the same shirt and khakis he'd had on yesterday, and an open bottle of Chivas Regal dangled from his right hand. Toni frowned. She could smell the alcohol on him. Was that all he could do? Stand there looking stupid and sad?

"Chris, get in here," she ordered, yanking him through the door. While she locked it again, Chris headed for the living room. He staggered, tripping over his own feet.

"Chris, did you drive over here?"

"Vroom, vroom," he said, holding his hands out like he was steering a car.

"Sit down," Toni whispered, so as not to wake the children. She shoved him onto the couch just in case he was incapable of following directions. She caught the liquor bottle just before it hit the floor and set it on a nearby table. Chris grabbed the nearest pillow and hugged it to him. He curled himself on the couch, shoes and all. That's when Toni noticed the purplish bruise along his jawbone.

She had just seen him yesterday. And he had been fine, meaning he was still in the same funk he'd been in since the big blowup with Marshall. Toni sat down in the armchair. "Before you doze off, suppose you tell me what happened."

He turned half-closed eyes her way. Green pupils danced around, unable to find a focus. "You know the sound system in my living room?"

Toni regarded him evenly, surprised that he was capable of a complete sentence. "Yeah, what about it?"

"When I got home last night it was gone."

"Gone?"

"Yep, and the antique grandfather clock, half the artwork . . ."

Toni's anger and disgust were replaced by concern. "Was the house broken into? And you caught them at it? Is that why you have that bruise on your cheek? Chris, are you all right?" When she tried to touch his face, he waved her off.

"Robbery? Don't I wish?" Chris's laugh was bitter. He ran a hand through blonde tresses that were already standing on end. "You know, I thought it was a robbery, too, until I got upstairs to the bedroom and all of Marsh's clothes were missing. That stopped me cold in my tracks. I thought, why would a thief take only Marsh's clothes?"

Now Toni understood. "Oh, Chris, don't tell me Marshall came and took his stuff without telling you."

"Okay, then I won't tell you that," he said, burying his face in the pillow. He kept his face pressed against it so long, Toni worried he might accidentally smother himself. She tugged it away from him. Without his prop, he stared at her.

"So what happened?" she repeated.

"Once I got over the shock, I went back downstairs. Marsh left me a note on the refrigerator. Something about needing a complete break."

Toni ineffectively patted his shoulder. "What a coward! You mean to tell me he didn't give you any clue he was moving completely the hell out!"

He put his finger to his lips—not hers. "Shush, the kids, remember."

Toni lowered her voice. "I thought you were drunk." She felt him shrug where her hand rested on his upper back.

"Not drunk enough. Where's my Chivas?" Spying the bottle, he reached for it. Toni didn't protest when he took a swig. It was for medicinal purposes. To numb the pain.

She stared at his long, sad face. His eyes closed. The back pats turned to strokes. She hoped he took some comfort from them. "Chris, if he took the stuff last night, why didn't you call me? I left messages on your machine. Why didn't you call me back?"

"I didn't get them," he mumbled, burrowing deeper into the couch. "When I saw Marsh's note, I drove straight to New York." His eyes popped open. "And when I got to New York, guess what I found."

"What?" Toni whispered, pushing Chris's legs farther back so that she could sit more comfortably.

"Good old Seth, helping Marsh rearrange the furniture he'd stolen from our house."

"Oh, Chris." This story kept getting worse and worse. "Don't tell me you got into a fist fight with him."

"Let's just say, when it was all said and done, the cops escorted me from the building." He grabbed Toni's hand. "Me? Can you believe it?"

Chris was a lover, not a fighter. He must have been hurting bad. "Well, I hope you got in a few punches before they threw you out."

Chris laughed and reached for the Chivas again. After this gulp, Toni took the bottle from him. It was almost empty anyway. "I got in a punch or two," he said. "But to tell you the truth, I'm glad the cops hauled me out of there, before Seth did some serious damage. The man is an accomplished triathlete, you know." The next laugh came out more like a sob. "I came back to Delaware, but I just couldn't bring myself to go into the house. I drove around all night. Then I passed a liquor store. Finally, I checked my mas . . . ages, mes . . . sages . . ." He was tripping all over his words. ". . . from the car. Thought Marsh might have called."

She clicked her tongue sympathetically. So, Chris had avoided going to an empty house, drinking himself into a stupor. No wonder he hadn't gotten her messages until now. Toni put an arm around his shoulder and hugged him. She knew just how he felt. If she hadn't had Sanji to think about, she probably would have done the same thing when she found out about Marvin and all his lies.

Chris pressed into her. Holding on tight. Toni was just grateful he didn't start sobbing. A drunk man was bad enough. A crying drunk man would have been too much.

Chris relaxed against her, sighing. "Just a few months ago

Marsh was talking to me about wanting a commitment service. Now he's so uncommitted it ain't even funny."

Toni held him. The smell of sorrow and alcohol swirled around her. "Chris, it may not feel like it now, but everything will be all right."

He nodded against her shoulder blade. "Men may come and men may go, but we still have each other, right?"

From any other man it would have sounded off-the-wall, but coming from Chris it made perfect sense. Even if he *was* drunk. A slow smile curved Toni's lips. "Right," she said.

"And if we can't find anybody else, we can always marry each other," he said so softly she barely heard him.

This time Toni laughed. "I don't think so, Chris. I can't marry anybody prettier than me." She expected a smart-ass remark from him, but silence followed.

Chris had fallen asleep.

Toni eased away from him, took his shoes off. She covered him with a throw blanket. Heavy feet took her back to her own room.

Toni got into bed and closed her eyes, hoping to be quickly and thoroughly embraced by sleep. The kids would be getting up soon.

c h a p t e r
<u>22</u>

"Honey, I'm so happy that you're here," Lynn said as she reached out to grasp Bruce's hand. He was lying on the bedspread next to her. She brought his hand closer until it touched her swollen stomach. She wanted him to feel the life growing in her. Wanted him to touch it and know that they had created something special.

When Bruce's big hand splayed between hers to slowly rub her belly, she felt an incredible joy. She smiled into his eyes. This is what it should be like.

"So has Junior been kicking up a fuss lately?" Bruce asked as he moved his hand over her in circular motions.

They knew this one was a boy. Lynn hated to be sexist, but she hoped Bruce would try to bond more with their little boy than he had with Dakota and Montana.

"Oh, I think this one is a soccer player or a kangaroo. He's been kicking and punching up a storm. I'm sure if you leave your hand there long enough, you'll feel him moving around."

Bruce nodded. "That's good. If you don't come into this world kicking and ready to do battle, you end up getting kicked."

The harshness of this made Lynn look down at the dark hairs on the back of his hand. She didn't agree. She didn't think you had to live like you were doing battle every single day. That would be exhausting. Which is maybe why Bruce was so tired all the time.

Bruce's hand moved up from her hand to stroke her arm. Lynn closed her eyes. It was nice having him touch her like this. Bruce had been visiting Lynn at her parents' house a little more often since her last stint in the hospital. He didn't stay very long, but he was nicer, more considerate, making Lynn wonder if Mama or Daddy had said something to him. She hoped not. She hoped Bruce was acting this way because he chose to, not because he'd been shamed into doing it.

Suddenly his hand cupped her breast, and her eyes popped open in surprise. Bruce had shifted on the bed, his face much closer to hers. "Bruce?" she said, her voice questioning.

He pushed the flimsy material of her nightgown to one side and kissed the fuller than usual slope of one breast. Then she felt the heat of his tongue mark a wet trail across it and flick her nipple, which already was hard and extra sensitive due to the pregnancy.

Not unaffected by the erotic swirls against her skin, Lynn sucked in a breath.

Then a twinge in her stomach brought her back to reality. She placed a hand on the side of his head to still him. "Bruce, you have to stop. We can't." Ignoring her soft protest, he greedily moved his mouth to the other breast. When she felt him trying to push her nightgown up past her thighs, Lynn pulled his head away from her chest. "Bruce, stop," she said more firmly.

He resisted the pressure on his head for a moment but then straightened up. Lynn shrank from the anger lurking in his eyes. "Honey, it's not that I don't want to—" she began.

He groaned in frustration, "Lynn, do you know how long it's been?"

Bruce was a very sexual man, and when she had been pregnant with Montana and Dakota, they'd had sex almost up until the very end. "Honey, it's been just as long for me—"

"It's different for you. Men need sex more than women do," he said, dismissing her feelings with lightning speed.

Lynn collapsed against the pillows at her back. She couldn't speak for all men, but *Bruce* definitely wanted sex more than her. Just to keep him happy, Lynn often went along with it whether she was in the mood or not. But not this time. "Bruce, the doctor said we can't. We have to think of the baby."

"Think of the baby. Think of the baby. I can't tell you how tired I am of hearing that. What about me? You're supposed to be a *wife* and a mother. Not just a mother," he muttered, flinging off the calming hand she had placed on his arm.

Lynn felt herself freeze. She knew he didn't want to hear this. But one thing was certain, Bruce was not going to bully her into doing anything that would jeopardize this baby. Mama and Toni had questioned her relentlessly the last time the baby was in distress. *Did something happen to upset you? Did Bruce do anything or say anything to upset you?*

Lynn had lied to protect him because having her family at Bruce's throat would only cause her more stress. But after fighting to keep this baby alive for eight months, she was not going to endanger him now because Bruce had a woody.

Finding the words to tell him that, though, was easier said than done. Bruce's eyes, which had been cloudy and heavy with desire only moments ago, were drilling a hole through her.

The phone rang, interrupting the tense silence between them. They both looked at it, but neither one reached for it. After the second ring it stopped. Someone downstairs had picked up.

"Bruce, I'm sorry. I know you have needs. But I have to think about what the baby needs, too."

"You act like I was gonna rape you or something. Did I say we had to have sex? Maybe I just wanted to touch my wife. Was it too much to hope that you would want me to touch you?"

Lynn bit her lip. Had she misunderstood his intentions? A few moments ago, Bruce had looked like he wanted sex. Had he really just wanted to hold her? She didn't know what to think. Being with Bruce was like being on a runaway roller coaster. She didn't know up from down or topsy from turvy.

Her mother's voice floated up the stairs. "Lynn, phone for you. It's Toni."

She reached blindly for the phone, her eyes never leaving Bruce's face. Lynn cleared her throat. "Hello?"

"Hey, little sis," Toni said. "I was thinking about you. Are you about ready to pop yet?"

Normally, Toni's bluntness would have made her laugh. This time Lynn softly replied, "Three more weeks."

"What's wrong with you? You don't sound right."

Her sister knew her too well. "No . . . I'm fine. Bruce . . ." Her eyes flicked over her husband's rigid stance. "Bruce is here."

"So Mama said," Toni said. Three little words, but her dislike for Bruce was evident in each one.

Bruce got up from the bed and started prowling around the room. Lynn's eyes followed him. She hated when he paced like a caged animal. She wished she could get up from this bed. It made her feel trapped, like prey.

"Lynn? Are you still there?" Toni asked, her voice concerned.

"Yes. Yes."

"So then, answer my question," Toni said with a touch of exasperation.

"I'm sorry," Lynn said, then realized that it was a phrase she used with too much frequency. "What was the question?"

"I asked if you were taking care of yourself."

Bruce walked back over to the bed and looked down at her from his great height. The coldness in his eyes invaded her. Lynn ran a nervous hand through her already tousled hair. Cradling the phone with her neck, she pulled the covers back over her, more tightly this time. "Yes, Toni. I've been good. I only get up to go to the bathroom, and even then I have someone help me. And the kids can't come in the room unless Mama or Daddy is with them."

"Lynn, are we gonna finish this conversation or what?" Bruce asked.

She put a hand over the mouthpiece. "Honey, just give me a sec. I won't stay on long. Do you want to say hi to Toni?"

Bruce looked at her like she was crazy. The way his moods kept changing, she certainly felt that way a lot of the time.

"I'm glad you're taking it easy—" Toni began.

"Lynn! I can't stay here all day," Bruce said.

"He can't let you talk to your sister for five damn minutes without interruption?" Toni said, her voice incredulous. "Tell him to take his impatient ass on, then."

This was just what Lynn didn't want: Toni sniping on one end and Bruce scowling on the other. Lynn closed her eyes and made herself take a calming breath. She would not, could not, get worked up.

"Since you don't have time to talk to me, I'll leave," Bruce announced. At that, she opened her eyes to face him again.

"Toni, hold on. Bruce, wait," Lynn called after him. His hand was on the door. "Wait," she repeated. "Toni, I'll call you back later," she promised, and then hung up before she could hear Toni's indignant protest. Toni was mad, but she could deal with Toni's anger a lot better than Bruce's.

"Oh, so you decided I'm important enough after all," Bruce said, turning around and crossing his arms in front of his chest.

"Bruce, you *are* important. I don't know why you would ever think that you're not."

He slowly shook his head. "Girl, do you know how empty the house is without you . . . and the kids," he added, almost as an afterthought.

It was nice to hear he missed her, but Bruce's shifts in moods confused her. A minute ago he was angry. Two minutes ago he was horny.

"Bruce, do you think I want to be here? I want to be in my own home. In my own bed. Sleeping next to you."

When he scoffed as if he didn't believe her, Lynn felt compelled to convince him. "Honey, I don't want you to be lonely. Why don't you move in here until the baby comes? That way you can be with me and the kids."

"You know I don't feel comfortable in this house," Bruce said, squelching that idea. "And it's not just about being alone. I'm working all the time. I'm behind on the laundry, and I'm tired of eating food from the restaurant every night."

"Well, then maybe you could come over here for dinner," Lynn suggested. "The kids would love that."

"What would be the point in that, Lynn? They would be in bed by the time I got in."

Lynn sighed. Why was he making this so hard?

"But I was wondering if Mother Rollins would be willing to throw a couple of loads of laundry in the washer for me. I could drop them off tomorrow."

He couldn't be serious? Mama was doing too much as it was. Surely he could see that. "Bruce," she said, choosing her words carefully. "Mama's got her hands full with the kids, me, work, and studying for that GED. I would hate to ask her to do any more for us."

Bruce's arms came away from his chest. Lynn thought it was a sign that he was opening up to what she was saying—until his hands balled into fists at his sides. "What is a load of laundry? She could throw it in with everybody else's stuff. It's not like I'm asking her to scrub my clothes by hand."

Determined not to argue with him, Lynn simply nodded. If he wanted to ask Mama, he could. She wasn't going to, and she hoped Mama turned him down. "I can't stop you from asking her," she said.

His eyes narrowed. "What's that supposed to mean? Do you want to stop me?"

"Bruce, let's not argue. But if you are coming back in the next day or so, could you pick up some needlepoint supplies for me? I'm working on a piece for one of Mama's friends, and I'm running low on yarn—"

Not letting her finish, he said, "I thought you weren't supposed to be doing anything."

"I can move my hands and arms. I'm just not supposed to be walking around. Please do this for me, Bruce," she said, hating the begging tone in her voice. "I'll be bored stiff if I don't have anything to do."

"Lynn, I ain't got time to be running all over town for some needle and thread."

"Bruce, it won't take but a minute. There's a craft store I go to at Randall Park Mall, and I can write out exactly what I need." She reached for the pen and pad on the stand next to the bed.

Even as she began scribbling the brief note, Bruce was backing up. "I told you, Lynn. I'm too busy. And I never said I'd be back in a couple of days."

"But what about the laundry?" Hadn't she heard him say he was bringing that by tomorrow?

"There's no rush on that. I still got a few clean pairs of drawers left," he chuckled.

"So, you're not going to do this for me?" she asked.

"Look, Lynn. Do you want me to take time from my job to buy you stuff for your little hobby? That's like taking food out of our kids' mouths and clothes off their backs."

Lynn's hands gripped the edge of the bedspread. "It's not just a hobby. I get paid to do it," she said hotly.

Stunned by the heat in her voice, Bruce didn't say anything at first. Then he moved closer to the bed, looming over her. Pointing a finger in her face, he said, "Ha! Fifty dollars here or there. You call that money? You don't handle the money. I do. We got the stack of bills coming day after day. Rent, the car note, food, utilities. What is fifty dollars gonna do?"

"Well, maybe once the baby is old enough, I'll go back to work," Lynn said.

Bruce erupted. "What the hell are you talking about? We both agreed that you wouldn't go to work until all the kids are in school full-time. I don't even like your mother keeping them. So I know you ain't talking about leaving them at no day care."

Lynn leaned away. She had promised herself she wouldn't get worked up, but Bruce had that effect on her. This was not the same man who had lain against her breast so lovingly only a few minutes ago. "Bruce, what do you want me to do? Everything I offer to do to help is the wrong thing," she whispered.

The echo of the door clicking behind him and empty silence that followed was the only answer she got. Lynn pressed her face into the nearest pillow but did not cry. She had to think of the baby. Crying wouldn't be good for him.

c h a p t e r
23

Over the weekend, Toni had given yet another customer service rep a piece of her mind. She wasn't taking any chances that another check might bounce. As soon as the bank opened, she withdrew money from the Shear Necessity account and transferred it to her personal account to cover all the outstanding checks she had written. She also took out enough to pay Flo in cash later in the day. Now Toni was waiting to discuss the discrepancies in her account with a real live person for a change. Those phone calls weren't getting her anywhere. And she wasn't leaving until she got some answers about those missing funds. A plump middle-aged brunette was the only other customer waiting in the sterile-looking bank lobby with Toni.

"I love your nails, honey," the woman said.

Toni looked up from the small business–management textbook she had been reading. She had an exam in two days. Closing the book, she held out her hands to display the full set of shiny acrylics that LaSandra, the manicurist she was thinking of hiring, had affixed to her nubs just yesterday.

"Very pretty," the woman said. "Just one color. And I love the gold star at the tip. Nothing too gaudy. I like it." The woman flashed her own nails of varying lengths. "I get my nails done all the time . . . but I'm a secretary, and typing all day really ruins them."

Toni reached into her purse and pulled out one of her business cards. "The manicurist at my hair salon is using some new gel tips that are very chip-resistant. Why don't you call for an appointment?" she said, handing the woman the card.

"Thanks," the woman said, reading over the card. "Maybe I will."

Technically, Shear Necessity didn't have a manicurist yet, but she and Chris had agreed to give LaSandra a month-long tryout after seeing her work. When she'd done Toni's nails, Toni had asked LaSandra to keep her nail design simple. No amount of fake nails would last on Toni, not with her dipping her hands in solutions and water all day. Still, it had been nice to be pampered. Toni just about purred while LaSandra gave her a pedicure. But then sanity returned. She and Chris still needed to see if LaSandra was reliable and professional when it came to dealing with customers.

Chris. He'd had one hell of a hangover on Saturday morning. Toni felt sorry for him. She didn't even tease him about his drunken marriage proposal. Instead, she insisted that he stay at her place and not come in to work. Toni took the kids with her, assuring Chris that she could handle things on her own for one day.

But his behavior had scared her. She hoped the drinking was not going to become a habit. They had had a long talk when she got home that night. Chris was embarrassed and angry with himself for acting like a lovesick fool. It was pretty obvious to Toni that despite the wild trip to New York and the drinking, Chris wanted Marshall back.

Toni couldn't believe Chris was blaming himself or Seth for the problems he was having with Marshall. When Toni had found out about Tiara and Marvin, she had been hurt and angry—at him, not herself. She believed that people cheated because they were selfish.

Toni fingered the pages of her textbook. It felt heavy on her lap. She frowned, thinking about how she was still three classes away from graduation instead of two. Toni had to drop her accounting class when the frantic search for Joy in the summer had caused her to miss the first two weeks. Now accounting had been postponed until the spring, when she would take that along with another class she dreaded even more—econ. Uncrossing her legs, Toni sighed. She'd be so glad when she graduated. This working six to seven days a week had to go.

Toni darted a look in the direction of the banker's office. What was taking so long? She didn't want to be here all day. It was bad enough that she was taking a sick day to get this done, and she still had to register Jesse for school now that Joy had faxed the papers. Chris was watching Jesse while she got these errands done, but she didn't want to burden him when he was already feeling down in the dumps.

"Who's next?" a cheery male voice inquired.

"Me," Toni said while quickly rising. The man beckoned for her to follow him.

He was a fair-skinned black man with an early eighties, before he became "The Artist," Prince pompadour. He was skinny like Prince, too, only he didn't need the five-inch heels to boost his height. A little peach fuzz posing as a mustache was above his upper lip. The name plate on his massive oak desk identified him as James Roush.

Toni quickly explained the problems she'd been having with her account, then watched as his bony fingers flew across the keyboard, entering her account number.

"Ah, I see that your account has been flagged."

"It's been 'flagged' for months. But that doesn't tell me anything. I want to know what black hole my money seems to be disappearing into."

"I don't blame you. Now, how much did you say is missing?"

Toni opened her purse and took out copies of her bank statements for the past five months. She had used a highlighter to mark the discrepancies. "The individual withdrawals ranged from twenty to a hundred dollars in one case. Over the last five months, I'd estimate that about six hundred dollars has gone missing."

He whistled softly at that figure, then glanced over the statements. "That's a tidy little sum. Let's see what we can do to solve this mystery."

"Thanks. I want to get this cleared up ASAP."

"First we'll check the account security system," he said in that cheery voice that was starting to irk her. Would he be so chipper if it was his money that was missing?

James Roush began typing again. "Let's see if anyone other than yourself has been using your card. I'm going to enter the transactions you mentioned into our system, and then I'll be able to download pictures from the surveillance cameras to catch our culprit, if there is one."

This was all very James Bond. Toni sat back in her chair and let him do his thing. She scratched the back of her head. The long nails did wonders for her itchy scalp. But what she really needed was to get some more eczema medication from her doctor. Toni kept forgetting to call for a new prescription. *I need to wear a little notebook with a pencil on it on a chain around my neck. That way I can keep up with all the things I'm supposed to do,* Toni thought. This was followed by: *Who am I kidding? It'll never happen. I'd have to remember to buy the darn notebook first.*

"Ms. Carleton." Toni's eyes swung over to him. "I think we've got something." He angled the monitor so that she could see.

"What?" she asked, staring at the small photos displayed on the screen.

"This person doesn't look like you, does it?"

She shook her head. "Of course not. It's a man. But the picture is so small, I can't make out his face."

"Not to worry. I'm enlarging and printing out what I've found."

The printer next to his desk hummed as it slowly emitted black-and-white copies of the photos. So her earlier suspicions were correct. Someone had gotten a hold of her ATM card. But how? The only thing she could think of was the spare card she kept in her bedroom.

After a brief glance at it, Mr. Roush handed Toni the first picture: a black male with a baseball cap pushed down low over his forehead. His eyes were hidden in the grainy picture, but Toni instantly recognized Marvin. The paper fell from her numb fingers, landing at her feet. The room wavered before her eyes.

"Ms. Carleton."

Toni blinked, then passed a bloodless hand over her face.

"Are you all right, Ms. Carleton?"

No, she wasn't. But she nodded anyway. Toni retrieved the photo from the floor. Her eyes cleared. In front of her were more photos of Marvin. One . . . two, three, four . . . eight in all, Toni counted. Marvin had gone into her account eight times!

"It's someone you know?"

Toni nodded, not trusting herself to speak.

"Who is it?"

She tried to speak but had to clear her throat first. "Uh . . . My ex-husband."

"Your husband?"

"Ex!"

The banker murmured, "I see." He fiddled with his reading glasses, opening and shutting their handles.

During the separation, Toni had switched banks. *But you didn't switch PIN numbers, you idiot*, she castigated herself.

She didn't think she had a reason to. Marvin wasn't living with her. Didn't even have a cause to know where she did her banking.

She looked at the date stamps at the bottom of the pictures. The oldest went back to May. She scratched her head trying to remember. She'd asked the no-good bastard to take care of Sanji. . . .

"Ms. Carleton, do you want to press charges? The bank's security department will cooperate in whatever way we can. Provide these photos, for example."

"What?" Toni said, distracted from her thoughts. She shook her head. "No, I don't want to press charges. I just want to get my money back." I'll handle Marvin myself, she silently vowed. Jail was too good for him.

"I can see that you're upset. But you need to understand that the bank won't replace the money unless you press charges."

"Why not?" she asked wearily. Marvin had stolen from her. They had caught him red-handed, taking money out of his own child's mouth.

James Roush tapped the glasses against the blotter. "The bank isn't liable. You have to report the card as stolen and press charges since you know who took it. If you are unwilling to press charges, how do we know you didn't just give him the card?"

At her glare he hastily added, "Couples have these temporary reconciliations all the time, Ms. Carleton. Then when they break up again, they try to get back at the other person by getting them into trouble. Or maybe they decide they want their money back."

Wordlessly, Toni snatched the pictures off the desk and stuffed them in her purse's side pocket. "Thanks for your help. I'll handle it from here," she called over her shoulder as she hightailed it for the parking lot.

*   *   *

Toni pounded her fist on the already splintered wood of the door of the rented town house Marvin sometimes shared with Tiara.

A female voice on the other side yelled, "Knock it off! I'm coming."

Maybe so, but not quickly enough to suit Toni.

Seconds later, Tiara yanked open the door. Irritation changed to outrage when she found Toni standing there, the dangling wire of the ribbed screen door behind her. Tiara reared back, then snarled, "What are *you* doing here?"

Tiara's skin, the color of warm molasses, was marked with occasional dark acne scars. Thick hair was pulled into one bulking French braid in the middle of her head. She was petite, with fine facial bones, her teeth small like a child's. Her woman-child prettiness was spoiled by her dislike for the woman darkening her door. Toni wasn't surprised to find Tiara home in the middle of the day. Her work ethic was like Marvin's.

"What do you want?" Tiara repeated.

"That's between me and Marvin."

Not liking that answer, Tiara tried to slam the door. With equal swiftness Toni pressed a shoulder against the door. "Tiara, I don't have time for these games." She was prepared to knock Tiara over if necessary. Sticking a foot in the door, she pressed with all her might.

Grunting, Tiara tried to hold her off, but Toni's determination prevailed. Conceding, Tiara opened the door a crack wider, but still did not let Toni into the house. The smaller woman's nostrils flared.

"Anything you say to Marvin, you can say to me. He's my man now. So tell me what you want, and I'll give him the message and then you can be on your way," Tiara said.

Toni impaled her with a venomous look. "I swear to God, Tiara, if you don't shut up and get the hell out of my way, I'm gonna hit you hard enough to send you into next week."

While Tiara absorbed this fact, Toni muscled by her. "Believe me, what I have to say to Marvin won't take long." Toni disappeared down the shadowy hallway.

Tiara yelled after her, "Bitch, you can't just come in my house and tell me what to do."

Ignoring her, Toni ventured into the living room. The couch had an assortment of grimy, mismatched cushions on it. Talk show losers aired their dirty laundry in muted tones. Three-year-old Daisa dozed nearby on the floor, surrounded by newspapers, toys, dirty dishes, and soda cans that served as ashtrays.

Toni proceeded to the kitchen. Nothing but more dirty dishes.

Tiara caught up with her in the dining room. "What do you think you're doing? Get out of my house!" she said, grasping Toni by the elbow.

Toni gave her a look of impatience and shook free of her. Marvin must be upstairs. She retraced her steps. The stairs leading to the second floor were near the front door. Toni began climbing them.

"Marvin!" she called out. She heard Tiara's feet thundering behind her. "Marvin!"

Toni found him still in bed, buried under a mountain of crumpled clothing. She began throwing stuff off the bed, trying to get to him. "Marvin! Marvin, get up, you son of a bitch!" Then Tiara was pulling her arm again.

"What the hell are you doing? Stop it!" Tiara yelled. Her presence was akin to a fly on a horse's butt, and Toni flicked her away.

"Wh—What?" Marvin cried, coming awake. He bucked when Toni's talons dug into his arm. "Hey!" he cried. The pain got him up quick and in a hurry. His pupils dilated at the sight of Toni leaning down in his face and pushing Tiara away with her free hand. Marvin scrambled away, wiping the sleep from his eyes.

Tiara was cursing like a sailor, and Marvin sought to make sense of it. But it was just a string of nonsense. Bitch . . . barging in . . . police . . . Daisa. "Tiara, will you please shut up!" Marvin said.

Tiara's mouth opened and closed like a fish out of water.

Marvin touched the red claw marks Toni had left on his upper arm. Confused, he raised his eyes. "Toni, what are you doing here? What's wrong?"

She stared at him. Now that she finally had his attention, she didn't know where to start. Her chest heaved. Fighting off Tiara had left her breathless.

"Is something wrong with Sanji?" Marvin asked.

"No." She managed to get that much out.

After hearing that Sanji was okay, Marvin quickly reverted to his usual joking ways. He slumped against a rickety headboard. Stretching his arms over his head, he asked, "Then why you come busting in here? Waking me up out of a dead sleep. Don't you know that kind of shock could give a man a heart attack?"

"We need to talk," she said. The words floated out calmly, totally at odds with the jumble of emotions inside. Was that really her voice sounding so normal?

"Now?" Marvin said, then smiled down admiringly at his start-of-the-day erection.

Then Toni noticed the erection, too. Behind her, she heard Tiara's sharp intake of breath. Toni was unfazed. It was nothing she hadn't seen a million times. "Now," she said. Marvin's self-absorption reminded her why she was here.

"Can't you at least let a brother get some clothes on?" he joked.

Tiara looked from Marvin to Toni, then rushed over to the bed. She yanked the covers around his waist. She glared at Toni. "Tell her to get out, Marvin. She ain't got no business in our house, much less our bedroom."

Marvin said, "Think about it, Tiara. This must be important. Toni ain't never come over here before. So chill."

"Chill? You want me to chill?" Tiara looked ready to cry. "Marvin, you better tell this bitch to get out right now before I throw her out, and if you don't like it, you can leave, too."

As if sensing Tiara was near the breaking point, Marvin took another tack. His tone was softer when he said, "Baby, calm down." Tiara shot Toni a proprietary glance and moved closer to Marvin.

Toni folded her arms across her chest. This jealous shit was pathetic. Both of them were pathetic.

From the bed Marvin said, "Baby, give me something to put on."

Tiara reached into the clothes heap that Toni had thrown on the floor. Toni heard the creak of the bed as Marvin got up and put on bleach-splotched sweats. Tiara continued to radiate hostility. Toni ignored her and focused on Marvin instead.

He glanced at the angry expressions of both women and wisely decided that Tiara would be easier to get rid of. He put an arm around her shoulder and guided her toward the door. "Give us five minutes, baby. You go downstairs with Daisa and let me see what Toni wants."

When Tiara opened her mouth to protest, he shushed her with a reassuring smile and ushered her out the door. He shut it behind her with a snap. He took a deep breath and then turned to face Toni. With a smile meant to disarm, he said, "So what's so important you've risked creating all this domestic strife?"

This was the moment she'd been waiting for. Ever since she saw those pictures at the bank. She lunged in his direction. "You want to know why I'm here? To kill you, to wring your stupid neck."

Marvin was still smiling, but he backed away from her. He knew from past experience that she didn't make idle threats. "Toni, I don't know what you're all pissed about but"—he glanced nervously toward the door—"you better tell me what's up and get out of here before Tiara changes her mind and calls the cops."

"Marvin, Tiara can call the police if she wants. Yeah, in fact, that's a great idea. And when they get here, you explain to them and me why you've been stealing money out of my bank account. For months!"

"Stealing?" He jumped as if she'd hit him.

"Yeah, stealing, motherfucker! Did I stutter when I said the word?"

"Toni, I don't know what you're talking about. I ain't stole nothing from you—"

Toni threw the crumpled security photos at him. "Marvin, shut your lying mouth! These are pictures of you using *my* card at ATMs all over Delaware and Pennsylvania."

Marvin looked at the photos, then at his bare feet. Toni bet he was sorry he'd closed the door. She bet he was wishing he could run out of the room, just like he ran away from every other mistake he'd made. Not this time.

After a while he stopped, looked her way, then shrugged. Toni hated him in that moment. She had felt hurt, anger, betrayed over some of the things he'd done in the past. But never hate. Marvin had stolen from her and all he could do was shrug?

"I ask so little of you . . ." Toni stopped, horrified that her voice was shaking. *God, please don't let me cry*, she prayed. "I ask so little of you . . . really I do."

Marvin couldn't took her in the eye. He shoved his hands deep into the pockets of the sweats. "Okay, okay . . . I took the money," he admitted.

He took a step toward her, but she backed away. She held up a hand, a stop sign. Who did he think he was dealing with? She was not Tiara, some desperate little nitwit that he could pat on the head.

Marvin stopped dead in his tracks. "But, Toni, I didn't *steal* the money. I—I was just borrowing it," he explained.

"Borrow? Borrow? Do I look like a fool to you? Last time I checked, borrowing meant asking someone's permission to use something with the intention of giving it back." Now she advanced toward him. "Did you ask permission to use my ATM card? Hell, no! Did you talk to me about how and when your unemployed ass was going to pay me back? I don't think so!"

Toni's hand balled into a fist. Marvin grabbed her wrist before the punch landed.

"Let go," she said between gritted teeth. His hands fell away, then Marvin moved out of striking distance. Tears were shining in Toni's eyes. "Do you think you're some modern-day Robin Hood, robbing from the rich to feed the poor? Well, here's a news flash. I *am* the poor, you son of a bitch . . ."

The tears began to fall, making Toni angry. She rubbed them away with the back of her hand. She didn't want to cry. She wanted to hurt something. Ram her fist into something. Hard. Toni turned toward the dresser and cleared all the junk off in one swoop. Brushes and jewelry and perfume bottles and an alarm clock hit the floor with a satisfying crash.

She whirled back around to continue unleashing her fury on Marvin. He had edged closer to the door. "I can't believe that while I was out busting my hump, for our daughter, you . . ." She pointed an accusing finger at him. ". . . were doing shit to set me back. I take one step forward and your bullshit pulls me two steps back. Do you know how much trouble your last round of 'borrowing' caused me?" A sob from the heart prevented her from saying more.

Toni licked at salty tears and wished she had something to blow her nose on. Marvin tried approaching her, but again she quelled him with just a look. He moved over to the bed and sank onto it as if his legs had given out. He wrung his hands as if not sure what to do with them. "Toni, I am sorry. I didn't mean to cause problems for you. I did not set out to take anything from you. The idea just sort of popped in my head. I honestly . . ."

Honestly? How could he even let that word pass his lips?

". . . didn't think you would miss twenty bucks here and there." He eyed her warily. "Most of the time . . . I was spending the money on Sanji. I got tired of not being able to take her out, buy her nice things. That's why I don't come around much. It's not because I don't care. I know that's what you think."

Toni couldn't believe it. Now it was all about Marvin. The downtrodden black male. Well, she wasn't standing for it. "Whose fault is it that you don't have any money?" she cried. "Is it my fault that you choose to quit every fucking job that you've ever had? I have the same choice, but guess what? I choose to get up every morning to see our child off to school whether I'm tired or not. I choose to work two jobs and further my education so I can provide her with a good life. I want to buy her nice things, too, but I am not always able to. But does that mean I go out and steal so that I can? I could, but I choose not to. We all have choices to make. But for you to think that stealing from me is the right choice"—Toni slapped her hands against her thigh—"well, that just takes the cake."

"Toni, it's not the same for a black man. We catch more hell on the job than you could ever imagine."

Toni blew out a sigh. Then looked him in the eye. "You know what, Marvin? It's tough all over! So you need to deal with that and stop thinking it's going to go away."

Toni leaned on the dresser for support. Her head was pounding. The tears were like a tub that had overflowed. Even when the water is turned off, it takes a while to clean everything up. And her tears hadn't quite stopped flowing. Toni sniffed, wishing again she could blow her nose.

Marvin watched her with a pained expression on his face. "Toni, baby, please stop crying."

Baby? The same endearment he used with Tiara. That refueled Toni's anger. "All these years, you've acted like I was asking so much of you. When all I was asking was for you to spend a little time with your daughter. To be involved in her upbringing. It was never about how much money you were spending on her." She fixed him with a hard look. "Well, you know what, Marvin? You don't have to worry about that anymore. If I can't leave you alone with her in my house without you stealing from me, she doesn't need to be around you."

Marvin rose from the bed. "Toni, what are you saying?"

"I'm saying, I'm not asking you for anything anymore!" Toni's chest ached with the effort of yelling, crying, and trying not to cry all at the same time.

"C'mon, Toni, don't start tripping. I'll pay you back. Every red cent," Marvin vowed.

"Marvin, you can't pay me back."

"Yes, I can. I'll start looking for a job today. Toni, don't be like this. Please accept my apology. I'm truly sorry. I just wanted Sanji to have a little fun when we were together—"

"Don't you know that just having you around was all Sanji needed? If you really wanted to do something with her that cost money, all you had to do was ask. All you had do was ask," she repeated softly. Her cheeks, however, were salt-streaked, and her eyes were swollen and red. "The last time I offered you money, you just about bit my head off." Her accompanying laugh was hollow. "Now I get it. Your guilty conscience must have been eating at you." She started crying again.

Marvin crossed the room and stood as close to her as he dared. "Toni, please stop. You're gonna make yourself sick."

Too late. She was already sick. Sick at heart. Sick of his lies and promises. Toni stared at him with cold eyes to match her frozen heart. "I'm sick of you, Marvin." Before he could interrupt, she added, "You're dead to Sanji. Don't call, don't write. And don't even think about trying to see her."

Toni walked away. She reached for the door handle with chipped, broken nails that were missing most of their gold stars. When she opened the door, she almost collided with Tiara. She gave the woman a pitying look. "Obviously, you heard. You've been wanting him all to yourself Now you got him."

c h a p t e r
<u>24</u>

Toni placed a poinsettia plant on the reception desk and then another on the coffee table in front of the couch. Beale had been Shear Necessity's last customer of the day. He had surprised Toni by finally bringing by the pictures he had taken at Sanji's dance performance, which earned him a free haircut. She had almost forgotten about the photos.

Toni sighed as she absently stroked the deep red leaves of the plant. It wasn't surprising that he had made jokes and kept the conversation casual. He had asked her out three times over the last couple of months, and she'd turned him down three times. Three strikes and she was out, she guessed. She'd just had no time once the school year got underway.

After Beale's departure, she and Chris had stuck around to put up Christmas decorations. Chris was now framing the mirrors at their stations with ropes of silver tinsel. He was also trying to outdo Donny Hathaway as he sang along to "This Christmas." Though he sounded like a member of the worst glee club in Delaware, it was wonderful to see him in a good mood again. And it had been Chris's idea to make the place look more festive for the holiday season.

She looked at the small pine tree lying on its side in the

corner. There were also a set of lights, a tree skirt, ornaments, and a stand. His holiday spirit had cost them a pretty penny. But when Toni complained, he told her to think of it as an investment. Except for the tree, they could use the same decorations year after year.

Toni glanced at her watch. She was supposed to pick the kids up from the Boys and Girls club in an hour. She and Chris had better get a move on. First, though, she wanted to finish putting snowflakes on the windows. She hoped they had enough canned snow left. They had already sprayed holiday greetings on the door, windows, and mirrors: Merry Christmas, Happy Kwaanza, Holy Ramadan, Happy Hanukkah. She wondered if she had forgotten anybody. Did the Buddhists or Hindus celebrate any holidays this time of year? Wouldn't want to leave anybody out.

She grinned.

Where had all this enthusiasm come from? she wondered. This was supposed to be Chris's project. She was just one of Santa's elves. Toni put her hands on her hips and looked around. The begging lyrics of "Please Come Home for Christmas" played on the radio. Chris had disappeared into the back of the store. Maybe we should get a menorah candle, too, she thought. Now, where did she put those cans of snow? Was that them sticking up out of the box of decorations? Toni walked over to it and reached inside. Bingo. She took the cap off and began shaking the can.

Her finger was slightly touching the can's nozzle when the bell above the front door chimed. "We're closed," Toni said, turning around. She involuntarily pressed down on it when she saw Marshall standing on the threshold, brushing snow off his bomber jacket. A stream of fluffy chemically engineered snow spread forth, then eventually joined the real flakes left by Marshall on the floor. Marshall's lackluster brown eyes were watchful, his face red. Was it from the cold or the shame of showing his cheating face? she wondered.

Chris's tenor came floating down the hall ". . . Then won't you please tell me, you'll never more roam . . ."

Her eyes never leaving Marshall's, Toni walked over to the radio and turned it down.

"Hi, Toni," he said as he unzipped the jacket. His eyes were just as wary as hers.

"Marshall." She took a seat in one of the client chairs. She could see Chris headed this way, still singing. She turned her head, wanting to signal him with her eyes, but he wasn't looking at her. He was playing with a handful of stringy silver tinsel. What had he been doing with that? Decorating the bathroom?

". . . If not for Christmas by New Year's night," he crooned.

Toni willed him to look up. He didn't.

"It's cold outside," Marshall remarked. She stared past him. Snow had piled atop the hoods of the cars outside. When Marshall cleared his throat, she swung her gaze around to him again. "As the song says, the weather outside is frightful. But it's nice and toasty in here," he added.

Then you're not feeling the waves of cold I'm sending your way, Toni thought. "Did you come here to talk about the weather?"

The arc of his smile thinned to a flat line. "You know I didn't."

Chris joined them. Did a double-take. Something glowed, then darkened in his green eyes. "Marsh?" Then, "What are you doing here?" He came closer, his eyes searching. He blinked a couple of times, as if worried that Marshall was a mirage.

Toni didn't blame him. He hadn't seen hide nor hair of Marshall in weeks. Now he came walking in as bold as day.

"I went by the house," Marshall said. "My keys didn't fit in the locks."

"I changed them." At his wounded expression, Chris said, "I couldn't have you coming in and out, taking whatever you saw fit."

Toni mentally scored one point for Chris.

"Where's Seth?" Chris looked out the glass window of the store as if he expected to find Seth waiting in a running car. When he didn't, he collapsed into the seat next to Toni's.

"In New York," Marshall replied. "Hooking up with Seth again was a mistake."

"Hooking up?" Toni snorted.

Marshall frowned. "That was a poor choice of words. Toni, I'd like to talk to Chris alone, if you don't mind."

She sought Chris's eyes to see what *he* wanted.

When she would have stood, Chris grabbed her by the wrist. "No, Toni stays. She was the one here for me when you threw me out of your apartment like yesterday's garbage." Side by side, they faced Marshall. A united force.

Marshall jammed his hands deep into his pants pockets. Toni could see the balled imprint of fists pressed against the fabric. "Dammit, Chris, I didn't throw you out. I didn't call the cops. My neighbor did. Besides, you were so furious. You went straight for Seth's throat. I was worried somebody was going to get hurt."

Toni couldn't stop herself from asking, "So why didn't you ask Seth to leave instead of Chris?" Marshall's aggravated breath was audible, though his lips barely moved. Chris stared at Marshall, awaiting his answer.

Again Marshall looked at Toni. Despite Chris's request, they wouldn't be able to talk freely with her here. And she had already proven that she couldn't contain herself. She was too pissed. Why did he have to show up just when Chris was starting to pull himself together? Toni said, "I need to straighten up in back." She touched Chris's arm. "I'll be close by if you need me."

Toni briefly locked eyes with Marshall. Her brown eyes flashed a warning: Do not mess with Chris's head, or you'll have me to deal with. Marshall looked away first. Toni quickly gathered used towels and smocks and took them with her.

Marshall moved closer to Chris. He stopped inches away from his chair. After Toni disappeared into the storeroom, Marshall said in his quiet voice, "Toni's right. I should have made Seth leave. Like you suspected, Seth *was* trying to break us up. He actually admitted recently that he went after me because he wanted to see if he could break up 'the perfect relationship.'"

Chris blew out a sigh of disgust and slowly shook his head.

"I never realized it, but Seth resented that I was able to meet someone new—someone better—so quickly. I had moved on, but I guess he hadn't," Marshall said.

Chris ran his hands through his hair, then down his face. He rubbed under his chin. I need a shave, he noted absently. So Marsh finally realized what *he* had known all along. "Well, Seth must be pretty proud of himself. He succeeded in breaking us up."

"No, he didn't," came Marshall's swift denial.

Chris's answering look was skeptical. He watched Marshall become temporarily distracted by the sight of his own regretful face fragmented by the "Happy Holidays" wish scrawled in the mirror behind Chris's head.

"I'm not proud of how I handled things," Marshall said. "At first I honestly didn't notice that Seth was coming on to me. I thought he was just trying to be a friend. Then when I did begin to notice, there was a part of me that was still angry at him for dumping me. So I let him flirt with me and flatter me. You haven't had as many serious relationships as

I have. They get complicated. But, Chris, you have to believe me, nothing happened."

Chris forced himself not to swivel like an unsure boy in the green vinyl-covered chair. In the past Marsh had used their ten-year age difference to make him feel younger, and he wouldn't play that role anymore. Chris ran his tongue across his upper teeth, giving himself time to find his voice. "And you expect me to believe that?" he finally said. His chest swelled at how strong and firm he sounded.

"But it's true. I accepted all that attention from Seth to get back at him for hurting me."

"And to get back at me!"

"You're right. I was angry because I wanted you to come out to your family. I understand now that you aren't ready. I was unhappy and hurt, so I let Seth get in between us. But you've got to believe me, Chris. It wasn't a conscious thing. I didn't realize what I was doing—and how wrong it was—until recently. Until you refused to answer my phone calls. I've missed you."

"It's only a two and a half hour drive from Manhattan. Even less on the train."

"I know. I know. But I didn't want to come down here until I was absolutely sure about what I wanted to say."

"And now you know what that is?"

Marshall nodded. "Chris, do you think maybe we could spend the weekend together?"

Chris was confused. He didn't know exactly what he had expected Marsh to say, but it sure as heck wasn't this. How was spending a weekend together going to resolve months of misery and, according to Marsh, misunderstandings? "And do what?" Chris asked.

"Just talk. Try to sort things out."

Chris folded his arms across his chest and leaned back into the chair. "I can't."

"Chris, please."

He shrank away from the persuasive hand Marsh was about to lay somewhere on his person. "I can't. I'm going skiing in the Poconos with my cousins."

"Can't you cancel?"

"I could, but I'm not going to." Seeing Marshall's surprised expression, Chris added, "For months I chased after you like a sick puppy, begging you to work on our relationship. Well, you know what? This puppy got tired of the chase. I'm going skiing this weekend. If you still want to talk things out, I'll be back on Sunday night. You can call me then . . . if you still want to."

"So, it's not okay for me to stay at our . . . the house and wait for you."

Chris shook his head in the negative. That was out of the question. He didn't want his weekend clouded by images of Marsh making himself comfortable in what used to be *their* home.

Marshall's face had turned red at Chris's refusal. "I suppose I deserve that."

Chris watched as Marsh retrieved his brown suede gloves from his coat pocket. He pulled them on, jerking the edges to ensure a tight fit. "Chris, I know I messed up, but I'm not giving up on us this easily. Please, please talk to me when you get back."

The pleading in Marsh's voice melted a chunk of the not quite solid ice around his heart. But Chris didn't say anything to ease his mind. After weeks of imagining a scene like this, one where Marsh would beg his forgiveness, Chris found himself very reluctant to kiss and make up. This was too out of the blue. He needed some time to sort out his feelings.

Rising from the chair, Chris silently followed Marshall over to the door. Though Marsh was smiling, his brown eyes were sad. "It was great seeing you, hon. It's been too long." His arms then snaked around Chris's waist. And Chris's arms slowly, of their own accord, went up to reciprocate the hug.

Abruptly, Chris broke contact. It felt too good.

Marshall left the salon, then stomped through the inch-thick snow. When he reached his Saab, he gave a final wave. Chris held up a hand as well, wondering why he felt so alone. Fat flakes of snow blown by a forceful wind touched his lips. The heat of his tongue melted them away. He slowly closed the door.

When Toni came out of the storeroom, she found Chris still standing, his head pressed against the cold glass of the door. She gave him a hug from behind.

"You okay?" she asked.

His head bobbed up and down.

Grasping his shoulders, she slowly turned Chris around to see for herself. She stepped back to take a close look at him. He still looked like he was in one piece. "I have a confession to make. I didn't close the storeroom door all the way. I was eavesdropping."

"I knew you would. You're like a mother hen. But I had it under control."

"I know . . . but . . . but you were so . . . so . . . strong. I thought you'd cave at the sight of your precious Marsh begging for forgiveness."

"Me, too," Chris said wonderingly. "Look at my hands. They're shaking."

"Yeah, but he didn't see that. How do you feel?"

"Exhausted. This expressing your emotions stuff is hard work. I don't know how you women do it."

"It's either do that or shoot somebody."

He laughed. "Tell me you're joking."

Toni walked over to the coat rack and pulled on her jacket. "I ain't telling you nothing, except it looks like you're gonna be putting this tree up by yourself. I gotta go pick up the kids," she threatened.

Actually, she had decided to bring the kids back to Shear Necessity. They would have a ball putting up the tree. Besides, Chris probably shouldn't be alone right now.

As Toni left the shop, Chris peered out the window. But he wasn't watching her depart. He was staring at the empty spot where Marshall's car had been.

chapter
25

The phone had become Toni's enemy. Marvin had been calling almost daily. She was tired of his apologies. She was tired of him asking for Sanji. She was tired of his promises. "I've changed." "This was a wake-up call for me."

Fed up, she had started screening her calls. And up until today, Marvin had known better than to show his face. Then he had left a message, saying that he was on his way over.

Toni had heard it and fled. She had to. Time was supposed to heal all wounds, but hers was as fresh as if the knife had just been pulled out of her back. Hearing his pissed-off attitude over the answering machine unleashed a desire to do him violence. *What does he have to be upset about? Who is he to have an attitude?* she fumed. Marvin wasn't the one who had been hurt.

At least not yet. Toni had been ironing clothes at the time and could easily imagine smashing him over the head with the iron. That's why she had bundled up the kids and headed for the mall.

The automatic doors of the toy store slid open, revealing long lines that snaked from the registers and trailed down the aisles. Bright, noisy, crowded. The floor an obstacle course of picked-over, damaged, and discarded merchandise. Many of the remaining games, buzzers, and whistles protruded from the sides of shelves, destined to hit the floor if jostled by one more passing body. The sale-fueled chaos had Toni considering an immediate about-face. But she couldn't. For one thing, Sanji had already surged forth into the sea of Christmas shoppers, and second, this was the chain where Lynn was registered.

There hadn't been a baby shower. Toni had talked Lynn into having showers when she was pregnant with Montana and Dakota. Small ones. The family and a few of Lynn's friends from her old job. This time Toni didn't bring up the subject. The pregnancy had been so iffy, she thought it might jinx Lynn to presume anything.

But after all the stress and strain of the pregnancy, the birth of her new nephew had gone off without a hitch. Houston was a healthy, if slightly underweight, baby boy. Toni couldn't wait to see him at Christmas. And other than sounding exhausted, Lynn had been fine when Toni teased her about the baby's name. "What, did you run out of states to name your kids after?" Lynn hadn't been strong enough for a vaginal birth, so the doctors opted for a C-section. She had stayed in the hospital a week instead of the usual two days. Only now could Toni stop holding her breath and buy her nephew a few gifts to welcome him into the world. *And avoid dealing with Marvin at the same time*, she reminded herself.

Jesse double-clutched Toni's hand. She looked down. With eyes more owlish than ever, he gazed around the store in awe. Predictably, Sanji was taking a more interactive approach. Tugging on the hood of Sanji's coat, Toni pried her away from the video game counter. Sanji's smudged fingerprints were left on the glass case. They joined those of hundreds of other kids eager to behold the latest Nintendo or Sega or whatever mess they were selling these days. Well, thought Toni, she hoped Sanji didn't expect to find one of those under the Christmas tree. They were too expensive and the games that went with them too violent.

Toni stopped a harried-looking blue smock–wearing teen. "Excuse me, but could you tell me where I could find the new baby registry?"

The girl pushed stringy dishwater blonde hair out of her eyes. "Next to the customer service desk."

Before Toni could ask where that was, the girl had moved on. Swallowed up by the crowd.

"Mommy, will you buy me this doll?" Sanji held up a boxed baby. According to the package advertising, Mealtime Molly could say fifty phrases. Most of which had to do with what Molly preferred to eat.

Toni promptly put the doll back. "Sanji, I told you before we came in here that we're not buying for you. We're getting something for your new cousin and then we're leaving. So stop begging."

Seeing her daughter's face fall, Toni relented. It was pretty cruel to bring kids into a toy store, then expect them not to want anything. "Okay. Both of you can have something. But it has to cost under ten dollars each." That wouldn't cripple her budget.

Sanji crushed Jesse in what was supposed to be a hug. "Yeah! We gonna get something! We gonna get something!"

"Under ten dollars," Toni reminded her. Not that Sanji made much distinction between a ten-dollar toy and a hundred-dollar one. Toni suddenly noticed she was sweating under the layers of cold-weather clothes. She unzipped her jacket. Either the thermostat was set on eighty, or there were too many damn people up in here. Time to get the baby gift and then get the hell out of here before she was trampled. People had that shopping-fever glazed look to them.

A huge orange and yellow sign was suspended above the customer service desk, so it was not hard to find. The people in the checkout lines held their positions as if defending against a game-winning touchdown. Equal to any NFL full-back, Toni bulldozed her way through them, dragging Sanji and Jesse through the hole she had made.

Toni printed out Lynn's baby registry at the kiosk next to the customer service desk. She studied the list. It wasn't very long. With a child still in diapers Lynn probably didn't need much.

"Hmmm, it's a toss-up between the baby monitor and a car seat. She probably needs a second car seat more." Dakota was only two, so she would need hers for a while yet. "What do y'all think?" Jesse was nearby sorting through a basket of toys that people had returned but that hadn't been put away yet. Sanji . . . was nowhere in sight.

Toni's fingers tightened on the slip of paper. This was exactly why she used to put one of those leash thingies on Sanji's wrist. This was not the first time she'd strayed away. But Toni thought she had lectured, threatened, and heated up her daughter's behind enough times for Sanji to get the message: Don't wander off. She grabbed Jesse's hand, her eyes searching for Sanji the whole time. Toni wasn't too worried about Sanji being snatched by someone. Sanji would scream to high heaven if someone tried to take her out of the store. At least, she hoped she would. In any case, Sanji had no business running around by herself in the store. How was she supposed to find her in this madness? She never should have let Sanji out of her sight. Toni walked over to the aisle nearest to her—baby cribs, bassinets—but no sign of Sanji.

Toni stopped to think for a moment. Which aisle would hold the most appeal for a hardheaded six-year-old girl? she wondered. The doll department? Or maybe Sanji had gone back to the video game counter. Either way, Sanji could forget about that ten-dollar toy. Toni released an angry breath. She would search for a few minutes, and if she didn't find her wayward child, she would get security in on the action.

"Jesse," she said, stooping to his height, "did you see where Sanji went?"

He pointed directly in front of him. "She went over there."

Toni sighed, then straightened up. "There" could be anywhere between where they were standing and the front doors. Jesse's vague eyewitness account covered just about all of the store.

Since Sanji wasn't in the immediate vicinity Toni geared up to fight her way through the crowds. Then she spotted a flash of red about two aisles down. Was that her? "Sanji!" Toni sprinted in that direction. She almost tripped over a box of Huggies somebody had left in the middle of the floor. "Watch out, Jesse," she said. *Just wait until I get that little missy home*, she vowed.

When Toni got to the doll aisle, it was in worse shape than the main walkway. Blank spaces where some products had been completely snapped up. Opened boxes. Wall-to-wall people, still searching for the perfect baby doll. But Sanji was there, about midway down the aisle, wedged between a leather-clad man whose back was to Toni and a woman in her thirties who was reading a description on a box with the intense concentration of an anorexic reading the nutrition facts on a Twinkie wrapper.

Toni's heart resumed its regular beat, and her grip on Jesse's hand eased. Anger replaced relief as she watched her daughter deliberate over which item to pull from the shelf in front of her. Sanji was already holding an ugly Cabbage Patch doll in the other hand.

"Sanjari Marita Carleton, get your butt over here now!"

Sanji pulled her hand back as if from a hot stove. She found herself caught in the vortex of her mother's stormy eyes. Nothing moved on her except a pair of dangling wool mittens that were attached to her coat by suspenders.

Toni said, "Sanji, you are in so much trouble, it ain't even funny." The woman next to Sanji gave her a sympathetic look, then moved out of the way. Other shoppers paused only long enough to note that it was just another lost child–furious parent scene.

"It's okay, Toni. She's with me."

That's when Toni noticed the man whose back had been turned to her. Marvin. Toni could smell the new leather of his coat from where she stood. Beneath it he wore jeans, a thick navy wool sweater, and a pair of Timberland boots. Though it was hot in the store, Marvin looked the epitome of cool. Smiling. Relaxed.

What the hell is he doing here anyway? "I thought you were on your way over to my place."

"I was. Until I saw your car heading the opposite direction on Route Forty. I made a U-turn at the next light and caught up with you here at the mall." He saluted the little boy at her side. "Hi'ya, Jesse. What's up, buddy?"

"Hi," Jesse said shyly. Toni released his hand because, unlike Sanji, Jesse could be trusted to stay put.

"So what, are you stalking me now?" Toni demanded to know.

Marvin laughed. "Girl, be for real. I thought maybe you hadn't got the message." He rubbed his chin and studied her with a little smirk on his face. "But I guess you did. Does that mean you were running away from me?"

She wanted to slap that smirk right off his face. "I ain't got to run away from nobody. I just didn't want to be bothered."

"You still drive like a bat out of hell, I see. You almost lost me when you got onto Route One."

"I drive like someone who has some place to be."

Sanji stood between her parents, glancing worriedly from one to the other. "Mommy . . ."

Toni snatched the doll from Sanji and threw it back on the shelf "Not now, Sanji. You're already in enough trouble."

Her eyes challenged Marvin. "Well? Did you follow me here?"

He shrugged. "Don't yell at Sanji. It's not her fault." He held out a hand to Sanji, beckoning her over—to his side. She went without hesitation. "I saw y'all standing over by customer service. I was headed that way. Then I saw that Miss Behavin' was wandering off. Luckily, I was able to grab her before she could get too far."

He ruffled the top of Sanji's head. She leaned back against him, tilting her head up. Smiling. "It was good to see Miss Behavin'." He gave Sanji a wrestler's one-armed hug. She tucked her neck into the curve of his arm. "Anyway, since Miss Behavin' wanted to look at dolls and since you looked busy—"

Busy? Since when was she too busy not to care that her child was missing? "If you had any sense, you would have brought her back over to me or at least told me that she was with you. Instead, I had to come looking for her." Why was she wasting her breath talking to him? she wondered. "Come on, Sanji," Toni ordered. Even if Marvin's arm hadn't been around her, Sanji didn't try to move toward her as Toni had expected she would. *What the hell is going on? Sanji is getting a little too big for her britches if she thinks she can ignore me just because her father is here.*

Marvin's left eye twitched. "If you had been paying more attention, maybe she wouldn't have wandered off in the first place."

Toni had been about to grab Sanji and drag her away from Marvin if she had to, but his accusation rooted her to the spot. She blinked. "What did you say?"

A snicker. A girl who looked barely past the age of playing with dolls herself had a baby strapped to her stomach in a cloth papoose and a runny nosed toddler at her side. Great, they had an audience.

Toni put her hands on her hips. Marvin had a lot of fucking nerve, criticizing her parenting skills. "I don't need to tell you how difficult it is to keep *your* daughter out of trouble. She's just like you." Toni immediately wished she could take back the words. It was a lousy thing to say in front of her child. She stole a look at her daughter. Sanji was stroking Marvin's arm where it rested lightly around her neck. It was almost as if she was trying to soothe him in the face of the charged energy between her two parents.

When Toni looked at him again, Marvin's eyes were glittering dangerously. One eye continued to twitch like an on and off switch. "Thanks. I'm glad you remember that she is my daughter," he said.

Toni flung her hands to the side. "Okay, that's it. We ain't even having this conversation. Sanji, Jesse, let's go."

"But Daddy's—"

Toni silenced Sanji with a look. "No buts, I'm getting what I came for, and then we're going home." Sanji reluctantly moved away from her father, resentment filling every step she took toward Toni.

Toni saw this and tried to remind herself that Sanji was just a child, and by definition, she didn't always know what was good for her. Marvin was like candy. Irresistibly sweet but gorge yourself on it and you end up with a stomach ache.

Marvin shook his head. "Toni, I've been trying to talk to you for weeks. How you gonna just walk out on me?"

Toni let her actions speak for her. She grabbed each child by the hand and turned away.

Sanji twisted around for a final wave. "Bye, Daddy." It took every bit of self-control not to yank Sanji down the aisle.

Marvin was waiting beside her car when she got to the parking lot. Ignoring him, Toni unlocked the doors and popped the trunk. "Get in and buckle up," she told the kids. Sanji had to be told twice because she seemed to be having trouble tearing herself away from her father. Toni threw her bags in the trunk and closed it. She brushed by him and was about to open her door when Marvin took hold of her arm. Toni looked down at the hand on her jacket, then up at his face. He removed his hand. "Toni, we need to talk," he said.

Sanji had her face pressed up against the window. Hot air from her breath was fogging it up. She wiped away the condensation with the sleeve of her coat. Jesse was looking through one of his picture books.

Toni sighed. She might as well let Marvin have his say. Then maybe he would quit bugging her. She folded her arms across her chest and leaned against the car door. "About what?"

"Well, for one thing, I have your money." He took out his wallet and peeled off some bills and held them out.

She turned her palm up. Marvin hesitated, then handed the bills over. After quickly counting it, Toni stuffed the money—seven hundred dollars, a hundred more than he had stolen—in her coat pocket. Marvin's look of surprise when she took it almost made her laugh. Did he think she wouldn't? Hell, he owed her that much, with interest!

Marvin made no move to leave. What was he waiting for? Her to say thank you? Toni hoped he wasn't holding his breath.

"Don't you want to know where I got the money from?" he asked.

"Not particularly."

He shook his head at her lack of enthusiasm. His smile was knowing, as if he'd expected her to say something like that. "I got a job."

He rubbed his hands together. She watched as he balled a hand into a fist and tried to warm his fingers by blowing it.

Between puffs, Marvin continued to talk about his new job. "It's a good one. Benefits and everything."

"How nice for you."

"Sanji showed me which doll she wanted for Christmas. With the new job I'll be able to get her that, and I was thinking about buying her a laser tag game, too. That way her and Jesse would have a game they could play together."

Toni had nothing to say. Did he really expect her to believe all this? With his track record, he probably wouldn't still have the job by Christmas. And why was he trying to play Daddy all of a sudden? She had to shame him into buying Sanji a Christmas present last year.

"So when is the best time for me to get together with Sanji on Christmas?" Marvin asked.

"Marvin, I told you. Sanji doesn't need anything from you. And for your information, we will be with *family* at Christmas." Toni turned away from him and climbed into the driver's seat, slamming the door closed.

Marvin rapped on her window. Hard.

Toni's jaw clenched. He was getting on her nerves. Sanji poked her head around Toni's head rest. Toni told her to get back in her seat belt. She jabbed the power window switch. When it was about a third of the way down, she spat out, "What?"

Marvin hunched down, bringing his face level with hers. His angry brown eyes under the cover of thick brows bored into hers. Before speaking, he glanced at the kids in the backseat. His words heated the air, coming at her in spirals of gray mist. "Stop being such a . . . a . . . bitch," he said, his voice barely above a whisper.

Toni's neck snapped back. Did he call her a bitch? She must have misheard him. She stared at the frost on the hood of her car, then turned the key in the ignition.

"Mommy, tell Jesse to let me play with his book," Sanji whined.

"Quiet, Sanji. Look at your own book. It's in the pouch behind the seat." Toni watched in the rearview mirror as Sanji reached toward the back of the passenger seat. She nudged Jesse with her elbow. The move looked deliberate. When Sanji straightened, she had a box of crayons and a coloring book. Her seat belt was off. "Sanji, if I have to tell you one more time to fasten that seat belt . . ." Toni warned.

Smoke trailed out of the tailpipe and snaked toward the front of the car. Leaning on her door, Marvin scratched his chin. If he'd been trying to get on Toni's good side, he had failed miserably.

Sanji waved to him from the backseat. He pressed the palm of his hand against her window. Smiling, she touched the window on the other side. Her much smaller palm was hidden behind his. Marvin sought Toni's eyes but found only her profile. He tapped on the window again, this time softly, with only one finger. She faced him. Cold, expressionless eyes. "Toni, I have every right to see my own child. You can't do this."

"Watch me." Toni rolled the window back up and stomped on the gas. Marvin barely had time to jump out of the way before his foot was flattened.

Toni stuck her hand under the faucet. Fingers dripping, she turned up the hot water a notch. She swished the water to thoroughly mix the generous dollop of vanilla-scented bath oil she had put in it. Toni put on a terry-cloth robe and gathered her discarded clothes from the bathroom floor and put them in the hamper. It was half full. Dirty clothes multiplied like rabbits around here. She had just washed three loads yesterday.

Sanji and Jesse had started watching a video about ten minutes ago, which meant Toni had at least an hour to relax and try to put Marvin out of her mind.

Her phone rang. With a sigh, Toni turned off the tap. She'd have to get it. Jesse and Sanji had been forbidden from answering it. If it was Marvin, she was going to curse him out. She had been "polite" earlier today, she thought. But no more.

She shouldn't be forced to monitor her calls because of him, and she was going to tell him so. Toni picked it up before the answering machine clicked on.

"Hello," she said with an edge to her voice.

A computerized voice informed her, "You have a collect call from—"

A pause, then "Joy Rollins."

"Press one if you will accept the charges," the voice instructed.

Joy had been calling a lot lately. Apparently, she'd forgotten that long-distance calls were not free. Toni suspected she was bored. Still, she was reluctant to refuse a call because it could be important. And as a mother, she'd feel like the bitch Marvin had called her if she deprived Jesse of the opportunity to speak to his mother.

Toni pushed the requested button.

"Hi, Joy."

"Hey, Sis." Flat. Monotone. Not like Joy.

Toni rubbed under her nose and took a seat on the bed. "What's wrong?" she asked.

Heavy sigh. "Sis, I can't take this place anymore."

"Why not?" Toni asked, but she was thinking, it wasn't like Joy had much choice. She could either "take it" or go to jail.

"They treat us like kids. We never get to go anywhere. We have to earn privileges for the stupidest little things. Like to use the phone or watch TV. It's whack. The food is bad. Half the people who work here are ignorant. Somebody should give me their jobs. I asked this kid who works in the kitchen for celery. He didn't even know what it was. How dumb is that? And can't nobody around here fry no chicken. I offered to cook some up for them. But they won't let us near the kitchen. Scared we gonna drink up the vanilla extract or anything that's got alcohol in it."

Toni was sorry Joy was bored and lonely at the rehab center, but she wasn't in the mood to listen to her sister's pity party. "Listen, girl, you being at that place is like a 'get out of jail free' card. You could be doing hard time somewhere with gates, barbed-wire fence, and cells."

Joy snorted. "I don't need a lecture, Sis. I should have known you wouldn't understand."

"Then why did you call me?"

"It's Christmas." Sigh. "I'll still be here over Christmas. I want to be with Jesse and the rest of y'all."

That Toni could understand. Christmas at the Rollinses' was such a fun time. The kids got so excited, and the grown-ups started acting like kids. "I'm feeling you, Joy. I know it's hard to be away, especially right now. Hang in there a few more weeks and you'll be a free woman."

"Toni, it's not that easy. You just don't know."

"It'll be over soon," Toni said, trying to comfort her.

"Not soon enough," Joy muttered.

Join the reality club, Joy. Nothing anybody wanted ever came soon enough. "I'm sure it sucks to be away from everybody at this time of the year, but don't do anything rash. That nasty fruitcake that Aunt Dot sends every year will still be waiting for you when you get home," Toni said, knowing that would get a laugh out of Joy. And it did. Nobody ate Aunt Dot's fruitcake or anything else she made. She was a horrible cook.

"Child, please, if I wanted to eat bad food, I might as well stay here."

"My point exactly. There will be other Christmases," Toni promised.

"So where is my little peanut head?" Joy asked.

Toni was glad for the change of subject. "Watching *Hercules* with Sanji. Do you want me to get him?"

"In a minute. Uh, Sis, do you think you could send me a couple of bucks? Cigarette money."

"Okay, I'll send something out tomorrow."

"Money order. You can't send cash with all these thieves around. I ain't just talking about the residents, either."

"I'll go get Jesse," Toni said, rising from the bed. Maybe talking to Jesse would remind Joy that her top priority should be to get better, so that she could be the kind of mother the boy needed and deserved.

chapter
<u>26</u>

Toni wrapped a cottony blue-and-white-striped towel around herself and quickly padded from the bathroom to Darius's room. The drive through the mountains of western Pennsylvania in holiday traffic with two kids in the back had left her nerves frayed. The blowing snow, while pretty, had been slippery and blinding at times. She probably shouldn't have waited until Christmas Eve to head home, but she and Chris hadn't wanted to miss out on all those customers who wanted to beautify for the holidays.

A gaping yawn escaped Toni as she tossed her towel over the back of a chair. She should have taken a nap after the long drive but couldn't resist making the acquaintance of her new nephew. Lynn's family, including Bruce, was staying at Mama's over the holiday to make it easier on her. She had expected Houston to be frail and wan like Lynn. But he wasn't. He was strong and active. The little fella didn't want to miss anything. In his snapped-up outfit, his fat legs and arms were in constant motion. It was as if all Lynn's energy had been unselfishly transferred to him.

Toni visited with Lynn only briefly. Her sister had looked drained, so Toni volunteered to take Houston off her hands. She cooed to him and walked him until his father showed up from parts unknown. When she put the fretful boy in

Bruce's arms, his trapped look was pathetic. If he couldn't handle an infant for a couple of hours so his wife could get some much needed rest, then he should stop making babies.

The excitement of Christmas Eve and younger cousins to boss around was like a shot of pure adrenaline to Sanji's system. Mama fussed over everybody. Darius blared his music. Daddy was smart: he had holed himself up in the basement and wouldn't let anybody under eighteen down there. One big happy family. Except for Joy. She still had three more weeks to go in her rehab program.

Toni slipped into a pair of satin PJs. A steaming bath had soaked most of the tension right out. Toni removed the scrunchy band from her hair and threw it on Darius's dresser. She and Sanji were sleeping in his room. Darius had been relegated to the sofa bed in the basement. Jesse had wanted to sleep with Toni, but Darius had persuaded him that they'd have more fun watching videos in the basement.

Sanji was now sprawled diagonally across Darius's bed. Her red Minnie Mouse nightgown was bunched around her waist, and her braids were loose, sprouting tufts of hair in thick black clumps against blue sheets. The blanket and comforter had been pushed to the floor by restless feet. Sighing, Toni dragged her sleeping child's dead weight to one side of the bed. She pulled the covers up and tucked them around Sanji's shoulders. Seconds later, Sanji flipped onto her side, knocking a pillow to the floor. Toni tossed it back on the bed. She smiled to herself. *A good night's sleep is a long shot with a wildcat lying next to me.*

Postponing the inevitable, she decided to make herself a cup of cocoa. As she made her way downstairs, though, she heard a rustling sound from the living room. All the kids were supposed to be in bed. Who was being naughty, not nice? Toni wondered. When she poked her head around the comer of the living room, she saw her brother under the Christmas tree. Darius was on his knees, wearing only a pair of plaid flannel boxers. Red and white lights blinked, spot-lighting the gift that he was shaking next to his ear.

"Darius Isaiah Rollins, you're pitiful," Toni said.

Darius whirled around. His smile was shame-free. The sheen from his newly shaven head glowed in the lights from the tree. He had also grown a skimpy goatee while at school. "You got me, Sis."

Toni moved closer. She took the foil-wrapped box from his hands. Wagging a finger at him, she put it back under the tree. She looked at the tag on it. MONTANA. "This ain't even your gift," Toni said.

"I know. I was trying to find one with my name on it. There aren't as many as there used to be," he lamented.

"Here I was thinking one of the kids was trying to sneak a peek at the presents, and who do I find? Your grown rusty butt," she said, laughing.

"Hey, I'm still a child at heart."

"Obviously," Toni said. Mama had always had to hide the Christmas presents from Darius—and Joy. They would scour the house in the weeks leading up to Christmas, unable to wait to find out what they got.

"You must have X-ray vision. How did you know I was in here?"

"My bionic hearing. You were shaking that box like a rattlesnake's tail."

"Aw, come on. I wasn't that loud. I was trying to be quiet." He eyed her suspiciously. "And what are you doing creeping around in the middle of the night?"

"Unlike you, what I'm doing is perfectly innocent. I was about to have a cup of hot chocolate. Want some?" Toni already knew what his answer would be. The boy was a chocoholic.

In no time they were settled in at the kitchen table. Toni regarded him over a piping hot mug. She blew on the surface of the brown liquid to cool it. She grimaced as Darius added two lumps of sugar. It was a wonder the boy had a tooth left in his mouth. "So, college boy, how did your first semester of school go?"

"Two A's, one B, and a C."

Toni was surprised. A lot of freshmen struggled their first semester. "Not bad," she said.

"Very good. College is a piece of cake. If you don't watch out, I'll catch up and maybe even pass you."

"I don't think so, buddy. Two more classes to go and I'm outta there." Finally. The A that Toni had gotten in her small business–management class had come as a big surprise. She'd been so happy, she actually went out and bought herself a new outfit. A wool pantsuit. She didn't know where she was going to wear it, but she felt she deserved it.

Darius's big hands engulfed the mug. Was this really the same little boy she used to boss around? She remembered a time when she'd tossed his race cars out of the window because he was keeping up too much racket. Darius was afraid of the dark, and he started crying. Lynn had volunteered to go get them.

Toni smiled and shook her head. Darius was a man now, and he'd probably put a hurting on her if she tried to order him around. She inhaled deeply. The kitchen always smelled like home. Mama liked to get most of her cooking done for Christmas the night before.

The stairs creaked as someone slowly crept down them. Toni and Darius smiled at each other. Which kid's curiosity had gotten the best of her? The footsteps didn't head away from the kitchen, though, but toward it. Clarence Rollins was tightening the belt of his knee length robe as he stepped into the kitchen. Long, bony feet were encased in fake leather slippers. The light was on, so he didn't seem surprised to find them there.

"Y'all still up?" he said, stating the obvious.

"I wanted some cocoa," Toni replied, then jerked her head toward Darius. "And he was unwrapping his gifts early."

Clarence chuckled. "Boy, you worse than the kids."

Darius gulped down his drink. "Well, if we didn't open our gifts with the youngest going first, maybe I wouldn't be so impatient. Since my big sisters keep having babies every year—"

"Hey, that's Lynn, not me," Toni said. "I only got one."

"Whatever. Since *I'm* not the youngest anymore, I didn't want to have to wait until Christmas afternoon before I got to open my gifts."

"If you have to wait to the afternoon," his father said, "as the oldest I guess I'll have to wait till New Year's Day."

"Daddy, what are you doing downstairs? Couldn't sleep?" Toni asked.

He rubbed his flat stomach. "Naw, I was feeling a little hungry."

Toni smiled. She knew exactly what her father craved in the middle of the night when he was "a little hungry." "Have a seat," she said. "I'll get you some buttermilk and cornbread."

Clarence smiled in thanks. As he moved toward the table, Darius stood up. "Since y'all ain't going to let me open any gifts, I'm going to bed." His hopeful look belied the words.

Toni's eyes flicked over her brother. What a con artist. "Guess we'll see you in the morning, then."

He pretended to be hurt. "Ice water in the veins," he muttered as he headed for the basement.

Toni handed her father a bowl of cornbread floating in a sea of milk and a tablespoon. She sat down across from him. He ate slowly, like he did everything else. After he swallowed a few spoonfuls, she asked, "So how is everybody? I barely had a chance to say two words to Mama, and you've been hiding out in the basement all day."

"Things have quieted down since Lynn had the baby. Before that it was Grand Central Station in here." Clarence broke up one of the larger chunks of bread with his spoon. He submerged it in the thick milk. "Your mama and me really appreciate you taking Jesse in. Your mama felt real bad about sending him away. But it really helped a lot."

"So everything's calm around here."

"'Bout as calm as they ever get." Those sad, tired eyes lowered. "Anna didn't make her deadline, though."

"The deadline?" The GED. How could she have forgotten the December deadline? That was the main reason Jesse had been sent to Delaware. "Oh, no, Daddy. When did she find that out?"

"Last week."

Last week? Mama hadn't said a word. Every time they talked, Mama seemed like her old self. Even today, cooking until she was dead on her feet, running from room to room making sure everyone had what they needed. Last-minute gift wrapping. Smiling. "Does that mean she lost her job?"

A small shake of the tight salt-and-pepper curls. "Once she explained all the family problems we been having, they gave her more time—until the end of March. It's the math section. I know she can do it. She just didn't have time to study up on it."

Toni scratched the top of her head. Her mama was something else. It was just like her not to say anything. She probably hadn't wanted to spoil Christmas for the rest of them by sharing her bad news. She sighed. "Well, once Lynn is back at her own house—for the most part—and Jesse is with me, maybe she will have the peace and quiet she needs."

Her father's bowl was empty. He took it over to the sink and rinsed it out, then turned to face her. "This whole family will be back on track soon. Your mama will pass her test. Joy will get out of that place. We'll help her be a better mother to Jesse. Lynn will get her strength back. And you will be the first business tycoon in the family."

Toni smiled up at him. Daddy said all of that like it was fact. A lump formed in her throat. He was so cool. So wise. In low moments, when her responsibilities threatened to overwhelm her, she longed for her father's quiet confidence that everything was gonna be all right.

Her father leaned against the sink. His slender hands rested against his robe. Toni envied his stillness. Perpetually sleepy eyes. He was so relaxed. It was as if he could nod off standing there. "You forgot Darius. What about him?" Toni said, breaking the silence.

A slow smile. "Darius will learn that good things come to those who wait. And who work for it."

Amen. "Let's go upstairs, Daddy." When she was young, Mama used to tell them that Santa wouldn't come if they didn't go to bed. Linking her arm with her father's, Toni now knew that Santa had been with her every day of the year.

The stairs leading to the second floor were narrow, so Toni walked behind him. When they got to the top, she gestured for him to bend down. She hugged him and gave him a peck on the cheek. "Merry Christmas, Daddy," she whispered.

As they tiptoed down the hall, she noticed a light under Lynn's door. They weren't the only ones up apparently. It was dark in Toni's old room. Dakota and Montana were in there. Her parents' room was at the other end of the hall across from Darius's room.

A thud came from behind them. Then hushed voices. Their feet stilled. Toni glanced back at Lynn's door. At the second thud, her father moved over to the door and tapped on it. "Lynn?" he said softly.

Silence.

"Lynn, is everything all right in there?" Toni came up behind him, resting a hand on his back. More silence. Toni twisted open the knob of the door.

"Lynn? We were passing by and—"

The light from a bedside lamp cast a frightening silhouette. Bruce looming over Lynn. A hand over her mouth. A forearm pressed against her throat. Lynn's curled fingers were unable to loosen the pressure of his massive arm. Her thrashing body went still at the sound of Toni's voice.

Once she got over her first shock, Toni rushed forward. Her sole intent: to kill the bastard. What the hell did Bruce think he was doing? But her father got to the bed before she did.

"Son, take your hands off my child," he said with deadly calm. Veins throbbing at his temple, Bruce whipped his head around to see who was giving him orders. Though he looked at them, it was like he was in another world. He was breathing hard, and a thin layer of sweat glistened on clumpy chest hairs. It took him a moment to recognize his father-in-law. Only then did Bruce's arm fall away from Lynn's neck. Lynn slumped against the headboard. Her breathing was quick. She clutched her throat.

Toni shoved Bruce out of the way. She gently took her sister by the shoulders. "Lynette, are you all right?" Lynn nodded weakly but kept rubbing her throat. "What's going on?"

Lynn automatically looked to Bruce. For guidance? Toni wondered. But her father now stood between Bruce and the bed. And Clarence's feet were firmly planted. He was prepared to physically keep Bruce from his daughter if necessary. "Nothing," she croaked.

"Nothing? How can you say that? That asshole was trying to choke you."

Bruce took a step toward the bed. His face no longer contorted in a mask of rage but still threatening. "Toni, why don't you stay out of this? Me and my wife were just having a disagreement."

Clarence blocked any further forward movement. "A disagreement involves exchanging words, not blows. You need to leave this house."

"Leave? It's the middle of the night. It's practically a blizzard out there."

His self-centeredness incensed Toni. She spun around. "You should have thought about that when you started beating up on a woman." She stared at his bulked-up body, wanting to hurl herself at him, but that would mean waking up the entire house. Some Christmas Eve. Whatever happened to Silent Night, Holy Night?

She couldn't stand to look at him any longer. Turning away, she smoothed Lynn's hair back from her overheated face. Her eyes were wide, shell-shocked. "Here, Lynn, get back under the sheets."

As Lynn eased lower on the bed, Bruce ordered her to get up. "Go wake up the kids. We're going home," he said.

Clarence strong-armed his son-in-law's chest. "I'll say this once more. *You* need to leave this house."

Bruce's hand clenched into a fist at his side. Clarence stared him down. The fist uncurled and went limp.

The baby whimpered in his bassinet. Lynn tried to sit up, but Toni gently pushed her back down. "I'll get him," she said. Toni walked around to the other side of the bed. She picked him up, blanket and all. Poor baby, I'd be crying too if I had an idiot for a father, she thought as she rocked him.

"Lynn?" Bruce said.

Lynn's eyes swung away from Toni and the baby. Fear lurked in them. "Let's go."

Lynn looked from Bruce to her father, then back again. Clarence came over to the bed and sat down. "Lynette." It was a command. She looked up, meeting her father's eyes. "I don't know what this is all about. I try to stay out of my kids' business." Clarence's voice roughened. "But I almost lost one child to drugs doing that. I will not stand by this time. I won't. Do you understand me?"

Lynn lowered her gaze. "Yes, Daddy."

"Marriage is a serious thing. Y'all can try to work it out. But not tonight. You and my grandkids are not leaving here until I believe in my heart you will be safe."

The baby's whimper grew to a wail. "I think he's hungry," Toni said.

Lynn held her thin arms out for Houston. The sleeves of her gown fell back, revealing ugly bruises on her wrists and upper arms.

Toni's breath caught in her throat.

Lynn bowed her head to avoid the questions in Toni's eyes. "He's probably hungry. Could you go downstairs and fix him a bottle?" Lynn was not breast feeding. She couldn't produce enough milk.

"I'll get it," Bruce said.

"No." Lynn chewed her lip, then said, "Maybe you should get dressed. Daddy can lock up the house after you leave."

Until this moment Toni hadn't noticed that Bruce was dressed only in his drawers. She gathered the jeans, flannel lumberjack shirt, socks, and boots he had left strewn about the floor and threw them at him. "You can change in the bathroom," she said.

Toni stayed with Lynn awhile, but her sister would not talk about what was happening with her and Bruce. Instead, Lynn fussed with Houston for a while until Toni finally took the sleeping child out of her arms. Once she was certain he was definitely asleep, she crept back to her own room and crawled into bed with Sanji. She wrapped her arms around her daughter to warm the chill she felt. In vain Toni tried to match the unburdened rhythm of her slumbering child's breathing.

Darius was able to open his presents well before noon. Dakota and Montana scarcely missed Bruce. They were too busy tearing through wrapping paper and trying out new toys. Toni hadn't gotten much sleep. Unfortunately, the mini-xylophone was the most popular gift, so she wasn't likely to get in a nap either. At first light, Daddy had told Mama what had happened.

During the Christmas prayer, Toni's eyes popped open when her mother asked God to bless Lynn's marriage. She prayed Bruce and Lynn would forge a strong and lasting bond in the coming year.

Later, Toni asked why she had even mentioned Bruce's name. Mama told her, "That's what Lynn wanted for Christmas."

"And you support that?" Toni asked.

"I support the notion that everybody is in need of prayer. And Lord knows, Bruce and Lynn need all the prayers they can get."

chapter
<u>27</u>

Toni took the lid off the crock pot and slowly stirred the black-eyed peas. She had put them on early this morning. Black-eyed peas on New Year's Day was an old Southern tradition Mama had passed on to her. They were supposed to bring you good luck. Toni smiled as she replaced the top. She didn't even like black-eyed peas. They were too dry. Though she had laughed at Mama's silly superstitions when she was little, some of them had managed to become a part of her life as an adult.

Supposedly, washing clothes on New Year's Day meant you were washing someone out of your life. So Mama used to have them wash loads and loads on New Year's Eve. Toni humphed. She had not washed clothes yesterday and wasn't planning on washing any tomorrow either. She barely felt like washing her body this morning. That's why she was still in her robe at eleven in the morning. And why the kids were getting themselves dressed. It didn't matter what they put on.

None of them were leaving the house today. She wasn't tired, just feeling lazy. There were only a few days left before she started work again. She wanted to spend them relaxing. Today she and the kids would maybe play Uno and some of the games they had gotten for Christmas. Chris was coming over later to watch the Rose Bowl.

He was bringing Marshall.

He might have shown Marshall the door when he first came crawling back, but that door was thrown wide open now. If it had been her, she would have made Marshall work a little harder.

Mama used to tell Toni she was like an elephant. Her memory was long and surrounded by "Keep Out" signs for people who had hurt her. Like Marvin.

When she'd gotten back from Cleveland, he'd called her about bringing some presents over for Sanji. She'd told him he could keep them. He hadn't bothered to bring her any gifts last Christmas or the Christmas before that. She told him to give them to his other kids. Tiara would be sure to appreciate that.

Despite that, he still dropped off some presents and left them at her door. Sanji saw them, so Toni couldn't very well send them right back. Which was what she wanted to do. She allowed Sanji to call her father to thank him, but a visit was still out of the question. Sanji didn't understand. Toni didn't really expect her to. But Marvin just couldn't be trusted. Toni had reached the point where she felt it was better to have no father influence in Sanji's life than an unstable one.

Using a sauce brush, Toni coated the ham with glaze. She topped that with pineapple rings and fresh cloves—Sanji loved pineapples. After wrapping it in foil, she put it in the oven. Toni wasn't cooking a whole lot, but her upbringing just wouldn't let her have company without fixing them a little something to eat. Not that Chris and Marshall were really company. Well, maybe Marshall was. She still wasn't convinced that "nothing happened" between him and his ex. Still, the bottom line was that it really didn't matter what she believed. If Chris had forgiven Marshall, she would have to learn to as well.

Wiping her hands on a dish towel, Toni scanned the kitchen to see what else needed to be done before she got dressed.

There was a knock at the door.

It couldn't be Chris. It was too early. Maybe it was Kathleen Bishop from downstairs. The elderly woman said she might drop by with some treats for the kids. Toni liked the retired schoolteacher, but she hoped it wasn't her. According to Mama, it was bad luck to have a woman be the first person to enter your household on New Year's Day. Sexist? No doubt. But tradition was tradition. And Toni didn't need any bad luck to start off the new year.

Toni headed for the door. If it was Mrs. Bishop or another female, Toni would ask Jesse to leave the apartment and then reenter it before she let a woman in. She probably was nuts, but she wasn't taking any chances. Not after the year she'd just had.

From the living room, she saw Jesse was wrestling with the lock on the front door. Why was he still in his Power Rangers pajamas? He and Sanji were supposed to be getting dressed. "I'll get it, Aunt Toni!" he said when he noticed her.

"Jesse, wait!" But he had already yanked the front door open. Oh, shoot. Let it be a male, Toni thought.

The little boy stood there, his mouth gaping open. The sunlight reflected off his glasses onto the hallway walls. He didn't move a muscle.

"Jesse, who is it?" Toni said.

"Hey, baby, ain't you gonna tell your mommy Happy New Year!" a woman's laughing voice inquired.

Joy! Toni hurried down the hall. *Oh, my God, it is her*. Engulfed in a yellow parka and jeans, she pulled the hood away from her hair. Her face was thinner, less made up, and the weave was gone. She grinned at Toni. "Hiya, Sis. Happy New Year!"

Jesse came to life. Rushing into Joy's outstretched arms, he yelled, "Mommy! Mommy!"

Joy picked him up, laughing. "In the flesh, baby. Give Mama some sugar. Oh, you so sweet, I could eat you up," she said as she planted kisses all over his face and neck. He started giving his mother the same enthusiastic welcome.

Toni couldn't decide if the sight of her wayward sister at her door or Jesse's outpouring of affection was what left her speechless. She had never seen Jesse light up like this. No matter what Joy had or hadn't done for him, the kid absolutely worshiped her.

As Joy carried Jesse over the threshold, Toni stepped aside to let her in. "Joy, what are you doing here? Did you finish the program early?"

Jesse was clinging to his mother, his legs wrapped around her waist. "I'll explain in a minute," Joy said as she stroked Jesse's head. "I got my hands full now." She hefted her son over her shoulder and began walking toward the living room. "Boy, you getting so big," she told him. "I can barely pick you up."

Jesse giggled.

Toni trailed behind her. What had Joy done? Something was rotten in the state of Delaware. Was it bad luck if a male and a female crossed the threshold at the same time? she wondered. Toni decided to stop grasping at straws. When Joy was the female, it could only be a bad omen.

It was nearly impossible to separate Jesse from his mother. He insisted on showing Joy his report card, his Christmas presents, his room. Then when he went off to get dressed, Sanji took his place. Sanji and Joy always had gotten along like two peas in a pod. This time they tried to see who could tell the corniest joke. Toni didn't want to spoil it for the kids, especially Jesse, by grilling Joy. But in between all the fun and games, she managed to pry some basic information out of her sister. Apparently, Joy had felt this overwhelming urge to be with Jesse, so she had walked out of the rehab center yesterday evening. She had hitchhiked a ride to Pittsburgh, which further confirmed Toni's belief that Joy didn't have two teaspoons' worth of common sense. Who hitchhiked in this day and age?

Joy was lucky whoever picked her up didn't slit her silly throat. Then some man at the Pittsburgh bus station had felt sorry for her and paid her fare to Wilmington, where she managed to bum another ride to get to Newark. Joy claimed she was starving, and by the time she and the kids had polished off the big breakfast Toni hadn't planned to cook, it was past noon. Toni had to rush to get herself dressed before Chris and Marshall showed up. She had loaned Joy some clothes because she hadn't brought any with her. Toni supposed it would have been a no-no if she was sneaking off.

Toni turned the oven off to keep the ham from drying out. She took a storebought pecan pie out of its plastic bag. She glanced over at Joy, perched on the edge of Chris's chair. She had been fawning over him all afternoon. Acting like they were old friends when in actuality she'd only met him once before. Toni's lips tightened. That vamp actually had her legs draped between his. The blue sweat pants she had loaned her—the only clothing Toni had that was long enough for Joy—brushed slowly back and forth where her legs touched Chris. Shameless!

Scowling, Toni turned to check out Marshall's reaction to this. He was sitting at the dining room table, helping Jesse and Sanji put together a jigsaw puzzle. He held a piece in his hand, frowning in concentration. Hell, he needed to be keeping an eye on his man. He had just barely gotten him back. Toni knew she was being ridiculous. Chris was gay, after all. She looked back at the chummy picture her sister and best friend made. No matter where Chris's heart belonged, that didn't keep him from being a big flirt.

"Now, tell me again, Chris," Joy cooed. "What is the difference between a wide end and a tight receiver?"

Before he could answer, Toni pointed at the players on the screen. "That's a wide receiver and that's a tight end. Now, get your wide, tight end off Chris's chair. You're practically sitting in his lap." She gave Joy a little shove in the direction of the couch.

"Damn, still rude as ever, I see," Joy said, fluffing a pillow behind her.

"And you're still as obvious as ever. Leave Chris alone. He's taken."

Both Joy and Chris laughed. "Big sis, I don't know what you're talking about. I just figured if we were going to watch the stupid football game, I might as well learn some of the rules. I'm a B-ball fan myself."

Chris winked at Joy. "And since when do I need you to defend my virtue?"

"You tell her, Chris," Joy said. "She's just mad because she can't stand seeing people having a little fun. Am I wrong or am I right?"

"You're right!" Chris agreed. "I tell her that all the time. Toni, have a little fun. I say, Toni, kick your heels up. Go out and meet some people instead of working like a dog twenty-four seven. Has she always been this . . . this sexless?" he asked, lowering his voice to a whisper. But Toni heard him just the same.

Oh, she definitely didn't need this abuse. Not Joy *and* Chris ganging up on her. "I'm going in the kitchen to clean up, since no one else seems inclined to do so."

"Oh-oh . . . I think we hurt her feelings," Joy giggled.

Chris started to follow Toni into the kitchen, but Joy grabbed his arm. "No, stay. She'll be fine. Toni never could take a joke."

The plates clattered as Toni threw them in the dishwasher. *Can't take a joke?* Having her show up out of the blue, if that wasn't a joke and a half, Toni didn't know what was. She slammed the dishwasher's door shut and twisted the On knob.

"Did I hear something about you needing help?"

Marshall had appeared with some plastic cups the kids had used. Shit, she'd forgotten to get the dishes left around the coffee table. Toni took the cups from him and put them in the sink. "No, I'm fine. Joy just works my nerves sometimes."

"You two not close, huh?"

"Not even living on the same planet." Toni turned on the tap and squirted the glasses with dishwashing liquid. "Are there any more dishes out there?"

"Just the popcorn bowl, and the kids are still working on that."

Toni turned her back then and gave the cups an unnecessarily forceful scrubbing. When she finished them and turned around, Marshall was still there.

He leaned against the fridge. His pale amber eyes regarded her levelly.

"What?" she asked.

"Is it my imagination, or is Joy not the only one who is working your nerves?"

"What do you mean?"

"Whenever I try to talk to you, the temperature in the room drops by ten degrees."

Toni pulled a couple of paper towels from a nearby roll. She studied Marshall while she dried her hands. The sandy hair sprinkled with gray. Average height, nondescript eyes and nose. Preppy clothes suited him, though. Prior to all this crap she had liked Marshall all right. But she did not see why Chris was so enthralled by him. And did he really want to get into this now?

From the unwavering look he was giving her, Toni supposed he did.

She tossed the used towels into the garbage can. "If I haven't welcomed you back with open arms, what did you expect? You messed with my best friend's mind . . . and heart."

"Guilty as charged. But I was messed up myself."

"So you say."

"You say that as if you don't believe me. In all the years you've known me, have I ever deliberately done anything to hurt Chris?"

She shook her head but still eyed him warily. "You weren't around to witness how much damage you did."

"True, but if it makes you feel any better, I'm paying for that now."

Toni raised an eyebrow. She didn't see how.

"Just because Chris and I are seeing each other again, don't think everything is hunky dory. There is a distance there. Question marks and walls that didn't used to be there before."

Toni's surprise showed in her eyes. Chris had said they were taking things slowly. But it hadn't seemed that way to her. He always beamed when he mentioned Marshall's name and had cheered up considerably since he started seeing him again. But who knew with Chris? He wasn't one to share his problems. Which was why she'd been so worried about him when he couldn't get it together during the breakup. She shrugged. "I'm sorry you guys are still struggling. And I don't mean to freeze you out. I just don't want you hurting him again." She gave him a pointed look, as if daring him to even try it.

Marsh smiled. "Chris is lucky to have a friend like you."

Damn straight, Toni privately agreed.

"Toni, if you don't trust me, trust Chris. He's not stupid. He's definitely not all starry-eyed about me the way he used to be." There was a trace of wistfulness in his voice. He held out a hand to her. "So, can you turn up the heat toward me a notch or two? I know it would make Chris happy . . . and me, ecstatic."

Toni grasped his fingers, giving them a bruising squeeze. Shaking on Chris's happiness, yeah, she could do that.

Toni sat in the breakfast nook with Joy. She watched impatiently as her sister devoured a slice of the pecan pie. The kids were finally in bed, and it was time to get some answers.

Joy took another bite of pie. "This is the bomb! Do you know how long it's been since I had a home-cooked meal?" She licked the sweet goo off the fork. "Months!"

It was supposed to be months plus two weeks. "It's not homebaked. I got it at Super G."

"Whatever. It's good."

"Joy, I have just one question. Am I harboring a fugitive?"

"Since when is wanting to see your child a crime?"

"When you leave a court-mandated drug-treatment program to do it!"

Joy tapped her fork on the counter. "To be honest, you probably are harboring a fugitive." She laughed. "Just like that Harrison Ford movie. I'm on the lam."

Toni did not smile.

Joy rubbed her nose uncertainly with the side of the fork. "That place I was at . . . it's pretty much like a jail without all the barbed wire fence. We aren't supposed to leave the premises without permission."

Toni closed her eyes. She knew it. She knew it, but some masochistic streak in her needed to hear Joy confirm it. How could Joy be so stupid? And how dare she bring trouble to her front door? She poked the side of Joy's head with a finger, the way she used to do when they were younger and Joy pissed her off. "Why couldn't you just stop and think before you acted?"

Joy ducked her head and batted Toni's finger away. "Stop it. You know I hate when you do that."

Joy should count herself lucky she didn't smack her upside the head. That's what she felt like doing. "Fine, I'll keep my hands to myself. But you've got to realize that this stunt might land you in more trouble than you were in before. For God's sake, you only had two more weeks to go."

"Obviously, I wasn't thinking about that, I just wanted to get to Jesse."

"Yeah, but that's in the short run. What good will you have done Jesse in the long run if you have to spend even more time away from him because you're in jail?" Toni could see Joy was tuning her out. How could she sit there calmly eating that damn pie? She banged her hand on the counter, and Joy's head jerked up. Her fork clattered on the plate. Good, she had her attention now. "What you did was so damn stupid!"

"I'm sorry that we can't all be as perfect as you are, Goody Two-Shoes," Joy muttered.

"I'm so sick and tired of you criticizing me to take the focus off of *you*. I never professed to be perfect. I'm just out here trying to make it. Believe me, I have made plenty mistakes."

"Just not 'stupid' mistakes like me, right?"

Toni leaned back in her chair and sighed. "I don't mean to judge you. But I can't begin to understand you. We both started off the same way, same parents, same upbringing. You just weren't raised to act like this. It's not like you've had any great tragedies in your life growing up—"

This time it was Joy's palm that smacked the counter. "How would you know?" she demanded.

"What do you mean, how would I know? I was right there with you."

"What would you say if I told you that when I was twelve, some sweaty, cologne-dipped old man held me down in the backseat of his car and screwed me like a lightbulb!"

"What? When?"

"You probably won't even remember this." Joy reached for the pack of cigarettes that were never far from her.

Toni threw her hands in the air. "I can't believe you gonna drop a bomb like that and then calmly take a cigarette break. Tell me what happened," she demanded.

Joy made her wait until after her first puff. Her eyes fixed on the gray clouds of smoke twirling up from her lips, then slowly dispersing. "It was the time I went to visit Aunt Laura. Remember when I spent most of the summer there . . . and then I begged the folks to let me catch the bus from downtown by myself?"

Toni put a trembling fist to her mouth as Joy told her about the man who'd offered her a ride to the bus station and ended up robbing her of trust—in other people and in herself. She folded her arms across her chest, suddenly cold. The sour taste of bile rose in her throat.

Joy was wrong. Toni did remember that summer. Clear as a bell.

She had been jealous. She was the oldest, and she'd never been allowed to take the city bus by herself. And she'd hated that Mama and Daddy had let Joy do it first. Toni gnawed at her knuckles, remembering how mean she'd been to Joy when she got home that day. She'd talked about how ugly all the new clothes Aunt Laura had bought her were. She talked about how messed up Joy's hair and clothes were after the bus ride. And Joy hadn't said anything. She just asked Toni to leave her alone so she could finish unpacking. She had skipped dinner and had gone to bed early that night. That had pissed Toni off even more. She couldn't take out her frustration on Joy if she was asleep.

Wiping her spit-dampened knuckles on her blouse, Toni said, "Joy, I don't know what to say. Does Mama know?"

Joy shook her head. The smoke from the cigarette whirled in front of her, creating a cloud that hid her eyes. "I didn't tell anybody."

"Why didn't you tell somebody? What happened to you was horrible. It was criminal!" When her sister didn't respond, Toni added, "Joy, you shouldn't have kept this to yourself. You should have at least told Mama and Daddy. They would have helped you through it."

Joy tapped her cigarette on the side of the plate. Toni reached behind her and pushed an ashtray toward her. Joy nodded in thanks. "Of course, I realize that now," she said, "but at first, I couldn't believe what had happened. I walked around like a zombie for days . . . weeks! Later, when it hit me, I was too scared and feeling too guilty to tell Mama and Daddy." She gave a mirthless laugh. "I was the one who told them I was old enough to take care of myself, remember."

"Well, you could have told me or Lynn. We were your sisters!" Toni cried. Joy could have at least given her *the chance* to help.

"Lynn was too young. And . . . and you were too . . . you. The big sister who was always right." Joy's smile was pulled down on one end when she said, "Toni, you were the last person I'd tell."

"But I'm not always right!" Toni protested.

Again the sad smile. "See, still correcting me. Even now."

The accusation silenced Toni. Was she really so unapproachable? Even though she'd been awful to Joy that particular day, before then she had thought they were close. They didn't argue much—because Joy used to be so accommodating, she reminded herself. They were close enough in age that they had some of the same friends. They swapped secrets and gossip. Why hadn't Joy come to her?

Joy said, "Toni, don't look so sad. Everything you're saying is true. I fucked up then, and I fucked up now. I could only see how miserable I felt in the moment. I wasn't thinking about tomorrow."

Toni's eyes misted. Her stomach was a balled fist, clenched in the grip of guilt. Confusion. She ached for all that Joy had been through. Toni felt like she'd just gotten off that amusement park ride where the floor drops beneath your feet and only the centrifugal force of the wall spinning round and round kept you from falling to the ground. "Joy, I'm not going to argue anymore about who's right and who's wrong. I'm just glad you finally did tell me—even if I had to provoke you into doing it."

Then Toni did something she hadn't done in a long while. She reached out to her sister. She entwined her fingers with Joy's. Strong, brown fingers. Nothing dainty about them. A tiny scar on Joy's ring finger. Perhaps a deep scratch that had healed over, jagged, a lighter brown than the rest of her skin. Toni could feel the small, hard calluses on the pad of her thumb where it rested against Joy's hand. Shear Necessity. Her hand was ashy gray in the deep valleys where fingers met palm. In need of lotion. A hand that pressed, straightened, weaved, dyed, braided, curled. Always in need of lotion. Both of their hands had been through a lot, Toni mused. Had done their fair share of labor. Had experienced pain and hurt.

It had been so long since she had felt anything but anger, annoyance, and fear when she'd touched her sister or, more likely, when Joy had touched her. At this moment she felt a connection, one she hadn't felt since they were kids. Probably not since Joy was that twelve-year-old who thought she could trust a stranger to take her to a bus stop that was only two blocks away. Her gaze moved to her sister's face. Joy was staring at their linked hands. Did she feel the connection, too?

Joy had been raped! It explained so much. Why she

treated men with such contempt yet couldn't seem to do without them. Even today she couldn't resist flirting with Chris, a man who could never seriously pay her any attention. Was being raped the reason Joy cared so little for herself, living every day like it was the last? Toni swallowed a lump in her throat. Maybe that's the way it had felt to her. "Thanks for telling me what happened to you. It helps me understand," Toni said softly.

A slow, cat-eyed grin from Joy. "Aw, girl, you can do better than that. I was molested as a child. I deserve at least a hug."

Even as Toni smiled at Joy's frankness, a tear spilled down her cheek. Only Joy could make her laugh and cry at the same time. They stood up then. Arms around waists, chest to rib cage. Joy rested her chin on Toni's shoulder. Toni tightened her grip on a sister who was stronger—who had been through more than she could imagine. When they finally let go of each other, Toni's cheeks were damp. Joy was dried-eyed, making Toni feel like she didn't have the right to her tears. If anybody had a right to cry, it was Joy. Toni wished she would. Joy reached for another cigarette. Taking her sister's hand, she guided her over to the couch. Joy sat down crossed-legged next to her.

"Did you tell the counselors at the rehab center about this?" Toni asked.

Joy gave a little laugh. "Like you, they 'provoked' me into it. When I first got there, everybody kept harping about how your family can mess you up early in life, how if you don't have the proper learning environment, you develop 'antisocial' values and low self-esteem. I finally told them if they didn't lay off my family, I'd show them antisocial behavior, all right." She paused to light her cigarette.

"They have us do this group counseling thing. And everybody in group jumped all over what I said like it was a juicy bone. Called me defensive. 'If your family ain't the problem, then what is? We're all born good and with the capacity to love ourselves. Joy, why don't you love yourself?' " Joy's voice took on a lecturing tone as she mimicked the group members. "So I told them—just to shut them up."

"Well, I don't care how they got you to do it. I'm just glad it came out. I don't know anything about how to deal with being raped . . ." My God, Joy had been a little kid. Toni shuddered at the thought of something like that happening to her own daughter, sleeping safely down the hall. "But I know keeping it to yourself for years couldn't have been good for you."

"It wasn't." Joy put her half-smoked cigarette out in the kids' popcorn bowl. Toni forced herself not to utter a word about it. "Actually, talking about it has helped in a way." She scratched the back of her neck, searching for the right words. "For years I felt like I had a fire inside me. It was burning me alive, and I did everything I could to put it out, to distract myself from it . . . but I couldn't, ya know. Now I think the fire is still there, but it's smaller. It flickers from time to time." Joy held up a pack of matches and struck one. It flared to life. "More like this," she said, then blew it out just as quickly. "Not like the incinerator it used to be." Joy laughed. "But sometimes the big flames do get stirred up, like when I couldn't be there with the rest of the family for Christmas. I was burning up inside. All I knew was I had to get out of that place. I wanted to be with my baby." She gripped her knees and leaned toward Toni. "A mother should be with her child. Especially around the holidays."

Joy had never spoken with any seriousness about anything as an adult. Toni was glad to see the change. There was hope for her. But leaving the rehab center on impulse showed she had a ways to go. "What are you gonna do now?" Toni asked.

"Call New Beginnings. Tell them where I am. What else

can I do?" She shrugged. "I just hope I haven't screwed up too bad."

Toni nodded. She hoped the same.

Joy got up from the couch, taking her bowl with her. "But first I am gonna have me another slice of that pecan pie. Want some?"

Toni laughed. How could Joy still be thinking about food? The fear of future punishment would have robbed Toni of her appetite. But then Joy had always been pretty fearless.

Joy put the bowl in the sink and turned to Toni, who had followed her into the kitchen. "And while I eat my pie, I want you to tell me just how gay your friend Chris is. I mean, does he bat from only one side of the plate, or is he a switch hitter?"

Toni shook her head. Joy was a trip. She laughed again. *Wait until I tell Chris he has an admirer.*

Joy cocked her head to one side. "Whatcha laughing at? He is *fine*—for a white boy. Never had me one of them. I could probably turn him . . . to the dark side." Joy chuckled at her own joke.

Joy had to be horny as hell if she thought she could entice Chris. He wasn't about to turn to the dark side or any other side as long as Marshall was around. But, Toni thought as she ordered Joy to wash the bowl, there was no harm in fantasizing. Joy had avoided dealing with reality this long. One more evening without it wouldn't hurt.

c h a p t e r
<u>28</u>

Anna Mae's heart was in her mouth as she and Clarence walked into the too bright room hand in hand. Forty or so people had already crowded into the classroom at Cuyahoga Community College, where Anna Mae had come to take the GED for the third time.

She was very aware that this was her last chance to pass the test before her end of March deadline. God, I hope I do okay, Anna Mae silently prayed. She really liked working at Hayworth. She would hate to have to leave there. Being around the kids kept her young—and paid the bills.

Her teacher had recommended that people not take the test until they got at least a forty-five on the pre-test. Anna Mae had gotten a forty-three on her last math pre-test. That would have to be close enough. She had run out of "practice" time. This was the real deal. She'd find out in about six weeks whether she had averaged high enough on all five sections to pass.

She tried to focus on the strength and security of clasping hands with Clarence instead of thinking about numbers and scores. It was only gonna give her a headache.

Think positive, she told herself. *I'll do fine on the math. I scored above a forty-five on all the other sections of the test*, she reminded herself. And Joy, who had gotten out of rehab a few weeks ago, had been helping her study. She had quizzed Anna Mae every day on her algebra and geometry equations. She also had been able to attend her classes at Tri-C more regularly after Lynn and her kids moved back home.

Now, that was something she didn't want to dwell on. Shortly after the new year, Lynn had decided to move back in with Bruce. Concerned about his unpredictable temper, Anna Mae and Clarence had pleaded with her to hold off. But Lynn could be determined when she made up her mind about something. While Lynn was upstairs packing, she and Clarence had a little talk with Bruce. Clarence warned him to keep his hands to himself And Anna Mae informed him that she would be paying Lynn regular visits. She knew he didn't like what either of them had to say, but that was tough.

Well, she couldn't be worrying about Lynn now, Anna Mae reasoned. She had to pass this test.

Anna Mae shivered. In fact, she felt chilled all over, and it wasn't due to the February weather, either. Clarence's arm was around her waist. She snuggled against him and tried to absorb some of his warmth and strength. She had asked Clarence to come with her this time. She knew Toni would probably think she was being a superstitious old woman, but Clarence had brought her luck for over thirty years. Maybe he'd bring her good luck this time, too.

Anna Mae stopped at a desk near the front of the class. She didn't want to see a room full of bowed heads as she was taking her test. It would only feed her anxiety. She tugged her leather gloves off one fingertip at a time, and then Clarence helped as she shrugged out of her overcoat. After she'd stuffed the gloves in her coat pocket, he took the coat from her and put it over the crook of his arm.

His eyes searched her face. "How you feeling, Anna?"

"Nervous."

"Well, let's see if we can get you to relax some before you take the test. Sit down." Anna obeyed. Clarence put her coat on her lap and then removed his billed hat. He handed it to her. After loosening the buttons on his pea coat, he walked in back of her. Anna Mae winced, then smiled as knuckles cracked behind her.

Seconds later, Clarence placed his hands on the tense muscles of her shoulders. Anna Mae let her head fall forward to her chest. Strong yet gentle fingers kneaded, then smoothed knots that had bunched just beneath the surface of her skin. She felt his hands move up, splay at the base of her neck. The chill within her began to thaw under his knowing touch. Anna Mae closed her eyes and allowed his familiar touch and smell to soothe her. Big hands glided over her, from her neck to the rounded corners of her shoulders, then down to the middle of her back. Circling, pressing just hard enough.

A deep moan of pleasure passed her lips.

An amused voice from behind her called out, "Hey, mister, I'll pay you ten bucks if you can make me moan like that."

"Yeah, me too," another voice said. A male one! Clarence's hands continued to move as if no one had spoken. Several people started laughing, and Anna Mae felt her face grow warm. Her eyes popped open. She chuckled. What a picture they must make, Clarence stroking her and her moaning like a fool in a room full of people.

She straightened some and said, "You can stop now, honey."

"Are you sure?"

She nodded, then reached up to pat his hand. "That was nice," she said. "Just what I needed."

The door opened, and a young man in heavy hiking boots, a down jacket, and a mountain of papers entered the room: the test proctor. He stopped at the instructor's desk in front of the blackboard, his face red from the cold. His short-cropped dark brown hair was brushed away from his forehead.

"Hi, everybody," he greeted them with a smile before relieving himself of his burden. He looked out on the group and began taking his jacket off. "We'll be starting in just a few."

"I'll be right back," Clarence said. A couple of strides took him to the proctor's desk. Clarence said something to the man that Anna Mae couldn't hear. The young man slowly shook his head. Clarence sighed, then came back over to her.

"What was that all about?" Anna Mae asked.

"Oh, I just asked him if I could sit in the room while you took the test. He said no. It would violate the uniformity of the testing situation or something like that," he muttered, clearly disappointed.

"Clarence, have I told you that you're the best husband a woman could have?"

"Yes."

"Well, I'm telling you again."

A slow smile from him.

"I'll be fine," Anna Mae said with more confidence than she felt. "Just having you here for moral support was all I needed, and the massage helped a lot."

"Sorry, folks, but I'm gonna have to ask all visitors to leave now. And for you who are taking the test, please put away all your books and notes," the proctor said.

Anna Mae handed Clarence her coat and his hat. He took them, then crouched down next to her. He leaned forward, giving her a peck on the cheek. "Good luck, Anna." She nodded absently, already thinking about the upcoming test. Clarence tipped her chin up.

The concern in his eyes made Anna Mae smile. She had fallen in love with those eyes. They were the most expressive part of his face. When he didn't have the words to tell her how he was feeling, all she had to do was look into his eyes. Like now. She saw love for her. Faith in her. Clarence was quiet in so many ways, but had never been shy when it came to showing her—and anybody who happened to be around—how much he cared about her. She touched his cheek with her hand.

"I'll be sitting right over there," Clarence said. Anna Mae's eyes followed his pointing finger. Beyond the window in the classroom door, out in the hall, was a brown wooden bench.

"Okay." This time she kissed him before he left. "For an extra helping of good luck," she explained when he looked surprised. Truth was, she just felt like kissing him.

It took the proctor a while to sort out who was taking which sections of the test. Anna Mae stared at the exam, lying facedown on her desk. At first, fear of losing her job had been her motivation for passing. But now passing the dam thing was a personal goal. She wanted this GED—for herself.

The proctor finished handing out the first set of exams and returned to the front of the classroom. He carefully explained the testing procedures. But Anna Mae already knew them from past experience. She had ninety minutes for the math exam. "I'll write the time on the board every thirty minutes so that you know how much time you have left. For those of you leaving after the first forty-five minutes, please do so quietly. You may now turn your exam over and begin."

Anna Mae closed her eyes in silent prayer. "God, please help me do what needs to be done." After she opened her eyes, they drifted from the proctor standing behind his desk to the classroom door. Leaning forward on the sturdy bench, Clarence was staring straight at her. Just as he had promised. He gave her the thumbs-up sign. Anna Mae signaled back— then attacked the first question.

* * *

Clarence dropped Anna Mae off at home and then left directly for the plant. Anna Mae left the test feeling optimistic. It hadn't looked like total gibberish to her, and she hadn't gotten stuck as much. She shrugged, knowing she'd done her best. If worse came to worst, she wouldn't be the first person who had to look for a new job.

When she pushed open the front door, the unexpected aroma of a cake baking in the oven greeted her. "Joy, I'm home," she said. No one answered. Anna Mae deposited her coat in the downstairs closet and headed for the kitchen.

She grinned at the sight of her least-domesticated daughter wearing a flour-smeared apron around her waist and holding a cake with the same tilt as the Leaning Tower of Pisa. "Joy?" she said, not quite believing her eyes. "What on earth are you doing?"

Joy set the cake pan on the butcher block cutting board. "What's it look like I'm doing?" she said, putting her hands on her hips. Her voice had a teasing quality, so Anna Mae didn't take offense. "You act like you ain't ever seen me cook before," Joy said.

Actually, Anna Mae hadn't. Not since all the girls were in the house and had to take turns cooking once a week. And from the looks of that cake, Joy was a little out of practice. "I know you can cook. I taught you. But what are you baking a cake for? What's the occasion?"

Rather than answer her, Joy plopped down in a chair at the kitchen table and reached for her pack of cigarettes. Her hair had started to grow back since Toni cut the weave out and relaxed it. Joy blew a strand of hair out of her eyes. "Whew! I'm tired."

Anna Mae joined her at the table. "Well," she said as Joy lit up the cigarette, "aren't you going to answer my question?"

"The special occasion is you. Daddy wanted to do something to celebrate you taking the test today. So he told me to make your favorite cake." She gestured toward an unopened can of lemon frosting.

"Just because I took the test doesn't mean I passed it."

"Now, you need to take that up with Daddy," Joy said. "All I'm doing is following orders."

Clarence always could get the kids to do whatever he wanted. Probably because he rarely asked anything of them.

She leaned over and kissed Joy on the forehead. "Well, thanks, sweetie." She took in the used mixing bowls and utensils sticking out of the sink. *The Joy of Cooking* lay open on the table, splattered with flour like its namesake's apron. Anna Mae's eyes lit with pleasure, appreciating the trouble Joy had gone to. "I can see you been working hard. You want me to put the icing on?"

Joy shook her head. "Naw, that's the easy part. I'm just waiting for it to cool. Tell me how the test went. Did you kick ass?"

Anna Mae shrugged, too tired to tell her daughter to watch her language. "I don't know about that, but I felt pretty good when I left. Just the same, I had my fingers, toes, and legs crossed while I was taking it." Changing the subject, Anna Mae asked, "So what did you do all day?"

"Not much. Daddy dragged me out of bed before you left so that I could start on the cake. I had hoped to have it finished before you got back."

"Don't worry, it was still a nice surprise. What are your plans for the rest of the day?"

"Ain't got none."

Anna Mae frowned. Joy hadn't been out of the house much since she got home. A few of her friends had come over. Though she seemed happy to see them, she hadn't gone out with them. And considering the fast life that many of them led, Anna Mae thought that was probably a good idea. Joy had been looking halfheartedly for a job in the classifieds. She wasn't so down that Anna Mae would call her depressed, but she hadn't been her old, fun self, either.

"Joy, is everything all right?" Anna Mae asked.

Joy reached for the can of frosting and pulled off the pop-up top. "I guess," she said with a sigh. "It's just that everything feels so weird . . . now that I don't have any chemicals in my system."

Anna Mae bet it did. And Joy seemed at a loss as to how to build a new life.

Joy scooted her chair back until she could reach the cutlery drawer. She opened it and took out a butter knife. She moved back to the table and stuck the knife in the can. Under her mother's scrutiny Joy dropped her eyes and with slow circular motions blended the frosting. "I'll be glad when Jesse gets home," Joy said. "I've missed my little peanut head."

Anna Mae knew all about how much Joy missed Jesse. Joy's case worker had called when she ran away from the place. Thank God, Toni had persuaded her to take her butt back there and finish out her sentence. Joy didn't even get penalized for taking off—because she had come back of her own accord. "Toni said the marking period is over in a couple of weeks," Anna Mae said by way of consoling her. "But Jesse isn't going to take up all your time. You gonna have to get on with your life . . . without chemicals, as you put it."

Another sigh, then a few furious puffs of the cigarette. "I know," Joy said. But she didn't sound too happy about the prospect.

When Joy first got home, she was spouting all these twelve-step slogans that until recently Anna Mae had seen only on bumper stickers: "One day at a time." "Keep it simple, stupid." "Live and let live." But as time went on and the cocoon of being in rehab with people who were in the same boat began to wear off, Joy had stopped peppering her conversation with those phrases. Come to think of it, Joy hadn't been to any meetings since she got home. Wasn't she supposed to be "working the program"?

"Maybe you should go to an AA meeting. It might help you figure out how to get going again," Anna Mae suggested.

"I don't know, Mama. Drugs and alcohol weren't ever really the problem."

This was news to Anna Mae. Her eyes searched her daughter's. "What do you mean?"

Joy looked like she wanted to say something, then shook her head. "Nothing," she mumbled as she got up from the table. She centered the lopsided cake on the plate. "I don't know how I'm ever gonna thank Toni for all she's done for Jesse."

Anna Mae didn't miss the change of subject. But if Joy wasn't ready to explain herself, she wouldn't push. "I don't think Toni pitched in because she wants to be thanked. You're her sister."

Joy stopped fussing over the cake. Her brief look made Anna Mae feel like she'd said something outrageous. Family did for family. It was as simple as that.

The first knife full of creamy icing glided over the top layer of the cake. When the knife was clean, Joy dipped it back into the can. Anna Mae tapped her foot on the gray tiles of the kitchen floor. Joy could pretend like that cake needed her undivided attention if she wanted. But this was her mama she was trying to fool. And Anna Mae could see that she was troubled about something. Tired of playing games, Anna Mae walked over to the counter and moved the cake out of Joy's reach.

Joy jumped. Anna Mae's expression was grim as she said, "If you don't want to tell me what's on your mind, that's fine. But, Joy Rollins, don't think I'm gonna let you backslide. You been doing good. And though you got a tendency to shoot yourself in the foot, I ain't gonna let that happen.

I'm taking the gun right out of your hand. I want you to go find that list of meetings your probation officer gave you and then tell me which one we're going to."

Joy's eyebrow shot up. "We?"

"So, in addition to being hardheaded, you hard of hearing, too?" Anna Mae said.

Joy laughed, then shook her head. "I'll be right back, Mama." She put the knife down and went in search of the list.

Anna Mae grunted in satisfaction, then reached for the frosting and the knife. At the rate Joy was going, it would take her all day to get this cake frosted.

In the end, Joy decided to go to a Narcotics Anonymous meeting instead of AA. She said crack was her "drug of choice"—whatever that meant. And though Anna Mae was sincere in her offer to go with Joy, she wasn't prepared for the blue smoke haze that greeted her at the front door of the Glenville Community Center. As Anna Mae took a seat in the room where the meeting was to be held, she thought she had never seen so many chain smokers in her life. Though Joy had never been to a meeting here before, she actually knew some people, so Anna Mae left her to socialize. She felt like a fish out of water. She had attended maybe two family meetings at the rehab center, but that was different. There were other non-addicts there and counselors. And of course, Clarence was right by her side.

Joy said it was an open meeting, so anybody could come. Anna Mae wished there was some way to tell the addicts from the non-addicts. Then maybe she wouldn't feel like such a foreigner. But everybody looked normal to her. It made her want to laugh at her own expectations. Did she think that the addicts would all be huddled in a corner with the shakes?

Somebody eventually called the meeting to order, and Joy took a seat in the chair Anna Mae had saved for her.

Joy leaned over and whispered to her, "This is a speaker's meeting." Seeing Anna Mae's blank expression, she added, "That means somebody is going to talk to the group about how drugs and then the program changed their lives."

Anna Mae nodded her understanding. A couple of people stood up and read from a book. They read "the steps," "the promises," and "the traditions" of NA and AA. It seemed like a lot to aim for, but at least it gave people a constructive focus. Something drugs could never do. After that, people were invited to introduce themselves. When they got to Joy, she stood up and said, "Hi, my name is Joy, and I'm an addict."

For the first time Anna Mae didn't flinch, didn't want to hang her head in shame when that label was attached to her child. Instead, she relied on the faith that always kept her going. As the Bible said, "And the truth shall set you free."

When Joy was done, Anna Mae stood up. "I'm Anna Mae, and I'm Joy's mother," she said proudly.

Neither Anna Mae nor Joy said much in the car on the way home. Anna Mae didn't know about Joy, but listening to what the speaker had been through was a very sobering experience for her. She glanced at her daughter's profile as they neared the house. She thought back to Joy's earlier comment about drugs and alcohol not being the real problem. In her gut, Anna Mae knew Joy probably hadn't scratched the surface as far as telling "her story." This suspicion gnawed at her, but it was Joy's story to tell, not hers to demand.

Bruce's old Porsche was in the driveway, and Anna Mae pulled in behind it. This day was just full of nice surprises. Her eyes danced in anticipation. Lynn hadn't been around lately, and seeing her grandbabies and their innocence might take the edge off the sad tale she had just heard.

They found Lynn in the family room. Sitting in the dark.

Frowning, Anna Mae turned on a lamp. Lynn didn't even blink. "Lynn, what you doing in the dark? Where are the kids?"

Lynn was dressed in purple stretch pants that bagged at the knees and thighs. Her stick-like arms hung loosely between her legs. One look at the rings under her eyes and Anna Mae's stomach contracted as if someone had slammed a fist into it. Something was wrong.

"Mama, is it okay if me and the kids move in here for a while?" Lynn asked, her voice devoid of emotion.

Frightened, Anna Mae fired off a series of questions that Lynn couldn't possibly answer all at once. "What? Why? What's happened?"

"Last night Bruce dislocated Montana's shoulder."

"What! Where is that punk-ass nigger?" Joy demanded. "I can get some of my posse to jack his ass up."

"Calm down, Joy," her mother said. She gave her younger daughter another worried look. There were patches of dry, flaking skin on her cheeks. Her lips were chapped. There were red scratch marks on her arm as if she had a rash. "Is Montana all right?" Anna Mae asked.

"Yes, we took her to the emergency room, and they popped it right back into place. But not until after they asked a million and one questions about what had happened." She started crying, and Anna Mae sat down next to her and gathered her in her arms. "Mama . . . it was humiliating. I . . . I was so scared. I thought they might take the kids away from us if I told them what really happened. I made up some lie. I don't even remember what it was."

Anna Mae met Joy's eyes over Lynn's head. Joy had taken a seat in her father's recliner. "So what really did happen?" Anna Mae softly inquired.

Lynn shook her head as if she wasn't really sure. "The kids were playing. Running around like they always do. Bruce had been asking—yelling at them to quiet down all evening. And then Montana knocked a glass off the table . . . it just had water in it. And . . . and he snapped." Lynn squeezed her eyes, trying to shut out an unwanted image. In a faltering voice, she went on, "He ran over and jerked her away from the table by the arm and started shaking her . . . he was screaming at her. I had to fight him to get her away from him . . . that's when I noticed she wasn't holding her arm right. It was kinda hanging limp. But she wasn't crying." Lynn swiped away her tears. "Mama . . . I honestly think she was too scared to cry. I told Bruce I was taking her to the hospital. That's when he stopped screaming at us and came to his senses."

Lynn lifted her head and glanced at the two of them. "He had to come with me. I couldn't handle all three kids by myself, and I didn't want to leave Dakota and Houston there with him."

Anna Mae simply nodded. Then after a moment she said, "Why didn't you call us? Me and your daddy would have gone with you. Joy could have kept the kids."

Deep sigh. "Mama, I couldn't call you. I knew you were taking your exam today. And I didn't want to be responsible for you flunking it again."

"Lynn, I don't know *what* you're talking about. And my child and grandchildren are more important than any test. You got that?"

"Yes, ma'am."

"Where are the kids?"

"Believe it or not, they're all upstairs sleeping. They had a long night."

"And Montana is okay?" Anna Mae asked for the second time, her voice full of doubt.

"She's fine." Lynn looked at Joy. "She's a little toughie,

like her aunt. She didn't even cry. Just looked at the doctor like he was crazy or something for pulling on her arm."

"I can't believe you went back home with that idiot," Joy said.

"Bruce didn't stay. I asked him to go to a hotel, and he did. He was feeling really guilty about hurting Montana."

"He should have been," Joy remarked. "The big bully. I'd like to see him try that with someone his own size."

"I think he scared himself. He's always been impatient with the kids. Yelling and probably spanking them more often than they deserved. But he's never lost control with one of them." She paused, her eyes unfocused, then murmured, "I can't believe he hurt my baby . . . I thought working out the way he does would help reduce his stress."

Joy scowled. "If he was into taking care of his kids half as much as he's into hanging out at the gym, maybe y'all would be in better shape."

"I don't know what's wrong with him. He didn't used to be like this, Joy." At her sister's doubtful took, Lynn turned to her mother, then shrugged her bent shoulders. As Anna Mae gently massaged them, she only felt bone, no meat. "I just don't know," Lynn repeated, her voice husky from crying. "Bruce says he will get help."

Lynn raked the already inflamed skin on her arm. Anna Mae reached out to still her agitated fingers.

"It's about time," Joy said. Then with a snap of her fingers she followed with, "Maybe Bruce is on drugs. He must be on something if he thinks he can put his big mitts on somebody in this family and not get his ass kicked. Why don't I invite Bruce to one of my NA meetings?" she suggested sarcastically. "Then again, I can't see Bruce turning to anyone for help, because that would mean he'd have to admit that he was wrong about something."

Lynn pulled away from her mother and quietly contradicted her. "I believe he's gonna get help, Joy." Despite

Joy's skeptical look, she remained firm. "But I couldn't stay there. I . . . I have to think about the kids. I told Bruce I was moving back home for a while." Her eyes darted to Anna Mae's. "If it's okay with you and Daddy, that is."

"Lynn, I don't even know why you're asking for permission. There is a reason why every one of my kids has a key to this house. This will always be your home."

"Mama, don't misunderstand me. I'm not giving up on my marriage."

When Joy snorted in disgust, Anna Mae sighed. Joy was not helping. She said to Lynn, "I never thought you were. Ain't no quitters in this family." She hugged her tighter. "But, baby, remember that old party song."

"What old song?"

"It takes two to make a thing go right. It takes two to make it out of sight." Anna Mae pretended not to see Joy's astonishment that she knew any song that came out after 1979. "Bruce needs to make some effort here, too. And saying I'm sorry just ain't gonna cut it."

"I know, Mama. I know," Lynn murmured. "Mama, I'm so tired. I didn't sleep at all last night, and then this morning I was packing our stuff."

"Why you gotta move out?" Joy asked. "Make him leave. He's the child abuser."

Anna Mae shot her a look, and Joy subsided in the chair. It was a good thing Lynn had come back home. It was time for her to deal with Bruce's actions rather than his empty promises. Anna Mae's eyes took in the colorless face, the loose-fitting clothes, the stringy hair pulled back into a ponytail. It was heartbreaking. Lynn used to be willowy, not washed out. Anna Mae took the scrunchy out and redid the ponytail.

"You look about ten years old," she said to her youngest daughter. "I used to carry you upstairs when you were little and looked this tired." She chuckled. "You're too big for me to carry now. But I'll go up with you. I want to check on the kids and see that everybody gets settled in for the night."

"Thanks, Mama. You've done so much for me, especially these past few months. I know I can't ever pay you back."

Joy answered for her mother: "I don't think she's doing it for pay back. She's doing it because you're her daughter."

Anna Mae smiled. She never thought she'd see the day when Joy was quoting her words of wisdom. The Lord did indeed work in mysterious ways.

c h a p t e r
<u>29</u>

Beep-beep. Beep-beep. Toni grabbed her portable alarm clock and turned it off. She felt like tossing it out the window. But it wasn't fair to punish a clock just because she was having academic troubles. She and Chris had been studying for econ all morning. She hoped they had done better on this group of questions than they had on the last set. "Put your pen down, Chris. Stop cheating," Toni said.

"Who's cheating?" Chris asked as he quickly scribbled a few more lines in his spiral notebook, then tossed his pen on top of the page.

Doubling up on accounting and economics in her last semester was killing her. Accounting wasn't nearly as bad as econ. She was averaging a B minus in that, but she'd failed one econ test and got a C minus on another. And it wasn't from lack of trying. If that had been the case, she would be out enjoying this unusually warm and sunny spring day and not cooped up in the house with Chris doing timed word problems. She had taken both micro and macroeconomics years ago and been so traumatized by the experience, she had put off her final econ course until the last possible minute. She was paying for that now.

As Toni flipped to the back of the textbook to check her answer, she envied her classmates who could afford to sun themselves in Cancun or overcrowd the Florida beaches during spring break. Actually, she would have been happy just to be able to sleep during her week off. But she couldn't. She still had to get Sanji off to school. At least the bookstore was closed for break, too. That gave her more time to study. And Jesse was back in Cleveland with his mom.

Ugh! Her answer was wrong. Again.

"Well?" she said. Chris was playing with a flaxen strand of hair, twirling it around his finger, then untwirling it.

"Well what?" he said.

"Were you able to predict how a five percent change in the index of leading indicators would impact the economic conditions in Botswana?"

Chris covered his answer with his hand when she tried to take a look. "Did you?" She pushed the book over to his side of the table. He turned it around to read the correct answer.

Chris laughed. "I didn't even use the right equation."

Toni tapped her pencil back and forth along the edge of the table. It was fine for him to laugh about it, but this was serious. Business majors had to get a C in this course. Anything less was considered failing. There was a test coming up after spring break and then the final in May. If she got less than a C in the course, she would have to retake it. She could still march at graduation, since she was only three credits short. But all she would get was a blank piece of paper. And where was the joy in that? Everybody else would be running around showing off their degree, and she'd have nothing.

An image of graduation had been in her mind for eight long, hard years. She pictured herself walking across the football stadium, shaking hands with the dean of the Business School as he handed over her prize: a real diploma with some words written in Latin to emphasize its importance. Graduation should be a big, family-oriented affair that had at least one speaker that people had actually heard of. That was the May graduation. The dinky January commencement ceremony just wouldn't do justice to the pomp and circumstance that Toni felt her hard work and persistence deserved.

Of course, studying with Chris was like the blind leading the blind. She had a D average, and Chris had a D+. And that was probably only due to the fact that he got extra help from Marshall with his problem sets. Like her, he was taking two classes, but only econ required any work. His other class was international ballroom dancing, which he was taking to fulfill the multicultural course requirement. His main dilemma there was deciding which female dance partner to turn down. As only one of three men in the class, his services as a partner were in high demand despite his two left feet.

Toni pushed away from the table. "I'm going to fix myself some tea. You want some?"

"Hell, no. Real men don't drink tea. But I'll take a beer if you have one."

Toni looked at her watch. "At two o'clock in the afternoon?"

"It's eight o'clock at night in Paris."

"You see anybody speaking French up in here?"

"*Mais, oui.*"

Still continuing her conversation with him from the kitchen, Toni replied, "Yeah, right. From the way we keep screwing up on these problems, I'm not even sure about our English-reading skills. In other words, since you're as dumb as dirt when it comes to this stuff, you can't afford to have a fuzzy mind—any fuzzier than usual, that is."

"Don't be snapping on me. Just 'cause you got the problem wrong," Chris said.

Snapping. That was Chris's slang term of the month.

Toni opened the cabinet above the sink and took out a mug, filled it with water, and stuck it in the microwave. She set it for two minutes. She kept a box of herbal teas on the counter and began looking for a flavor to match her mood. She said to Chris, "Isn't chamomile tea supposed to relax you?"

"A nice cold Coors does the same thing," he replied.

Ignoring him, Toni pulled out an Earl Grey. After taking the mug out of the microwave, she added a dollop of honey and cut a wedge out of a three-week-old lemon.

Once she took her seat at the table again, she said, "Remind me again why we're business majors."

He yawned, then replied in parrot-like fashion, "Because we want to become highly successful entrepreneurs in the hair-care industry."

"But we're trying to run a small company, not a small country," she grumbled. Toni opened her book to the chapter they'd been studying. She stared morosely at a circular flow diagram. When was she ever going to have to worry about the relationships between the major economic sectors? People would get their hair done no matter how the economy was doing. "I still don't see why we have to know this crap." She slammed the book closed.

Toni took a sip of her tea. It was still too hot. It burned her tongue.

They were in deep doo-doo. "Chris, I think we need a tutor. Do you think Marshall would set up some review times with us when he comes down for the weekend?"

Chris shifted in his chair uncomfortably. "He probably would . . . but I'd rather he didn't."

Was he kidding? They needed all the help they could get. "Because?"

"Well, you know how doctors aren't supposed to operate on relatives?"

Toni nodded.

"And how parents shouldn't try to teach their kids to drive?"

Toni hadn't heard that one, but she nodded anyhow.

"Well, the same applies to lovers helping with homework. The other day, when Marsh was supposedly helping me, he told me I was learning impaired. He's convinced something is wrong with my brain since I can't pick this stuff up as easily as he does."

Toni laughed. "Well, I don't want to cause strain in your relationship." Especially since it was just getting back to solid ground. Thanks in large part to Chris's forgiving nature.

"Having him around does help me with my studies in a way."

"And what way is that?"

"Well, a little nookie every now and then helps me relax. In fact, it's the only thing that makes me relax. I'd bet it's better than chamomile tea and a Coors combined."

Toni said dryly, "Spare me the details, if you don't mind."

Chris raised an eyebrow, as if questioning her judgment. "You should get a little nookie yourself. Might take the edge off."

The edge? He meant the edges, plural, didn't he? She had edges and angles and arcs that needed smoothing out. Toni ran a finger around the rim of her cup. Thinking aloud, she said, "I don't know. When this is all over I'm going to be in the mood for some post-divorce, ain't-had-a-man-in-years sex." At Chris's shocked expression, she added, "And it's gonna take a hell of a man to handle all the pent-up sexual energy I've got. I might actually hurt somebody."

Chris put his hands over his ears. "Stop. You're embarrassing me."

"*Please*, nothing embarrasses you. You invented the word *shameless*."

Toni squeezed the pulpy juice from the lemon slice into her mug and stirred. Her mouth watered as she licked the remaining juice from her fingers. She tried the tea again. It slid past her already scorched tongue without further damage.

Chris had stretched his legs out in front of his chair and put his hands behind his head, as if contemplating Toni's depiction of him as shameless. His eyes were closed and a wide Cheshire cat grin covered his face. He looked utterly unconcerned about their poor academic performance or anything else.

There was no doubting that he was indeed relaxed. It made Toni both jealous and curious. "If your sex life is as hot as you say it is, it sounds like you and Marsh are getting serious again."

Chris nodded. "I know you think I'm crazy for giving him a second chance . . ."

Wasn't that the truth. But so far Chris had been riding high on the waves of reconciliation. He'd stopped dragging around like he had the weight of two worlds chained to his ankle. The old twinkle was back in his eye.

". . . but we're taking the time to work out some of the differences that drove us apart in the first place. I haven't seen any sign of Seth when I go to NYC. No calls. No strange boxers in the laundry basket," he joked. "And Marsh has definitely decided that he's moving back in when his contract is up."

No surprise there. It was about time Marsh realized how lucky he was to have someone like Chris. "I thought Delaware didn't have enough gay people for him. And what about you coming out to your family?"

"Toni, Toni, Toni. It's all about compromise. I told Marsh that I was willing to get a little more involved in the community."

"What does that mean? You're going to your first LGB meeting?" she asked, referring to the campus group for non-heterosexuals and their straight allies.

"No, we're looking for an older crowd. We'll probably look for stuff to do in Rehoboth Beach or Philly. And besides, I won't be a student for much longer."

"You hope." Chris could be so cocky sometimes. Or maybe it was just optimism. Toni wondered if it was catching. The goings-on of the past year would have tested even Job. But Chris and Marshall were an item again, and if Chris was happy, so was she. Joy was out of the slammer and still off drugs. She had even landed a job at a music store in Tower City. And in the week-hell-freezes-over category, Lynn was starting to see what a loser Bruce was. Their recent scuffles had really shaken her up. Maybe this crazy world was finally spinning on its axis the way it was supposed to.

"Toni, you gotta have faith."

"No, what I gotta have is a tutor working with me twenty-four seven to help me get through this class."

He winked at her. "Or a little Afternoon Delight."

"Enough with the sex talk already. Unlike you, I don't have any nookie lined up."

"I don't know. Beale has been coming into the shop getting his hair cut an awful lot. And he specifically requests you every time."

Beale? Toni shook her head. She didn't think so. Her chance with him had passed. Though Beale came to the shop, he hadn't asked her out again. He hadn't even made any more business offers. "Chris, you don't know what you're talking about," she said. "Beale barely says two words to me. He just asks for me 'cause I can hook him up better than any white boy."

"You're not going to distract me by throwing out racial slurs," Chris told her. "I'm a man and I'm telling you, Beale's interested. Never underestimate the power of the poontang," he said solemnly.

Toni shook her head. What did Chris know about poontang? How could he even say the word with a straight face? "Okay, that's it, Mr. Lover-Lover. It's obvious where your mind is, and it ain't on studying. It's time for me to pick up my child anyway."

But Toni felt a stirring of female-male interest that had been inactive for far too long. All that talk about nookie had reminded her what she'd been missing. She made a mental note to pay more attention to Beale when he came in for his next haircut. She'd be checking him out, because she wasn't kidding, when she finished this semester, she was gonna put a sexual hurting on somebody. Maybe Beale had the right stuff.

A U.S. mail truck was parked by the back-to-back row of silver metal boxes when Toni and Sanji pulled into the apartment complex's parking lot. For some reason, Toni couldn't let go of the expectation that mail got delivered in the morning, not the early evening. She popped the trunk before getting out of the car, to get the groceries.

A moving vehicle was an open invitation to take a nap as far as Sanji was concerned. She inherited that trait from her daddy. Toni leaned over and gently shook her daughter's shoulder. "Wake up, Sanji."

Toni was surprised when Sanji awoke with very little prodding. "We're home," Toni said, stating the obvious.

Instantly alert, Sanji said, "Can I have my Pudding Pop now?"

Toni laughed. What a one-track mind. "After dinner." And it wasn't going to be anything fancy, either. Though Toni had the whole day off, the studying had frustrated her to no end and she just wasn't in the mood to be cooking.

"Sanji, will you run over and get the mail?" she said.

She didn't have to ask twice, Sanji was already skipping off in that direction. Her teddy bear backpack, slung low on her back, bounced with every step she took. Her eagerness reminded Toni of Jesse and how much she missed his old soul. He had really started to come out of his shell in the past couple of months. He had to, or Sanji would have trampled all over him. He laughed and giggled and argued more than she ever imagined possible. Jesse was finally acting like a six-year-old should instead of like an old man.

Toni took the two bags of groceries out of the trunk and waited for Sanji on the walkway that led to the apartment. Sanji tugged the female postal worker's blue-gray jacket to get her attention. She came about waist high to the thick-hipped woman, who held two bundles of mail in one arm. At Sanji's request, she began searching through the bundles. She paused, said something, and Sanji came skipping back over empty-handed.

"No mail today?" Toni said.

"The lady wants you to come over, Mommy." The words came out spitty and breathless. That tooth was still missing.

A dash of irritation. Why couldn't the woman just hand Sanji the mail? Toni thought.

Her annoyance diminished when the letter carrier said, "Thanks for coming over, Miss Carleton. You have a registered letter here, and I need you to sign for it." She held out a brown business envelope. She took a pen from behind her ear and offered that as well.

Toni took both pen and envelope and scribbled her name on the slip of paper attached to the letter. "Thanks," she mumbled as she gave the woman her pen back. *Who could be sending me a letter that is so important they sent it registered mail?* she wondered as she began walking away.

Her hands began to shake when she saw an attorney's office stamped as the return address. Toni nervously thumbed the letter open.

It read: "We are writing this letter on behalf of Marvin Carleton. Our client informs us that you have violated the terms of your divorce by denying him visitation rights. You have two weeks to respond to this request. Failure to respond will result in our client filing a petition with the Family Court for joint custody."

Joint custody. The words leapt off the page. Toni gasped for air. It was like someone had socked her in the gut. Marvin was threatening her? After all the shit he'd pulled, he was threatening *her*? *He* was demanding a response?

Toni crumpled the paper in her hand. He'd get a response, all right.

She hurried over to Sanji and snatched the bags up off the pavement. Sanji had to run to keep up with her as Toni took the stairs to the apartment two steps at a time. Cursing, she fumbled with her keys. She couldn't get in the apartment fast enough to give Marvin his response. Marvin could go straight to hell.

c h a p t e r
30

Lynn planted a kiss on Houston's soft cheek before gently putting him down in the playpen in her parents' family room. Houston curled a small fist under his chin. The smell of milk, baby powder, and innocence filled her senses. The sound of his relaxed breathing tugged at her heart. *I could spend all day just watching him and listening to him breathe*, Lynn thought as she straightened, her hands resting lightly against the side of the mesh-covered square.

Houston had stolen her heart from the moment she laid eyes on him. Maybe it was because she'd gone through so much to have him. Houston slept on his stomach with his little butt tooted up in the air. That he was here at all was a miracle. That he was a sturdy, healthy, and perpetually grinning little boy was a blessing. Lynn leaned down, unable to resist stroking his soft baby's hair one more time before she went to finish dinner while Montana, Jesse, and Dakota were still occupied with their afternoon cartoons.

Now that Lynn was feeling stronger, she had taken over most of the household chores. It was funny, watching Mama not know what to do with herself when she came home to a cooked meal and clean house.

Lynn felt it was the least she could do. Though they had settled into a routine, she knew it couldn't last. She was a married woman with children of her own. She couldn't stay holed up here, playing house forever. Bruce stopped by to see the girls at least once a week since she'd moved in, but he hadn't said anything about what he was willing to do to fix their problems. And Lynn wasn't bringing it up. The ball was in his court.

She took a pan of perch fillets out of the refrigerator and placed it on the table. She picked up a garbage can near the table and returned it to its normal spot in front of the window between the sink and stove. Lynn had dragged the garbage can closer to the chair she had been sitting in while she'd shucked sweet corn earlier. The ears of fresh corn were boiling in a big pot of salted water.

She liberally sprinkled the fish with salt, pepper, and Old Bay seasoning, then coated it with yellow cornmeal. Lynn debated whether she should start frying the fish now or wait a bit. Joy's new job at the record store was only part-time, so she usually got in first, around five-thirty. And then Mama, who had a twenty-five-minute drive from Shaker Heights, usually got home a little later than Joy. And there was no telling when Daddy would roll in. Seven or seven-thirty.

It was next to impossible to get everybody together for dinner on a weeknight. *So, I might as well finish cooking*, she decided. There was no telling when Houston would decide to wake up from his nap, and fish was something that could be easily reheated. Mama kept most of her pots and pans in a lower cabinet. Lynn squatted down, opened the cabinet, and withdrew a large cast-iron skillet. Mama favored the heavy, clunky pans over lightweight non-stick ones.

When she turned around, she saw Bruce leaning casually against the door that separated the kitchen from the family room. She gasped and clutched the skillet to her chest. "Bruce, you almost scared me to death." He wore a white dress shirt and blue dress pants. A solid blue tie was loose around the collar of his shirt. He must have just come from work. Usually he called before he came over.

"Sorry, I didn't mean to," he said, then grinned. "I would have said something, but I just got caught up admiring the view."

Admiring the view? Oh, when she was bending over. His appreciation of her backside failed to move her as it would have a year ago. A lot had happened in a year.

She didn't respond to the compliment but said, "I didn't hear the door. How did you get in?"

He reached in his pocket and dangled a small key ring with a single key. The spare key to the house that every "family" member had been given.

Lynn did not like the thought of him being able to come and go as he pleased in her parents' house. The whole point in her being here was so she and the kids could feel safe. Lynn set the skillet down on the table next to the pan. She grabbed a nearby dish towel and wiped her hands, which still had cornmeal clinging to them. "Bruce, under the circumstances, I think you should give me the key back," she said, then held out her hand.

Bruce did not move. The smile left his eyes. His fist closed around the key. "I'm still family. Unless you know something I don't."

"I just don't feel comfortable having you waltz in this house whenever you feel like it."

"Why not? My wife and kids are here. Ain't I welcome?"

He was so skilled at twisting her words. Lynn looked at him. She didn't want to provoke him. Not with just her and the kids in the house. "I didn't say you weren't welcome. I just don't think it's a good idea for you to just drop by whenever you feel like it. Like now. This is not a good time," Lynn said. To emphasize her point, she picked the skillet up. "I'm in the middle of cooking and—" Before she could finish her sentence, a large, punishing hand closed around her wrist.

"And you should be cooking at your own damn house," he said, squeezing her wrist even tighter.

"Let go of me!" she said in a tight whisper. She didn't want to wake Houston or cause a racket that would scare the other kids. When Bruce didn't move fast enough, she gave his chest a mighty shove. Lynn saw the surprise in his eyes as he fell back.

She wanted to rub her sore wrist, but that would mean putting the skillet down. And she wasn't going to do that. She might need it.

Bruce still looked stunned. Lynn had never fought back.

That made Lynn start reevaluating on the spot. Maybe she had been going about this the wrong way. Instead of trying to reason with him and feeling sorry for him, maybe she should have pushed back a long time ago.

She took a step in his direction and felt a surge of intoxicating power when he took a step back. "Coming in here and manhandling me? Is that your way of trying to win me back?" she asked.

"Lynn, I'm sorry. I just want our life back. I want you to come home."

"Why would I want to come home? You give me one good reason why I would want to come home to you." She truly wanted to know. Any good memories had been buried under the mountain of images of Bruce complaining about money, Bruce complaining about work, Bruce yelling at the kids, Bruce putting her down and making her feel small and stupid.

"Lynn, how can you ask me that? Everything I do, I do for you and the kids."

"When you grabbed me just now, was that for me? When you promised me you would get help and then turned right around and started acting like nothing ever happened, I suppose that was for me, too?" she cried, forgetting her earlier vow to keep quiet.

In the silence that followed, she heard footsteps running up from the basement. Jesse suddenly burst into the kitchen via the pantry entrance. He skidded to a stop when he saw the tense stances of the adults. His aunt was gesturing toward his uncle with a frying pan. "Auntie Lynn?" he said, the uncertainty in his eyes magnified by his glasses.

"Jesse, go back downstairs with the girls," she ordered softly but firmly. When he didn't move, she added, "It's all right. I'm all right. I'll be down in a minute."

"Okay," he said, and began edging out of the room. When she heard him starting down the stairs again, she turned back to Bruce.

She jumped when she saw he was only inches away from her. His eyes bulged and his mouth was a grim line.

"Pretty cocky now that your family's turned you against me."

A slap that she didn't see coming landed square on her cheek. Her neck snapped back and her teeth rattled in her head. Her face stung and tears sprang to her eyes.

Pure survival instinct set in. Lynn stepped down hard on the foot that was invading *her space*. Then she swung the skillet. First it landed on a kneecap. As Bruce hobbled forward, grabbing it, he bent until he was at her height. That's when she clocked him not once but twice on the forehead.

Bruce grunted in pain. Then there was another, less adult but very insistent, wail. *The baby*!

Lynn wanted to go to Houston, but she was afraid to turn her back on Bruce. Only a fool would do that in the presence of a wounded animal. Bruce grasped the back of a kitchen chair and spewed out a string of vile curses at her.

Lynn's heart started thumping in her chest. She looked wildly around the room. *What have I done?* she asked now that she was thinking straight. *What have I done? I'm no match for Bruce*. She could hear the seconds ticking by on the smiley-face clock behind her head as she waited to see what he would do next. It matched the pounding of the blood pumping in her veins. And her face was throbbing where Bruce had hit her.

She heard footsteps on the basement stairs again. "Go back downstairs!" she shouted. "Don't come up here." The footsteps came to a halt. She could hear Jesse saying something to the girls, but Lynn didn't take her eyes off Bruce. Not this time.

"I can't believe you fucking hit me," he said as he rubbed his head.

"And I can't believe you fucking made me." Lynn had the satisfaction of seeing his eyes widen. Not just in surprise but with a glimmer of fear. The burst of satisfaction was short-lived. Houston was still crying.

The front door slammed. "Lynn!" Joy called. "Lynn?"

Joy's shouts added to Houston's wails. Lynn was beyond words. She eyed Bruce warily, listening as the sound of Joy's voice grew closer. She was almost limp with relief that she was no longer alone with him.

"Lynn, why didn't you answer me?" Joy demanded as she came into the room. She held Houston propped on her hip, still crying a little. "The baby was screaming his head off—" She halted in mid-sentence as she saw Bruce gingerly touching a lump on his forehead and Lynn's death grip on a large black skillet. Her gaze moved up to Lynn's face, where the imprint of Bruce's hand had left angry red streaks.

"What the hell is going on in here? World War III?" she demanded. When neither Bruce nor Lynn responded, Joy walked over to Bruce and knocked his hand away from the chair he was leaning on for support. "I don't want you touching anything in this house. And that includes my sister," Joy snarled. She looked at the angry marks on Lynn's face again. "You been knockin' my sister around, you lousy son of a bitch? If I wasn't holding this baby, I'd kick your ass from here to Timbuktu. In fact, Lynn, you take Houston and I'll take out the trash—"

"Why don't you stay the hell out of it, you stupid crack head," Bruce said. The rageful look had come back into his eye. He was itching for a fight, needing to prove he hadn't been beat.

Lynn snapped out of it then. Even without the drugs Joy could be pretty crazy. And Lynn knew from experience she was not afraid to go up against any man. A kitchen was full of weapons, like the skillet, the pot of boiling corn, not to mention knives.

Joy was on probation. Lynn stepped between the two of them. Joy had fought many of Lynn's battles in the past, but it was time for her to take care of herself.

"No, Joy, you keep Houston. I can finish this . . . this discussion with Bruce. Would you go check on the kids? They're in the basement."

Joy looked at her like she couldn't believe she was for real. The lack of faith was justified. Up until now Lynn hadn't done anything to earn any respect. She gave Joy a slight nod and her sister left, but not before giving Bruce one last disgusted look.

Bruce took a step in her direction, trying to stare her down, giving her that menacing scowl that usually had her apologizing whether she'd done something wrong or not. Right now it simply made her sad.

Now that her burst of adrenaline had been spent, Lynn's knees suddenly buckled and she quickly sat down at the table. "I refuse to live like this, Bruce. First it was yelling, then intimidation, pushing and shoving. Now you've lost control with the kids and me." She lifted her head. "And worse yet, I lost control, too."

"You damn right about that," he agreed. He looked at Lynn like she'd dropped down from some alien planet. And he was half right. She certainly wasn't acting like her old peacekeeping self.

"I'm not going to live in a war zone," Lynn told him. "Because wars always end up with someone getting hurt. I don't want to be hurt, and I don't want to hurt anyone."

"You hurt someone?" he scoffed. Something in Lynn's flat eyes stopped him.

Her voice was soft as ever as she calmly informed him, "Not only will I hurt you, but I will try my damnedest to kill you if you ever lay another finger on me or my kids."

"Lynn, you don't know what you're saying," he said, talking to her like she was Montana or Dakota.

"I'm saying I can see into the future. I see you hurting me or one of my children because you haven't done anything to get your temper under control. And like I said, I don't want to kill anyone, especially not the father of my children."

In response, Bruce backed off. "Lynn, I'm sorry I lost my temper. I've never hit you before, and I promise you, I won't do it again."

Had he forgotten about Christmas Eve? Lynn wondered. But it didn't matter. Not really. She said, "I know you won't because I'm not giving you the chance." There was a click as the big hand on the smiley clock moved a notch. It was getting late. Mama would be home soon. Lynn grabbed the skillet, went over to the stove, poured cooking oil into the skillet, and turned the flame on.

He relaxed visibly when she put the skillet down. "I'll get help," he said.

Now, where had she heard that before? "I hope you get help. But do it for yourself. Not to get me back, but so that you can still be a father to your kids."

"What does that mean?" he asked. Her serenity had him off balance. Or was it her indifference?

"You figure it out, Bruce. You need to go now. Mama will

be here soon." She turned to face him square on. "The key," she said, holding out her hand.

Bruce slowly dropped the key in her open palm. His eyes searched hers, hoping for a last-minute change of heart.

Lynn tossed the key onto the table and turned back to the stove. He didn't move for several seconds; then she heard him leave the kitchen. She gently placed the first strip in the skillet at the sound of the front door closing behind him.

The fish was sizzling in the pan when Joy reentered the kitchen a few minutes later. She held Houston in her arms, and his bright eyes roved around the kitchen. The tears were gone. "Is it safe to come back in?" Joy asked.

Lynn waved her to a chair and then reached for Houston. She buried her face in the soft folds of his fleshy neck. Trying to absorb the essence of him. The untainted innocence.

"That was a pretty big lump Brucie was sporting," Joy said.

"Yes, it was," Lynn acknowledged with a sigh.

"Did you hit him with a frying pan?"

"Yes, I did."

"Damn, I wish I'd been here to see that."

"No, you don't," Lynn said, her voice cracking. Meeting violence with violence was nothing she felt proud of. Lynn trailed little kisses across Houston's face. He gurgled happily as she moved from the top of his head, to his eyes, to his father's nose, on to both cheeks.

"So what does it feel like?" Joy asked. Her face was propped between her hands, her elbows resting on the table, as she looked into her sister's eyes.

Lynn put a hand to her puffy face. Her eyes never leaving Joy's, she said, "It feels sore."

"No, I meant, what does it feel like to fight back?" Joy explained.

Lynn thought for a moment, then replied, "Liberating."

c h a p t e r
31

Marvin stunned Toni by being true to his word. A week after the blistering tongue lashing she gave him over the phone, he petitioned the court, asking that the custody decree be modified. A court date was set with surprising quickness.

The night before, she made a point to get into bed at a reasonable hour. A lot of good that did. She tossed and turned her way from night to daybreak. She didn't eat anything for breakfast. Couldn't. Her stomach was in knots. A lightheaded feeling made her wish she'd tried to get something down. She needed to have her wits about her.

She put on some makeup, thinking it might help her look and feel better. One glance in the mirror told her that splaying makeup on a haggard face was like trying to cover funk with Chanel. It only made it worse.

In the hall outside the courtroom, Toni slipped her brown satchel onto her lap and took out the bottled spring water she always carried with her. Food and drink weren't allowed, but her mouth was completely dry. It had gone as arid as a desert right around the time she caught sight of Marvin dressed in a conservative navy blue suit and tie. It unnerved her. She didn't even know he owned a suit. He flashed her a "let's be friends" smile. He took a step toward her until his lawyer placed a restraining hand on his jacket sleeve. His lawyer. That was another surprise. Toni had been sure he'd show up with some wet-behind-the-ears, sloppily dressed Legal Aid trainee.

The sister at his side was anything but. And she didn't look like she worked cheap, either. Forty-something. Wearing a tailored, tan suit that was professional looking yet feminine. Confidence exuding from every part of her. The clear, intelligent eyes. Her walk. The way she handled her client.

Marvin hadn't bothered to hire a lawyer for the divorce. He hadn't wanted a divorce, but knowing that his wants didn't hold any water with Toni, he hadn't contested it, either. He had not asked for custody, visitation. Nothing. This time, Toni feared, he meant business. The thought of shuttling Sanji between the two of them and having her spend time with that whacked-out Tiara was what she dreaded the most.

Marvin and his lawyer sat at a table nearby, their heads huddled close together. Conspiring.

Toni was using Bonnie Marmarosh, the same lawyer who'd represented her in the divorce. When Bonnie ran out to make a phone call, Toni felt alone, making her wish she'd accepted Chris's offer to come with her. Quickly unscrewing the top off the water bottle, Toni guzzled. A third of a liter was gone by the time she stopped. At the sound of the courtroom doors swinging open, she capped the bottle and hastened to stuff it in the satchel. When she turned around, Bonnie was trotting down the aisle, only a few paces behind the court clerk. Another creaking door had Toni whipping her head back around to the front of the room. A black-robed judge was emerging from his chambers.

Judge John Byron looked to be in his mid to late fifties. He was a trim man of average height, brown hair, graying at the temples and most of it missing on top. He moved with the brisk efficiency of a runner.

A male judge? Toni didn't know if that was good or bad.

He smiled at her as he moved over to his chair. Then again, he smiled at Marvin, too.

After a surprisingly thorough reading of the documents in front of him, Judge Byron began the case of *Carleton* v. *Carleton*. He said, "Mrs. Carleton, Mr. Carleton, my job is to ascertain what is in the best interest of the child and make appropriate recommendations based on that judgment. Since you are the petitioner, Mr. Carleton, you get to go first."

Marvin's lawyer stood and identified herself as Liz Hargrove. "Your Honor, my client is seeking joint custody of his minor child, Sanjari Marita Carleton, as a result of her mother's unwillingness to allow him visitation—"

"Ah-choo!" Like a judicial magician Judge Byron produced a cloth handkerchief from up his sleeve and then wiped his nose a couple of times, then balled it in his hand. "Sorry about that," he said with a smile. "Allergies."

Liz Hargrove nodded, then continued. "There was absolutely no reason for visitation to be denied. The child has never come to harm when in my client's care. They have a very close, loving relationship. We also have a letter from his minister attesting to his strong moral fiber."

His minister? Now, wait a minute. Since when had Marvin started going to church? Toni quickly glanced through her lawyer's copy of various letters and statements. There was one from Reverend LeRoy Weems. Marvin was using his uncle as a character reference!

Toni looked over at Marvin, her smile totally disbelieving. Uncle LeRoy wasn't even a real preacher. He hung out in Rodney Square in downtown Wilmington, harassing people on their way to work or waiting for a bus. The homemade flyers he waved under their noses proclaimed that the end of the world was nigh because women were wearing Wonder Bras and people were communicating over the Internet. The man was loony toons.

Toni couldn't help it. A guffaw escaped her. She clapped

a hand over her mouth. At the questioning look the judge gave her, Toni looked down at the table to keep from laughing. Uncle LeRoy? Marvin was really reaching on that one.

Liz Hargrove picked up a yellow legal pad and used the tip of a pencil to locate her next point. "I also have a statement from the Prosecutor's Office showing that Mr. Carleton is making child-support payments."

Toni looked up at that. She had received a check from the Prosecutor's Office *at the beginning of February* for a measly forty-three dollars. The first money from Marvin she'd seen in two years. She hadn't cashed the check. Nor had she the second one. She sent the letter back unopened. It was a case of too little, too late, as far as she was concerned.

"Well, Mrs. Carleton, how do you account for this change of heart? Has your ex-husband endangered the child in some way?"

Though he addressed the question to Toni, it was Bonnie Marmarosh who stood up. The motherly woman cleared her throat before speaking. "My client's decision to deny custody was based on the knowledge that Mr. Carleton was involved in criminal activity. He stole hundreds of dollars from my client over a period of several months."

Marvin's lawyer quickly interjected, "Objection. Irrelevant. Doesn't speak to his fitness as a parent."

"Your Honor, it speaks to his character. A strong moral character is extremely relevant to the issue of parenting. Ms. Hargrove just made the same point herself earlier, not five minutes ago," Bonnie said.

Toni settled back against her chair. *You go, girl*, Toni silently rooted.

"I'll allow it. Go on, counselor."

Marvin looked anywhere but at Toni or the judge while Bonnie was talking. She briefly described how Marvin had stolen from Toni over a period of months. She concluded with: "Despite Mr. Carleton's total disregard for the law and his ex-wife's personal property, not to mention her trust, for the sake of their daughter she did not press charges against him."

His attorney rose from her seat, her knuckles pressed against the heavy mahogany table. "Your Honor, my client immediately realized that what he had done was wrong. He has since paid restitution to his ex-wife for the full amount owed her. In fact, he gave her an extra one hundred dollars."

Immediately? Toni pursed her lips. *Marvin didn't do shit until he was caught. He'd probably still be robbing me blind today if I hadn't figured out what he was up to.*

The judge said, "Is it true that he paid you back?"

Toni thought for a moment about lying. Marvin had paid her in cash. If she said no, it would be her word against his. She sighed. *Two wrongs don't make a right.* Besides, she could win this thing fair and square. "Yes, your Honor. He did pay me back." She quickly added, "But only because he got caught. And as for the extra money, what is a measly hundred dollars when he owes me thousands in unpaid child support?"

Judge Byron made a notation on his notepad. Toni was disappointed. She had been hoping he would be as outraged by Marvin breaking the law as she had been.

"Thank you," the judge said, "Carry on, Ms. Marmarosh."

Bonnie continued, and at the end said, "In addition to his criminal behavior, we believe that joint custody poses a threat to the safety and welfare of the child because there is a history of harassment of my client by Mr. Carleton's common-law wife, a Ms. Tiara Marien. She has repeatedly threatened my client over the phone. She has slashed the tires of her car—"

"Objection. There is no proof that Ms. Marien has done any of the things she's been accused of. And she's not on trial."

The judge turned to Toni, "Do you have any proof? Perhaps a tape of the threats Ms. Marmarosh mentioned? Or has Ms. Marien, to your knowledge, ever threatened the child?"

Toni looked at her attorney and then slowly shook her head.

"Objection sustained."

Toni lurched forward in her seat, and the judge chuckled. "You look like you're going to bust a gut if you don't speak. What is it that you want to say, Mrs. Carleton?"

"Judge, my ex-husband didn't seek custody or visitation during the divorce. And he's pretty much been a deadbeat dad. He can't keep a job. And he hasn't supported Sanji financially for years. I had to beg him to spend time with her. Now he's coming in here acting like he's father of the year. Believe me, he's not."

"You may not be aware of this, but according to the uniform custody law, your ex-husband doesn't have to seek visitation. Unless it is contested by the custodial parent, the court grants it. That is what happened with your divorce. And employment is not a criterion for visitation rights."

Liz Hargrove signaled to get the judge's attention. He turned toward her. "Yes?"

"Your Honor, if I may respond to the charge that my client can't hold a job."

He nodded.

She picked up a piece of paper. "Your Honor, my client has held a job as a sales associate at Michael's Sporting Goods for seven months. I have a letter from his employer verifying that."

Marvin smiled when he saw the surprise on Toni's face. Seven months? That had to be a record for Marvin. But so what? *I've been working steadily for five years.* Marvin could grin all he wanted but he couldn't compete with her stable job history.

". . . My client's employer has been so impressed with his

reliability and sales record that he is likely to promote him to an assistant department manager within the year."

Toni did a double-take. A promotion? Marvin was doing a lot better than she'd expected.

The judge asked, "Is there anything else from either side?" Both lawyers said no.

"One last question, then. Mrs. Carleton, your daughter isn't here, which I'm happy to see because I hate it when kids are dragged through this process. However, Mrs. Carleton, if Sanjari were here and I asked if she wanted to spend time with her father, what would she say?"

Toni hated being set up. If he had been anybody else except a judge, she would have refused to answer. "She would want to see him, Your Honor," Toni admitted in a voice hardly above a whisper.

"Okay, I think I've heard all I need to."

Toni expected him to rise, go to his chambers, and seriously weigh all the evidence that had been presented, but he didn't budge. After a final perusal of the court documents, Judge Byron was ready to make a ruling.

Looking out on his small but attentive audience, he said, "This case can be summed up in two words. Irresponsibility and anger. All too often the two go hand in hand. Luckily for you, I'm here to put a stop to it before the whole situation turns ugly and your daughter ends up getting hurt. Given how hard the two of you are fighting for custody of Sanjari, it's obvious you love her.

"It appears from the statements provided by Sanjari's school, Mrs. Carleton's place of employment, and other character references that the child has a stable and loving environment with her mother . . ."

Toni's heart cheered.

"However, that does not give you the right to unilaterally deny visitation, Mrs. Carleton. From what I can gather, you and your ex-husband were on . . . well, maybe amicable is too strong a word, but he was allowed to visit. And you trusted him to care for your daughter in your absence. You also trusted him *not* to steal from you." He gave Marvin a stem look. "So naturally you'd be angry when he betrayed that trust. Your anger is justifiable. But that's just it. It's your anger, and not your daughter's. Your husband does not pose a physical or emotional threat to her."

Toni stared wide-eyed. Of course Marvin posed an emotional threat. If he was a thief, what kind of role model was that? She didn't like where the judge was headed with this.

"As for the petitioner, I am denying custody for the moment for several reasons." Tears of relief formed in Toni's eyes. This was not what she had expected to hear. Not after the way the judge was just criticizing her. "Sanjari is a young child who has her own room, friends at school, a routine. Mr. Carleton, you haven't provided sufficient cause for disrupting that routine."

The judge turned to Marvin. "Is it true that this is your first attempt after your divorce to be a regular presence in your daughter's life?"

Marvin fingered his shirt collar as if it was too tight at his neck. "Your Honor, I tried to see Sanji whenever I could. When I was working it was hard to get away. . . . Then I totaled my car . . ."

The judge sniffed, and Toni didn't think it was because of his allergies, either. "You mean to tell me, you don't have a friend or relative with a car?" the judge said. "No need to answer that, Mr. Carleton. You know and I know that buses run every day. Back to the matter of custody. Though it is laudable that you have held a job for seven months, that does not sufficiently prove consistency and dependability. Mr. Carleton, you need to contact the Prosecutor's Office to set up some type of payment schedule for reducing your arrears child-support payments. Also, any tax refund or sum of money beyond your salary that is reported to the IRS will be attached."

"What!" Marvin cried. His lawyer immediately shushed him.

The judge paused, trying to remember where he was before Marvin made him lose his train of thought. "You also failed to adequately establish a legal residence."

Judge Byron's eyes were full of disdain as he added, "Try paying a bill other than the cable before you show your face again in my court, Mr. Carleton."

Looking miserable, Marvin nodded.

"Given the fault on both sides, I am granting liberal visitation. However, your daughter is to have limited contact with Ms. Marien since it appears she pretty much hates your ex-wife and her absence today makes me question whether she'll be welcoming your daughter into her home with open arms. You can work out the details about visitation with a domestic-relations counselor."

Toni couldn't believe she was smiling like sunshine after a rainstorm. But she was. She felt downright giddy. It could be her empty stomach, but more likely, it was relief. After months of hating Marvin's guts, not allowing him within a two-mile radius of Sanji, visitation seemed like a small price to pay.

"Mr. Carleton, I will reconsider the petition for custody in six months if you still wish to pursue it. Case dismissed." Gathering his papers, Judge Byron rose and disappeared behind the heavy oak door that led to his chambers.

After the hearing, she and her lawyer met with Marvin and his lawyer to talk about the domestic-relations counseling. To his credit, Marvin didn't gloat. But then again, neither one of them were walking away a total winner. Sanji was the only winner. She had both of her parents back in her life again. The hearing had put Toni in a more cooperative frame of mind. She had almost lost what she had by putting herself rather than Sanji first. The judge's condemnation of both her and Marvin—what were his words: anger and irresponsibility?—had been the dose of cold water she needed.

"Marvin, it's over. I shouldn't have stood between you and Sanji," she reluctantly admitted prior to leaving the courthouse. His answering grin said all was forgiven. Unlike Toni, Marvin was not one to hold a grudge.

c h a p t e r
32

The dental school students were passing the naked inflated doll around again. Her flaming hair and pasties dangled as she flew over the crowd. Tacky, but a commencement ceremony tradition. Something to entertain themselves with while they sat through the dry preliminary speeches before the main commencement speaker came on. Being more conservative, the business school students tossed around a multicolored beach ball. When it got to Toni, her hands automatically went up in the air to keep it going.

Her eyes scanned the U-shaped stadium, looking for her family. They had rented two mini-vans and the whole crew—her parents, sisters, brother, nieces and nephews, even a couple of aunts and uncles—had gotten in late last night. They were staying at a hotel near the campus. Toni was supposed to meet up with them after the ceremony. Marvin had come by for Sanji this morning in his newly purchased used car. He'd invited her out for breakfast with them, but Toni was so excited she couldn't eat. So they'd gone on without her. She still couldn't believe she was sitting here.

As soon as Professor Abdoo sent out an e-mail that grades were posted outside his office, Toni had torn out of the bookstore. Her feet had slowed, though, the closer she got to the bulletin board. She could see the grades from several classes tacked up. With a trembling hand she had searched for the last four digits of her Social Security number, then found it. Seventy-five percent! She had done it—with one percentage point to spare! Toni had fallen to her knees and started bawling right out there in the hallway. Her legs were trembling so badly, she couldn't even stand up. A secretary had come out of an office to ask if she was okay and Toni cried all over her, too.

And when she was done crying, she walked down Main Street to the nearest church. It didn't matter that she wasn't Catholic. She fell on her knees once again, thanking the Almighty because that's who had truly helped her get the B she needed on the final.

Toni shaded her eyes with her hand, still looking for her family. Being here among thousands of smiling people who were about to graduate was a dream come true. And she still felt like she was dreaming. She wasn't sure when it would feel real to her. Maybe when she actually got the diploma in her hand. Or when she got more than five or six hours of sleep a night. Or when she could give Sanji some honest to goodness real attention rather than say, "Shush, Mom's studying." Or maybe when she could hand in her two-weeks' resignation at a job that had been a means to an end. Maybe then it would feel real.

Toni sighed. She was surrounded by folks but still alone. She wanted to share every moment of this day with the people who cared about her. The people who had been encouraging her since day one. She knew they were here, but where? Toni wished she'd thought to tell them exactly where to sit. Then she'd know where to look for them. Other people were waving to their family members, making her jealous. Even Chris was lost in the sea of mortarboard-covered heads behind her. They had marched in by college and in alphabetical order. The business college was one of the largest, so there were hundreds of students separating the Cs and the Vs.

Just as the main commencement speaker was being introduced, a flash of white on the visitors' side of the field caught her eye. About midway up the stacked rows, she saw a sign. The words ROLLINS FAMILY IN THE HOUSE! had been spray-painted in red on a white sheet.

Toni started laughing. Her family had brought ghetto fabulousness to Newark, Delaware. They had to be blocking someone's view. Acting like they were at a football game or something. Even if they had stolen the sheet from the hotel, she wasn't embarrassed. Far from it, she felt herself relaxing.

Toni hugged the program to her chest. Now she finally could listen to the commencement speaker explain why she and her classmates were the pioneers for a new millennium.

When the College of Business and Economics was called, Toni thought she was going to burst into tears as she'd done when she got her econ grade. And though her legs felt wobbly, the momentum from the students in line behind her kept her feet moving. As she shook hands with the dean of the college, a cry went up: "Toni! Toni!" The Rollins family banner was really moving up and down. Like whoever holding it was jumping for joy.

Toni knew the feeling. She gave one of those Miss America waves—she had always wanted to do that—and blew her cheering family a kiss. More jumping up and down. Her smile was wider than the Grand Canyon. *This is what I waited eight years for.*

Toni was supposed to meet everybody at the gate leading to the west parking lot. Marvin and Sanji reached her first. Sanji ran over to her, the ribbons on her pigtails flapping in the wind. "I saw you on the field, Mom," Sanji cried. "We were way, way up in the stands. Almost as high as the clouds. Did you see us?"

Toni nodded and gave Sanji a kiss. When she was done, Marvin held his arms out. She reared back in surprise, then figured, What the hell? It was a special occasion. Toni stepped forward into his waiting arms. He enveloped her in a brief hug. "Congratulations, Tone. If anyone deserves this, it's you. I know you worked your butt off for it."

"Thanks," she said.

"Mom, I want a dress just like yours," Sanji declared, fingering Toni's blue graduation gown.

"Oh, believe me, honey, you will have a dress just like mine. Maybe two or three dresses just like mine," Toni assured her, and put her mortarboard on Sanji's head. It was lopsided and too big, but Toni liked the look. She figured Sanji would grow into it. High school. College. M.D., J.D., Ph.D. Who knew? The sky was the limit.

"Toni!" A bunch of people were calling her name. Her family as well as Chris and Marshall all converged on her at the same time. Her father's hug was so fierce, it lifted her off the ground. By the time she had accepted all of her congratulations, she was sure her face was just as lipstick-smeared as all the people standing around her.

Joy's clothes were as tight as ever, but her eyes were clear. Mama had said she was doing well. Sanji, the perpetual center of attention, was showing off her new hat—the mortarboard—to her cousins. Lynn had baby Houston on her hip and was minus Bruce. As Toni hugged her baby sister, she was happy to note that she had regained some weight, and her smile was full and true. Toni stepped back from her to continue her perusal. Lynn's hair had some oomph to it, too. She was looking like the young, pretty woman she was instead of tired and worn out.

Toni grabbed Darius's camera and took Lynn's picture. If Lynn ever lost herself in her marriage again, Toni wanted her to have a reminder of what she looked like without Bruce.

Ever the practical one, Mama was passing around tissues so that everyone could wipe the lipstick off their faces. When she got to Daddy, Toni noticed that Mama personally did the job herself.

Toni punched Chris in the shoulder. The lucky dog had done even better than she had on the final. He claimed she must have gotten her B by cheating off of him.

"Ow, what was that for?" he complained.

"Just a love tap."

He looked at Marshall for confirmation that Toni was nuts. Marshall shrugged. He was staying out of it. "Congratulations, Toni."

"Thanks." She grinned at Chris. "Well," she said, "we did it."

"Praise God," her mother said.

"Chris," a commanding female voice called from behind him. A tall, bony lady with a cadaverous face and the bearing of a queen was leading a pack of blonde-haired, equally tall, but considerably younger representatives of the same family toward them.

He turned around. "Oh, looks like the Van Akens have arrived." Chris's entourage was even bigger than hers. But then again, he was local. Toni had met some of them but only one or two at a time.

"Well, I'd better get going. See you guys at our place tomorrow for the cookout."

Toni and her family were going to a restaurant for lunch, and there were no specific plans for dinner. All Toni knew was that she wasn't cooking, Not that Aunt Hester Ruth and Mama would let her get near her own kitchen while they were around—even if it hadn't been a special occasion. She couldn't get all these folks in the little apartment anyhow. But tomorrow the whole family was invited to Chris and

Marshall's for a barbecue. It should be quite an experience, because while the women in the family had not given it a second thought, Daddy and Darius were decidedly leery about hanging out with two gay guys.

Maybe she should have them talk to Marvin. He could break it down for them: Chris was her friend. He wasn't going anywhere.

"See y'all tomorrow," Toni said.

Chris waved to his family and then smiled uncertainly at Marshall. Toni's eyes bugged out when Chris slowly extended a hand to Marshall and said, "C'mon, Marsh." Marshall's eyes bugged, too, but he linked his hand with Chris's and allowed himself to be pulled in the direction of the Van Akens.

Toni stared open-mouthed as Chris stopped in front of his family, his hand still in Marshall's. Toni couldn't wait until tomorrow to get the 411 on that introduction. She was calling him tonight.

"Well, don't you have something to show me?" her mother said.

"I'll show you mine if you show me yours," Toni said.

She watched as her mother reached into her purse. Mama always carried a big purse. She withdrew an eight-by-five leather frame.

"Bam!" Toni said as they simultaneously exchanged diplomas.

As Toni read her mother's name on the GED certificate, her eyes began to water. She knew how much this little piece of paper meant to her mother. There were unshed tears in her mother's eyes as well. "Mama, I'm so proud of you," she said as she pulled her close for a hug.

"I'm proud of both of us," Anna Mae said with a smile that could light up Times Square. "Whew, child, it wasn't easy. We both struggled."

No lie, Toni thought as she handed the certificate back. Anna Mae eased it carefully into her purse.

As she was about to do the same with Toni's, her daughter held out her hand, "Uh, Mama, give me back my degree," Toni said.

"But my collection . . ." Anna Mae said, her brow wrinkling in confusion.

"You don't need my diploma, Mama. You got your own," Toni softly reminded her.

Anna Mae paused as if surprised, then handed the degree back to Toni, who held it tight against her chest. A smile of pure joy lit Anna Mae's unlined brown face. "Sure, you're right. Baby, sure you're right," she murmured, then held her arms out for yet another hug of mutual congratulation.

"Toni!" A male voice rose above the din of the growing crowd of graduates and their well-wishers. Toni scanned the mass of humanity. Her eyes passed a guy holding a bouquet of orchids and then swung back to him. There was something familiar about the shape of his head. He raised a hand over his head and waved to get her attention.

"Beale?" she whispered. It was definitely him, and he was looking good, too. She'd never seen him in a suit before. She already knew his hair looked good because she had cut it herself last weekend. "Wait here, Mama," Toni said. "I'll be right back."

Beale stayed close to a steel pillar near the entrance of the stadium. When she reached his side, she said, "Hey, Beale, what are you doing here? Who do you know that's graduating?"

"You."

Me? The last time Toni had cut his hair, she had mentioned that she had taken her exam, but she hadn't said anything about graduation because she didn't want to jinx herself. "But how did you know that I'd be here or where to find me?" she asked. "I mean, with all these people running around?"

A shy grin, then he leaned toward her in a confidential whisper. "A little birdie told me." That's when Toni learned that he smelled as good as he looked. That fact had her mind wandering in all sorts of directions.

She smiled at him and asked, "A birdie named Chris, I suppose?"

"Yep. I think Chris took pity on me since you didn't seem to notice I was alive—"

"Of course I knew you were alive," Toni protested, but she couldn't meet his eyes. Was she that bad? She thought he had given up on her. He hadn't been acting interested lately. But how would she know? When was the last time she had paid any attention to vibes from a man?

It humbled her that he was still hanging around, given how she'd kept putting him off.

"Chris told me not to take it personally. He said the average nun could flirt better than you."

Toni gave a little laugh. It sounded like Chris had said entirely too much.

"Chris also said that if I was going to get anywhere with you, I needed to be direct. So I hope you don't mind me showing up here." A question was in his eyes as he held out the flowers. "Here, these are for you."

His uncertainty was endearing and completely unnecessary. "No, Beale, I don't mind you showing up. In fact, it would make my day if you joined me and my family for lunch." Then she took the flowers. And since they were being direct, she pulled him close for a hug. She didn't want him thinking she didn't know he was alive. She wanted him to know she was ready to live again. More than ready.

SIGNET   (0451)

SANDRA KITT

☐ **CLOSE ENCOUNTERS**   (200489 / $6.99)
Tense, thoughtful, & sensual, this is the richly emotional story
of two people struggling to make sense of their lives in the
aftermath of a violent chance encounter.

☐ **FAMILY AFFAIRS**   (191854 / $6.99)
When the owner of a New York City art gallery meets
an artist at her opening, she recognizes him as the man who
was a surrogate child to her mother decades ago. Now that he
has returned to her life, she may learn that this archnemesis
can turn out to be someone special.

☐ **BETWEEN FRIENDS**   (191846 / $6.99)
Two women, one African-American, one white, have been the
best of friends since childhood, having grown up together in
the same neighborhood. When they attend the funeral of a
mutual friend, they both fall in love with the deceased's brother, testing the boundaries of their friendship as well as their
mutual love for one man.

Also Available:

☐ **THE COLOR OF LOVE**   (184270 / $6.99)
☐ **SIGNIFICANT OTHERS**   (188241 / $6.99)

Prices slightly higher in Canada

Payable by Visa, MC or AMEX only ($10.00 min.). No cash, checks or COD. Shipping & handling:
US/Can. $2.75 for one book, $1.00 for each add'l book; Int'l $5.00 for one book, $1.00 for each
add'l. Call (800) 788-6262 or (201) 933-9292, fax (201) 896-8569 or mail your orders to:

Penguin Putnam Inc.   Bill my: ☐ Visa ☐ MasterCard ☐ Amex _____ (expires)
P.O. Box 12289, Dept. B   Card# _____
Newark, NJ 07101-5289   Signature _____
Please allow 4-6 weeks for delivery.
Foreign and Canadian delivery 6-8 weeks.

Bill to:
Name _____
Address _____ City _____
State/ZIP _____ Daytime Phone # _____

Ship to:
Name _____ Book Total $ _____
Address _____ Applicable Sales Tax $ _____
City _____ Postage & Handling $ _____
State/ZIP _____ Total Amount Due $ _____

This offer subject to change without notice.   Ad # SFIC1 (4/00)

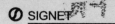 SIGNET

(0451)

"Hot, sexy, and funny."
—*Library Journal*

ERIC JEROME DICKEY
New York Times Bestselling Author

❏ **SISTER, SISTER** (188020 / $6.99)
Totally fresh, in-your-face, and outrageous, depicting a modern world where women may have to alter their dreams, yet never stop embracing tomorrow.

❏ **FRIENDS AND LOVERS** (188039 / $6.99)
A soulful tale of love, betrayal, and friendship set in modern-day Los Angeles, in which the gender gap isn't merely investigated, but celebrated.

❏ **MILK IN MY COFFEE** (194063 / $6.99)
A sexy, sassy, laugh-out-loud novel of intimacy and identity—with an amazing twist.

❏ **CHEATERS** (194071 / $6.99)
Take a dip into the dating pool, as six friends win, lose, and cheat at the game of love.

Prices slightly higher in Canada

Payable by Visa, MC or AMEX only ($10.00 min.), No cash, checks or COD. Shipping & handling: US/Can. $2.75 for one book, $1.00 for each add'l book; Int'l $5.00 for one book, $1.00 for each add'l. Call (800) 788-6262 or (201) 933-9292, fax (201) 896-8569 or mail your orders to:

Penguin Putnam Inc.	Bill my: ❏ Visa ❏ MasterCard ❏ Amex _____ (expires)
P.O. Box 12289, Dept. B	Card# _____
Newark, NJ 07101-5289	Signature _____
Please allow 4-6 weeks for delivery.	
Foreign and Canadian delivery 6-8 weeks.	

Bill to:
Name _____
Address _____ City _____
State/ZIP _____ Daytime Phone # _____
Ship to:
Name _____ Book Total $ _____
Address _____ Applicable Sales Tax $ _____
City _____ Postage & Handling $ _____
State/ZIP _____ Total Amount Due $ _____
This offer subject to change without notice. Ad # EJD2 (4/00)